WAR STORIES

Other books by Joe Haldeman

Novels:
The Forever War
Mindbridge
All My Sins Remembered
Worlds
Worlds Apart
Tool of the Trade
Buying Time (AKA *The Long Habit of Living*)
The Hemingway Hoax
Worlds Enough and Time
Forever Peace
Forever Free
The Coming
Guardian
Camouflage
Old Twentieth
There Is No Darkness (with Jack C. Haldeman II)

(writing as Robert Graham)
Attar's Revenge
War of Nerves

Collections:
Infinite Dreams
Dealing in Futures
Vietnam and Other Alien Worlds
None So Blind
Saul's Death and Other Poems

WAR STORIES

JOE HALDEMAN

NIGHT SHADE BOOKS
SAN FRANCISCO & PORTLAND

"Introduction: You Have to Start Somewhere" © 2005 by Joe Haldeman.
War Year © 1972 by Joe Haldeman. First published by Holt, Rinehart and Winston.
"Introduction: Fragments" © 2005 by Joe Haldeman.
"Time Piece" © 1970 by Joe Haldeman. First published in *If*, Jul/Aug 1970.
"The Private War of Private Jacob" © 1974 by Joe Haldeman. First published in *Galaxy Science Fiction*, June 1974.
"To Howard Hughes: A Modest Proposal" © 1974 by Joe Haldeman. First published in *The Magazine of Fantasy & Science Fiction*, Nov 1974.
"The Monster"© 1986 by Joe Haldeman. First published in *Cutting Edge*, ed. Dennis Etchison, Doubleday, 1986.
"Graves" © 1992 by Joe Haldeman. First published in *The Magazine of Fantasy & Science Fiction*, Oct/Nov 1992.
"A Separate War" © 1999 by Joe Haldeman. First published in *Far Horizons*, ed. Robert Silverberg, Avon EOS, 1999.
"Giza" © 2003 by Joe Haldeman. First published in *Asimov's Science Fiction*, March 2003.
"Saul's Death" ©1983 by Joe Haldeman. First published in *Omni*, Feb 1983.
"DX" © 1987 by Joe Haldeman. First published in *In the Field of Fire*, ed. Jack Dann and Jeanne Van Buren Dann, Tor, 1987.
"Introduction: A Tangled Web" © 2005 by Joe Haldeman.

First Edition

ISBN
1-59780-022-8 (Hardcover)
1-59780-023-6 (Limited Edition)

Night Shade Books
http://www.nightshadebooks.com

To Gay, who heard all the war stories first.

CONTENTS

INTRODUCTION:

YOU HAVE TO START SOMEWHERE

I actually started writing my first novel while I was still in combat in Vietnam. I'd gotten a bound blank book from my mother for my birthday, and so I started to fill it up.

The novel wasn't about Vietnam itself, though; that would be far too direct. It was a fantasy romance set in some sort of Conanesque imaginary battlefield. It wasn't prose, either; that would be too easy. It was in linked rhymed quatrains, ABAB/BCBC/CDCD and so on.

A North Vietnamese literary critic delivered his opinion in the form of a 122-millimeter rocket. It hit our bunker and totally destroyed it. American letters lost a curiosity of dubious value, but I also lost my other birthday presents, a neat chromatic harmonica and a Swiss Army knife the size of a potato, with everything from a swizzle stick to a decoder ring.

My three squad-mates and I should have been killed. In the late afternoon we'd been ordered away from our not-too-comfy bunker on Brillo Pad, onto a chopper with chain saws and gas cans, and flew to an adjacent hill to cut down a bunch of trees that were bothering the artillery battery there.

We stayed too late to get a ride back, and so had to sleep on the cold ground, bitching. We didn't get much sleep, though, because sometime after midnight the artillery started pounding away as fast as it could shoot. We shouted at them, asking what was up, and a guy pointed across the valley and shouted back, "Human wave attack on Brillo Pad!"

I got some 7X35 binoculars and looked at our erstwhile home, about a mile away, and in the light of flares and explosions it did look like there were an awful lot of enemy soldiers. I'm not sure how many people it takes to make a "human wave," but it was far and away the most Vietnamese I'd ever seen, and they got over the multiple strands of concertina barbed wire we'd set out, some close enough to be incinerated by the "foo-gas" defensive devices we engineers had buried in front of the machine-gun positions. A few even got inside the fire base, and lived long enough to raise some hell.

By dawn, the Americans had won the day, though there were a lot of casualties. Talking to people who were actually there, later, most agreed that a lucky coincidence may have saved most of them: people had dug a deep garbage sump in front of a good-sized artillery piece, I think 155-mm, and the crew was able to push the gun down into it at an angle, so that it would actually fire downhill, straight into the enemy charge. They had canister rounds, like huge shotgun shells, for the purpose, and just traversed left and right, delivering mayhem.

That I had lost my first novel didn't really loom very large. My outfit left Brillo Pad a week or so later, under heavy fire, and I don't think I've ever been so glad to leave a place, even if I did have to leave a manuscript buried behind there.

I wrote a lot the year I was in Vietnam, roughly half in combat and half in hospitals, but it was almost all in the form of letters. The idea was to sort of kill two birds with one stone: I would write home to my wife every day, each letter containing something like a diary entry, and she would keep them in chronological order, material for my eventual Vietnam novel.

That worked, but it didn't work.

I hadn't written many letters before really horrible things started happening, no surprise, but what I hadn't thought through was what the effect would be of sending back an accurate record of it all to a woman who was powerless to do anything but worry. So I toned them down.

I had two older friends in science fiction fandom, Ray and Joyce Fisher, to whom I said I'd write the unalloyed truth, no holds barred, and they promised to keep it secret until I came home or died. But after the one letter establishing that premise, I couldn't bring myself to follow up on it. I wrote an occasional column for their fanzine, *Odd*, instead — "Notes from the Jolly Green Jungle" or "Atheist in a Foxhole." But they didn't really express how terrified and hopeless I felt. At this distant remove I can't say honestly whether I was ashamed to admit it. My excuse at the time, in the vernacular of the time, was that I didn't want to "lay a bad trip" on friends and loved ones.

I took pictures and sent them home to my wife to be developed, but never pictures of the dead or maimed. On one occasion, I did shoot a roll of the aftermath of a firefight, and sent it to my brother (who worked in the trauma ward of a hospital), asking that he develop them and keep them hidden till I came back. He later said he never got them.

So I had lots of material for a novel, about 500 pages, but most of the interesting stuff was self-censored, so I had to reconstruct the truth. Maybe that was just as well. Hemingway pointed out that journalism was interesting because it told you what had just happened, but it was less interesting the next day and useless a year later. He thought that to make fiction work, you had to forget the things you had experienced, and then reinvent them to make them more real, with a reality that lasted longer than a simple recitation of facts could.

I had already written the first two stories I would publish; in the thirty days' "compassionate leave" the army gave you when you returned from combat (so your family could deal with you, rather than the army). I rewrote those stories and sent them out to magazines. One sold while I was still in the army, three months later.

I kept writing stories after I left the army, while doing graduate work in mathematics. Most of the stories sold, but I considered them serious beer money rather than a profession. I kept tabling the novel, putting it off until I had time.

A lot of writers sell their first book because they met the right person at the right time, and that definitely happened to me. I was invited to the Milford Science Fiction Writers Conference, a roundtable workshop that typically comprised fifteen or twenty experienced writers with two or three newcomers.

The experience was life-changing. Here I was surrounded by people I'd been reading for years — Damon Knight, Harlan Ellison, Gordon R. Dickson, Kate Wilhelm — and they were treating me provisionally as an equal. Just as important, I saw they were all making a living just by their writing, and if they could do it, maybe I could too.

One of the last nights of the conference, I was having a beer with Ben Bova, and I told him about the Vietnam novels I wanted to write, one mainstream and one science fiction. He was interested in the idea, and offered to read a couple of chapters and an outline; if he liked them, he'd send them along to his editor with a note.

That was a tremendously generous favor. I wrote the outline and two chapters as soon as I got home, and then went back to being a graduate student. I only enrolled half-time, to give myself some time to write. The first day of classes, though, I found out that my most important course, Artificial Simulation of Physical Systems, was going to be taught by a graduate student who would try to stay a week ahead of us, reading the departed professor's notes. I decided, hell, I'd drop out for a semester and concentrate on writing.

Just then I got a letter from Bova's editor, agreeing to buy *War Year*. I never went back to mathematics.

War Year was meant to be part of the publisher's Pacesetter series, a line of books destined for adult education programs. The idea was to provide books with adult themes that were not difficult to read, so that people going back to school later in life could have material that had meaning for them. The restrictions were that the novels had to be short, and they had to be written using Basic English (a list of 500 of the most common words) plus whatever technical vocabulary was needed.

That sounded like a good idea, and still does, but the program fizzled out before *War Year* was finished. Nobody told me, though. I wrote the novel in a white heat, six weeks, and the final result of those constraints was that critics called my writing "Hemingwayesque."

War Year did well critically, a full page in the *New York Times Book Review*, which surprised the publisher. It was the last remnant of an abandoned series, so they had only printed a couple thousand copies and dumped them with no publicity or promo.

The nadir of my disappointment came the month after the book was released. I went incognito to the American Bookseller's Association book fair, which was being held in Washington, D.C., where I lived at the time. An editor friend couldn't go, so he sent me his nametag, to save me the registration fee.

I went straight to the Holt, Rinehart and Winston booth. They must have had a hundred titles on display, but not mine. I asked the salesman about *War Year* by Joe Haldeman.

"Hey, I read that," he said. "Damned good book. But nobody wants to read a novel about Vietnam. We didn't bring any copies."

I went back to writing science fiction.

WAR YEAR

I almost slept through that first enemy attack.

I'd been on KP all day, washing dishes, on my feet from dawn to dark. When it was over, I went to my bunk and just slept like a rock. So I didn't hear the sirens when they went off. I woke up with this big guy shaking me.

"Incoming, man, wake up! Goddammit, incoming!" And he made for the door.

I didn't know what "incoming" meant, but he looked pretty shook. Then I woke up enough to hear that the sirens were blasting the way they warned us would happen in case of an attack on Cam Ranh Bay. I jumped out of bed and nearly caught that guy at the bottom of the steps.

I could hear something going *crump—crump* off in the distance. I didn't know how far off they were, but at least I couldn't see any explosions. Followed the big guy to the nearest bunker—that's just a big sewer pipe sitting on the ground, covered with sandbags—and crawled in after him.

It was right crowded, and the pipe wasn't big enough for a tall Oklahoman, like yours truly, to sit without cracking his head on the top.

"You fellas are a little late for the party. Decide to catch a few more minutes shut-eye?"

"Man, I was on KP all day," I said. "Never even heard the sirens until this guy woke me up."

"Maybe he should've let you sleep. Those're 122's comin' down—one of 'em hits this bunker and we'll all be blown away anyhow."

"Tell 'em all about it, hard-core," somebody else said.

I got this weird feeling in my stomach. I guess everybody who goes to Vietnam knows there's some chance he'll get killed. But the first week? For Christ's sake!

There was a high, thin whistle. You could hardly hear it over the sirens. Then a loud *crump!*

"Gettin' a little closer. Like I say, those're 122-millimeter rockets from China; they'll go through ten layers of sandbags just like they weren't there.

This bunker's got four, maybe five layers. So if one hits us, we won't even know what happened."

I was so scared I wanted to puke. Wanted to run, too, but I knew there wasn't any place safer than here.

There was another loud one, and then they stopped. The sirens stopped, too, after a while. In about half an hour, a guy stuck his head in the bunker and said, "All clear, boys." We got out of the bunker and went back to our bunks. But I was still too nervous to sleep.

I was still awake, just staring at the ceiling, when they called the first formation of the day. It was about ten o'clock.

There were a couple of hundred of us lined up on what they called the "hot sheet." Sheets of steel soaking up the Vietnam sun and pushing it back through the soles of your boots. You stand at attention while a sergeant yells at you through a bullhorn.

"Following named personnel," he yelled, "line up over in the shade. You're goin' to Play-koo tomorrow morning, 14 January, uh, 1968."

Pleiku, I thought. It's been in the papers.

"Adams, Donald, RA 67948563. Barnes, Abraham, US 23746894. Brown, Leon…"

I stood and waited for the F's to come up. We'd done this for over an hour every day for nearly a week, and my name hadn't been called yet.

"… Farmer, John, US 11575278."

That's me. I broke out of the formation and carried my gear to the bunch standing in the shade. Off the hot sheet it must have been thirty degrees cooler. A buck-sergeant—three stripes, nothing to be afraid of—was in charge of us. When they finished the alphabet, he led us away. We went into a big white-painted shack, same kind as I'd stayed in the past week.

"This is your billet for the night, men. Tomorrow morning at 0400 you'll be leaving for Pleiku. You've been here long enough to know the rules—if you hear the siren, high-tail it into the bunker next door. If you hear shots and no siren, take the mattress off the bed and roll up in it and pray. No John Wayne stuff, right? You'll get your chance, where you're headed."

He really knew how to make a fella feel good.

I didn't feel like waiting in the chow line, so I went over and waited for the club to open. The club was just another white shack, but you could get hamburgers and beer there. I was getting used to beer—in Oklahoma a nineteen-year-old can't get it, but here, nobody asks how old you are.

There were about a dozen of us waiting when they opened the door. I got a hamburger and a warm beer and sat down at a table. Took out a tablet and started to write a letter to my girl, Wendy.

"Mind if we sit down here?" Two guys; dark tan and shaggy moustaches showed they must've been in Vietnam a while.

"Suit yourself." I went back to writing my letter.

"You a new guy?" one of them asked after a minute.

"Yeah, I've only been here a week."

"Where you headed—got your orders yet?"

I took the orders out of my pocket, unfolded them, and laid them on the table. "Pleiku—Fourth Administration Battalion."

They both laughed. "You poor fucker—you might wind up in our outfit!" the taller one said. "Fourth Engineers—I'm Smitty and this runt's Shakey; we're both in Company C."

"What makes your outfit so bad?"

"Oh, there's nothin' wrong with it—if you don't mind gettin' shot at."

"Come on, Smitty, it's not that rough."

"Sure, it isn't—you tell him how you got the name Shakey!"

"So I get nervous sometimes…"

"Nervous is the only way to *be*—" I noticed something a little stronger than beer on Smitty's breath— "be first in the hole and last out. Behind a tree if there's no hole, diggin' a hole if there's no tree…"

"Cut it out, Smitty, you're plastered. You're gonna scare the poor guy to death. It's not all that bad, buddy."

"Name's John Farmer."

"Way you talk, they'll call you Tex."

"I'm from Oklahoma…"

"Man, this is the army—they'll *still* call you Tex."

Smitty got up from the table and walked away, not too steady. "Back in a minute," he mumbled.

Shakey watched him wander out the door and shook his head. "He's gonna go pass out. He'll wake up sick in the morning and be hittin' that bottle again before noon."

"He do this all the time?"

"Nah—for one thing, there's no liquor out in the boonies. Even if there was, Smitty wouldn't get drunk. Not too many people would. Everybody depends on everybody else.

"But Smitty's on vacation—he's headed for Bangkok for R & R."

"R and R?"

"Yeah, rest and recreation—didn't they tell you about that? After you've been in Vietnam long enough, you get a week's vacation. Bangkok, Hawaii, Australia—there's a couple of dozen places you can go. Can't go back to the world, though. Guess they're afraid you'll stay."

We sat for a minute without saying anything. "Shakey, if you don't mind me asking—why *do* they call you that?"

"Good reason. The first fuckin' day I was out with the company, they ran into an ambush, lost thirty men. I didn't see how anybody could live through a *week* of that, let alone a year. Things are pretty cool most of the time, everybody told me, but I couldn't make myself believe it. I was pretty shook for a month or two."

He took out a pipe and started loading it with tobacco. "I learned, though. Doesn't pay to sweat it. You'll either make it or you won't. Most people do make it."

He lit the pipe. The warm sweet smoke reminded me of my father. "I've been kind of hoping they'd make me a clerk," I said. "I took typing in high school; passed the army typing test."

"Wouldn't bet on it. What's your MOS?"

Yeah, that was the bad part. My MOS, Military Occupational Specialty. "Combat Engineer."

"Hmmm…you might wind up in our outfit, at that. But I don't think they'll make you a clerk. Hell, we've got a college graduate out there humpin' the boonies with us."

"Humpin' the boonies?"

"Man, don't you know anything? Humpin' the boonies—that's what you'll probably be doing the next twelve months. You put a monster pack on your back, a gun in one hand and a shovel in the other, and you go out in the woods—the boondocks, man, the boonies—lookin' for trouble. Find it, too, sooner or later."

"Really bad, then?" and he was talking about Smitty scaring me.

"Oh, I dunno." He smiled. "I got through a whole year of it without a single scratch."

"What, you're headed home?"

"That's right, man, I'm a real short-timer. *Really* short. Two more days and I get on that bird and kiss this hole goodbye. You might even be my replacement."

"That'd be funny."

"No, happens all the time. You figure everybody goin' to Pleiku spends a week here at Cam Ranh Bay first, and everybody leavin' has to hang around here for a week… a guy's replacement almost has to be here when he's checkin' out. Just a question of running into him."

"You ever meet the guy you replaced?"

"Nah." Shakey drank the rest of his beer in one gulp and set the empty can down carefully. "He went home in a box."

"Sorry; I…"

"Don't be—get sorry over strangers dying and you'll spend the rest of your life being sorry." He relit his pipe and stood up. "Well, better go check on Smitty. Take it easy, Tex. Hope you have half the luck I did."

"Have a good trip home." Kind of a dumb thing to say.

"No such thing as a bad trip home." He gave me a peace sign and walked out the door.

Going home in a box, I had to think, would be a bad trip home.

I stuck a beer under my shirt—you aren't supposed to take them out of the club—and walked out into the cool night. I swear the temperature here must drop fifty degrees when the sun goes down. You can wake up cold and be frying by nine.

They were fighting a few miles south of Cam Ranh Bay. Something was going on there every night since I landed. They told us not to worry about it. Guess I was in a worrying mood, though.

I sat down on the sand behind our billet and watched the fireworks on the horizon. There were a couple of planes, propeller jobs, and a helicopter shooting up the landscape with machine guns and rockets. Looked impressive, red and orange flames, but you couldn't hear anything. I guess it'd even look pretty if you didn't know what was going on. I watched for maybe half an hour, until I finished the beer, then went back to my billet and sacked out.

Only got a couple of hours' sleep. The buck-sergeant came stomping in, turned on all the lights, and started hollering the most godawful language I'd ever heard—and I've heard some fine stuff. Then he started tipping over bunks when people didn't get up. I squirmed out just in time to keep from getting dumped. The buck-sergeant wasn't happy at being up at three in the morning, and he wanted everybody to know it.

He calmed down a little bit after everybody was up and getting their gear ready. "All right, you fuckers, there's a bus outside the door. Hand me one copy of your orders before you get on. The last ten fuckers gotta stand all the way to the airport, so get a move on."

I was the second one on the bus, but it turned out nobody had to stand. Never trust a sergeant. It was only a ten-minute ride, anyhow.

The airport was a big metal hut filled with bored soldiers, and not much else. It had a refreshment stand and a *Stars and Stripes* bookstore, but they wouldn't open until 0900. I sat on my duffel bag and started writing letters.

Wrote a long one to my girl and one to Mom. I was halfway through writing my brother when the buck-sergeant made us line up to go out to the plane. He took a roll call, opened the door, and we trotted onto the field. There was a big old C-130, a "flying boxcar," and we got on in no particular order. No seats—we just flopped our bags on the metal floor and sat on them. We couldn't get everybody on at first, but they juggled us around and packed us in tight as sardines, and managed to fit everyone in.

An Air Force guy with captain's bars and a tough-looking .45 in a shoulder holster poked his head in from the front of the plane. "I'm your pilot, Captain Platt. I hope none of you guys get airsick too easy—this is gonna be a rough ride.

"This airplane is older than some of you. It'll probably outlive some of you, too. If you got anything to say to your neighbor, you better say it now. 'Cause once I start these engines, you won't be able to even hear yourself think until you get to Pleiku. It's about one hour's flight. If we land any sooner than that, you better start praying. You can smoke as soon as the light goes on." Then he yelled something out a window and the engines started. The noise was incredible, so loud it made my teeth hurt.

I'd flown lots of times before; my Dad had a license. We'd go out on weekends, out by Turner Field, and rent a plane for a few hours. But we'd always get the little Pipers or Cessnas, nothing that made a tenth as much noise as this did.

We stood still for about five minutes before the plane started to move.

After we rolled down the runway a while, the noise doubled and we were in the air. Without windows you could only tell by the upward tilt of the plane and the fact that the air was less bumpy than the ground. Still, the airplane sounded like it was going to shake itself apart.

After a boring hour—nothing to do but look at the other guys turning green—the plane started to come down. I could feel the pressure in my ears, and there was a loud bump when the landing gear came down. We bounced several times before the plane started rolling on the ground.

The rear door fell open before the plane stopped taxiing. You couldn't see much, except that everything was covered with red clay. All over everything was a thick white fog, bright in the morning sunlight.

We rolled to a stop and the unloading ramp clanked down. Everybody scrambled out of that plane as fast as they could.

Sure enough, there was another buck-sergeant there on the runway. He herded us into a line and marched us over to a bus. As we got on the bus, he checked our names off a list.

The bus had metal screens, like thick chicken wire, over the windows. One of the windows had a bullet hole in it. The bus had a name painted over the fender. It was called "Last Chance."

Two guards, armed with machine guns, got on the bus. One of them spoke up: "All right, listen up! If there's any shootin', just get down under the seat and make like a turtle. We'll take care of everything—right, Killer?" The other guy laughed in a dumb kind of way. "We're goin' through Pleiku City. There's lots of VC there who'd just love to knock off a bus fulla green troops. No sweat, though. We ain't lost a bus all week."

Guess we were supposed to be impressed. But I'd been in the army too long—less than a year at that—and seen too many phony tough guys.

Have to admit I was getting a little scared when we went through the town of Pleiku. It took a long time to get through, too; seemed as big as Tulsa. Half the buildings were demolished. Bullet holes and shell craters everywhere. But there wasn't any fighting going on, just lots of skinny little Orientals who stared at the bus as we went by. None of them smiled.

There were fewer and fewer buildings and after a while we were out in the country. Nothing but red dust and a few scraggly looking bushes on both sides of the road—looked like the worst part of Oklahoma in the middle of the summer. And this was January.

After a while we got to Camp Enari. A sign said "Welcome to the Fourth Division," but I didn't feel too welcome. It seemed more of a prison camp than an army camp—barbed wire everywhere, sentries with machine guns in towers all around the edge of the camp. A couple of privates rolled aside a big barbed-wire gate, and we drove through.

TWO

"I'd like to welcome all of you to Camp Enari." The major was pacing up and down, looking at the floor. We were lined up all around the walls of the big plywood building. A private was passing out clipboards and a thick wad of forms to each person.

"...and I'd like to be able to say that you're going to enjoy your stay here. Unfortunately, you *won't* enjoy it—nobody ever has. And you might as well start getting used to the fact that there's a war going on, on the other side of that barbed wire. Nobody's ever gotten killed inside Camp Enari, though we've been attacked a few times. But most of you aren't staying in Enari.

"I'll give you the facts right now. You're going to spend a year—most of you—someplace here in the Central Highlands of Vietnam. Some of you are going home early. About one man in twenty goes home dead. There are about forty men in this building, so figure it out. Maybe the guy standing next to you, maybe the guys on both sides of you...maybe you.

"Now I'm not saying this just to scare you—but if you're scared, you're smart. You've got a much better chance to get home in one piece if you're scared—careful scared, healthy scared—every day of the next three hundred and fifty-some. The guy who gets cocky, the careless one, he's the one who doesn't watch where he puts his foot and steps on a mine. He's the one who lights up a cigarette at night and gets a sniper's bullet through his brain. Or doesn't keep his weapon clean and has it jam up when it could save his life.

"That's your first warning. You'll get lots more in the next week. There'll be training every day from 0600 in the morning—pay attention to every word these men tell you. They're all combat veterans, and they'll be trying to teach you how to stay alive for a year.

"Now I'm going to turn you over to Sergeant Ford, who'll help you fill out the forms. Good luck."

A short blond sergeant, with a face like a monkey, who had been sitting on the floor, walked to the center of the room. "Okay, troops, listen up!" A sergeant knows nobody ever listens to him, so he has to say "listen up" before he says anything important.

"The pink slip of paper on top there is what they call a release. The army's going to send a telegram to your old lady if you get killed or hurt really bad. If you can read, you'll see that this pink form asks whether you want a telegram sent if you're 'lightly wounded.' Just check 'yes' or 'no' and sign it. If you're smart, you'll check 'no.' You don't want your old lady to freak out just because you got a little hole in your head. Right?"

That made sense, even if I didn't care for the way he said it. I checked "no" and signed it.

It went on like that for a couple of hours, while we filled out the rest of the forms. Some of them could scare you if you stopped to think about what they meant, like that first one, and the one that took care of where to send your body… but most of them were just regular army stuff, about your pay and where you were born and how old your mother is and all that stuff.

I must have written my address a hundred times. When we finally got up to leave, my hand was ready to fall off from writing so much.

We left that place and walked through the scorching sun to Supply, another big shack like all the others. We just walked through in a line and they piled stuff in our arms—some clothes, first-aid packet, a canteen and mess gear so we could eat and drink, a steel helmet— steel "pot," they call it—to keep our brains inside in case there was an attack, and for sleeping, a couple of sheets, a mosquito net, and a blanket—must be 130 degrees out there, and they give us a blanket! We each got two boxes of malaria pills and a little bottle of pills for purifying water.

Then they led us to our billet and showed us how to tie the mosquito nets over our bunks, to keep from being eaten alive during the night. I hadn't noticed any mosquitoes around, but they said they really get thick after sundown.

By the time I got my bed made and the net strung up, almost everybody else had left for lunch. I took my mess kit—just a metal bowl with knife, fork, and spoon attached—and went out to find the chow hall.

Turns out I walked right by it, on the wrong side. I waded through the thick dust for a couple of blocks—the dust was fine as talcum powder, dark red, and piled up in drifts above your ankles. Finally I stopped a guy and asked directions. He sent me back to the mess hall, and this time I passed the right side. There was a long line, not moving, and I went to the end of it.

Just then a siren started to blow. I nearly jumped out of my skin and started looking for a bunker to run to.

The guy in front of me turned around and smiled. "Man, don't sweat it… that's just the noontime whistle. Don't mean anything unless it blows some other time—then you wanta jump."

"Thanks—guess I'm a little jumpy." I stuck out my hand. "Name's John Farmer."

"Wally Lewis." He was short and stocky. "Guess you're new around this place—been assigned yet?"

"No, just got here today. They say we've got to go to a bunch of classes before we get assigned."

"Right… you get to play soldier for a few days. Just hope you don't have to *be* one, though. A lot of guys get assigned here in base camp. Never have to shoot a gun again, after that first week."

"That'd suit me fine. I never asked to be part of this war."

Wally laughed. "Man, who ever did?"

We talked for about twenty minutes, while the line moved up. Wally was a clerk for one of the infantry companies. Wasn't always a clerk, though—he started out as a rifleman. After six weeks in the boonies he got shot in the arm. He showed me the scar, bright pink against his brown skin. When he got out of the hospital, the clerk job was open and he grabbed it. He'd been behind a desk ever since.

Like the major, Wally said nobody had ever gotten killed inside the base camp, Camp Enari. But it still paid to be careful. People had been hurt in three rocket and mortar attacks, and it was just luck that nobody had died.

There was a rumor, Wally said, that Enari would get another attack around midnight. But that rumor came around at least twice a week. He said it wasn't worth worrying about.

Wally was only in this part of camp—Fourth Admin—to round up some new men who had been assigned to his outfit. After chow he went off to find them and I went back to my billet.

Some guys were sitting in little groups talking, and a bunch of old sergeants were sitting in the back playing cards and passing around a bottle of whiskey. I flopped down on my bunk and tried to get some sleep. It was too noisy and too hot.

After a while a sergeant came in and rounded us up. We walked out to a black metal shed in back of our billet.

"This here is called a tock," the sergeant said. "There's enough M-16's in here to give you each one and have some left over. Now who's the highest ranking man here?"

One of the sergeants who'd been drinking whiskey, almost bald with a little fringe of white hair, stepped up. "That'd be me, I guess. Master Sergeant Jack O'Donnell."

He opened the tock and gave the key to O'Donnell. "Sarge, you're in charge of givin' these weapons out. Two different times you give 'em out."

He walked inside the dark tock and came out with a clipboard. "When you give 'em out for training, have somebody write down everybody's name and the serial number on the weapon he gets. Use this clipboard and have him put it back in the tock when he's through.

"If there's an attack, just open it up and pass out the guns as fast as you can. I'll come by with ammunition if Charlie gets inside the camp.

"If you leave the area at night, to go to the NCO club or somethin', give the key to someone who'll stay around 'til you get back. Charlie doesn't usually attack before midnight—try to be back by then.

"Now this goes for everybody. Any time you go out after dark, take your steel pot, canteen, and first-aid packet. If there's an attack, get in the nearest trench or bunker. Try to get back here. This is the only place you're goin' to get a gun. Be back here by midnight ev'ry night.

"That's about all for today. You can do whatever you want as long as you're back by midnight. The PX closes in an hour and a half. You probably won't get there for another couple of days, so better go now if you need cigarettes or shavin' stuff. The clubs open at six—that's 1800 for you hard-core types. There'll be a movie outside here soon as it gets dark. Dismissed."

I really wanted something to drink after breathing that dust all day. Since we had a couple of hours before the Enlisted Men's club opened, I followed a bunch of guys down to the PX. I thought maybe I could get a Coke there.

The PX was huge, the size of a big supermarket, and it had just about everything. Everything but Cokes, that is. I picked up some comic books and a little can of pineapple juice. The little Oriental checkout girl opened the can for me.

The juice was good but it just made me thirstier. I went back to the Admin company area and emptied my canteen down my throat. Then I went up to the mess hall to beat the line for dinner. I should have known better.

I was sitting in the shade in front of the mess hall with two other guys, reading about the Fantastic Four. The mess sergeant grabbed the three of us and put us on "serving detail." So I got to eat early, but spent the next hour spooning out mashed potatoes to guys who were smart enough to come late.

After he finally let us go, I was dead tired. I stumbled back to the billet and flopped in my bunk. It had been a rough day, but it was still so hot and noisy that I just couldn't sleep.

A bunch of guys came in wearing just towels and boots. They were actually clean. I looked at myself—red dirt ground into every bit of skin—and asked one of them who told me where the shower was. So I stripped down—looked like a cartoon Indian; the dust goes right through your clothes—locked up my wallet and watch, and went to find the shower.

It was a pretty crude arrangement, but it worked. Just a wooden floor with plywood walls, and water dripping down from a discarded jet fuel tank overhead, the kind that goes on the wing-tip. I wondered what had happened to the rest of the jet. There were twelve or thirteen guys standing shoulder-to-shoulder under the tank, scrubbing like mad. When one of them popped out I squeezed into his place. Then I found out why everyone was in such a hurry—the water was freezing! I lathered up, rinsed off, and jumped out, my teeth chattering. While I was drying myself, one of the guys waiting in line for the shower spoke up.

"Seems pretty cold, doesn't it?"

"Like ice water!"

"Man, it's not that cold. Just that your blood's gettin' thin. It's livin' in the tropics that does it. I've been here a week, and if I wasn't so fuckin' cruddy you couldn't *pay* me to get under that thing."

"That's great. That's really great."

"Well, they're supposed to heat it—see that little oil burner underneath the tank? Whoever's in charge of it's been slackin' off—we got hot water one time this week. And it didn't last long."

I got dry and walked back to the billet, walking carefully so as not to stir up dust onto my clean skin. The sun was setting, and I had to admit it looked real pretty. We had good sunsets in Oklahoma, too, but nothing like this; bright splashes of crimson and purple just glowing in the dark sky. Must have been all the dust in the air.

Back in Basic, somebody had told me that Vietnam used to be a vacation spot for rich Europeans. I guess it *would* look pretty nice if you got rid of all the barbed wire and guns and mickey-mouse army shacks. While I was getting dressed I tried to picture what Cam Ranh Bay would look like with the army gone… suntanned dolls in bikinis, fat old rich men sitting under beach umbrellas with frosty tropical drinks, speedboats pulling water skiers through the bay…weird.

With a brand-new uniform, I felt like a human being again. It was ten minutes to six—1750 if you want to get technical—so I gathered up my comic books and went off to wait for the club to open.

I waited about half an hour—nothing good ever starts on time in the army—and this rough-looking master sergeant walked up to unlock the place.

"Ain't none of you guys comin' in here without you got yer canteen, yer pistol belt, yer first-aid pack, and yer steel pot. So jus' high-tail it back to yer billet an' get straight.

"What you gonna do if ol' Charlie, he decides to hit tonight while yer in there gettin' drunk? You gonna stroll back t'yer billet and get yer stuff? No, you ain't. You gonna carry it with you all the time.

"And soljer, get them sleeves rolled down. Ev'y day at 1700 you gotta roll yer sleeves down cuz that's when the skeeters come out. One o' them malaria skeeters bites you and yer gonna wish you had that sleeve down.

"Them comic books ain't gonna keep the frags outa yer head, soljer. Go on back and getcher stuff."

I went back to the billet, feeling kind of stupid, and got out my stuff. I fastened the first-aid packet and the canteen to the pistol belt, rolled it all up and stuffed it in the steel pot. After all, he didn't say we had to *wear* the junk.

The beer was fairly cool. Somebody had managed to get some ice. The club was just a shack, but they actually had a juke box. I listened to the music for a while, reading my comics. Then a guy sat down across from me, dropping his helmet on the concrete floor with a loud clatter. "You're a new guy too, aren't ya?" he asked.

"Sure… how can you tell?"

"Take a look around. We're the only ones in here carryin' *this* shit around." He gave the helmet a kick. "They say this is the safest place in the whole fuckin' Central Highlands."

"Well, that's good to hear."

"Yeah." He stuck out his hand. "Willy Horowitz."

"Farmer, John Farmer. Just come in today?"

"Yeah, same plane as you, I think." He sucked down about half the can of beer. "What you do, back in the world?"

"Nothin' much. Just got out of school last June. Pumped gas for a few months, then got a job typing at the courthouse in Enid, Oklahoma."

"Didn't wanta go to college?"

"Thought about it—didn't have the grades to get a scholarship, though. Said the hell with it. How 'bout you?"

"I went for a year. City College, New York—guess I partied too much, flunked chemistry and got kicked out, for half a year, anyhow. Plenty of time to get drafted—you didn't *join up,* did you?"

"Hell, no. All I did was turn nineteen."

"Where'd you do Basic?"

"Fort Leonard Wood. That's in—"

"Yeah, I know, Missouri. Asshole of the world. I got my Engineer training there."

"Me, too," I said. "Bet we were there about the same time."

"Our cycle got out the end of December."

"Same here—what company?"

"Bravo."

"How 'bout that—I was in Charlie. We were practically next-door neighbors."

"I'll drink to that… hell, I'll drink to anything." He crunched the beer can double and stood up. "Ready for another?"

"Yeah—here." I pushed a dollar at him.

"Shit, keep it. I been playin' poker, got more damn MPC's than I know what to do with."

MPC's, Military Payment Certificates, were what everybody used for money in Vietnam. They had different colored bills for tens, fives, and ones, then little bills like Monopoly money instead of coins. You could buy slugs at the bar, to operate the juke box.

"Budweiser OK?" He had two cans in each hand, set them down in the middle of the table.

"Sure." I slid one over and sipped it. "How do you like it so far?"

"Like it?"

"The war, Vietnam."

"Shit." He took out a cigarette and tapped it on his thumbnail. "It wouldn't be so bad… you know, army-wise. They don't hassle you like they did Stateside—but God, that rocket attack—were you in Cam Ranh Bay when—"

"Yeah, that was bad."

"Bad… scared me shitless. Wonder how often, how much of that shit we're gonna get."

"Don't know," I said. "Guy told me that was just a picnic compared to the real thing."

"Yeah, but ya never know. Some guys like to act hard-core, scare the shit out of ya."

"Guess we just wait and see."

"Yeah." He looked at his watch. "Look, there's a movie on in a few minutes, outside by the billet… wanna go check it out?"

"Sure." We got a good supply of beer and split.

It was pitch dark on the way over, and I managed to step into a ditch. They had these three-foot-deep ditches all over the area; you're supposed to dive into one when the shooting starts. I turned my ankle and limped the rest of the way to the movie.

It was one of those Italian-made Westerns, about some guys blowing up a bridge. Pretty good.

When they turned off the movie it was almost pitch-black—just a little bit of starlight—but we had pretty much figured out where the ditches were. Managed to get back to our bunks without breaking my neck.

It had gotten right cool and I didn't have any trouble falling asleep. But I don't think I slept more than a few minutes when some guy pulled on my leg, nearly yanking me out of bed.

"Incoming! We got incoming!" Then I could hear the faint *crump—crump*, just like it'd been in Cam Ranh Bay a few days before. I jumped down, scooped my steel pot off the floor, and ran for the door. It was a mess, everybody trying to get out at once. I finally got outside and ran for the nearest ditch. Cut my bare foot on a rock but hardly felt it. I jumped into the ditch and laid down lengthways.

You could hear the rockets whistling in, but you couldn't see them. The explosions got louder and louder. My throat got dry and I started shaking.

Then a bright blue flash and the ground jumped, and a noise like somebody slapped your ear with a baseball bat. It must have been real close; you could smell the smoke and hear clods of dirt falling out of the sky.

Someone down at the end of the ditch yelled, "Medic! Jesus Christ—Medic! I been hit!" The medic ran by me, out of the ditch, crouched low. Another round whistled in and the medic jumped in the ditch, but it landed pretty far away. He got back out and ran down to the wounded guy. Watching him, I decided there were worse things than being a combat engineer.

"Pass it down!" The guy on my left handed me an M-16. I gave it to the next guy and told him to pass it down. I passed about twenty of them and then got one for myself. It wasn't loaded. I remembered the sergeant saying he'd bring ammo if there was going to be trouble. But I wondered whether he'd actually come from wherever he was, with rockets dropping all around. I knew I wouldn't.

The attack lasted about fifteen minutes. None of the other rounds came as close as that one. They told us to stay in the ditch—there could be another attack any time. That was all right with me at first—I felt pretty safe where I was—but after a while I was ready to get out and take my chances. I was just wearing the shorts I slept in, and it was cold. I was also grimy from lying in the ditch and my foot throbbed where I'd cut it on the rock.

We must have laid there for hours. Finally they told us to get out and turn in the guns. I went and washed off my foot. It didn't look bad, but it sure hurt like the dickens. I found the medic and he bandaged it for me.

About dawn they said we could turn in. They said we could have two extra hours of sack time—get up at 0800—and acted like they were doing us a favor. I could have used two extra *days*, but I was too tired to complain. My head hit the pillow and I was out.

THREE

I thought I'd been dirty before, but the next morning when they rolled us out of bed, I was caked and crawly-feeling with red grime. Sleeping on it kind of grinds it in.

Decided to skip breakfast and take a shower, but the water was all gone by the time I got there. So I got dressed and headed for the chow hall. The food was all gone, of course. I got a cup of coffee that tasted like diesel fuel. It woke me up a little, but I still felt like I'd had only two hours' sleep after cowering in a ditch all night.

Refilled my canteen cup with coffee and dumped enough sugar in it to kill the taste, then carried it back to our billet. It was 0845; we didn't have to report for training until 0900.

I sat on a pile of sandbags and watched the people mill around. There was a line of about fifty guys doing a police call, walking in a straight line picking up cigarette butts and such. They seemed more interested in it than usual (usually you just walk along looking at the ground, picking up something when you think someone's watching). A couple of them were really excited, showing off their finds to each other. What's so interesting about a cigarette butt?

The coffee was making me sick, so I tossed out the last half-cup of it. Where it splashed, I saw a glistening piece of metal.

That's what they were picking up. I brushed the dust off the thing and looked at it. Everybody'd talked about shrapnel in Basic—it's the stuff that causes the most casualties—but this was the first actual piece of it that I'd ever seen. It was a chunk of lead about an inch square with razor-sharp edges. I handled it carefully, but it still made a little nick on my finger. It looked like it could go right through a person without slowing down.

Here in 'Nam they called them "frags" instead of shrapnel. That's what they were—fragments—like when an artillery shell goes off, the explosive inside shatters the lead casing into hundreds of frags.

This one must have been one of the frags that had been whistling over my head last night. I wrapped it up in a scrap of paper and put it in my shirt pocket.

They were lining up in front of the billet, so I walked over to join in the fun.

"Awright, listen up." Old Sergeant O'Donnell stepped in front with a clipboard in his hand. "Today yer lucky. We just gotta go across the street for half-a-day's training. I know you guys didn't get much sleep last night. Tough shit. Neither did I. Anybody falls asleep, he goes on KP tomorrow morning." Some of the guys looked like they couldn't stay awake in the middle of a rock band.

We marched more or less in step to a bunch of wooden benches across the street. Whoever was supposed to teach us hadn't showed up yet—probably getting some sleep!—so I just sat down and smoked to stay awake.

"Why the fuck did we have to get a master sergeant?" Willy slumped down next to me on the bench and lit a cigarette. "He's gonna be nothin' but trouble."

"Maybe every bunch has to have one."

"Fuck, no—billet next to ours has a corporal in charge."

The sergeant came back with a captain walking in front of him. O'Donnell looked at us flopped around on the benches and yelled, *"Tench-hut,* god-dammit!" We came to attention in a creaky sort of way.

"At ease, men." The captain waved a hand in our general direction. "Sit down. Smoke if you want to.

"I'm Captain Price, Artillery, here to tell you how the army uses artillery to support the infantry in the field. Any artillery boys in the crowd?" A couple of hands went up. "Well, you two might just as well close your eyes and get some sleep—if you don't know everything I'm tellin' these guys, and more besides, your ass is grass anyhow.

"You were supposed to get instruction on the .45 automatic this morning, from Sergeant Something-or-other. But one of the rocket rounds last night hit the shed where we keep all the demonstration .45's—so you're just gonna have to learn about that on your own, if you get issued a .45. Doesn't make any difference to me one way or the other, of course, except that you'll get off two hours earlier, and I had to get up two hours earlier to give you my talk. I know that just breaks you up." Even Willy chuckled. Captain Price seemed to be all right, for an officer.

"Artillery comes in two varieties, ours and theirs. Either one can kill you dead. All you have to do is be standing in a spot where a frag wants to go.

"Jungle warfare's almost always close range. You grunts, you infantrymen, are going to have Charlie so close you'll be able to smell his BO." People laughed. "I'm not kidding! And even when he's that close, you'll be having artillery dropped in on him, and be damned glad it's there, too. Otherwise, he might be in your foxhole with a knife.

"When it's coming down right in front of you like that, just keep your head down and you'll be OK. Most of these rounds could fall a few meters away; if you're scrunched down in a foxhole you won't get hurt.

"Of course, maybe one time in a hundred, in a thousand, that round's gonna fall short and land right in your lap. Don't waste time worryin' about that. If it happens, you won't feel a thing.

"Now, we have several kinds of artillery, broken down according to how big around the shell is. Biggest one is the 8-incher…"

He went on for about an hour, telling about the different kinds of artil-lery, their "kill radius," how fast they can shoot, and such. I don't think I remembered a tenth of it.

We had a break for coffee and then piled onto an open truck. It took us about a mile, to Camp Enari's perimeter. We got off and stood around while Captain Price talked into a hand radio, getting clearance to drop a few shells into the valley below us.

"Now these 105's will be about the smallest rounds you'll see in combat, not counting the mortars. First comes the smoke round—watch!"

There was a ragged, rustling sound, then a distant pop (the sound of the gun catching up with the shell), and a louder pop, then a puff of white smoke in the jungle below.

"Drop fifty and fire three HE," the captain said into the microphone. I could remember that meant to crank the gun down so it would aim fifty meters closer, and shoot three HE, high explosive, rounds.

"Now look at that little clearing down there." The rustle was much louder than before, followed by pop-pop-pop, and the clearing exploded in three fountains of dirt and gray smoke. The noise of the explosions was loud rolling thunder.

"Well, that's the show, boys. Wish you could see more, but we can't spare the ammunition." He got into his jeep. "Want a ride back, Sergeant?" Our truck had already left.

"Yes, *sir*—Specialist, you march these people back to the billet." They left in a cloud of dust.

"All right, quit bitchin'." The guy was a specialist fourth class, a Spec/4; not quite a sergeant. "At least that's all we're gonna do today. We can go back and hit the sack."

"You ain't gonna make us march, are ya, Specialist?" That was Willy.

"Hell, no. We'll just walk down to the main road and see if we can catch a ride—but fer Chrissake don't forget to salute everything that moves!"

It was a couple of blocks to the road. We stood there for half an hour (long enough to walk it, actually), breathing dust and saluting every couple of minutes, until an empty dump truck pulled up and hauled us to the Admin area.

The specialist advised us to fade out of sight; there was bound to be somebody cruising around looking for detail men. 'Most everybody hiked up to the PX, but I was too tired. Decided to take my chances and headed straight for the sack. It took me about three seconds to fall asleep.

"What the *fuck* do y'think yer doin', soljer?" I looked up bleary-eyed and saw three stripes. Buck-sergeant.

"Just gettin' a little shut-eye, Sarge. Training's over for the day."

"Trainin' might be over, but work ain't over. Yer on my sandbag detail."

"I'm not even in your platoon, Sarge."

"What, you givin' me lip, soljer? Wanna see the captain?"

I knew when I was licked. I sat up and tried to shake the sleep out of my head. "Where's your fuckin' detail?"

"That's more like it. Follow me." We walked out of the billet into the blazing sun. Four men with their shirts off were sitting on a pile of sandbags.

"Awright, goddammit, get to work. Nobody leaves 'til you fill ev'ry fuckin' one of those bags."

I took off my own shirt and joined the group. The sergeant walked off, and a wiry little colored guy handed me a gray burlap sack. Seemed like every other guy in Vietnam was Negro.

"Here, you hold for a while. I'll dig."

"Suits." I held the bag open and he dumped a shovelful of dirt into it. "How'd you get on this detail?"

"Same as these other guys. We got some Cokes at the Class-Six store and came back to drink 'em—found a nice cool bunker, then that asshole of a buck-sergeant found us."

"Yeah," said another guy with an Alabama drawl. "This fuckin' army—we gotta spend all day fillin' sandbags we'll never get t'use."

"I don't know," I said. "We might be behind 'em tonight."

"Might. Might not. How'd he get aholt of you?"

"Just tryin' to get some sleep."

The Alabama boy kicked his shovel in deep and leaned on it. "This goddamn fuckin' army. Charlie keeps ya awake all night and the fuckin' sergeants won't let ya catch up in the day."

It went on like that for several hours. We wound up putting empty sandbags inside the ones we were filling—otherwise we never would've gotten through. Guess it was about four when we put the shovels back in a shed and went our separate ways. I was going to hide somewhere and catch a nap, but first I checked the billet. There were a dozen guys snoring away inside, so I said the hell with it and went to my bunk and flopped. I didn't even wake up for chow.

The next morning we went out to a rifle range and learned how to use an M-16. Some of the guys had them in Basic Training, but most of us hadn't ever shot one before. The stock and grip are hollow fiberglass, so the gun's really light, as light as my .22 at home. But it can really shoot 'em up—put the selector on AUTO and hold down the trigger, and eighteen bullets come out all at once. We learned how to zero them in so the bullets went about where you aimed, and spent the rest of the time murdering tin cans.

In the afternoon we learned how to use explosives. That was kind of interesting, since, being a combat engineer, I'm supposed to know all about them. But I was on KP all the time we'd studied explosives in training, so it was all new.

"These are the things you're gonna be using most often." The guy teaching the class was a Spec/5 not much older than me.

"TNT." He held up a block about half the size of a brick, covered with green paper.

"C-4 plastic explosive." It looked like an overgrown piece of taffy, a white rubbery stick about a foot long.

"Det cord, detonation cord." Looked just like plastic clothesline.

"Time fuse." Looked like the det cord, but orange.

"And, of course, blasting caps." Skinny silver tube.

"Mostly you're gonna use the C-4, because the TNT doesn't work too well if it gets wet. And everything gets wet during the monsoon season.

"Now here's all you have to do, to make a big noise. First you take the crimpers"—he held up a funny-looking pair of pliers—"and crimp a blasting cap onto some fuse." He blew in the end of the cap and slipped a length of fuse into it. Then he squeezed the end of the cap with the jaws of the crimpers, and gave it a couple of tugs to show that it was securely fastened to the fuse.

"Now when you get out in the field you're gonna see hard-core engineers crimp these caps with their teeth, like in the movies. If you're *real* lucky you might see one of them get his jaw blown off. Don't do it.

"In all this bag of tricks," he waved an arm at the pile of various explosives behind him, "the only things really dangerous to *you* are the blasting caps. The rest of it, you can burn or shoot full of holes, nothin's gonna happen.

"But drop one of these blasting caps on the sidewalk—if you can find a sidewalk—and you'll be lookin' for a new pair of balls.

"Now to put the cap in the C-4"—he broke off a piece of C-4 a few inches long—"you just punch a hole in it with the pointy-ended handle of the crimpers. The other handle's a screwdriver, which you'll never use.

"Make the hole about as deep as the cap and push the cap in. Like this. Now follow me." He led us over to a hole in the ground, big enough to hide a truck in. He set the piece of C-4 inside the edge of the hole.

"Let me use your cigarette." He took a cigarette from a guy and touched it to the fuse and blew on it. "You can use matches, but a cigarette works better."

The fuse started to sputter and he said calmly, "Get away and get down." I ran like hell, not knowing whether to expect a firecracker or an H-bomb.

"That's far enough," he shouted. I hit the dirt and the thing went bang, a little louder than a rifle. We went back and sat down again.

"Most of you prob'ly won't ever use this stuff. Explosives are the engineers' job. But you've all gotta know how to do it in case of an emergency, like all your engineers getting killed." Oh yeah.

"You almost never use these things as weapons—you've got plenty of explosives made for that purpose. Mostly you use the C-4 for blowing down trees, either to make an LZ—helicopter landing zone—or to clear away enough of the jungle so that Charlie can't come too close without you seeing him.

"You don't want to blow down your trees one by one, so you use the det cord to make all the charges go off at once.

"This stuff"—he held up a coil of the white cord—"is nothing more than hollow plastic tubing filled with an explosive similar to C-4. If something goes bang at one end, the bang travels down the cord to the other end. To make sure everything goes off all at once, you ought to put a cap on each end of the det cord. But in a pinch, you can just wrap it around the explosive a few times."

He used the det cord to string together a bunch of different kinds of explosives, to show us where the caps went in each one. There were cratering charges, a Bangalore torpedo, a Claymore mine, a dynamite stick, and a number of other things that I never saw again. At the end of the session, he blew the whole thing up. Even scrunched down in a foxhole a block away, it was so loud it made my ears hurt. They rang all the next day.

The week went by pretty fast. We learned about weapons, booby traps, jungle survival—even spent a night out in Charlie's Country, on the other side of the barbed wire. Nothing happened, but it was spooky.

It was like Basic Training all over again, but boiled down and concentrated and with all the bullshit taken out. In Basic they treated you as if you were a boy, and a moron at that—but there's no room for tots or stupids in the jungle.

When the week was over, they posted lists telling where everybody was assigned. Willy and I both drew B Company, Fourth Engineers.

FOUR

The supply sergeant just looked at us when we walked into the supply room, stood there behind the counter and looked at us without saying anything. He rolled a dead cigar butt from one side of his mouth to the other, and back again.

"New guys." It wasn't a question.

"Yes, I'm—"

"Lemme see a couple copies of yer orders." We handed them over.

"Farmer. Horowitz." He took the cigar out of his mouth and looked at Willy. "Joosh?"

"Huh?"

"You Joosh or what?"

"Oh. Yeah, I'm a Jew. What about it?"

"Lucky sumbitch." He shuffled the papers around.

"Lucky?"

"Yeah, we gotta let ya go t' Long Binh fer those crazy holidays. No synagogue around here.

"Had a Joosh guy till a coupla months ago. Useta go ta Long Binh fer a coupla days an' come back really fucked up. Lucky sumbitch."

He got out two copies of a list titled "COMBAT ISSUE—B Company, Fourth Engineers." At the bottom there was a place for your name. He printed our names in the blanks, slowly and carefully.

"Says here plain as day, 'please print,' but none o' you fuckers c'n read so you just put some squiggly fuckin' line that's s'posed to be yer name. So *I* gotta write it.

"Okay." He started at the top of the list. "Rifle, M-16, Serial number such-and-such." He clumped over to a rifle rack, unlocked it, and pulled out the first two M-16s.

"Take good care o' these." He tossed them on the counter with a plastic-sounding clatter. "Gon' save yer life someday."

He slapped two pens on the counter. "Serial number's on th' enda th' barrel. Write it inna blank."

He put his finger on the second item on the list. "Ammunition, 5.63 mm, 100 rounds. You don't get none o' that."

"No ammo?" I said.

"Tha's right. Otherwise you fuckers get drunk an' start shootin' each other in th' ass—"

"Then what the hell are we going to do in case of an attack?" Willy was indignant.

"Son, I been here goin' on twenty-one months—"

"You came back?" I couldn't believe *anybody* would spend more than a year here.

"Shit, yeah. Twenty-one months, like I say, an' I ain't once had to shoot my M-16. Don' even know if th' fucker works." He put a finger on his chin and frowned. "Hey, jus' a second.

"HEY, FUCKFACE!" he yelled.

"Yeah, Sarge," came a tired voice from a back room.

"Where them fuckin' manifests come in this mornin'?"

"Second drawer down on your right. Where I always put—"

"None o' yer fuckin' lip, Private." He opened the drawer and fished out two little tickets.

"Yeah, you get ammo. Yer shippin' out in th' mornin'." He went back to the gun rack, unloaded a box, and brought back two cartons of ammunition. Then he added four hand grenades.

"The rest o' this shit, we already got made up." He pointed to two big plastic bags, the kind laundries use, standing up in a corner. They were filled with various objects, mostly green.

He turned the lists around so we could read them. "That oughta be it."

The rest of the list went like this:

1	BANDOLIER
1	HELMET, STEEL
1	LINER, HELMET
1	NET, CAMOUFLAGE
1	BAR, MOSQUITO
2	JACKETS, FATIGUE, JUNGLE
2	TROUSERS, FATIGUE, JUNGLE
2	UNDERSHIRTS, GREEN
2	DRAWERS, GREEN
1	BOOTS, TROPICAL, PROTECTIVE SOLE, PAIR
4	SOCKS, GREEN, PAIR
1	PACKFRAME, ALUMINUM
1	RUCKSACK
1	PONCHO
1	LINER, PONCHO
1	MATTRESS, AIR
1	PACKET, FIRST-AID
1	BELT, PISTOL
2	GRENADES, HAND, FRAGMENTATION
1	BAYONET
2	CANTEENS, FIBERGLASS, GREEN

"What are we supposed to *do* with all this crap?" Willy asked.

"Do with it? Lemme see." He looked at the list. "Well, y'carry the gun. Stuff the ammo in the bandolier and sling it across yer chest, like a Mexican bandit. Put the liner in the helmet and the camouflage net over the helmet and dump it all on yer head. Put the bayonet and the first-aid packet on the pistol belt and hang it on yer hips. Then buckle the rucksack on the packframe and stuff everything else into the rucksack. Got it?"

"Then you put the rucksack on your back and try to walk. Right?"

The sergeant laughed. "You poor fucker. Son, that ain't thirty pounds worth of stuff. Wait'll you get out in the field and they give you a week's worth of C-rations and 200 more rounds of ammo. Lemme see, and a carton of butts and ten pounds of C-4 and an ax and a few more grenades—when you go back to the world you'll have the strongest back on the block.

"Anyhow, I'll show you how to put the rucksack on the packframe. Get everything together tonight—you're leavin' bright an' early tomorrow for Ban Me Thuot. You oughta take shavin' gear and stationery, but leave the rest of your personal shit here, in your foot locker. Remember, everything goes on your back."

We managed to get the stuff together and staggered out to where the supply sergeant said the billets were. *Had* to be more than thirty pounds!

I had a pretty good night's sleep, but it was still dark when a guy came in with a flashlight and shook us awake.

"Farmer and Horowitz? Saddle up—there's a jeep waiting for you outside." The guy smoked a cigarette in the darkness while Willy and I dressed.

"Who're you?" I asked.

"Masters, PFC Masters. I'm the supply clerk."

"Don't suppose you need another supply clerk… or anything clerk."

"Nah. We got clerks out the ass in this company. You oughta be glad you don't hafta stick around here and put up with all the bullshit." He ground his cigarette out on the floor. "Yeah, I kinda envy you guys. Out where the action is."

"Trade you all the action for your typewriter," I said.

"Man, you don't *know*—half the guys out there go all year without ever gettin' shot at. Just sit on their butts an' take it easy. Free cigarettes, lotsa beer, Red Cross broads…."

"Still trade. Somebody's gettin' shot. I'd just as soon it was somebody else."

He lit another cigarette. "Yeah. Guess I could get reassigned to combat if I really wanted to. Think about it, too, every time the supply sergeant gets a bug up his ass."

I heard Willy grunt as he hoisted the pack. "Ready to move out, Willy?"

"Ready as I'll ever be. Still asleep, though, goddammit."

By the time the jeep got to Pleiku it was getting light. Masters suggested we should poke our guns out the window, just in case, as we drove through. We did, but nobody paid much attention to us.

When we got out of the jeep, Masters handed us a manifest, a plane ticket, to Ban Me Thuot. I took it into the little stucco building by the airstrip, and the guy at the desk told us it'd be loading in another hour or so. We sat and wrote letters until he called us.

The pilot of the C-130 made us leave our hand grenades behind—the supply sergeant should have known they wouldn't allow them on the plane—and we had about a half-hour's ride to a run-down airstrip in Ban Me Thuot. The strip was full of holes, filled with gravel.

There was a sign on the airstrip: INCOMING FOURTH DIVISION PERSONNEL REPORT TO FOURTH DIVISION TRAINS AREA. That was us, but neither of us had any idea what the hell a "trains" area was. There were a bunch of tents at the end of the airstrip, so we headed for them. It turned out that the whole shmear, about a hundred tents, was the trains area. We wandered around for a while—nobody else in sight—'til I finally stuck my head in a tent and some sergeant gave us directions to the engineer's outfit. He was shaving, looked like he'd just gotten up.

"This place don't look too fuckin' dangerous," Willy said as we walked down the dirt road.

"What do you think made those holes in the airstrip—termites?"

"Well, yeah. Still, you don't see anybody gettin' ready to fight a war."

"I don't see anybody at *all*. It's only seven o'clock—maybe they don't fight until after lunch."

"That must be the place." Willy pointed at a tent with a sign that had the Fourth Division cloverleaf and said ENGIN. B CO. We went into the tent.

Inside, there was a guy asleep in a chair in front of a radio set. Willy went over and shook his arm. "Hey, fella, wake up."

He sat up straight and looked around. "Jesus Christ—was I asleep?" He looked at his watch. "Captain'd have my ass in a sling… thanks. Who are you guys, anyhow?"

"I'm Willy Horowitz and this is John Farmer. New guys."

"Just two? They said five or six… you just get in?"

" 'Bout fifteen minutes ago."

"Hey, do me a favor, the mess tent's just across the street. Get us some coffee, OK?"

"Sure." Willy went out the flap.

"Take off your pack and have a seat. I gotta find the papers for you guys."

I sat down and took out a cigarette, decided to wait and smoke it with my coffee. "How is it out here?"

"Here? Oh, pretty much like base camp. Not as much spit-'n-polish. Three hots a day and beer at night, if we're lucky. Only had two attacks all the time I've been here. Nobody hurt."

"Sounds pretty good."

"Oh, it is—hell of a lot better than where *you're* goin'. "

"We aren't gonna stay here?"

"Nah, you're goin' out to either Brillo Pad or, uh, two-one-two-four."

"Where's that?"

"Hills nearby. Fire bases."

"Fire bases. So what's a fire base?"

"Man, a *fire* base. That's where they keep the big guns, artillery. Safest place in the world, forty, fifty big guns and mortars, two grunt companies—two hundred men, man, no way Charlie's gonna fuck around with you. That's a fire base."

"How come one has a name and the other has a number?"

"Oh, the number *is* the name—the '2' means infantry; '21' means A Company and '24' means D Company, that's the two infantry companies on the hill."

Willy came back with the coffee. It tasted terrible.

A tall man, the first guy I'd seen with creases in his pants, came into the tent. "Morning, David."

"Morning, Captain." Willy and I started to come to attention but saw that the guy at the radio stayed in his seat. We stood up anyhow.

He grabbed my hand while I was still deciding whether to salute. "I'm Cap'n Brown, your company commander." He shook hands with Willy, too. "You must be replacements—where are the others, getting chow?"

"Uh, sir, we're the only ones they sent."

He bit his lower lip and picked up a clipboard. "I see. What're your names?"

We told him. "Yes, you're on this list. But so are four others." He sat down on the table and leafed through the papers. "We're under strength. Way under. Those God-dern base camp commandos. We need men out here for *soldier* work—and they grab half our replacements for permanent KP and paper-shuffling."

Why couldn't I have been one of those lucky four? I can wash a mean dish.

"Well, you-all go get some breakfast. Then get a couple of cases of beer from the mess sergeant and head out to the helicopter pad. Tell the pad man to put you on a slick to 2124."

Breakfast wasn't too awful, but we had to go back and get a note from the captain before the mess sergeant would give us any beer.

The pad was quite a ways away from the trains area. That case of beer was getting mighty heavy by the time we got there.

No helicopters, just a bunch of supplies lying around, and the dirtiest guy I'd ever seen, sitting on a crate, drinking beer.

"You the pad man?"

"Nah, he went to get some chow." He gave us the once-over. "New guys?"

"Yeah," I said, "Bravo Company engineers."

"You won't be clean again for a long time. Better enjoy it while you can—pull up a box and crack a beer."

It sounded like a good idea. He let us use his church key. It was on a chain around his neck, all wrapped up in green tape. His dog tags were wrapped the same way; I asked him about it.

"That's so they won't jingle, man. You gotta be quiet. Don' want to jingle in the jungle." He laughed, a dry cackle. "Where you two goin'?"

"Place called 2124."

"2124? Oh yeah—2124!" He cackled again. "That's where I'm headed, too—but that's not what we call it."

"Place has a name?"

"Yeah." Cackle, cackle.

"Alamo. Alamo Hill."

FIVE

The first "slick"—that's a helicopter big enough to hold about six people—was headed for the Alamo. He didn't even shut off the engine; we three just piled in and he lifted off again.

The bird was equipped with sliding doors for both walls, and both of them were open (imagine riding in a convertible going 100 miles an hour, a half-mile up in the air). Door gunners were strapped on either side, leaning on .30 caliber machine guns. They looked bored. The pilot and copilot looked bored. I was scared shitless.

After about fifteen minutes we dropped down to treetop level and roared up the side of a hill. It was green bamboo jungle all the way up to the top, and all of a sudden, dirt—Alamo, a brown scab covering the mountaintop. Barbed wire and bunkers. Heavy artillery all over. On a low-level patch not much bigger than the helicopter, a guy was waving his arms. The helicopter set down gently and kept roaring away, kicking up dust while we helped unload two flame throwers, a mailbag, and lots of C-rations.

So I got my first good look at a fire base through a cloud of whirling dust, dry sticks, and bits of paper kicked up by the helicopter blades. Most people do, I guess.

First, it was really filthy. Everything and everybody was covered with that reddish dust. It had a temporary look; no buildings except for a couple of steel tocks that were probably dropped in by helicopter. I guessed people lived in the bunkers, holes in the ground with crude log roofs piled high with sandbags.

The artillery pieces were clean, black metal shiny with oil, and I could see why; half the crews seemed busy wiping rags over the metal. Looked to be about twenty real artillery-type guns, plus another dozen mortars, each one a black stovepipe about waist-high.

There wasn't any order to the place; the bunkers seemed to be just scattered around all over the hill. The guns were all together in one place, though, and so were the mortars.

Finally the slick lifted and fell away, down the side of the hills. Everything was eerie quiet, like cotton stuffed in your ears.

Speaking, I realized I was more than half-deaf from the noise. "Hey, buddy," I asked the pad man, "where do the engineers hang out around here?"

He pointed up the hill to what looked like a wooden shack on wheels, with a tattered American flag fluttering above it.

"If you swallow hard a couple of times, you'll be able to hear OK," Willy said. I did and it worked.

Right by the shack (which turned out to be a trailer with walls and a roof built over it), there were four guys digging a hole and filling sandbags.

"This Bravo Company engineers?"

An old guy, about thirty-five, dropped his shovel and climbed out of the hole. "That's us." He stuck out his hand. "Sergeant Pobanovitch, call me Pop. Which of you is Farmer and which is Horowitz?"

We got straightened out and he introduced us to the others. "The tall one's Doc Jones, the medic." Jones was the only Negro in the bunch. "Guy with the pick is Fats—Fats, what the hell is your real name?"

"Don't matter. Fats is OK."

"And I'm John Williamson," the last one said. "They call me Professor." He *looked* kind of like a professor, too; horn-rimmed glasses and bald halfway up his head. But he was just as dirty as the rest, and unshaven to boot.

"All right, men, take a break," Pop said. "We'll help you get rid of some of that beer."

"Yeah, it's lunchtime anyhow."

"You ever think about anything else, Fats?"

"You betcher sweet ass I do!" He went over to a cardboard box and fished out a green tin can. "None of them around, though."

"Let me show you guys how to eat C's," the Professor said. He pulled out three C-ration cans and started opening one with a P-38 Army issue miniature can opener. "You don't want to open it all the way—leave enough so you can use the top as a handle." He bent the top over so it made a kind of messy handle. "Then you find yourself a stove, like this." He picked up another tin can with both ends removed to make a hollow stand, with holes punched in the side. "Now. You take some C-4"—he took a stick of the white plastic explosive out of his pocket—"pinch off a piece the size of a marble, put it in the stove and light it." It flared up with an orange flame, and he put the C-ration can on top of the stove. "It heats up real fast but you've got to stir like mad to keep it from burning on the bottom."

The can he brought over for me turned out to be frankfurters and beans; Willy got spaghetti and meatballs. Not bad. For dessert, we opened cans of fruit.

"Farmer, you and Horowitz are going out with the Prof tomorrow to relieve the engineer squad with A Company, First of the Twelfth. Prof'll be in charge, and your squad's code name is Two-One-X-ray. That's what we'll call over the radio when we want to talk to you.

"Reminds me—we've gotta get code names for both of you. Can't use real names over the air. Either of you have a nickname?"

I remembered Smitty at Cam Ranh Bay. "Anything but Tex. Call me

Okie."

"Okie it is." Pop wrote it down in a little notebook. "Horowitz?"

He puffed on his cigarette. "Hmm… how 'bout 'Whore'?"

"Fine." He wrote it down. "Now—good thing you came so early; didn't think we'd get this bunker done by nightfall. Fats, you get a chain saw and Doc, get an ax; go out an' get us some overhead. Rest of us'll keep digging here. Including the lieutenant, if he ever gets back from that goddamn meeting."

"Meetin'!" Doc snorted. "You *know* they's up there drinkin' beer and tellin' dirty stories. Lieutenant's not comin' back 'til the work's all done."

" 'RHIP' Doc—remember what that means?"

"Yeah… 'rank has its privileges'—too many fuckin' privileges, if y' ask me."

"So who asked you? Take a couple of beers, but don't let any officers see you drinkin' on the other side of the perimeter. If they do, I'll swear I don't know where you got 'em."

"OK, Pop." Doc put a beer in his leg pocket and tossed one to Fats.

"Also, don't fuck around out there, y'hear? Get *big* logs—you two're gonna be stayin' in this bunker."

"We know, Pop," Fats said. "The life you save…"

"… may be your own. Goddamn right." Pop watched them gather up their tools and start down the hill, then turned to us.

"So that's the way we run things around here. Free an' easy, no bullshit. Long as everybody follows orders. Anybody starts to fuck around, we lean on him. I lean on him. The lieutenant leans on him. And life can get pretty sorry. Understand?"

We both nodded. "OK—Farmer, get on the pick for a while, break up the ground in the bottom of the hole. Horowitz, shovel the dirt onto that pile. Me an' Prof'll fill sandbags."

I picked away for half an hour and my palms started to blister. Willy traded with me, and the shovel seemed to put blisters everywhere the pick hadn't. After an hour we took a break for a beer.

"Pop," I said, "how dangerous is it out in the field? Many engineers get hurt?"

"No, not many. Too many, but not many compared to the infantry… you'll be part of the 'command group,' always in the middle, infantry all around you."

"It's like this," the Professor added. "The company moves through the jungle in three lines, right flank, left flank, and center file. We'll be in the middle of the center file. Charlie's got to get through a flank before he can get to us."

"But sometimes he does," Willy said.

"Sometimes." The Prof took a big swig of beer. "And sometimes he pops mortars or rifle grenades into the center file. But it's nothing like being on the line, smelling his breath."

"How often?" I asked.

"Hmn?"

"How often do you run into Charlie?"

"Oh, we make contact, what, about twice or three times a month, on the average. A Company hasn't made any contact in two weeks or so, now."

"Means they're due?" Willy asked.

"Doesn't mean anything, except they've been lucky for two weeks. Maybe they'll be lucky for two weeks more. Maybe for the rest of the year."

"Still sounds bad," Willy said.

"Ah, don't sweat it, Horowitz. I'm *glad* I'm goin' out in the field again. One heck of a lot safer than it is here—Alamo's been hit twice this week."

"Jesus Christ!"

"Not all that bad, just mortars. Couple of guys hurt, but nobody's been killed yet. They're bound to try a ground attack, though. I'd just as soon be someplace else when it comes." Prof wiped his forehead with a filthy rag.

"Ain't gonna be no fuckin' ground attack," Pop said.

"That's what they said on Brillo Pad, Pop."

"Tell y'what, Prof. Those Intelligence boys been sayin' we're gonna have a ground attack, three days in a row now. I'll bet you ten bucks there won't be an attack tonight, ten there won't be one Friday night, and ten there won't be one Saturday night."

"I'd hate to collect, Pop."

"You won't collect. Intelligence's got its head up its ass, as usual—hi, Lieutenant. How'd the meeting go?"

A guy not much older than me sat down on a pile of sandbags and took off his hat, wiped his forehead. "Same as usual, Pop. Except Intelligence—no attack tonight."

"Bet's off, Professor!" The Prof laughed.

"Let me guess," the lieutenant said. "You're Horowitz and you're, uh, Farmer."

"Sorry, sir. I'm Farmer and he's Horowitz."

"Glad you could make it. Another dozen and we'd be all set. Anybody got a butt?"

Pop threw him a pack of Winstons. He took out one and tossed it back. "Reminds me—we've got an SP pack down at the pad. Somebody wanta go get it?"

"On my way," Professor said.

"What's an SP pack?" Willy asked.

"Mostly cigarettes and candy," the lieutenant said. "Pop, you about ready to put overhead on this bunker?"

"Yeah, I've got Doc an' Fats on it."

"OK... what can I do besides drink one of those beers?"

"Thought we'd just take it easy until we get the overhead."

"Suits." He cracked a beer. "See, that's the way it is. I command this platoon, but Pop leads it. Pop, if I ordered you to eat a pile of shit, would you do it?"

"With a grin on my face, sir."

"I just bet you would. Anyhow, anything Pop says, goes. Anybody else tells you to do something, you can try to reason with him."

Doc and Fats came puffing up the hill, balancing two eight-foot logs on their shoulders. They dropped them by the hole and flopped down panting.

"Got six more this size," Doc said. "Afternoon, sir." Pant, pant. "How 'bout lettin' us take a break while the new guys haul up a couple?"

We got to our feet. "Just show us where they are," Willy said.

"I'll go with yuh," Doc said, getting up. "Oh, my achin' back."

"Give yourself a Darvon, Doc."

"Fuck, sir, I'll stick to aspirin. Let's go."

We found the logs, and Doc showed us how to get one on each shoulder. They didn't start to get heavy until we'd gone about ten steps. We barely made it to the top.

"Good job," Pop said. "OK, Fats, you an' Doc get the next two. Then Farmer and Horowitz again."

"What kind of cigarettes you smoke?" Prof was opening a cardboard box with his bayonet.

"Pall Malls for me," I said.

"Same."

He opened the box and tossed a carton to us. "That's all we got, you'll have to split it. Won't get any more for a week."

"Five's plenty."

"Not for me," Willy said. "What else you got?"

"All the menthols you can smoke. Everything else is pretty much spoken for."

"Ugh. Gimme a coupla packs of menthols, then. Just in case."

"Have a carton. You can always throw 'em away."

Willy and I helped Pop and the lieutenant stack sandbags around two sides of the hole. When Fats and Doc came back, all of us wrestled the six logs into place on top of the sandbags, then we went back to get the last two.

By the time we brought the two logs back, they'd covered half the bunker with three layers of sandbags. We placed the logs and finished piling up sandbags; wound up with four layers.

"Well, what do you think, Pop?"

"Four layers'll probably stop a sixty-millimeter mortar. Not much else. It'll do for tonight, though."

"Let's get some chow and call it a day."

"Goddamn it, Fats; get some chow, get some chow!—everybody else *hates* C-rations."

"Lieutenant Byrnes!" A private came running down the hill.

"Yes?"

"Command post wants you on the double!" He came to a staggering stop. "A Company's made contact, out in the boonies. Company-size ambush."

"Holy shit!" The lieutenant scrambled up the hill.

Pop grabbed the guy's arm. "Any casualties?"

"Yeah. Don't know how many yet."

"Prof, better get ready to blow an LZ. Your demo bag up tight?"

He picked up a bag and rummaged through it. "Plenty of caps, fuse, det cord. We'll get a box of C-4 down at the pad."

Then the artillery roared, BLAM BLAM BLAM-BLAMBLAM; I jumped out of my skin and so did Willy, but the others didn't seem to notice.

"Farmer, Horowitz, go with the Professor. Wait on the pad 'til we send word."

We put on our packs, picked up rifles, and walked down to the pad. While we were on our way, three jets in tight formation streaked over the hill.

"That'll be air support," Prof said. "Watch."

Two of the jets peeled away and climbed, while the third went on for a half-mile, shot two rockets and a long burst of machine-gun fire, and climbed. A minute later the other two, about ten seconds apart, screamed over the hill again. The first dropped a load of bombs and the second dropped a large barrel that burst into an orange-and-black flower at treetop level—napalm. They made a tight U-turn, rejoined the first jet, and sped for the horizon in tight formation.

"Whew! How do they know they aren't getting our boys?"

"Sometimes they do. Can't be helped."

Doc and the lieutenant came down the hill, carrying two chain saws and two axes. "Prof, you can scratch the C-4, they've got a natural LZ."

"Thank God for that."

"Yeah—look, the ambush dropped back after first contact, but they expect a night attack. They're digging in; you three got to go drop trees for their overhead."

"Coming back tonight?"

"No, you better count on staying. Doc's going along; they've got twenty casualties already. Sure to pick up more tonight.

"You new guys got plenty of ammo?"

"Two hundred rounds."

"Ammo dump's over there—better get another 500 apiece."

"Sir, our weapons aren't zeroed yet."

"Doesn't mean anything," the Prof said. "Never see your target out there anyhow."

"That's right. You get the first slick out—it's still a hot LZ, you'll probably have to jump."

I ran to get the ammo—I could hear the soft thrumming of a helicopter coming up the hill. Hot LZ? Jump?

How far did they expect us to jump without a parachute?

SIX

The slick brought us down, dropping like a rock, to within five feet of the clearing below. The copilot jerked his thumb and we jumped out.

Five feet isn't a long way to fall unless you happen to have a fifty-pound pack, a rifle strapped on your back, and a heavy chain saw in each hand. I hit hard, and fell over on my face. One chain saw ripped a chunk of skin out of my right leg. The chopper zoomed away, straight up.

"Hot LZ" means the pilot won't land, for fear of getting shot up. A couple of feet more couldn't have made that much difference, though. Besides, nobody was shooting anybody.

"Over here! Keep down!" A GI waved from the edge of the clearing.

The four of us got up and ran in a low crouch to where he was standing. "Are we glad to see you. You a medic?"

"Roger." Doc was staring straight ahead while he took the medic bag off his shoulder. I came up even with him and saw what he was looking at.

They had all the wounded and dead gathered in one place. The dead men, three of them, were wrapped in ponchos. Blood had leaked out and settled in a pool under the three corpses.

Two of the wounded were sitting up, smoking; one with the side of his head all bandaged and the other with an arm in a makeshift sling. The other wounded were lying down, some of them unconscious. One man was naked from the waist down. Both his legs were blown off at the knee, stumps covered with scarlet bandages held in place by web-belt tourniquets. I heard Willy puke and clamped my jaws shut and swallowed hard again and again.

"God *damn* it, you didn't bring any blood?"

"Man," Doc drawled, "ain't *got* no fuckin' blood at the fire base. We come from Alamo."

"Sorry. We need it though, man, need it bad. Got any morphine?"

"Yeah, twelve syrettes, maybe fifteen."

"More'n all of us put together. Wanna go down the line and see if anybody needs another shot—but go easy, no tellin' what's gonna happen tonight."

"Ain't nothin' gonna happen tonight, man. The engineers is here. Charlie's scared of the engineers." He grinned and the grin was a skull's leer in a gray Halloween mask. I didn't know Negroes got pale.

"Let's go find some trees," Prof said, and clapped Willy on the shoulder. "Gonna be all right, Horowitz?"

Willy knocked his hand away. "I'll be OK." We went on into the woods.

About ten yards in, we hit the perimeter. Two guys were digging like mad while the third stood in front of them with an M-16. "Hands up, Prof," he said.

"Friendly, goddammit," Prof smiled. "Long time no see, Benson. Where's the captain?"

"That way." Benson gestured with his gun. "You gonna cut us some overhead?"

"Long as you keep Charlie away," Prof said.

"Hell, I thought you engineers was tough—chop 'em up with your chain saws."

"Must have been some other engineers you heard about. I'm chickenshit through and through." Prof didn't smile when he said that.

We walked on through the woods. "Last time I saw that guy I helped put him on a Medevac chopper with a bullet in his arm."

"They made him come back?"

"Yeah. Nice thing about the infantry, they don't let you get soft. Engineers who get wounded stay back in base camp the rest of their hitch."

"Glad to hear *that.*"

"Mm-hmn. Best not to get wounded in the first place, though. There's the captain."

"You boys took your time." He was sitting by a radio with a map unfolded on his knees. He looked pale and his voice shook a little.

"Had to wait for a slick, sir, got here as…"

"OK, Prof, I know—drop your trees in the usual pattern, in a circle around the perimeter. Work fast, it'll be gettin' dark in a couple of hours."

"Yessir." We kept walking in the same direction. "Either of you know how to use a chain saw?" Prof asked. I didn't.

"Yeah, I worked on a farm one summer in high school," Willy said. "We cleared away some woods with 'em."

"Good. You know how to tell what direction it'll drop?"

"We always just made a notch on the side you wanted to fall, and then cut through from the back."

"Kee-rect. You take the yellow saw, the McCullough, and I'll take the green Remington; it's kinda cranky if you aren't used to it. Farmer, you'll be our security. Carry our guns and let us know if any shooting starts. We won't be able to hear a blessed thing once we start up the saws."

It was almost dark by the time we had dropped enough trees and cut them up into sections two ax handles long. While we were working two Medevac choppers landed—hot LZ or no—and took away the wounded men. Doc Jones left on the second one.

We didn't have time to dig a hole, but the artillery lieutenant said we could hop in his if caps started poppin'. We put our bedrolls under a tree by the artillery bunker and started to blow up our air mattresses. I was bushed, and I hadn't done much but stand around with three guns and a gas can, although they let me saw a couple of times to cut up logs.

"Now let me show you what every seasoned trooper takes onto the battlefield," the Prof said, reaching into his pack. He pulled out three beers.

We drank the beer and tried to relax, but it was hard to keep calm and collected while the artillery bursts walked in a circle around our perimeter. That was supposed to keep Charlie away, and I guess it worked. I fell asleep about three o'clock in the morning, and there was no attack.

A godawful racket woke me just as the sun was coming up; birds and monkeys (and lizards, I later found out) screeching at each other. The Professor was already up, heating a can of C-rations the way he'd showed us yesterday.

"Morning, Farmer, drink coffee?"

"Yeah, sure." He tossed me three little brown paper envelopes. Instant coffee, sugar, and powdered milk.

"Use one of those beer cans for a cup, heat it up with some C-4." I had a steaming can of coffee in less than a minute.

"I forgot to bring any C's," I said. And I was hungry.

"They've got a couple of boxes down by the command bunker. But I wouldn't advise eating anything unless you're starving."

"I am, just about. Why not?"

"We're goin' on a burial detail this morning. Smell anything unusual?"

There was a faint sickly sweet smell, mixture of molasses and shit. "Dead people?"

"Dead and half-rotten, in this heat. We've gotta put 'em under the ground, so don't eat anything if you don't have to."

"I thought they sent your... sent people's bodies back to the States."

"Sure, American bodies. Those are Vietnamese you smell. We search 'em, then bury 'em."

The coffee didn't taste so good. "Why do the engineers have to do it?"

"Sometimes the bodies are booby-trapped. Booby traps're our job, not the infantry's."

"We gonna have to disarm booby-traps?"

"Nothing so fancy. We just blow 'em up from a distance."

"Sounds messy...."

"Yeah."

I poured my coffee out on the ground. It had too much cream anyhow.

"There's one over here. X-ray?" That was one of the infantrymen who came with us to help with the pick-and-shovel work, and provide security. They all called us X-ray, as if to remind us that we weren't heroic grunts like them.

"Okay," Prof said. "You two stay here for a minute. I'll check it out for booby-traps." He went into the woods where the guy had yelled, and came back a couple of minutes later, wiping his right hand on his fatigues.

"All set. Here." Prof handed each of us a cigar and lit one up himself.

"Thanks anyhow, Prof. I don't smoke the things."

"No time like the present to start, Horowitz. Keep it in your mouth and it cuts the smell." Willy lit up and so did I.

The body was lying on its back with arms and legs stretched out all the way. The Prof called it rigor mortis. The skin on his face and hands was black, blacker than a Negro's. His body was all puffed up to where it filled his uniform like a balloon. His mouth was stretched open wide, a swollen black sausage of a tongue forced between even yellow rows of teeth. His eyes were wide open and filled with ants. His body was covered with ants and flies.

"You guys are lucky. Don't have to start out with a bad one." Prof took a deep drag on his cigar and kneeled beside the body.

"This is how you check it out. First, make sure there aren't wires or strings attached to the body. Don't see any, do you?"

"Uh uh." I couldn't keep myself from looking at the eyes.

"Okay. Now you have to check underneath. They can pull the pin on a grenade and prop it under the body, so it won't go off 'til you move it. Sometimes you can tell by just looking. Usually you gotta feel." He put his hand palm down on the ground and slid it under the body's back, sliding it back and forth. "Okay. He's clean. Now, Farmer, you do it."

"Aw, Prof, I get the idea..."

He stood up. "Still, you gotta do it."

I kneeled down where the Prof had and slid my hand under the corpse. Through the tight cloth of the uniform, I could feel the dead skin. Cold, spongy, slimy. I spit out the cigar and puked all over the dead man's chest. Prof put a hand under my arm and pulled me to my feet.

"Okay. It's a hard job, I know. Here, wash your mouth out." He handed me a canteen.

Horowitz kneeled down where the Prof and I had and repeated the action.

Somehow, he didn't puke, though he looked a little green when he got up.

The infantry was digging a hole about ten feet away. "This deep enough, X-ray?"

Prof went over and checked it out. "It'll do. One of you guys want to give us a hand with the stiff?"

"Hell, no. We just dig the hole, man. That's *your* job."

Prof stomped back. "Horowitz, take one sleeve. I'll take the other. The grunts don't want to get their hands dirty."

"I'll help," I said.

"Don't have to if you don't feel up to it. Nothin' to be ashamed of."

"It's just a piece of meat. I don't mind." Like hell I didn't. But I know, if a horse throws you, you gotta get right back up on him. Or you'll never ride.

He was heavy. Horowitz took one sleeve and I took the other. Dragging him to the grave, my stomach tried to heave a couple of times, but it must have been empty.

We buried corpses all morning and through half the afternoon. After a while we saw what the Prof had meant, that we didn't "start out with a bad one." There were some bad ones, later on. Chunks of bodies we had to gather up onto a poncho and dump them into the hole. Man-shaped charcoal lumps, feather-light, burned crisp by napalm. And worse…

Finally we worked our way back around to the first grave and walked back up to the perimeter.

"Christ, Professor," Horowitz asked, "why don't we just move on, let them bury their own if they want to?"

"Usually, we do move on, never stay in one place longer than overnight. Took too many casualties, though. Have to stay here a couple of days, get replacements sent out."

"Still, why couldn't we just leave 'em—the smell's not that bad, back where we're camped out."

"It's a public health problem, Horowitz. The flies. If a fly lands on your C-rations… just remember where he's been."

"And open another can."

"Yeah."

SEVEN

We spent three days at the grave-surrounded "patrol base," with helicopters coming in almost hourly, bringing in new replacements, mail, and supplies from Alamo, and twenty-five cases of beer from God knows where. I managed to take it easy the last couple of days; once the base was dug in and the dead were buried, there wasn't much work for the engineers.

Our X-ray squad that had been with A Company all left that first day—one dead, two "lightly wounded." In fact, most of the casualties in the ambush had come from the center file, which was very unusual... normally, an ambush comes from one or both sides, and the flanks take most of the punishment.

So Willy and Prof and I were the engineer squad, and would be for at least a month. Prof assured us that it couldn't be as bad for us; engineers were the safest people in the whole company. But I couldn't help thinking that if Willy and I had come a few days earlier, it would've been *us* going out on that Medevac, wounded or dead.

A couple of days of sitting around, drinking beer, and reading (most of the guys were playing cards, but I only had ten dollars, which wouldn't last a minute) just about cured me of the shakes. The company set up ambushes all around the camp, but they didn't catch anybody, day or night.

We broke camp on the morning of the fourth day. Took about an hour to fill the holes—emptied sandbags, rolled 'em up, and tied them to our packs—and destroy all of the supplies we couldn't take with us.

We walked, and we walked, and we walked some more. Just like the Prof said, we walked in three lines; right flank, center file, left flank. I couldn't see the flanks very often, though, for all the jungle. Sometimes it was so thick—big trees, little trees, vines and underbrush—that the only guy I could see was Willy, walking in front of me. I hoped *some*body knew where we were going.

After a week or so it got to be routine. We'd walk all day and dig in a couple of hours before dark. The bunkers we dug each night weren't as fancy as the ones we had at the original patrol base—but we didn't have chain saws to cut overhead; a good man with a dull ax (they were all dull) takes ten minutes to cut down a small tree.

Then Thursday or Friday, I'm not sure which, the routine was over, all of a sudden.

The captain decided we'd stop on the side of a little hill that afternoon. The top of the hill was bald except for a half-dozen trees; we could cut them down for overhead and make an LZ at the same time.

Prof and Willy started digging the hole and I took the ax outside the perimeter, up the hill to cut down one of those little trees. I figured that one would give us just about enough overhead.

I took one whack and the forest below exploded in gunfire. I hit the dirt and crawled over to my rifle—I had propped it under another tree—jacked a round into the chamber and looked for something to shoot at. Couldn't see anything.

The shooting kept up, in short spurts, but it sounded like it was all on the other side of the company. At any rate, I couldn't see anything. I decided to crawl back down the hill.

The perimeter was about fifty feet away—think I set a new speed record for the low-crawl. All the men had dropped where they were working. They looked a little silly, trying to hide in holes no more than two inches deep.

Willy and Prof were in their little hole, Willy lying flat on his stomach, Prof on his back, smoking a cigarette and running a cleaning rod through his M-16.

"What's happening?" I flopped into the hole next to him.

"Cap'n sent out a couple of patrols, down the hill. One of 'em ran into some trouble. Don't know how many, yet." Another rattle of machine-gun fire, and Willy and I scrunched down into the dirt.

"Relax. They're still pretty far away. Probably don't know where we are, either."

The radioman came crawling over. "X-ray?"

"That's us," Prof said.

"Which of you was up on that hill?"

Oh, shit. "That was me."

"Come on, the captain wants to talk to you." We crawled to the captain, hiding behind some trees about ten feet away, talking on a radio.

"This the guy?"

"Yessir."

"X-ray, how many trees were up there?"

"Six or seven, sir."

"You've got to get them all down, right now. We've got at least two wounded, one dead—going to need a dustoff as soon as they can get back." I guessed that by "dustoff" he meant "Medevac."

"Find Sergeant Davis and have him detail you six men with axes. Run up there, chop 'em down, and run back. Better get a squad for security, too."

I went back to Prof. "Where's Sergeant Davis?"

"Left flank—guess he's out that way somewhere. Why?"

I told him what the captain said. "Well, Horowitz and I'll go, right?" Willy nodded. "Guess we need about ten more, with the security. Let's go."

Sergeant Davis was on the line closest to the shooting. "Can't give you no squad, man, I don't care *what* the captain said. If Charlie's comin' through, he's comin' through right here—I need every man I can get."

"Look, Sarge," Prof said. "They've already called for a Medevac"—which was a lie—"and those wounded men might die if we don't get 'em right away."

"Bullshit. I've seen guys shot in the stomach hang around all day—'sides, if Charlie breaks through a weak line here, he'll wipe us all out."

"Okay, okay—give me two men with axes, I'll see how many I can get from the right flank."

"Simpson! Rodri-gez! Get axes and follow these X-rays." Simpson and Rodriguez scrambled over, looking relieved. Don't guess I'd care to stay on that line, either.

A buck-sergeant named Moselle was in charge of the right flank. "*Ten fuckin' guys?* Yer outa yer gourd, Professor. They's a war goin' on—can'tcha hear?"

"God damn it, Moselle. Nobody's firing on your flank. Anyhow, captain's orders."

"Awright, awright. B team! Up that hill—on the double!"

"Thanks, Moselle. Have 'em back in a couple of minutes."

"I'm comin' with ya to make sure."

"Bring an ax."

"Roger." He picked one up and the six of us ran up the hill in a low crouch. B team was already there, in a circle around a grove of trees. There were seven trees. We saved the smallest for last.

All but one of us dropped our trees, and Prof was working on the smallest one, when a grenade burst halfway down the hill, on the "enemy" side. We hit the dirt and rifle fire roared all around us, most of it from B team—maybe all of it.

"Get back!" Moselle shouted. "Back to the line!"

"Us, too," Prof said. "Go!" We ran like hell.

Prof went straight to his demo bag, started reeling out det cord.

"Can the dustoff land with those two trees there?" Willy asked him.

"Hell, no. Foul the blades. We gotta go blow 'em down." He cut off about eight feet of det cord and crimped blasting caps on each end. Then he snipped off about a foot of orange fuse and capped one end of it.

"Now, either of you ever blown a tree?"

"Not me," I said. Neither had Willy.

"Nothin' to it. One of 'em's cut halfway through, the other's little. A pound of C-4 each would knock 'em to Kingdom Come."

He got two bricks of C-4 out of his pack. "We'll use a pound-and-a-half each, just to be sure.

"You use the pointy end of the crimpers here, poke a hole in the C-4 to make a place to put the cap." He put a hole in one of the bricks, two holes in the other. His hands were shaking.

"Now get this. Don't have time to repeat it. Put one block at the base of the little tree, and one in the notch where Moselle was cutting the other. Connect the two with det cord, that'll make 'em go off at the same time. Then put the fuse in the other end of the block that has two holes. Light the fuse and *crawl* down the hill. Ninety-second fuse, plenty of time to crawl. If you get up and run, you might get shot."

"Which of us is gonna do it, Prof?"

"I am, of course—but if I don't make it, Horowitz tries, if you don't make it, Farmer tries. Farmer, if *you* don't make it, some poor yoyo's gotta go up there with an ax."

I was a little disappointed that he put Willy ahead of me. Also a little relieved. We went back to the right flank.

"Moselle, I'm going up to blow those trees. Give me some cover, okay?"

"Sure. Jus' a second—Hey, Pig! Got that 60 set up?"

"Yeah, Moser—want I should shoot somebody?"

"Professor's goin' up the hill. Lay down a field of fire on his right."

The belt-fed machine gun chattered twice.

"Whenever you're ready, Prof. I'll get a couple of 16's to cover your left."

"Use my new men, Horowitz and Farmer."

"Okay."

Moselle put us in a "foxhole" (about a foot deep) on the edge of the perimeter, facing the hill. "One of you guys start poppin' as soon as Pig starts the M-60. Bursts of three, about five seconds apart; aim anywhere to the Prof's left."

"That's this side?"

"Yeah, yer military left. Don't hit the Prof if you can help it. One reloads while the other fires—got it?"

"Sure, Moser." We set our ammunition in front of us. Together we had twelve magazines, clips with eighteen rounds each, plus 800 rounds in boxes. That was plenty, but refilling the magazines would slow us up.

It was my turn first. When the 60 started blasting—also short bursts, but about a second apart—I laid down a field of fire the way they taught us at Camp Enari. To get a burst of three you had to just touch the trigger, and get right off—if you held the trigger down any length of time, you'd empty the magazine, all eighteen rounds coming out right on top of each other. There wasn't any sense shooting close to Prof, there wouldn't be any enemy on the hillside. I sprayed the edge of the woods that started about fifty feet to Prof's left.

"Fer shitsake Farmer, don't shoot so fast! Five seconds!"

Guess I had fallen into the same rhythm the 60 was using. I sat down to reload and Willy got up to shoot. "Okay, Willy, I'll be more careful."

Pop-pop-pop. "You better. We might—" Pop-pop-pop. "—need this ammo more—" Pop-pop. "—after Prof gets back." Pop-pop-pop-pop. He was shooting just as fast as I had.

"Hey, Willy, slow down yourself!" He started counting to five between bursts. Seemed like a good idea, so I did the same.

Seemed like it took Prof an age to get up the hill. But I was just starting my third turn when he got to the top, so I guess it was about two minutes.

In the movies, I guess Prof would get shot and Willy'd go up to rescue him, and Willy'd get shot and I'd go up and save the day, or maybe get shot, too… but actually, whoever had fired at us earlier was either gone or keeping his head down, because Prof set the charges, lit the fuse, and crawled back down the hill without drawing any enemy fire. When he got back to the perimeter he yelled, "Fire in the hole!" three times, to warn everybody that the big boom wouldn't mean the Russians were coming.

It wasn't such a big boom anyhow—about as loud as one of the artillery shells we had gotten so used to hearing. The little tree flew away like a toothpick, and the bigger one gave a lurch and fell over. Lots of gray smoke and splinters flying.

The firing on the left flank had stopped before Prof went up the hill. When we went back, everyone was digging furiously, trying to build some kind of bunker while it was still light. Prof and I set to digging while Willy took the ax and got us some saplings for overhead.

It was almost dark by the time we finished. We were heating up some C's when we got word that we had to supply perimeter guards all night; two men on, one man off. That meant each of us would only get four hours of sleep. And boy, had I looked forward to hitting that sack.

Shouldn't have worried, though. Nobody was going to get very much sleep that night.

EIGHT

They attacked during the watch when the Professor was getting his four hours' sleep. Willy and I were on top of a bunker on the perimeter. It was about two o'clock and totally black.

We had orders not to shoot until we absolutely had to; the muzzle flash and tracer rounds would give our position away. We had plenty of hand grenades, though; and even though you can't see where you're throwing them, at least they can't be traced back to you.

There was a little radio in each foxhole, a PRC-25 (which everybody called a prick-25). Every perimeter bunker had a code name, starting with Tiger-1, then Tiger-2, Tiger-3, and so on up to Tiger-15. Tiger-1 was the command bunker, where the captain was. We were in Tiger-7. There were three observation posts, Oscar Poppa One, Two, and Three; groups of four men each, sitting about fifty feet outside of the perimeter to give us early warning. Oscar Poppa Two was right out in front of us, and that was where the battle started. It started out real quietly.

The prick-25 whispered. "Tiger-1, this is Oscar Poppa Two. Over."

"Oscar Poppa Two, this is Tiger-1. Boss speaking." That was the captain's code name. "What's up? Over."

"We've got movement out front. Maybe fifteen meters. Over."

"How many? Over."

"Hard to say, Boss. More than ten. Over."

"Well, come back in. If they hear you, chuck some grenades at them. Out."

"Roger, Tiger-1. Oscar Poppa Two out."

"All stations, this is Tiger-1. Oscar Poppa One, Oscar Poppa Three, you come in, too. Tigers, hold your fire until all the Oscar Poppas are in. Over."

"Think we better go wake up Prof?"

"No," I said, "if anything happens, he'll be up soon enough—you scared as I am?"

"Shitless."

"Me too."

"Tiger-7, this is Tiger-1. Over."

Willy beat me to the radio. "Tiger-1, this is Tiger-7. Over," he whispered.

"Tiger-7, I want you to trade stations with Tiger-9; that's Pig's M-60 team. Over. Tiger-9, this is Tiger-1. Did you monitor that? Over."

The radio crackled. "Roger, Tiger-1, this is Tiger-9; we did monitor and we're on our way. Over."

"Well, at least we won't be so close if Charlie follows them in." I started gathering up grenades and ammo.

"Yeah, they'll walk right into that 60—think we oughta wait for Pig?"

"I guess so. Got everything of yours?"

"Six grenades, two bandoliers." Footsteps to our right. "That you, Pig?"

"Yeah. Y'all go on now, two bunkers over, leave your radio."

Took us about two minutes to find the place, even though we could see it before the sun went down. Pig's radio was squawking when we got there.

"… repeat, all stations, everybody, in your bunkers. We have friendly artillery coming in on the old Oscar Poppa Two position. Over and out."

I jumped into the bunker and landed on top of Willy. He was pretty fast when he wanted to be.

"Jesus Christ—that's only fifty feet away!"

"We'll be all right in the—" the world bucked and heaved and shrapnel sang through the air. I could feel the artillery explosions in my teeth and my eyes. Willy's face was chalk-white in the light from the explosions. It only lasted a few seconds.

"Goddamn—you could see the flashes," Willy said. I could hardly hear him for the ringing in my ears. "They've never been that close before."

"Yeah… but think of what it's doing to Charlie."

"Let's hope."

After a minute a bunch of grenades went off, over by Tiger-7. Then automatic rifle fire, with green tracers, coming *into* camp. The artillery barrage hadn't gotten all of them.

Pig answered the rifle fire with his M-60, pouring lead into the jungle at ten rounds a second. Every third round was an orange tracer; it looked like he was spraying a solid line of flame.

A hand grenade went off pretty near, and in the flash Willy and I saw a man walking toward us, not more than ten feet away. I picked up my rifle.

"Wait!" Willy whispered. He pulled the pin out of a grenade and threw it side-arm out of the bunker. "Down!" I was already down.

It went off with a flat CHUNK and Willy got up and threw another. It went off and Willy said, "I think we better get out of the bunker."

"Are you crazy, Willy? With all that shit flying around?"

"Look, Farmer, all they gotta do is roll one grenade in here, and they'll be scrapin' both of us off the walls. Let's get out and lie down *behind* the bunker." I could see the sense in that, so we laid our weapons outside and hoisted ourselves up.

Looked like the battle was just about over. Pig's 60 was shooting in short bursts, but there wasn't any return fire. Tiger-6 and Tiger-8 fired M-16's into the jungle.

Then there was a whooshing sound and an orange ball of fire blossomed in front of Tiger-7. Somebody screamed. Another whoosh, this time the machine-gun bunker exploded and whoever was screaming, stopped.

"What the fuck is that?"

"Sounds like a bazooka," I said. "Does Charlie have bazookas?"

"Look, anything we've got, Charlie can steal. Just hope he doesn't have too many rounds."

"Think we oughta get back in the bunker?" Another whoosh. Hit just behind Tiger-6.

"Hell, no—you get in if you want. I'd rather take my chances up here."

The bazooka, or whatever it was, blasted a round right on top of Tiger-8. I was glad that we hadn't been shooting. He seemed to have zeroed in on everybody who'd given away their position with tracers.

Then we had a stroke of luck. The infantry had rigged the woods outside of the perimeter with trip flares, bright super sparklers that would go off if somebody tripped over a wire. There was a loud pop! and the jungle was flooded with light.

We saw them right away—two enemy soldiers in front of where Tiger-7 used to be, one of them with a long tube balanced on his shoulder. The other one had a bazooka round in his hand and another tucked under his arm. Willy and I opened up on them with our M-16's.

The ammunition bearer ran for the woods, and I think he got away. The other man was braver; he swung the tube around to where it was pointing at us, then one of us hit him and he flopped over backwards, shooting his last round into the trees where it exploded right over him.

That was the end of the battle. No telling how many enemy were involved, how many got away. We only found three bodies in the morning.

But the choppers took away three badly wounded GI's and six bodies, including Pig. That round, we had to admit, went to Charlie.

NINE

Willy and the Professor and I spent another three weeks in the field, without getting into any more fire-fights. Then one evening a chopper came in with three engineers, guys I'd never met (though they knew Prof), who took over. The three of us took the chopper back to the fire base.

The fire base wasn't on Alamo anymore. They'd moved to a place called Plei Djaran, in the middle of a grassy field about a mile wide. They even had a landing strip for light planes. There was a mess tent serving two hot meals a day, and a beautiful river just down the road where we could swim a couple of times a week.

Nothing much happened the month we were there. We spent most of our time putting up barbed wire around the perimeter. At night we'd sit in the dark and drink beer when we had it, listening to Radio 560, the army's Pleiku station, which played mostly soul music, and a little country and western. One of the guys had some pot, but there wasn't any place we could go to smoke it in privacy, and the Fourth Division is pretty strict about it; get caught and you'll spend a couple of months in LBJ, Long Binh Jail.

The three of us went back out to A Company on the first of May 1968. I was starting to feel like a real old-timer, especially since most of the guys recognized me and Willy from last time. They had had it pretty easy while we were gone; only one light contact. The brass said things were quiet because the 66th NVA (North Vietnamese Army) Regiment, who had been giving A Company such hell since February, had moved on south, toward Saigon. I didn't care what the reason was, but I was mighty glad that things were going to be less dangerous.

Sure enough, we moved around for a couple of weeks without so much as a peep from Charlie. Just walked around the boonies all day, dug in at night, got up in the morning, and humped all day again…

Things were going so easy that I guess I can't blame Prof for being careless. I might have done the same thing.

Prof and I were "walking point"; that is, we were at the front of the center file. I'd be in front for an hour, Prof second; then we'd switch and Prof'd be in front for an hour. This was the worst place to be in the center file, because you're usually the first one to go if you run into an ambush, and you get the first chance to step on any mines or booby traps that might be along the path.

So when you walk point, you're supposed to be especially careful to watch the ground and not step on anything peculiar-looking. Of course, you're supposed to watch the jungle, too, for whatever good it'll do. You can walk within five feet of a good ambush and not know it's there.

But the company hadn't ever come across a mine—they aren't common in the Highlands—and there hadn't been an ambush since the first day we joined the company.

We've got an antipersonnel mine, and I guess Charlie has it too, called a "Bouncing Betty." When a person steps on it, it doesn't just go off; first a little charge goes off that shoots it up to about chest-high, then it explodes.

I was looking off to the side when Prof stepped on the thing. It was pop-BANG! and I went down like I'd been hit by a truck. Pain like big bee stings up and down my left side. A big purple splotch was spreading along the inside of my leg. I clamped both hands over it and blood oozed out between my fingers. There was another stain welling out on my knee and while I watched I could see other, smaller ones, break out all over the leg. My left arm was covered with little bleeding pockmarks from tiny frags and blood started dripping from my chin. "Medic," I tried to shout, but it didn't come out too loud, so I tried again, and again, getting louder each time.

A medic came running up, crouched low. "Just lie down for a sec, Farmer, I've gotta check on the point man."

Prof was lying face-down in a puddle of blood. There was a hole in his neck so big that his head almost fell off when the medic turned him over. His face was blown away completely and his body was ripped open from throat to balls. I fainted.

I came to when they rolled me onto a stretcher. God, that hurt. My right arm was strapped to my side, blood feeding into it from a plastic bag a medic held over my head. There was a helicopter up the trail a ways, and they carried me there, walking very carefully. Guess somebody had told them to watch their step.

When they clamped the stretcher into the chopper, I saw that one of the guys carrying it was Willy. He grabbed my hand and said something, but I couldn't hear it over the roar of the slick's engine, so I just nodded.

It was a long ride. Seemed even longer when I saw what was on the floor, a rolled-up poncho with bloody boots sticking out from one end. Prof was going home early.

We landed in the Ban Me Thuot trains area, and two husky medics carried my stretcher down into a huge underground bunker, all lit up with fluorescent lights. They plonked me down on a table, and a man in a white coat came up with a clipboard.

"What's your name and serial number, son?"

"John Farmer, US 11575278." He wrote it down and put the clipboard away. He picked up a pair of scissors and started cutting away my trousers.

"Now we aren't gonna… take any stitches or anything, here—I just want to put new bandages on you and maybe give you a little shot. You'll be going to a regular hospital in about an hour." He also cut off my left boot. "Whoops—here's one the medic missed—son, did you know you'd been hit in the foot?"

"Can't say I did." It *did* hurt a little, now that he mentioned it.

"Well, it's just a little one. I'll fix it up." He took a big Band-Aid out of its paper covering and smoothed it over the wound. "Got your shot record in your wallet here?"

"I guess so."

"Mind if I dig through and find it?"

"Hell, no, go ahead." I wished he would just bandage me up and let me get some rest.

"Hmm… looks like I better give you a tetanus shot, just to be on the safe side." He produced a big wicked-looking needle and poked it in my arm. Funny thing, I hardly felt it. I asked him about that.

"Why, son, you're chock full of morphine… don't you remember the medic giving you a shot?"

"No, I was passed out most of the time."

"Oh. Well, that's why it doesn't hurt so bad. Let's take a look at these holes in you." He took the bandage off my head, and laughed.

"Just got a little scratch on your earlobe here, son; that always bleeds like a stuck pig. Doesn't mean anything, though; it'll be fine in a day or so."

He passed right over my arm and went to the large wound in my thigh. He started to untie the pressure bandage and some blood slopped out. "You're still leakin' a little bit there, partner—" He slapped a new pressure bandage on top of the old one and laced it tight "—but that one'll be okay, too, given time." The only other one that was still bleeding was the one on my knee; he put a new pressure bandage on it, too. The others he just wrapped up with gauze and tape. He wrapped a tube around my arm and took my blood pressure, and then pulled out the needle that was dripping blood into my other arm.

"You're in pretty good shape, son, all things considered." He took all the things out of my pockets and put them in a plastic bag. My wallet was covered with blood. He handed me the bag. "Now hang on to this until you get to the hospital in Tuy Hoa. They'll take it and lock it up for you, while you're in surgery."

"They gonna have to operate?"

"Sure, son, you don't want to go through life looking like a piece of Swiss cheese—and after they sew you up, you'll take it easy in bed for a few weeks.

Just read funny books and goose the pretty nurses as they go by." He squeezed my shoulder and smiled. "You'll be all right, John." And I wondered if that was what Willy said when he put me on the slick.

"Chavez! McGill!"

"Yessir?"

"Take Mr. Farmer up to the waiting room and manifest him on the next flight to Tuy Hoa."

They took me to a large room with a bunch of empty stretchers and set me next to a table with a pile of *Reader's Digest*s. I picked one up and leafed through it but had a hard time concentrating on the words. No need to give myself a headache on top of everything else. Besides, if I hit "Humor in Uniform," I'd probably puke.

With nothing else to do, I couldn't help but concentrate on the pain. It wasn't so bad, with the morphine, as I remembered it had been, first off; but it was still there—deep now, bone-deep and throbbing. "Medic?"

A guy came over, chewing gum, carrying the latest *Playboy*. "Yeah, champ?"

"You got anything for pain?"

"Just Darvon. Y'want a coupla Darvon?"

"If that's all you've got." He left for a minute and came back with two blue-and-gray capsules and a tiny cup of water.

"You don't wanna drink too much, now, not if yer goin' into surgery." He would say that. I was thirsty as a bitch.

By the clock, it was thirty-five minutes before Chavez and McGill came back to get me. They picked up the stretcher and one of them asked, "You ever ridden on an ambulance, fren'?"

"Never have." Ouch. My leg hurt every time either one of them took a step.

"Well, this will just be a short ride, but we'll put on the siren for you."

"Thanks a lot."

"Don' mention it."

They put me in the ambulance—it looked just like any other olive-drab army panel truck—and actually burned rubber on the dirt road, taking off. They switched on the siren. It might have been fun if I'd been in any condition to enjoy it.

There was a big bump—which hurt like hell—and we were on the airstrip, howling toward a C-130 that was all ready to go, engines roaring. They loaded me on and strapped my stretcher in place, and the plane was moving before the rear door had closed all the way.

I looked around. All the other people on the plane were sitting on the other side, perfectly well. There wasn't another wounded person on board—and for all the attention they paid to me, I could be just another piece of equip-

ment. Thinking about it later, I guess that was all right. What did I want
them to do? Stare?

TEN

The plane landed, not too gently, and there was an ambulance waiting for
me. The ride in this one was just as fast and bumpy, but they didn't use the
siren.

A couple of little Vietnamese unloaded my stretcher and jogged me down
a covered sidewalk. The way they grunted and carried on, I was afraid they
were going to drop me.

There was another building with bright fluorescent lights, this time
aboveground. They put me on a table and a doctor came over (holding a
clipboard, of course).

"John W. Farmer?"

"Yes, sir."

"Tell me in your own words what happened."

"We were walking down a trail... and the guy in front of me... stepped
on a mine."

"How do you know it was a mine?"

"Well, it sounded like one, you know, a little... pop before it went off. A
'Bouncing Betty.' "

"Did it kill the man who stepped on it?"

All of a sudden I could see Prof lying on the trail with his guts rolling out,
throat split open, after all the shit we went through together... and it could
just as well have been me. I couldn't make myself answer.

"He *is* dead, then, right?" I nodded.

He asked me other questions about my unit, rank, and so on. While he
was quizzing me an honest-to-God woman came over and cut away my
dressings. She was about as old as my mother. Her touch was very gentle,
but it still hurt when she peeled the dressings off.

She hooked my arm up to a bottle that said "Penicillin 10 million units
USP"—I guess that was a super-shot of penicillin. Must have been at least
a quart.

Then one of the Vietnamese rolled me away, stretcher, table, bottle, and
all. We went down the sidewalk about a block, and through double doors
marked POSITIVELY NO ADMITTANCE. I wondered whether the Vietnamese could read English.

He rolled me up to a white table under a huge X-ray machine. A medic
in a green tunic was talking on the phone.

"Right. He just got here. Okay... bye." He hung up.

"Well, Mr. John W. Farmer. Ready to get zapped by the Monster Machine?"

"Ready as ever, I guess."

"Hmm, that bottle's going to complicate things a bit." It was hanging on a rack attached to the rolling table. "We'll see what we can do, though." He motioned to the Vietnamese, and the two of them lifted me onto the cold enamel under the machine. "Now, we'll do the hard one first. Keep your arm stretched out so you don't pull the needle out, and roll over on your left side. Kick your good leg out to the left. Good. Hold it." He moved the machine around until the nose, a yellow plastic cone, was pointed at the biggest wound. It would have been an uncomfortable position even if I wasn't shot full of holes. He turned to the Vietnamese. *"Di di! Di di mao!"*

I don't know much Vietnamese, but I know that *"di di"* means "get outa here" and *"di di mao"* means "get the *fuck* outa here." The boy left in a hurry.

"Now hold real still until I tell you. Good." He went off into another room and flicked a switch. The machine hummed for a few seconds. "Okay," he said, and came out of the room. Then he took pictures in two other, slightly more comfortable, positions.

He poked his head out the door and said something in Vietnamese I didn't understand. The boy came back in, they put me on the cart, and he wheeled me another couple of blocks.

We went into another building marked NO ADMITTANCE. It was air-conditioned, deliciously cool inside. We went down a hall and into a gray room. The only other patient was a Vietnamese with his arm in a bloody sling, screaming. A medic was sitting at a desk, ignoring him.

The boy wheeled me into position next to the screaming Vietnamese (who was a soldier, or at least wore battle fatigues). The medic filled a needle from a little bottle and came over to me. "You just get X-rayed?"

"Yeah."

"Well, this little shot'll make you feel better. You *are* John W. Farmer, aren't you?" He poked the needle into my arm.

"Right." Twenty Questions again.

"Yeah. Well, I'm gonna shave yer leg, so the doc won't hafta look at all that hair." He soaped up an old shaving brush and lathered my leg. The Vietnamese soldier kept screaming.

"Look, shouldn't you be doin' something for that guy?"

"Nah. He's shot so fulla dope he can't be feelin' any pain. He's an enemy, though, NVA trooper they caught up by Kontum. Guess he thinks we're gonna torture 'im." Then I saw that he was strapped down, the buckles all out of his reach.

It's funny, I never could get up much hate for the enemy. Like I say, this is Johnson's fuckin' war, let him fight it. But I can't say I felt too bad about that guy, screaming bloody murder over a bullet in the arm. In fact, I'd rather have seen him lying on a jungle trail with his throat ripped out and giblets dribbling all over the ground. He couldn't have been the guy who buried the mine, not if they caught him in Kontum—but he'd do until the real thing came along.

The medic finished shaving me and I started to get a little woozy. Thought that shot was supposed to make me feel *better*. At least my ears were ringing so loud I could hardly hear the guy screaming, if he still was. For some reason, I couldn't focus on anything more than a few feet away.

The medic rolled me down to the other end of the room and through a door and into a room that seemed much darker and cooler. I remember an old guy with white hair and big bushy white eyebrows, wearing a green surgical mask, leaning over me, then everything shrunk away and I was out cold.

I woke up struggling against the straps that held me in bed, shouting and crying. A pretty little nurse held my hand and dabbed at my face with a piece of cotton.

"It's all over, soldier. You're gonna be just fine."

Nobody ever called me "soldier" before. But the way she said it, it was nice. She must have given me a shot—the world sprang into focus and I was wide awake. The first thing I saw was a big red NO SMOKING sign.

I looked up at her and asked, "Got a cigarette?"

"See what I can find." I watched her walk away. The white uniform was tight enough to give her a nice swivel. *That* was something I hadn't seen for a few months. Not that I'd stopped thinking about it.

She rummaged around in a desk drawer and came up with a stale pack of Kents. She brought them over with an ash tray and a pack of matches. First civilian matches I'd seen in a long time—they had a tomato sauce ad on the front and a recipe inside. I lit up, about the best cigarette I'd ever had.

She had gone back to her desk. "Say, is it all right if I undo these straps?"

"Sure. Just don't try to run around the block." She smiled. Jesus Christ.

I unbuckled the straps and looked under the sheet. All I was wearing was one big roll of bandage from ankle to crotch. There was a dark brown bloodstain on my thigh, over the largest wound. The whole thing ached, but I can't say that it bothered me too much.

"GI... ay, GI."

There was a Vietnamese strapped in the bed next to me. I didn't recognize him at first, because he was wearing blue pajamas. Then I saw the cast on his arm and knew he must be the NVA who was carrying on so much earlier. He made smoking motions, quick little jerks with an imaginary cigarette.

I lit one up and passed it to him—not the easiest trick in the world, with both of us all tangled up in tubes and bottles.

"*Cam on ong,*" he said. "*Toi la ban.*"

I didn't catch most of that, but "come on" means thanks. Didn't know how to say "you're welcome" or anything, so I just nodded and leaned back in bed and smoked, watching the chick shuffle papers around her desk.

Whatever kept the leg from hurting wore off real fast. "Ma'am?"

"What would you like?" She smiled again. God damn.

"Can you give me something for the pain?"

She looked at her watch, and at a clipboard on the wall. "Not for another half-hour, I'm afraid. You could have a couple of Darvon, but I don't think they'd help much."

"Anything's better than nothing." Actually, I just wanted to see her walk again.

I took the Darvon and chain-smoked for a half-hour. Then she came over again and gave me a shot. It stopped hurting before she even had the needle out, and I was asleep in a minute or two.

I dreamed that the NVA next to me was chasing me down a jungle trail, throwing lit cigarettes at me. My pack was full of blasting caps.

Somebody shook me awake; it turned out to be the medic who had shaved my leg earlier. "Wanna sleep yer life away, Farmer? It's breakfast time."

"Oh, man, go away." The leg was throbbing.

"Here, lemme crank you up." He turned a crank at the foot of the bed and the top half rose to put me halfway into a sitting position. "You'll feel better once y'get some chow inside."

The bed next to me was empty. "Where'd my buddy go?"

"Him? Oh, they took 'im to the POW ward last night. Here comes the chuck wagon."

A big Negro with a white uniform pushed a stainless-steel food cart down the aisle. "How 'bout some bacon an' eggs?"

"I have a choice?"

"Sure—you can have bacon an' eggs or a bottle o' sugar water, through another tube stuck in yer arm."

"Let me have the bacon without the eggs, then."

"Come on, man, just give 'em a try. You don't have to eat 'em." He fitted a tray to the bed, loaded up a plate, and set it down in front of me, with a glass of orange juice and a glass of milk. "Want coffee?"

"Ugh."

"Suit y'self." He rolled the cart away, clattering like a junkyard on wheels.

Army scrambled eggs are enough to make a well man puke. I scraped them to the side of the plate and ate the bacon. The orange juice tasted like sour water, but the milk was good and cold. The medic saw I was finished and took away my tray.

I lit up a cigarette. "Got anything to read around here?" If the nurse had still been around, I would've been happy to just sit and look at her—but the medic was no prize.

"Coupla papers." He brought over a *Stars and Stripes* and an *Army Times*. I read every word in the first one, trying to get my mind off the leg, and got halfway through the second one. Then in came another medic, pushing a cart like the one I went to surgery on.

"John W. Farmer?" I don't know who else he thought it would be; there wasn't anybody else around but the other medic. I told him I was John W. Farmer, last time I looked. "Takin' you to Ward 8."

He wheeled me out of that nice air-conditioned room into a ward full of disgustingly well people. At least nobody else there had a tube stuck in his arm. Some of them were sitting on beds, playing cards. It was so hot I could hardly breathe.

I got a couple of Darvon from the nurse on duty, and some writing paper and a pen. I tried to write letters to my folks and to Wendy, but the paper got so sweaty the pen wouldn't work half the time. I cussed and fumed, and the nurse gave me a couple of pencils.

Those were hard letters to write, trying to tell what happened without scaring the folks to death. So I lied a little bit here and there. I stuffed the letters into envelopes, addressed them, and wrote "free" up in the corner (that was the only advantage I'd found to being in Vietnam—didn't have to pay postage).

I slept until sundown and woke up with a start to the sound of a machine gun firing. There was a TV in the ward, and the patients were watching *Combat*.

Half a dozen GI's had to take a farm building full of Germans, I mean really *full*, twenty or thirty of them, talking English with funny accents. Machine guns poking out of every window. Did they call in for artillery and wait? No—the ol' sarge in charge took a grenade and crawled across the open farmyard, bullets thick as flies, and tossed the grenade in through a window. Killed 'em *all*. Guess they don't make grenades like they used to. Don't make bulletproof GI's anymore, either.

ELEVEN

I went to surgery again two days later (they had to wait until the smaller wounds were healing before they could close the big one), and stayed in Ward 8 until I could get around in a wheelchair. Then they moved me to another ward.

A week or so later, I graduated from the wheelchair to a pair of crutches. I still preferred the wheelchair, but with the crutches I could go across the sand to the PX, and out to the EM club at night for a few beers.

I pretty much settled into a routine. During the day I'd go down to the PX if I needed anything, then just lie in bed and read or write letters the rest of the day. Sometimes I'd wheel over to the next ward where they had a big percolator, and drink coffee. Every now and then I'd get into a checkers game or play some whist. It was a pretty soft life, except for the ache in my leg. I'd ask for Darvon during the day and save it, taking them all at night when I got in from the club. Otherwise, I couldn't sleep.

Then one morning they took out my stitches. I had about a hundred of them, and some were covered up with scar tissue—my leg was a bleeding mess when they were through. The doctor said that all of the wounds had healed well, and I'd be leaving in a few days for the Convalescent Center in Cam Ranh Bay, for rest and physical therapy.

Turned out I had to leave the next day, along with a lot of others. The VC had attacked a bunch of people on their way to the voting booths in Tuy Haq, and the hospital was suddenly very overcrowded. Waiting for the bus that would take us to the airstrip, I saw helicopters unloading the casualties. Horrible—mostly women and children. There was a little baby crying with an eerie scream, high-pitched as a whistle; you could even hear it over the roar of the helicopter. When two medics ran by with the baby balanced in the middle of their stretcher, I saw that both his arms had been blown off at the shoulder.

As many dead people as I'd seen, as many wounded GI's and enemy soldiers… I'd rather bury a hundred rotting corpses than see that baby go by again.

The plane was an Air Vietnam DC-3, much nicer than the C-130's we usually rode on. I was the only person aboard with a crutch. (I could get along on only one by then, but there was one guy strapped to a stretcher, wearing a straitjacket. He spent the whole flight staring at the ceiling; he never moved once.)

We landed in about half an hour and took a bus to the Sixth Convalescent Center. We filed into a big building where a sergeant took out medical records and gave us sheets and pillowcases. Ain't easy to walk with a crutch, carrying an armload of linen and a flight bag.

The bus waited while we were being processed and then took us to our billets. The driver called out names at each stop; I got off at the last one.

In front of the billet was an incredible beach—from horizon to horizon just as straight as if it had been laid down with a ruler. White sand and water so blue it was almost black. Two guys were riding surfboards in the breakers.

Inside the billet was like any army barracks, beds and lockers and not much else. I flopped my stuff down on the first bed I came to.

It's impossible to make a bed, standing on one leg with a crutch under your arm. I was just about to give up when a tall Negro came to my rescue.

"Heah, man, let me." It took him about twenty seconds to put the sheet on.

"Thanks—woulda been foolin' with that all night."

"Yeah. Say, you got a butt?"

I handed him one and lit one up myself. "What's it like around here? Beach sure looks nice."

"Shee-it. That all you gonna do, is look at it. Patients gotta get a pass to go swimmin'—but you don' get no fuckin' pass, 'cuz if you well enough to go swimmin', you well enough to go back to the boonies."

Sounded like I was back in the army.

"And that ain't the half of it, man—we got two mebee three formation a day, details all fuckin' day—PT in the mornin', man, gotta run a mile ev'ry mornin'—"

"No way nobody's gonna make me run. Can't half walk yet."

"Yeah, well, you safe long as you got that crutch. Fact, you just fall out in the mornin', push a broom around awhile. Then you free, rest o' the day."

Well, that didn't sound too bad. I found out that it was too late for chow, but there was an EM club that opened at seven. I hobbled over there and waited for it to open.

I managed to fill up on Slim Jims and beer. Watched TV until the place closed at eleven.

Army television in Vietnam is pretty strange. They show reruns of State-side shows, usually a year or so old. And the commercials are made by the army—telling you to keep your weapon clean, buy bonds, don't inflate the Vietnamese economy, and so on.

Seemed like I just barely got to sleep when they rousted us out of bed. My watch said quarter to six. It was still dark. I got my shaving kit and hobbled out to the shower.

It was almost worth getting up that early, though, because they had hot water. It was quite an experience, after shaving with cold water for four months. And the shower was pure heaven, even though I had to leave my crutch and hop across the slippery floor like some weird kind of bird.

The guy in the shower next to me looked at my leg. "Man, you really got fucked-up good."

"Yeah. Landmine."

"No kiddin'—you must be the only wounded guy in this barracks. 'Most everybody else's here for the clap or malaria."

"What about the other guys on crutches—some case of clap they must of picked up."

"Nah—broken legs. No other heroes."

Hero, that was a laugh.

We had a formation at six-thirty, everybody standing around in their blue pajamas while the first sergeant read off a bunch of announcements. I heard that I was supposed to report to room 101 at 1330 for physical therapy. After he finished the announcements he said, "Cripples, fall out and get yer brooms," and everybody who had a crutch or a cane went back into the barracks. It took us about five minutes to clean it up. Then some of the guys went to chow. I was so tired I just racked out for a few hours.

It was hotter'n hell when I woke up, about ten o'clock. There wasn't anybody else in the billet. I figured they must've gone someplace where it was cool, so I gathered up my crutch and set out to find them.

Went about a block down the main drag when I heard these monster air conditioners chuggin' away. It was the library. Sure enough, it was crowded—there were only three seats left. I found a bunch of books of cartoons and sat in the cool until noon, just diggin' it.

There was a formation at 1300, but we cripples didn't have to go to it. So I put off chow until about 1230, then walked over to the mess hall.

It was hot as a steam room in the mess hall. Can't complain too much, though. Since I had a crutch, I didn't have to stand in the line; I just sat down and a Vietnamese girl brought me a tray full of food. Not bad, either, by army standards; two hamburgers, french fries, and a salad.

After chow I wandered over to 101, the physical therapy building. It was air-conditioned there, too—but pure torture. I spent an hour lifting weights (little sandbags) with my bad leg, hurt like the very devil. They gave me a Darvon for my trouble and I limped back over to the library.

I felt better after sitting in the cool for a while, so I decided to go out and explore some. Would be a great place if you had any money to spend—snack bar (with pizza), big PX and a gift shop—but I only had eleven dollars, and I decided to save it for beer. That would be 110 beers, a couple of weeks' worth.

I wound up in a big recreation hall run by the Red Cross. They had all kinds of games and stuff. Played a few games of checkers with a Red Cross guy named Jerry. He beat me every time, but in return he told me how I could get some money—there was a man from the Fourth Division who could get me up to twenty bucks a week, that'd be taken out of my pay later. I decided I could afford a pizza tomorrow.

There was another formation about sundown, but all that happened was that the first sergeant called out the names of the guys who'd be leaving in the morning. Then he let us go to chow (which was pretty fair beef stew).

For a couple of weeks I did pretty much the same thing every day. Kind of made the rounds between the library, the Red Cross center, physical therapy, chow, and the EM club. Sometimes I'd hang around the PX and read the magazines. Not real exciting, but sure beat the hell out of being a combat engineer.

Then my leg got better and they took away my crutch. That made all the difference in the world. The next morning I couldn't fall out after the first formation, and I had to take PT.

The first exercise was jumping jacks, you know, where you jump up and down and swing your arms around—like a guy who's on fire and trying to put himself out. No way in hell I was gonna try one of those.

The guy who was leading them glared at me all through the exercise and, when they were finished, yelled out:

"Whatsamatter, soldier, you on vacation?"

"Have a heart, Sarge, I just started walking yesterday."

"So you don't think you can do jumping jacks."

"That's right, Sarge."

"What *can* you do?"

"Dunno, Sarge."

"Try twenty pushups. Right now."

That shouldn't have been hard; I was doing eighty every day in Basic Training—but I could only do twelve, and had to fake the rest of them, with everybody watching. A month in the hospital can really put you out of shape.

Had to fake most of the other exercises, too, except for the arm twists. And when they got out on the road to run their mile, I just limped along behind at a slow walk. A different guy was leading the running, and when he saw me lagging behind, he dropped back.

"Somethin' wrong with yer foot, fella?"

"Just got off a cane yesterday."

"Well, fall out and go to chow. Don't sweat the run."

First nice thing anybody had done for me in some time.

The work formation was right after chow. I got assigned to a sandbag detail, one of those jobs that never ends. Since we had more empty sandbags than we could fill in a week, we just took it as slow and easy as we could.

At 1300, I went to my physical therapy appointment. Didn't even think about the 1330 formation. But, since I wasn't a "cripple" anymore, I was supposed to be there. And people who skip the midday formation get put on the next day's shipping roster.

I didn't find out until the next morning, when the first sergeant called out the names of the people who were leaving. Instead of going to PT, I limped into the orderly room. The only guy there was a private, reading a comic book, feet stuck up on a desk.

"Hey, man."

"Yeah?"

"Can you tell me what the fuck I'm doin' on the shipping roster today?"

"Whatcher name?" I told him. He looked at a clipboard, hanging by the desk.

"Says here, 'AWOL 1330 formation.' Musta been yesterday—what, did ya skip out?"

"No, man, I couldn't make the fuckin' formation; I had a physical therapy appointment."

"Shoulda told somebody. Right now, you better find some doctor who'll give ya an excuse in writing. Otherwise you gotta leave at nine o'clock."

I went down to the infirmary. There was a fat sergeant at the admissions desk.

"Sarge, I gotta see a doctor."

"Your name on sick call?"

"No, it's not."

"Well, you better get on sick call or you won't see no doctor."

"But Sarge, it's after seven. I can't get on sick call this late."

He shrugged. "So don't die here. Go find a medic at the emergency room."

"Sorry, Sarge, a medic won't do."

"Oh, you gotta have brain surgery or somethin'. What's the score?"

"Well, they put me on the shipping roster today—"

"Congratulations."

"Goddammit, Sarge, I can't half *walk* yet!"

"Look, son, I get twenny guys come in here ev'ry morning tryin' to get off the shippin' roster. Tough shit, all of 'em. I ain't never let one through, never will."

"Sarge…"

"Yer all just a buncha chickenshits, don't wanna go back an' fight." He was shouting, and I could smell whiskey. "I was in Korea…."

"Bet you were tough, Sarge." I'd rather have killed that motherfucker than all the VC in the world. I slammed the door good and hard on the way out.

So at nine o'clock I rode a bus to the airport and got on a C-130 to Pleiku.

TWELVE

I walked in through the captain's door and came to attention in front of his desk. "Private Farmer reporting for duty, sir."

"At ease, Farmer. Have a seat." I sat down across from him.

"For one thing, you aren't a PFC anymore. Your orders for Spec/4 came in right after you were wounded."

"That's good news."

"Yes, and the army owes you some money. You can go down to Finance and get it, any time you want.

"Now, Farmer, you probably know I don't order men back into the field, once they've been seriously wounded. I've kept a job open here at base camp, assistant to the supply clerk. Don't suppose you want it."

"Sure do, sir."

He chuckled. "Can't say I blame you. He'll run you ragged, though… you were limping when you came in. Wounds still bother you?"

"Yes, sir. I had to leave the hospital before I was finished with physical therapy." I told him the story about the formation I missed, and how I got railroaded out.

"That's unfortunate, but I suppose it happens all the time. Tell you what, after you go to Finance, drop by the battalion aid station and see whether they have any physical therapy equipment. At least they should be able to set up some exercises for you to do.

"I'll put you on light duty status"—he pulled out a pad and scribbled something on it—"and you can do your physical therapy instead of coming to the morning formation." He handed me the paper. "This is good for three weeks. If anybody asks you to lift something heavy or walk any great distance, just tell them you can't. They can check with me."

"Thank you, sir." The slip said "Sp/4 J. W. Farmer, light duty to 30 June."

My back pay, with the promotion, came to almost 500 bucks. I pocketed fifty and put the rest in the company safe. It turned out they didn't have any physical therapy equipment at the battalion aid station, but the doctor there had a book that showed three exercises I was supposed to do for the leg. They weren't as bad as the sandbag-lifts at Cam Ranh Bay, but they did hurt some. Still, got me out of morning formation.

My new job, helping the supply clerk, was dull as hell. Most of the time I just cleaned equipment that wasn't really very dirty. Sometimes I'd make lists, type 'em up, and file 'em away where nobody would ever see them.

One day I was cleaning up, getting ready to close the supply room for the night, when the door opened—and a hand grenade flew in!

I started to roll under the counter when I saw it was harmless, the arming lever taped down securely.

"Awright, who's the wise fucker?"

"I cannot tell a lie. I am the wisest fucker in the company."

"Willy!"

He was just as mangy-looking as ever—conditions in the field hadn't improved any—so I got him a new set of fatigues and a bar of soap. After he cleaned up and changed, we went over to the EM club.

"Well, Farmer, how do ya like bein' a base-camp commando?"

"Beats the hell outa humpin'."

"Hmm—I don't know. It's been pretty easy since you left. With the monsoon coming up, we aren't humping as much. Mostly just stay in fire bases."

"And you don't have to shine boots or salute officers."

"That's right. I understand old General Stoner's a real sonofabitch for military courtesy."

"Yeah—shit, it's gettin' to be just like Stateside. Inspections every morning. If it moves, salute it. Have to go through the fuckin' chain of command to talk to anybody. What a bunch of bullshit."

"So why don't you volunteer for field duty again, man? We've got it easy."

I *had* thought of it, but... "No way, Willy. I can put up with anything for another four months. Just wanta get out of here alive."

"Yeah, I was just kidding, I guess. Half-kidding, anyhow. Showers every day and cold beer every night—fuck, you've got it made."

We talked for a long time, mostly about what we were going to do when we got back to the world. Just about talked each other into going back to school. Couldn't hurt.

Willy was dead tired, so we left before the club closed. The next morning I drove him down to the pad and put him on a bird to the fire base. He still looked pretty shot. I was doubly glad to be where I was.

Base camp life went along as usual for me, pretty dull and a little bitchy. Then one day I was walking along the road, coming back from the PX, when a jeep passed me, stopped, and hauled-ass in reverse back to me. There was a little flag with one star, fluttering on the bumper. I dropped my package and came to attention. General Stoner.

The driver, a captain, got out of the jeep and walked up to me. "Soldier, you are in trouble."

"Yes, sir."

"The general feels that, if a person can't be bothered with military courtesy in base camp, not even to the extent of saluting a general... he should be sent someplace where he won't have to worry about military courtesy."

General Stoner was sitting in the back seat, staring straight ahead, not looking at me. I'd heard of this; don't salute Stoner's jeep and zap, you're out in the boonies. Never thought it'd happen to me, though. Hell, I'd never even *seen* his jeep before.

The captain whipped out a leather-covered notebook. "What's your unit—who's your commanding officer?"

I told him and he wrote it down. Then he got my name and serial number (and checked my dog tags to make sure I wasn't lying).

"Report yourself immediately to your company commander and tell him what happened. Tell him you request immediate transfer to a field position."

Yessirs and salutes and all that bullshit, and he got back in the jeep and drove off. I went back to the company and reported to the captain.

"Jesus Christ, Farmer, you really blew it this time, didn't you?"

"Yes, sir, I did."

"Well, I'll send you out to the fire base where your old platoon is. They haven't had any action for over a month, so it shouldn't be too bad. But I don't know how soon we can bring you back... how short are you?"

"Three months, sir."

"Hmm—we'll try to get you back in base camp your last six weeks.

"Well, go get some field gear and run down to the pad before it gets dark. Better hope you can get a ride out, too. We'll both be in hot water if you're still here tomorrow."

So I requisitioned myself a pack and a gun, canteens and grenades (you can carry them on choppers) and all that junk. It took me a half-hour's wait to get a slick, and another half-hour to get to 2124, which the pad man told me was about thirty clicks—kilometers—west of Pleiku. That's about eighteen miles.

The fire base had moved to an old abandoned tea plantation. They were serving chow out of a falling-down farm building (still, better than C-rations), and the medics were set up in an old barn—just sitting around playing cards, which was a *very* good sign. There was even a dirt road leading into the place.

I found the engineers, but Willy wasn't there—in fact, the only guy I knew was Doc Jones, the engineer medic.

"What you doin' back here, man? Thought you was in some soft base camp job."

"If I told you, Doc, you wouldn't believe me. Where's Horowitz?"

"Out with D Company. S'posed to come in tomorrow."

"Thought they weren't humpin' anymore."

"Jes' overnight stuff, ambushes." Doc introduced me around to the new guys. Sergeant Miller, the new platoon sergeant, put me to work cleaning chain saws. Said he wished he had something better for me to do, but it was either that or fill sandbags.

The last chopper in was a big Chinook, or "hook," a boxcar-sized chopper with a monster load of beer and soft drinks. The engineers got six cases of beer and two of soft drinks. After we split them up and traded around (two beers for a soda), I wound up with twenty-one beers (and no sodas, never learned to like them warm).

We decided to do some serious drinking that night. Sergeant Miller produced a fifth of Scotch—God knows where he got it—and we sat in a circle, passing the Scotch around, washing it down with beer, tellin' lies.

Most of my memory of that night is pretty fuzzy, both because of all the drinking and because of what happened the next day. One thing I *do* remember, though, was when Doc Jones lit into me.

He was telling a joke about two Negroes on a motorcycle having a run-in with a white cop, and when he imitated the cop talking, he sounded like any regular white man, no black accent at all. I thought we were good enough friends, so I asked him straight out why, if he could talk regular English, he didn't talk that way all the time.

It must have been a sore spot, or maybe I was just stupid to ask in the first place—I didn't have any Negro schoolmates in Enid and was just curious—but he really blew up. Where had I been all my life, he asked, that I thought there was only one way to talk English—people talk the way it's most comfortable, the way they're brought up. Besides, he said, I sounded like Chester on *Gunsmoke*; half the time *he* couldn't understand a word *I* said! Everybody took Doc's side, and I felt like a real hick. Things got back to normal before we'd finished the bottle, though.

As the old saying goes, "beer on whiskey, mighty risky." I got to feeling woozy after a couple of hours, and went off to hit the sack. I remember starting to blow up my air mattress, but when I woke up in the morning I was lying on the cold ground, the air mattress on top of me without any air in it. Maybe that was because I forgot to put the plug in when I finished blowing it up.

"Wake up, Farmer. Just got time to say goodbye." Someone shoved a can of steaming black coffee under my nose. My head throbbed with every heartbeat.

"Willy—thanks. What time's it?"

"Little after seven. Everybody else is asleep down in the bunker. You decide to live dangerously? Or just hanker to sleep under the stars?"

"Musta passed out. Little party last night—you got an aspirin?"

"No, but I can probably find Doc's bag." He started rummaging around the pile of rucksacks and stuff alongside the bunker. "All that time I was lying out there in that ambush, trying to stay awake, you guys were lappin' it up—here we go." He brought over a couple of white tablets and a canteen.

"Thanks. Anything happen on the ambush?"

"The usual. One guy fell asleep and got chewed out. Otherwise, no excitement." He took a loud slurp of coffee. "Now, what the hell are *you* doing out here?"

"Oh, man, don't ask. It's so stupid."

"Didn't volunteer, did you?"

"Fuck, no! It was... well, General Stoner's jeep drove by me..."

"And you didn't salute?"

"Yep. So here I am."

"God damn—it's true, then. Always thought that was just a bullshit line they made up to keep you saluting."

"No way. I'm out here for six weeks at least."

"Probably won't be in the fire base much, either."

"Huh?"

"Fact—Miller'll probably have you take over my job, field squad leader. Nobody else here has more than a month's experience, except Doc. And he's not an engineer, not by training."

"Shit... trouble just comes in bunches, doesn't it." And the aspirin wasn't helping my head.

"Don't sweat it, man. We stay in fire base a couple of days every week. And in the field, well, we've only had one shootemup since June. Charlie's gone from around here."

"Let's hope. How much longer you stayin'?"

"Be on the first bird to base camp."

"That soon!"

"Yeah, man, I'm really short. Eight days. I'll be home before the next time you shave."

"Oh, you dirty fucker. And me with ninety days..."

"Right, John—next time you pick up that razor, think of me back home in Manhattan, in school, good threads and a pretty chick on each arm—wait!" Sound of a helicopter, pretty far off. "Think I hear the subway comin' in. Want to walk over with me?"

I was still trying to imagine what Willy would look like with clean clothes, civvies at that, and no whiskers on his chin. Just couldn't see it—let alone the two girls! "What?"

"Want to walk with me down to the pad?"

"Sure. Maybe I can knock you over the head and steal your papers."

"No way you'd ever pass for me, Farmer. You're too pretty."

What do you say to a guy who's going back to the world? We just stood on the pad, Willy watching the slick get closer and closer, me feeling a little bit jealous and sorry for myself.

Just before the chopper landed, Willy shook hands with me and wished me good luck. I wished him the same, though he was just about past the need for it.

The noise of the bird hadn't helped my head any, and it woke up the sleeping drunks in the bunker.

Drinking his morning coffee, Sergeant Miller said yes, I'd be doing Prof's job, at least until White, the assistant squad leader, had learned enough to take over.

He said we'd be humping out early in the afternoon, to set up a company-sized night ambush about two clicks away.

Turned out we left at noon.

THIRTEEN

Started out easy enough. We humped for about three hours and then set up a box-shaped ambush around a place where two jungle trails came together. We napped in shifts until dark, since Charlie doesn't travel much during the day. From sundown to sunup, though, we all had to be on alert.

This company had been setting ambushes for over a month without a single night of action, so nobody was surprised when the sun finally came up without a shot being fired. Tired as I was, I might as well have spent the whole night doing pushups.

The captain decided the hell with it, we'd hump back to fire base and get a day's rest. We could've stayed at the ambush place for another night, but I guess he didn't think it'd be worth it.

Maybe the captain should've let us rest before we started out. But everybody was anxious to get back to the fire base, get a hot meal, and sack out. So tired, careless, we started to hump back.

After about an hour, the jungle got less dense and the path we were following widened into a small clearing. I remember thinking it was strange to be able to see both flanks and the center file all at once, but it didn't occur to me that that was extremely dangerous.

Then one of the flankers yelled and fired. I hit the dirt and jacked a round into the chamber of my M-16 and all hell broke loose.

Ambush on three of four sides, just like we had sat in all night; a classic box. The gunfire mounted in a steady crescendo until it was just one constant unnerving roar. They had fifties, three fifty-caliber machine guns that traversed back and forth over the little clearing; perfect setup for a hundred careless idiots. A fifty is a hell of a lot of gun—all we had to fight back with was regular humping-infantry stuff; M-16's and grenades and one M-60 without too much ammo. You could barely hear our return fire over the chug of those fifties.

A minute ago I could see almost all of the company, seventy or eighty men. Now, lying in the grass, I could only see three, and one of them was dead.

The radio operator and White, my assistant squad leader, were lying in front of me. A rifleman whose name I'd forgotten, one of the flankers, was in the elephant grass to my left, his ribs glistening white and splintered where a rifle grenade had dug out his chest.

After a minute the enemy slacked off; fire started coming in short bursts. The radioman was hollering into the horn, trying to get us some artillery. The artillery observer, Lieutenant Hernandez, was thrashing around in the grass with a sucking chest wound, not interested in giving coordinates to the radioman. Finally, a shell crashed into the jungle, but it must have been a mile away.

The captain crawled up to me, moving on his back like a swimmer trying to do a backstroke with his shoulders.

"Where the fuck is that medic?" He had his left hand cradled in his right, blood gushing from the stump of a thumb.

"I don't know, Cap'n, he was back of me somewhere." The captain started to worm his way back. "Hold up—you stay here, I'll go back and find him. Got to check on my squad anyhow."

He opened his mouth to say something, then shut it and nodded. Not that I was bucking for a Bronze Star. They don't make engineer heroes. But I had to get my men together.

Squirmed out of my pack and demo bag and started crawling, rifle slung between my arms like some basic trainee on the "live fire" course. This was live fire, all right—but the bullets came in a little lower here.

"Medic!" I shouted once and rolled away, knowing they might zero in on the noise.

"Over here, goddammit," came a whisper to the left. It was Doc Dayton, the center-file medic. I found him in a shallow depression behind a stand of saplings, bandaging a tall Negro flanker whose lower jaw was shot off, thick blood drooling around the pressure bandage.

"Where you hit?"

"Not me, Doc—the captain's bleeding pretty bad from a hand wound and Lieutenant Hernandez got shot in the chest—"

"Motherfucker musta stood up."

"They're both up front. Ten meters or so."

A burst of machine-gun fire rattled through the saplings. The medic and I cringed down, but the big Negro just lay there, eyes filming. "Fuck 'em both." Doc pushed a morphine syrette through the dying man's sleeve, blood-slick and shiny. He tagged the man's collar and said, "Let's go."

"Gotta check my squad first."

"Man, you ain't *got* no fuckin' squad—go back there and you won't have no fuckin' squad leader, neither."

"All dead?"

"Dead, wounded—fuckin' half the company blown away 'fore they could hit the dirt."

The captain was lying beside the radioman when we crawled up. "Drop one-zero-zero and fire for effect. One-two over and out." He hung up the horn and saw us behind him. "Doc, go check the lieutenant, I think he's dead. Find your squad, Farmer?"

"Doc says they're all gone, all but me and White."

"Not White." The captain glanced at my assistant squad leader's body, less than five meters away, the back of his helmet blown open and bluish-grey brains splashed in a bloody streak down his back. "You'll have to drop back and try to blow the LZ by yourself."

"No way, Cap'n. That's suicide—I need a squad of riflemen with me while I set the charges, or—"

"That's an order, Farmer. Sorry. We need every man we can get on the line." He drew in breath with a hiss when Doc clamped a tight bandage over his hand. "Where the fuck is that artillery?" We all looked up automatically at the faint tearing sound that came in answer. "Get down that's coming right on top of—"

Everybody was already down, of course, but I held my helmet on with both hands and pushed my face into the dirt.

The ground fell away and came back to slap me, twice, three times and my ears rang, chimes, buzzers, bells… the captain shouting came through a whisper.

"Sergeant, round up a squad and try to punch through in the front. You go with them, Doc; see if you can find a place to blow your LZ."

It was useless to argue, and I supposed going up front with a bunch of riflemen was better than trying to get through the rear by myself. I picked up my demolition bag, put a couple of grenades on each side of my belt, and set out, ax in one hand and M-16 in the other.

We couldn't find a squad of whole people, but we got ten grunts and a medic, plus me and the sergeant. The fifty that had been spraying right down our column hadn't fired a shot since the artillery salvo hit. But they could just be playing possum. We circled around the gun's position and closed in.

I was crawling up the center between the medic and the sergeant when an AK-47 opened up on the right, a sound like dry sticks cracking. A couple of grenades went off and the AK stopped. That was all the resistance we hit.

One of the eight-inch shells had come in right on the fifty; nothing but twisted metal and gallons of blood scattered all over the area, with some barely recognizable human parts. Crawling up, I squashed an eyeball with my elbow.

There were a dozen or so shattered bodies just beyond where the salvo had hit. No telling how many had slipped away.

"Wanna blow your LZ here?"

I looked around. "No, it's too close to the perimeter. Those trees're too big anyhow. I don't have enough C-4 to drop all of 'em."

"Well, I can't send my boys out too far. They're still fightin' back there, back at the rear." I could hear spurts from the fifty that must have taken out my squad. "Might have to go back any minute."

"I know, goddammit." I could see daylight ahead about forty or fifty feet. The trees were probably more sparse there. "Leave me five men and take the rest back to the captain."

"Who's givin' orders here? I'll let you have three."

"Whatever you can spare, Sarge. But you know there's nothing more important than that LZ now—we're gonna need ammo, and we got thirty or forty wounded; a lot of 'em are gonna die if they don't get a dustoff, quick."

"All right, take the fuckin' five—but make it quick! I'm gonna need every one of 'em on the line."

We got to the sunlit area with no trouble, six of us moving up in a zigzag line. "Skinny, take three guys and post guards out, oh, thirty feet. Leave me Tex to help chop down that bamboo."

"How long a fuse you puttin' on it?"

"One minute—when I holler 'fire in the hole' you got a little less than that to take cover. Or you can head back to the perimeter; that's what I'm doin'."

"Minute's not too fuckin' much time."

"Nobody's gonna get blown away, Skinny—I don't have that much C-4. Just get far enough away that a tree won't fall on you."

"OK, Farmer—Tex, get to work on that bamboo. Rest o'you poor fuckers follow me."

Tex had just about gotten the bamboo down by the time I had set the first charge. It was a big one, ten pounds of C-4 set into a hole I chopped out of the base of a tree. I was crimping a cap when the sergeant came back.

"I need those five men. Need 'em *bad!*" He was panting hard. "Gooks broke through our rear, we're split in two."

"Well, they went that way. Leave me Tex, OK?"

"No way. Need all the firepower we can get—you're goin' on the line yerself, soon as you blow those trees."

Decided I'd take my time on the trees. I'm nobody's infantryman. Of course, I wasn't too happy about being left alone in the woods, either. The fighting was quite a ways away, but the enemy might decide to circle around, and run into me. In fact, they probably *would* circle around and try to surround us.

The sergeant took his men back and I continued setting charges, working as quietly as possible.

I was almost through, molding the last of my C-4 into the crotch of a tree that poked out of the ground like a giant wishbone, when I heard somebody coming down the path, from the wrong side. I got down behind a bush.

A Vietnamese wearing green jungle fatigues—probably an NVA regular, no VC would look that military—walked into the semi-clearing where I had set my explosives. He was carrying an AK-47 but also wore a pistol; probably an officer. I eased the safety off my M-16 and worked a hand grenade from my belt. Then I realized I couldn't use the grenade without setting off the whole thing—no matter what I told Skinny, it wouldn't be healthy to be near it when it went bang. I just wanted to kill the guy, I didn't want to share a grave with him.

Each charge was connected to two others with a length of white det cord, to make sure they'd all go off at once. The officer didn't see it at first, and just kept walking down the path. He'd pass about five feet in front of me.

Then he saw the stuff, turned and said something in a soft voice to the woods behind him. Four more men came out, following down the path. They knew what it was and wanted to get away.

I drew a bead on the officer, who looked like he was waiting for his men to catch up with him, and squeezed off a burst. Popped holes in his hip and back, and he flopped to the ground jerking. The others took cover but didn't shoot.

At first I didn't think they knew where I was hiding, so I held my fire, hoping they'd retreat. Then I heard the clink! sound of a grenade, the arming lever springing off as one of them threw it toward me. Shit, we're all dead, I thought—the whole fuckin' jungle's goin' up in—

FOURTEEN

Eight hours later, on the other side of the world, a cab rolled to a stop on a sleepy tree-lined avenue in a little Oklahoma town.

A captain in an immaculate dress uniform got out of the cab. He was holding the telegram by the corner because his hands were all sweaty.

Why do they have to use a captain to deliver the bad news, he thought; why not a lieutenant or even an NCO? He had to ride herd over a whole company of clerks at Fort Sill, on top of delivering these telegrams. It wasn't fair.

He checked the number on the house and compared it with the one on the telegram. Mrs. Beatrice Farmer, 2705 Central Avenue.

At least it was a son this time, not a husband. Widows are harder to calm down.

He started up the walk and told himself that he had the hardest job in the world.

INTRODUCTION: FRAGMENTS

Writers hate to be pigeonholed, and so I'm not wild about being called a "military science fiction writer." For one thing, the term has come to represent a distinct subgenre of science fiction, a lot of it glorifying war, which, surprise, I find repugnant. For another thing, only eight of the twenty-eight books I'm responsible for are war novels, and only six of them science fiction about war.

I'm primarily a novelist, partly because I like to eat regularly, but I have written six collections of short stories and poetry over the years. The novel is a natural vehicle for writing about war, since a war is a huge and complex undertaking, but you can use a short story or a narrative poem to look at one or two aspects of it. The pieces that follow are in that limited category.

Only two are set in Vietnam, but most of them have to be informed, or infected, by that war. The one that isn't, "Giza," was written the week after September 11, 2001.

"Time Piece" is the earliest one here, written right after *War Year*. It's a sort of trial run for *The Forever War*, my science fiction novel about Vietnam. That has been far and away my most successful book, continuously in print for thirty years, and if it's responsible for pigeonholing me, it's also paid a lot of the bills over those thirty years.

"The Private War of Private Jacob" is one of only three stories that I've written in one sitting. It's more like a weird parable than an actual story. I think I'd just read the fascinating anthology *Anti-Story* (Philip Stevick, ed., 1971), in which every story breaks one or several narrative rules, and I wanted to do something experimental.

There's an unsettling backstory and subtext to "To Howard Hughes: A Modest Proposal." Are there stories that you shouldn't write, because the information in them could be misused? From my experience as a demolition engineer, I know all sorts of neat things that would amuse my readers, like how to build an untraceable assassination weapon for pocket change, but I don't put them in my stories because people who are too technology-dumb to figure them out independently might read about them there and commit mayhem with the knowledge.

This story details how a wealthy enough person could build one or several nuclear weapons and use them for blackmail. Nowadays, with the web and the net, anybody could Google that information in a few minutes. When that story came out, that was a little harder, though anybody with a physics degree would know the science, and the rest is just imagination.

I understand that somebody used it, though no one was hurt. The mayor of Los Angeles got a letter that had a detailed description of how its anonymous author had made an atomic bomb and had hidden it somewhere in the city, and would blow it up tomorrow if the city didn't come up with a zillion dollars in a suitcase and deliver it to some public park at a certain time. The mayor showed the letter to his science advisor, who said it was just barely possible.

So a courier showed up with the suitcase. I assume it didn't have any money in it, because the park was swarming with plainclothes policemen. A young boy jumped out of the bushes and grabbed it, and was himself grabbed. The kid had gotten all of the details straight out of this story, in *The Magazine of Fantasy & Science Fiction*, which was evidently not widely read in the mayor's office.

"The Monster" and "Graves" are both nightmare fantasies of blood and gore from Vietnam. "Graves" sold to *Playboy*, at the time the highest-paying fiction market, but the managing editor refused to print it, on the grounds that it was "too gross," which is something of a distinction. The fiction editor held on to it for a year and tried to sneak it back in, but he remembered and said it was still too gross. So she generously let me keep the check and send the story elsewhere. It wound up in *The Magazine of Fantasy & Science Fiction* and won the Nebula and World Fantasy Awards for being the best short story of the year. But yeah, it is a little gross.

"A Separate War" was written for the Robert Silverberg collection *Far Horizons*, which was to be "All New Tales from the Greatest Worlds of Science Fiction." He was asking writers who had created classics in the genre to revisit their worlds, and write novellas set in them.

In my case it was *The Forever War*, and it was a wonderful opportunity. Editors and others had been after me for twenty years to write a sequel to the novel, and my response had always been no, the novel's complete as it stands. But I always wanted to write a novella about what happens after the novel ends, and here was Silverberg offering me the chance, and for more money than the novel's original advance.

I got twenty or thirty pages into it, though, a novella I was calling "Forever Free," when I realized that it begged to be expanded into a novel; an actual sequel. I wrote Silverberg and asked how soon the material could be re-used, and he said three years. That was too long; it was time for me to send out the next book proposal.

So I turned "Forever Free" into the book proposal, same title, and looked for another angle on the novella. It was immediately apparent. In the last part of the book, the main characters Marygay and William are separated, and we follow William's story. What happened to Marygay?

It was fun to write her story, both as a bridge to the sequel and as an oblique commentary on *The Forever War*, twenty years later.

"Giza" was a reaction to the events of 9/11, but it began as an assignment from my students at MIT. I always start out by giving them each a different science-fictional idea, like time travel or alien intelligence, and make them write the first few pages of a story about it. (This is to demonstrate that you don't have to wait around for inspiration; you can start writing anywhere.) During the break, I let them select a difficult topic, and I'll do the assignment myself. They were especially mean that year, and chose "asteroid psychology." I puzzled over that for awhile, since it's hard for a rock to have a psychology, but then realized that the *people* isolated inside an asteroid might have their peculiarities.

"Saul's Death" is the first poem I wrote after a ten-year hiatus — when I started writing fiction for a living, I regretfully gave up writing poetry, since it pays next to nothing. When I realized what a mistake that was, I went back to it and wrote this reaction to Ezra Pound's beautiful and terrible "Sestina: Altaforte." It sold to *Omni* for their short-story rate, which may have made me for one day the highest paid poet in America.

As I've written before, "DX" is a rarity, being a poem that is simultaneously science fiction and autobiography.

TIME PIECE

They say you've got a fifty-fifty chance every time you go out. That makes it one chance in eight that you'll live to see your third furlough; the one I'm on now.

Somehow the odds don't keep people from trying to join. Even though not one in a thousand gets through the years of training and examination, there's no shortage of cannon fodder. And that's what we are. The most expensive, best trained cannon fodder in the history of warfare. Human history, anyhow; who can speak for the enemy?

I don't even call them snails anymore. And the thought of them doesn't trigger that instant flash of revulsion, hate, kill-fever—the psyconditioning wore off years ago, and they didn't renew it. They've stopped doing it to new recruits; no percentage in berserkers. I was a wild one the first couple of trips, though.

Strange world I've come back to. Gets stranger every time, of course. Even sitting here in a bogus twenty-first-century bar, where everyone speaks Basic and there's real wood on the walls and peaceful holograms instead of plugins, and music made by men...

But it leaks through. I don't pay by card, let alone by coin. The credit register monitors my alpha waves and communicates with the bank every time I order a drink. And, in case I've become addicted to more modern vices, there's a feelie matrix (modified to look like an old-fashioned visiphone booth) where I can have my brain stimulated directly. Thanks but no, thanks—always get this picture of dirty hands inside my skull, kneading, rubbing. Like when you get too close to the enemy and they open a hole in your mind and you go spinning down and down and never reach the bottom till you die. I almost got too close last time.

We were on a three-man reconnaissance patrol, bound for a hellish little planet circling the red giant Antares. Now red giant stars don't form planets in the natural course of things, so we had ignored Antares; we control most of the space around it, so why waste time in idle exploration? But the enemy had detected this little planet—God knows how—and about ten years after they landed there, we monitored their presence (gravity waves from the ships' braking) and my team was assigned the reconnaissance. Three men against many, many of the enemy—but we weren't supposed to fight if we could help it; just take a look around, record what we saw, and leave a message beacon on our way back, about a light-year out from Antares. Theoretically, the troopship following us by a month will pick up the information and use it to put together a battle plan. Actually, three more recon patrols precede the troop ship at one-week intervals; insurance against the high probability that any one patrol will be caught and destroyed. As the first team in, we have a pretty good chance of success, but the ones to follow would be in trouble if we didn't get back out. We'd be past caring, of course: the enemy doesn't take prisoners.

We came out of lightspeed close to Antares, so the bulk of the star would mask our braking disturbance, and inserted the ship in a hyperbolic orbit that would get us to the planet— Anomaly, we were calling it—in about twenty hours.

"Anomaly must be tropical over most of its surface." Fred Sykes, nominally the navigator, was talking to himself and at the two of us while he analyzed the observational data rolling out of the ship's computer. "No axial tilt to speak of. Looks like they've got a big outpost near the equator, lots of electromagnetic noise there. Figures... the goddamn snails like it hot. We requisitioned hot-weather gear, didn't we, Pancho?"

Pancho, that's me. "No, Fred, all we got's parkas and snowshoes." My full name is Francisco Jesus Mario Juan-José Hugo de Naranja, and I outrank Fred, so he should at least call me Francisco. But I've never pressed the point. Pancho it is. Fred looked up from his figures and the rookie, Paul Spiegel, almost dropped the pistol he was cleaning.

"But why..." Paul was staring. "We knew the planet was probably Earth-like if the enemy wanted it. Are we gonna have to go tramping around in spacesuits?"

"No, Paul, our esteemed leader and supply clerk is being sarcastic again." He turned back to his computer. "Explain, Pancho."

"No, that's all right." Paul reddened a bit and also went back to his job. "I remember you complaining about having to take the standard survival issue."

"Well, I was right then and I'm doubly right now. We've *got* parkas back there, and snowshoes, and a complete terranorm environment recirculator, and everything else we could possibly need to walk around in comfort on every planet known to man—*Dios!* That issue masses over a metric ton, more than a bevawatt laser. A laser we could use, but crampons and pith helmets and elephant guns…"

Paul looked up again. "Elephant guns?" He was kind of a freak about weapons.

"Yeah."

"That's a gun that shoots elephants?"

"Right. An elephant gun shoots elephants."

"Is that some new kind of ammunition?"

I sighed, I really sighed. You'd think I'd get used to this after twelve years—or four hundred—in the service. "No, kid, elephants were animals, big gray wrinkled animals with horns. You used an elephant gun to shoot *at* them.

"When I was a kid in Rioplex, back in the twenty-first, we had an elephant in the zoo; used to go down in the summer and feed him synthos through the bars. He had a long nose like a fat tail, he ate with that."

"What planet were they from?"

It went on like that for a while. It was Paul's first trip out, and he hadn't yet gotten used to the idea that most of his compatriots were genuine antiques, preserved by the natural process of relativity. At lightspeed you age imperceptibly, while the universe's calendar adds a year for every light-year you travel. Seems like cheating. But it catches up with you eventually.

We hit the atmosphere of Anomaly at an oblique angle and came in passive, like a natural meteor, until we got to a position where we were reasonably safe from detection (just above the south polar sea), then blasted briefly to slow down and splash. Then we spent a few hours in slow flight at sea level, sneaking up on their settlement.

It appeared to be the only enemy camp on the whole planet, which was typical. Strange for a spacefaring, aggressive race to be so incurious about planetary environments, but they always seemed to settle in one place and simply expand radially. And they do expand; their reproduction rate makes rabbits look sick. Starting from one colony, they can fill a world in two hundred years. After that, they control their population by infantiphage and stellar migration.

We landed about a hundred kilometers from the edge of their colony, around local midnight. While we were outside setting up the espionage monitors, the ship camouflaged itself to match the surrounding jungle optically, thermally, magnetically, etc.—we were careful not to get too far from the ship; it can be a bit hard to find even when you know where to look.

The monitors were to be fed information from flea-sized flying robots, each with a special purpose, and it would take several hours for them to wing into the city. We posted a one-man guard, one-hour shifts; the other two inside the ship until the monitors started clicking. But they never started.

Being senior, I took the first watch. A spooky hour, the jungle making dark little noises all around, but nothing happened. Then Fred stood the next hour, while I put on the deepsleep helmet. Figured I'd need the sleep—once data started coming in, I'd have to be alert for about forty hours. We could all sleep for a week once we got off Anomaly and hit lightspeed.

Getting yanked out of deepsleep is like an ice-water douche to the brain. The black nothing dissolved and there was Fred a foot away from my face, yelling my name over and over. As soon as he saw my eyes open, he ran for the open lock, priming his laser on the way (definitely against regulations, could hole the hull that way; I started to say something but couldn't form the words). Anyhow, what were we doing in free fall? And how could Fred run across the deck like that while we were in free fall?

Then my mind started coming back into focus and I could analyze the sinking, spinning sensation—not free-fall vertigo at all, but what we used to call snail-fever. The enemy was very near. Crackling combat sounds drifted in from outdoors.

I sat up on the cot and tried to sort everything out and get going. After long seconds my arms and legs got the idea, I struggled up and staggered to the weapons cabinet. Both the lasers were gone, and the only heavy weapon left was a grenade launcher. I lifted it from the rack and made my way to the lock.

Had I been thinking straight, I would've just sealed the lock and blasted—the presence in my mind was so strong that I should have known there were too many of the enemy, too close, for us to stand and fight. But no one can think while their brain is being curdled that way. I fought the urge to just let go and fall down that hole in my mind, and slid along the wall to the airlock. By the time I got there my teeth were chattering uncontrollably and my face was wet with tears.

Looking out, I saw a smoldering gray lump that must have been Paul, and Fred screaming like a madman, fanning the laser on full over a 180-degree arc. There couldn't have been anything alive in front of him; the jungle was a lurid curtain of fire, but a bolt lanced in from behind and Fred dissolved in a pink spray of blood and flesh.

I saw them then, moving fast for snails, shambling in over thick brush toward the ship. Through the swirling fog in my brain I realized that all they could see was the light pouring through the open lock, and me silhouetted in front. I tried to raise the launcher but couldn't—there were too many, less than a hundred meters away, and the inky whirlpool in my mind just got bigger and bigger and I could feel myself slipping into it.

The first bolt missed me; hit the ship and it shuddered, ringing like a huge cathedral bell. The second one didn't miss, taking off my left hand just above the wrist, roasting what remained of my left arm. In a spastic lurch I jerked up the launcher and yanked the trigger, holding it down while dozens of microton grenades popped out and danced their blinding way up to and across the enemy's ragged line. Dazzled blind, I stepped back and stumbled over the med-robot, which had smelled blood and was eager to do its duty. On top of the machine was a switch that some clown had labeled EMER-GENCY EXIT; I slapped it, and as the lock clanged shut the atomic engines muttered—growled—screaming into life and a ten-gravity hand slid me across the blood-slick deck and slammed me back against the rear-wall padding. I felt ribs crack and something in my neck snapped. As the world squeezed away, I knew I was a dead man but it was better to die in a bed of pain than to just fall and fall....

I woke up to the less-than-tender ministrations of the med-robot, who had bound the stump of my left arm and was wrapping my chest in plas-tiseal. My body from forehead to shins ached from radiation burns, earned by facing the grenades' bursts, and the nonexistent hand seemed to writhe in painful, impossible contortions. But numbing anesthetic kept the pain at a bearable distance, and there was an empty space in my mind where the snail-fever had been, and the gentle hum told me we were at lightspeed; things could have been one flaming hell of a lot worse. Fred and Paul were gone but that just moved them from the small roster of live friends to the long list of dead ones.

A warning light on the control panel was blinking stroboscopically. We were getting near the hole—excuse me, "relativistic discontinuity"—and the computer had to know where I wanted to go. You go in one hole at lightspeed and you'll come out of some other hole; *which* hole you pop out of depends on your angle of approach. Since they say that only about one percent of the holes are charted, if you go in at any old angle you're liable to wind up in Podunk, on the other side of the galaxy, with no ticket back.

I just let the light blink, though. If it doesn't get any response from the crew, the ship programs itself automatically to go to Heaven, the hospital world, which was fine with me. They cure what ails you and then set you loose with a compatible soldier of the opposite sex, for an extended vaca-tion on that beautiful world. Someone once told me that there were over a hundred worlds named Hell, but there's only one Heaven. Clean and pretty from the tropical seas to the northern pine forests. Like Earth used to be, before we strangled it.

A bell had been ringing all the time I'd been conscious, but I didn't no-tice it until it stopped. That meant that the information capsule had been jettisoned, for what little it was worth. Planetary information, very few espionage-type data; just a tape of the battle. Be rough for the next recon patrol.

I fell asleep knowing I'd wake up on the other side of the hole, bound for Heaven.

I pick up my drink—an old-fashioned Old Fashioned—with my new left hand and the glass should feel right, slick but slightly tacky with the cold-water sweat, fine ridges molded into the plastic. But there's something missing, hard to describe, a memory stored in your fingertips that a new growth has to learn all over again. It's a strange feeling, but in a way seems to fit with this crazy Earth, where I sit in my alcoholic time capsule and, if I squint with my mind, can almost believe I'm back in the twenty-first.

I pay for the nostalgia—wood and natural food, human bartender and waitress who are also linguists, it all comes dear—but I can afford it, if anyone can. Compound interest, of course. Over four centuries have passed on Earth since I first went off to the war, and my salary's been deposited at the Chase Manhattan Credit Union ever since. They're glad to do it; when I die, they keep the interest and the principal reverts to the government. Heirs? I had one illegitimate son (conceived on my first furlough) and when I last saw his gravestone, the words on it had washed away to barely legible dimples.

But I'm still a young man (at lightspeed you age imperceptibly while the universe winds down outside) and the time you spend going from hole to hole is almost incalculably small. I've spent most of the past half millennium at lightspeed, the rest of the time usually convalescing from battle. My records show that I've logged a trifle under one year in actual combat. Not bad for 438 years' pay. Since I first lifted off I've aged twelve years by my biological calendar. Complicated, isn't it—next month I'll be thirty, 456 years after my date of birth.

But one week before my birthday I've got to decide whether to try my luck for the fourth trip out or just collect my money and retire. No choice, really. I've got to go back. It's something they didn't emphasize when I joined up, back in 2088—maybe it wasn't so obvious back then, the war only decades old—but they can't hide it nowadays. Too many old vets wandering around, like animated museum pieces.

I could cash in my chips and live in luxury for another hundred years. But it would get mighty lonely. Can't talk to anybody on Earth but other vets and people who've gone to the trouble to learn Basic.

Everyone in space speaks Basic. You can't lift off until you've become fluent. Otherwise, how could you take orders from a fellow who should have been food for worms centuries before your grandfather was born? Especially since language melted down into one Language.

I'm tone-deaf. Can't speak or understand Language, where one word has ten or fifteen different meanings, depending on pitch. To me it sounds like puppydogs yapping. Same words over and over; no sense.

Of course, when I first lived on Earth there were all sorts of languages, not just one Language. I spoke Spanish (still do when I can find some other old codger who remembers) and learned English—that was before they called it Basic—in military training. Learned it damn well, too. If I weren't tone-deaf I'd crack Language and maybe I'd settle down.

Maybe not. The people are so strange, and it's not just the Language. Mind-plugs and homosex and voluntary suicide. Walking around with nothing on but paint and powder. We had Fullerdomes when I was a kid; but you didn't *have* to live under one. Now if you take a walk out in the country for a breath of fresh air, you'll drop over dead before you can exhale.

My mind keeps dragging me back to Heaven. I'd retire in a minute if I could spend my remaining century there. Can't, of course; only soldiers allowed in space. And the only way a soldier gets to Heaven is the hard way.

I've been there three times; once more and I'll set a record. That's motivation of a sort, I suppose. Also, in the unlikely event that I should live another five years, I'll get a commission, and a desk job if I live through my term as a field officer. Doesn't happen too often—but there aren't too many desk jobs that people can handle better than cyborgs.

That's another alternative. If my body gets too garbaged for regeneration, and they can save enough of my brain, I could spend the rest of eternity hooked up to a computer, as a cyborg. The only one I've ever talked to seemed to be happy.

I once had an African partner named N'gai. He taught me how to play O'wari, a game older than Monopoly or even chess. We sat in this very bar (or the identical one that was in its place two hundred years ago) and he tried to impress on my non-Zen-oriented mind just how significant this game was to men in our position.

You start out with forty-eight smooth little pebbles, four in each one of the twelve depressions that make up the game board. Then you take turns, scooping the pebbles out of one hole and distributing them one at a time in holes to the left. If you dropped your last pebble in a hole where your opponent had only one or two, why, you got to take those pebbles off the board. Sounds exciting, doesn't it?

But N'gai sat there in a cloud of bhang-smoke and mumbled about the game and how it was just like the big game we were playing, and every time he took a pebble off the board, he called it by name. And some of the names I didn't know, but a lot of them were on my long list.

And he talked about how we were like the pieces in this simple game; how some went off the board after the first couple of moves, and some hopped from place to place all through the game and came out unscathed, and some just sat in one place all the time until they got zapped from out of nowhere....

After a while I started hitting the bhang myself, and we abandoned the metaphor in a spirit of mutual intoxication.

And I've been thinking about that night for six years, or two hundred, and I think that N'gai—his soul find Buddha—was wrong. The game isn't all that complex.

Because in O'wari, either person can win.

The snails populate ten planets for every one we destroy.

Solitaire, anyone?

THE PRIVATE WAR OF PRIVATE JACOB

With each step your boot heel cracks through the sun-dried crust and your foot hesitates, drops through an inch of red talcum powder, and then you draw it back up with another crackle. Fifty men marching in a line through this desert and they sound like a big bowl of breakfast cereal.

Jacob held the laser projector in his left hand and rubbed his right in the dirt. Then he switched hands and rubbed his left in the dirt. The plastic handles got very slippery after you'd sweated on them all day long, and you didn't want the damn thing to squirt out of your grip when you were rolling and stumbling and crawling your way to the enemy, and you couldn't use the strap, noplace off the parade ground; goddamn slide-rule jockey figured out where to put it, too high, take the damn thing off if you could. Take the goddamn helmet off too, if you could. No matter you were safer with it on. They said. And they were pretty strict, especially about the helmets.

"Look happy, Jacob." Sergeant Melford was always all smile and bounce before a battle. During a battle, too. He smiled at the tanglewire and beamed at his men while they picked their way through it—if you go too fast you get topped and if you go too slow you get burned—and he had a sad smile when one of his men got zeroed and a shriek a happy shriek when they first saw the enemy and glee when an enemy got zeroed and nothing but smiles smiles smiles through the whole sorry mess. "If he *didn't* smile, just once," young-old Addison told Jacob, a long time ago, "just once he cried or frowned, there would be fifty people waiting for the first chance to zero that son of a bitch." And Jacob asked why and he said, "You just take a good look inside yourself the next time you follow that crazy son of a bitch into hell and you come back and tell me how you felt about him."

Jacob wasn't stupid, that day or this one, and he did keep an inside eye on what was going on under his helmet. What old Sergeant Melford did for him was mainly to make him glad that he wasn't crazy too, and no matter how bad things got, at least Jacob wasn't enjoying it like that crazy laughing grinning old Sergeant Melford.

He wanted to tell Addison and ask him why sometimes you were really scared or sick and you would look up and see Melford laughing his crazy ass off, standing over some steaming roasted body, and you'd have to grin, too, was it just so insane horrible or? Addison might have been able to tell Jacob but Addison took a low one and got hurt bad in both legs and the groin and it was a long time before he came back and then he wasn't young-old anymore but just old. And he didn't say much anymore.

With both his hands good and dirty, for a good grip on the plastic handles, Jacob felt more secure and he smiled back at Sergeant Melford.

"Gonna be a good one, Sarge." It didn't do any good to say anything else, like it's been a long march and why don't we rest a while before we hit them, Sarge, or, I'm scared and sick and if I'm gonna die I want it at the very first, Sarge: no. Crazy old Melford would be down on his hunkers next to you and give you a couple of friendly punches and josh around and flash those white teeth until you were about to scream or run but instead you wound up saying, "Yeah, Sarge, gonna be a good one."

We most of us figured that what made him so crazy was just that he'd been in this crazy war so long, longer than anybody could remember anybody saying he remembered; and he never got hurt while platoon after platoon got zeroed out from under him by ones and twos and whole squads. He never got hurt and maybe that bothered him, not that any of us felt sorry for the crazy son of a bitch.

Wesley tried to explain it like this: "Sergeant Melford is an improbability locus." Then he tried to explain what a locus was and Jacob didn't really catch it, and he tried to explain what an improbability was, and that seemed pretty simple but Jacob couldn't see what it all had to do with math. Wesley was a good talker though, and he might have one day been able to clear it up but he tried to run through the tanglewire, you'd think not even a civilian would try to do that, and he fell down and the little metal bugs ate his face.

It was twenty or maybe twenty-five battles later, who keeps track, when Jacob realized that not only did old Sergeant Melford never get hurt, but he never killed any of the enemy either. He just ran around singing out orders and being happy and every now and then he'd shoot off his projector but he always shot high or low or the beam was too broad. Jacob wondered about it but by this time he was more afraid, in a way, of Sergeant Melford than he was of the enemy, so he kept his mouth shut and he waited for someone else to say something about it.

Finally Cromwell, who had come into the platoon only a couple of weeks after Jacob, noticed that Sergeant Melford never seemed to zero anybody and he had this theory that maybe the crazy old son of a bitch was a spy for the other side. They had fun talking about that for a while, and then Jacob told them about the old improbability locus theory, and one of the new guys said he sure is an imperturbable locust all right, and they all had a good laugh, which was good because Sergeant Melford came by and joined in after Jacob told him what was so funny, not about the improbability locus, but the old joke about how do you make a hormone? You don't pay her. Cromwell laughed like there was no tomorrow and for Cromwell there wasn't even any sunset, because he went across the perimeter to take a crap and got caught in a squeezer matrix.

The next battle was the first time the enemy used the drainer field, and of course the projectors didn't work and the last thing a lot of the men learned was that the light plastic stock made a damn poor weapon against a long knife, of which the enemy had plenty. Jacob lived because he got in a lucky kick, aimed for the groin but got the kneecap, and while the guy was hopping around trying to stay upright he dropped his knife and Jacob picked it up and gave the guy a new orifice, eight inches wide and just below the navel.

The platoon took a lot of zeros and had to fall back, which they did very fast because the tanglewire didn't work in a drainer field, either. They left Addison behind, sitting back against a crate with his hands in his lap and a big drooly red grin not on his face.

With Addison gone, no other private had as much combat time as Jacob. When they rallied back at the neutral zone, Sergeant Melford took Jacob aside and wasn't really smiling at all when he said: "Jacob, you know that now if anything happens to me, you've got to take over the platoon. Keep them spread out and keep them advancing, and most of all, keep them happy."

Jacob said, "Sarge, I can tell them to keep spread out and I think they will, and all of them know enough to keep pushing ahead, but how can I keep them happy when I'm never very happy myself, not when you're not around."

That smile broadened and turned itself into a laugh. You crazy old son of a bitch, Jacob thought and because he couldn't help himself, he laughed too. "Don't worry about that," Sergeant Melford said. "That's the kind of thing that takes care of itself when the time comes."

The platoon practiced more and more with knives and clubs and how to use your hands and feet but they still had to carry the projectors into combat because, of course, the enemy could turn off the drainer field whenever he wanted to. Jacob got a couple of scratches and a piece of his nose cut off, but the medic put some cream on it and it grew back. The enemy started using bows and arrows so the platoon had to carry shields, too, but that wasn't too bad after they designed one that fit right over the projector, held sideways. One squad learned how to use bows and arrows back at the enemy and things got as much back to normal as they had ever been.

Jacob never knew exactly how many battles he had fought as a private, but it was exactly forty-one. And actually, he wasn't a private at the end of the forty-first.

Since they got the archer squad, Sergeant Melford had taken to standing back with them, laughing and shouting orders at the platoon and every now and then loosing an arrow that always landed on a bare piece of ground. But this particular battle (Jacob's forty-first) had been going pretty poorly, with the initial advance stopped and then pushed back almost to the archers; and then a new enemy force breaking out on the other side of the archers.

Jacob's squad maneuvered between the archers and the new enemy soldiers and Jacob was fighting right next to Sergeant Melford, fighting pretty seriously while old Melford just laughed his fool head off, crazy son of a bitch. Jacob felt that split-second funny feeling and ducked and a heavy club whistled just over his head and bashed the side of Sergeant Melford's helmet and sheared the top of his helmet off just as neat as you snip the end off a soft-boiled egg. Jacob fell to his knees and watched the helmet full of stuff twirl end over end in back of the archers and he wondered why there were little glass marbles and cubes inside the gray-blue blood-streaked mushy stuff and then everything just went

Inside a mountain of crystal under a mountain of rock, a tiny piezoelectric switch, sixty-four molecules in a cube, flipped over to the OFF *position and the following transaction took place at just less than the speed of light:*

```
UNIT 10011001011MELFORD ACCIDENTALLY
DEACTIVATED.
SWITCH UNIT 1101011100JACOB TO CATALYST STATUS.
(SWITCHING COMPLETED)
ACTIVATE AND INSTRUCT UNIT 1101011100JACOB.
```

and came back again just like that. Jacob stood up and looked around. The same old sun-baked plain, but everybody but him seemed to be dead. Then he checked and the ones that weren't obviously zeroed were still breathing a bit. And, thinking about it, he knew why. He chuckled.

He stepped over the collapsed archers and picked up Melford's bleedy skull-cap. He inserted the blade of a knife between the helmet and the hair, shorting out the induction tractor that held the helmet on the head and served to pick up and transmit signals. Letting the helmet drop to the ground, he carefully bore the grisly balding bowl over to the enemy's crapper. Knowing exactly where to look, he fished out all the bits and pieces of crystal and tossed them down the smelly hole. Then he took the unaugmented brain back to the helmet and put it back the way he had found it. He returned to his position by Melford's body.

The stricken men began to stir and a few of the most hardy wobbled to their hands and knees.

Jacob threw back his head and laughed and laughed.

TO HOWARD HUGHES:
A MODEST PROPOSAL

Shark Key is a few hundred feet of sand and scrub between two slightly larger islands in the Florida Keys: population, one.

Not even one person actually lives there—perhaps the name has not been attractive to real estate developers—but there is a locked garage, a dock, and a mailbox fronting on US 1. The man who owns this bit of sand—dock, box, and carport—lives about a mile out in the Gulf of Mexico and has an assistant who picks up the mail every morning, and gets groceries and other things.

Howard Knopf Ramo is the sole "resident" of Shark Key, and he has many assistants besides the delivery boy. Two of them have doctorates in an interesting specialty, of which more later. One is a helicopter pilot, one ran a lathe under odd conditions, one is a youngish ex-Colonel (West Point, 1960), one was a contract killer for the Mafia, five are doing legitimate research into the nature of gravity, several dozen are dullish clerks and technicians, and one, not living with the rest off Shark Key, is a U.S. Senator who does not represent Florida but nevertheless does look out for the interests of Howard Knopf Ramo. The researchers and the delivery boy are the only ones in Ramo's employ whose income he reports to the IRS, and he only reports one-tenth at that. All the other gentlemen and ladies also receive ten-times-generous salaries, but they are all legally dead, so the IRS has no right to their money, and it goes straight to anonymously numbered Swiss accounts without attrition by governmental gabelle.

Ramo paid out little more than one million dollars in salaries and bribes last year; he considered it a sound investment of less than one-fourth of one percent of his total worth.

Our story began, well, many places with many people. But one pivotal person and place was seventeen-year-old Ronald Day, then going to high school in sleepy Winter Park, Florida.

Ronald wanted to join the Army, but he didn't want to just *join* the Army.

He had to be an officer, and he wanted to be an Academy man.

His father had served gallantly in WWII and in Korea until an AP mine in Ch'unch'on (Operation "Ripper") forced him to retire. At that time he had had for two days a battlefield commission, and he was to find that the difference between NCO's retirement and officer's retirement would be the difference between a marginal life and a comfortable one, subsequent to the shattering of his leg. Neither father nor son blamed the Army for having sent the senior Day marching through a muddy mine field, 1955 being what it was, and neither thought the military life was anything but the berries. More berries for the officers, of course, and the most for West Pointers.

The only problem was that Ronald was, in the jargon of another trade, a "chronic underachiever." He had many fascinating hobbies and skills and an IQ of 180, but he was barely passing in high school, and so had little hope for an appointment. Until Howard Knopf Ramo came into his life.

That spring afternoon, Ramo demonstrated to father and son that he had the best interests of the United States at heart, and that he had a great deal of money (nearly a hundred million dollars even then), and that he knew something rather embarrassing about senior Day, and that in exchange for certain reasonable considerations he would get Ronald a place in West Point, class of 1960.

Not too unpredictably, Ronald's intelligence blossomed in the straitjacket discipline at the Point. He majored in physics, that having been part of the deal, and took his commission and degree—with high honors—in 1960. His commission was in the Engineers and he was assigned to the Atomic Power Plant School at Fort Belvoir, Virginia. He took courses at the School and at Georgetown University nearby.

He was Captain Ronald Day and bucking for major, one step from being in charge of Personnel & Recruitment, when he returned to his billet one evening and found Ramo waiting for him in a stiff-backed chair. Ramo was wearing the uniform of a brigadier general and he asked a few favors. Captain Day agreed gladly to cooperate, not really believing the stars on Ramo's shoulders; partly because the favors seemed harmless if rather odd, but reasonable in view of past favors; mainly because Ramo told him something about what he planned to do over the next decade. It was not exactly patriotic but involved a great deal of money. And Captain Day, O times and mores, had come to think more highly of money than of patriotism.

Ramo's representatives met with Day several times in the following years, but the two men themselves did not meet again until early 1972. Day eventually volunteered for Vietnam, commanding a battalion of combat engineers. His helicopter went down behind enemy lines, such lines as there were in that war, in January 1972, and for one year he was listed as MIA. The North Vietnamese eventually released their list and he became KIA, body never recovered.

By that time his body, quite alive and comfortable, was resting a mile off Shark Key.

THREE: 5 DECEMBER 1969

Andre Charvat met Ronald Day only once, at Fort Belvoir, five years before they would live together under Ramo's roof. Andre had dropped out of Iowa State as a sophomore, was drafted, was sent to the Atomic Power Plant School, learned the special skills necessary to turn radioactive metals into pleasing or practical shapes, left the Army and got a job running a small lathe by remote control, from behind several inches of lead, working with plutonium at an atomic power applications research laboratory in Los Alamos—being very careful not to waste any plutonium, always ending up with the weight of the finished piece and shavings exactly equal to the weight of the rough piece he had started with.

But a few milligrams at a time, he was substituting simple uranium for the precious plutonium shavings.

He worked at Los Alamos for nearly four years, and brought 14.836 grams of plutonium with him when he arrived via midnight barge off Shark Key, 12 November 1974.

Many other people in similar situations had brought their grams of plutonium to Shark Key. Many more would, before the New Year.

FOUR: 1 JANUARY 1975

"Ladies. Gentlemen." Howard Knopf Ramo brushes long white hair back in a familiar, delicate gesture and with the other hand raises a tumbler to eye level. It bubbles with good domestic champagne. "Would anyone care to propose a toast?"

An awkward silence, over fifty people crowded into the television room. On the screen, muted cheering as the Allied Chemical ball begins to move. "The honor should be yours, Ramo," says Colonel Day.

Ramo nods, gazing at the television. "Thirty years," he whispers, and says aloud: "To *our* year. To our world."

Drink, silence, sudden chatter.

FIVE: 2 JANUARY 1975
Curriculum Vitae

My name is Philip Vale and I have been working with Howard Knopf Ramo for nearly five years. In 1967 I earned a doctorate in nuclear engineering at the University of New Mexico and worked for two years on nuclear propulsion systems for spacecraft. When my project was shelved for lack of funding in 1969, it was nearly impossible for a nuclear engineer to get a job; literally impossible in my specialty.

We lived off savings for a while. Eventually I had to take a job teaching high school physics and felt lucky to have any kind of a job, even at $7000 per year.

But in 1970 my wife suffered an attack of acute glomerulonephritis and lost both kidneys. The artificial dialysis therapy was not covered by our health insurance, and to keep her alive would have cost some $25,000 yearly. Ramo materialized and made me a generous offer.

Three weeks later, Dorothy and I were whisked incognito to Shark Key, our disappearance covered by a disastrous automobile accident. His artificial island was mostly unoccupied in 1970, but half of one floor was given over to medical facilities. There was a dialysis machine and two of the personnel were trained in its use. Ramo called it "benevolent blackmail" and outlined my duties for the next several years.

SIX: 4 APRIL 1970

When Philip Vale came to Ramo's island, all that showed above water was a golden geodesic dome supported by massive concrete pillars and arm-thick steel cables that sang basso in the wind. Inside the dome were living quarters for six people and a more-or-less legitimate research establishment called Gravities, Inc. Ramo lived there with two technicians, a delivery boy, and two specialists in gravity research. The establishment was very expensive but Ramo claimed to love pure science, hoped for eventual profit, and admitted that it made his tax situation easier. It also gave him the isolation that semi-billionaires traditionally prefer; because of the delicacy of the measurements necessary to his research, no airplanes were allowed to buzz overhead and the Coast Guard kept unauthorized ships from coming within a one-mile radius. All five employees did do research work in gravity; they published with expected frequency, took out occasional patents, and knew they were only a cover for the actual work about to begin downstairs.

There were seven underwater floors beneath the golden dome, and Dr. Philip Vale's assignment was to turn those seven floors into a factory for the construction of small atom bombs. Twenty-nine Nagasaki-sized fission bombs.

SEVEN: AUGUST 1945

Howard Knopf Ramo worked as a dollar-a-year man for several years, the government consulting him on organizational matters for various projects. The details of many of these projects were quite secret, but he gave as good advice as he could, without being told classified details.

In August 1945 Ramo learned what that Manhattan Project had been all about.

EIGHT: 5 APRIL 1970—3 FEBRUARY 1972

Dr. Philip Vale was absorbed for several weeks in initial planning: flow charts, lists of necessary equipment and personnel, timetables, floor plans. The hardest part of his job was figuring out a way to steal a lot of plutonium without being too obvious about it. Ramo had some ideas, on this and other things, that Vale expanded.

By the middle of 1971 there were thirty people living under Gravities, Inc., and plutonium had begun to trickle in, a few grams at a time, to be shielded with lead and cadmium and concrete and dropped into the Gulf of Mexico at carefully recorded spots within the one-mile limit. In July they quietly celebrated Ramo's 75th birthday.

On 3 February 1972, Colonel Ronald Day joined Vale and the rest. The two shared the directorship amicably, Day suggesting that they go ahead and make several mock-up bombs, both for time-and-motion studies within the plant and in order to check the efficiency of their basic delivery system: an Econoline-type van, specially modified.

NINE: TECHNOLOGICAL ASIDE

One need not gather a "critical mass" of plutonium in order to make an atom bomb of it. It is sufficient to take a considerably smaller piece and subject it to a neutron density equivalent to that which prevails at standard temperature and pressure inside plutonium at critical mass. This can be done with judiciously shaped charges of high explosive.

The whole apparatus can fit comfortably inside a Ford Econoline van.

TEN: 9 SEPTEMBER 1974

Progress Report
Delivery Implementation Section

TO: Ramo, Vale, Day, Sections 2, 5, 8.

As of this date we can safely terminate R & D on the following vehicles: Ford, Fiat, Austin, VW. Each has performed flawlessly on trial runs to Atlanta.

On-the-spot vehicle checks assure us that we can use Econolines for Ghana, Bombay, Montevideo, and Madrid without attracting undue attention.

The Renault and Soyuz vans have not been road-tested because they are not distributed in the United States. One mock-up Renault is being smuggled to Mexico, where they are fairly common, to be tested. We may be able to modify the Ford setup to fit inside a Soyuz shell. However, we have only two of the Russian vans to work with, and will proceed with caution.

The Toyota's suspension gave out in one out of three Atlanta runs; it was simply not designed for so heavy a load. We may substitute Econolines or

VW's for Tokyo and Kyoto.

90% of the vehicles were barged to New Orleans before the Atlanta run, to avoid suspicion at the Key Largo weigh station.

We are sure all systems will be in shape well before the target date.

(signed) Supervisor Maxwell Bergman

ELEVEN: 14 OCTOBER 1974

Today they solved the China Problem: automobiles and trucks are still fairly rare in China, and its border is probably the most difficult to breach. Ramo wants a minimum of three targets in China, but the odds against being able to smuggle out three vans, load them with bombs, smuggle them back in again, and drive them to the target areas without being stopped—the odds are formidable.

Section 2 (Weapons Research & Development) managed to compress a good-sized bomb into a package the size of a large suitcase, weighing about 800 pounds. It is less powerful than the others, and not as subtly safeguarded—read "booby-trapped"—but should be adequate to the task. It will go in through Hong Kong in a consignment of Swiss heavy machinery, bound for Peking; duplicates will go to Kunming and Shanghai, integrated with farm machinery and boat hulls, respectively, from Japan. Section 1 (Recruiting) has found delivery agents for Peking and Shanghai, is looking for a native speaker of the dialect spoken around Kunming.

TWELVE: NAMING

Ramo doesn't like people to call it "Project Blackmail," so they just call it "the project" when he's around.

THIRTEEN: 1 JULY 1975

Everything is in order: delivery began one week ago. Today is Ramo's 79th birthday.

His horoscope for today says "born today, you are a natural humanitarian. You aid those in difficulty and would make a fine attorney. You are attracted to the arts, including writing. You are due for domestic adjustment, with September indicated as a key month."

None of the above is true. It will be in October.

FOURTEEN: 13 OCTOBER 1975

7:45 on a gray Monday morning in Washington, D.C., a three-year-old Econoline van rolls up to a Park-yourself lot on 14th Street. About a quarter-mile from the White House.

The attendant gives the driver his ticket. "How long ya gonna be?"

"Don't know," he says. "All day, probably."

"Put it back there then, by the Camaro."

The driver parks the van and turns on a switch under the dash. With a tiny voltmeter he checks the dead-man switch on his arm: a constant-readout sphygmomanometer wired to a simple signal generator. If his blood pressure drops too low too quickly, downtown Washington will be a radioactive hole.

Everything in order, he gets out and locks the van. This activates the safeguards. A minor collision won't set off the bomb, and neither would a Richter-6 earthquake. It will go off if anyone tries to X-ray the van or enter it.

He walks two blocks to his hotel. He is very careful crossing streets.

He has breakfast sent up and turns on the *Today* show. There is no news of special interest. At 9:07 he calls a number in Miami. Ramo's fortune is down to fifty million, but he can still afford a suite at the Beachcomber.

At 9:32, all American targets having reported, Ramo calls Reykjavik.

"Let me speak to Colonel Day. This is Ramo."

"Just a moment, *sir*." One moment. "Day here."

"Things are all in order over here, Colonel. Have your salesmen reported yet?"

"All save two, as expected," he says: everyone but Peking and Kunming.

"Good. Everything is pretty much in your hands, then. I'm going to go down and do that commercial."

"Good luck, sir."

"We're past the need for luck. Be careful, Colonel." He rings off.

Ramo shaves and dresses, white Palm Beach suit. The reflection in the mirror looks like somebody's grandfather; not long for this world, kindly but a little crotchety, a little senile. Perhaps a little senile. That's why Colonel Day is coordinating things in Iceland, rather than Ramo. If Ramo dies, Day can decide what to do. If Day dies, the bombs all go off automatically.

"Let's go," he shouts into the adjoining room. His voice is still clear and strong.

Two men go down the elevator with him. One is the ex-hit man, with a laundered identity (complete to plastic surgery) and two hidden pistols. The other is Philip Vale, who carries with him all of the details of Project Blackmail and, at Ramo's suggestion, a .44 Magnum single-shot derringer. He watches the hit man, and the hit man watches everybody else.

The Cadillac that waits for them outside the Beachcomber is discreetly bulletproof and has under the front and rear seats, respectively, a Thompson submachine gun and a truncated 12-gauge shotgun. The ex-hit man insisted on the additional armament, and Ramo provided them for the poor man's peace of mind. For his own peace of mind Ramo, having no taste for violence on so small a scale, had the firing pins removed last night.

They drive to a network-affiliated television station, having spent a good deal of money for ten minutes of network time. For a paid political announcement.

It only cost a trifle more to substitute their own men for Union employees behind the camera and in the control room.

FIFTEEN: TRANSCRIPT

FADE IN LONG SHOT: RAMO, PODIUM, GLOBE

RAMO

My name is Howard Knopf Ramo.

SLOW DOLLY TO MCU RAMO

RAMO

Please don't leave your set; what I have to say is extremely important to you and your loved ones. And I won't take too much of your time.

You've probably never heard of me, though some years ago my accountants told me I was the richest man in the world. I spent a good deal of those riches staying out of the public eye. The rest of my fortune I spent on a project that has taken me thirty years to complete.

I was born just twenty-one years after the Civil War. In my lifetime, my country has been in five major wars and dozens of small confrontations. I didn't consider the reasons for most of them worthwhile. I didn't think that any of them were worth the price we paid.
And at that, we fared well compared to many other countries, whether they won their wars or lost them. Still, we continue to have wars. Rather…

TIGHT ON RAMO

…our *leaders* continue to declare wars, advancing their own political aims by sending sons and brothers and fathers out to bleed and die.

CUT TO:

MEDIUM SHOT, RAMO SLOWLY TURNING GLOBE

RAMO

We have tolerated this situation through all of recorded history. No longer. China, the Soviet Union, and the United States have stockpiled nuclear weapons sufficient to destroy all human life, twice over. It has gone beyond politics and become a matter of racial survival.

I propose a plan to take these weapons away from them—every one, simultaneously. To this end I have spent my fortune constructing twenty-nine atomic bombs. Twenty-eight of them are hidden in various cities around the world. One of them is in an airplane high over Florida. It is the smallest one; a demonstration model, so to speak.

CUT TO:

REMOTE UNIT; PAN SHORELINE

RAMO

VOICE OVER SURF SOUND

This is the Atlantic Ocean, off one of Florida's Keys. The bomb will explode seven miles out, at exactly 10:30. All shipping has been cleared from the area and prevailing winds will disperse the small amount of fallout harmlessly.

Florida residents within fifty miles of Shark Key are warned not to look directly at the blast.

FILTER DOWN ON REMOTE UNIT

Watch. There!

AFTER BLAST COMES AND FADES

CUT TO:

TIGHT ON RAMO

RAMO

Whether or not you agree with me, that all nations must give up their arms, is immaterial. Whether I am a saint or a power-drunk madman is immaterial. I give the governments of the world three days' notice—not just the atomic powers, but their allies as well. Perhaps less than three days, if they do not follow my instructions to the letter.

Atomic bombs at least equivalent to the ones that devastated Hiroshima and Nagasaki have been placed in the following cities:

MCU RAMO AND GLOBE

RAMO

TOUCHES GLOBE AS HE NAMES EACH CITY

Accra, Cairo, Khartoum, Johannesburg, London, Dublin, Madrid, Paris, Berlin, Rome, Warsaw, Budapest, Moscow, Leningrad, Novosibirsk, Ankara, Bombay, Sydney, Peking, Shanghai, Kunming, Tokyo, Kyoto, Honolulu, Akron, San Francisco, New York, Washington.

The smaller towns of Novosibirsk, Kunming, and Akron—one for each major atomic power—are set to go off eight hours before the others, as a final warning.

These bombs will also go off if tampered with, or if my representatives are harmed in any way. The way this will be done, and the manner in which atomic weapons will be collected, is explained in a letter now being sent through diplomatic channels to the leader of each threatened country. Copies will also be released to the world press.

A colleague of mine has dubbed this effort "Project Blackmail." Unflattering, but perhaps accurate.

CUT TO:

LONG SHOT RAMO, PODIUM, GLOBE

RAMO

Three days. Goodbye.

FADE TO BLACK

SIXTEEN: BRIEFING

"They didn't *catch* him?" The President was livid.

"No, sir. They had to find out what studio the broadcast originated from and then get—"

"Never mind. Do they know where the bomb is?"

"Yes, sir, it's on page six." The aide tentatively offered the letter, which a courier from the Polish embassy had brought a few minutes after the broadcast.

"Where? Has anything been done?"

"It's in a public parking lot on 14th Street. The police—"

"Northwest?"

"Yes, sir."

"Good God. That's only a few blocks from here."

"Yes, sir."

"No respect for… nobody's fiddled with it, have they?"

"No, sir. It's booby-trapped six ways from Sunday. We have a bomb squad coming out from Belvoir, but it looks pretty foolproof."

"What about the 'representative' he talked about? Let me see that thing." The aide handed him the report.

"Actually, he's the closest thing we've got to a negotiator. But he's also part of the booby trap. If he's hurt in any way…"

"What if the son of a bitch has a heart attack?" The President sat back in his chair and lowered his voice for the first time. "The end of the world."

SEVENTEEN: STATISTICAL INTERLUDE

One bomb will go off if any of twenty-eight people dies in the next three days. They will all go off if Ronald Day dies.

All of these men and women are fairly young and in good physical condition. But they are under considerable strain and also perhaps unusually susceptible to "accidental" death. Say each of them has one chance in a thousand of dying within the next three days. Then the probability of accidental catastrophe is one minus .999 to the 29th power.

This is .024 or about one chance out of 42.

A number of cautionary cables were exchanged in the first few hours, related to this computation.

EIGHTEEN: EVENING

The Secretary of Defense grips the edge of his chair and growls: "That old fool could've started World War III. Atom... bombing... Florida."

"He gave us ample warning," the Chairman of the AEC reminds him.

"Principle of the goddamn thing."

The President isn't really listening; what's past is over and there is plenty to worry about for the next few days. He is chain-smoking, something he never does in public and rarely in conference. Camels in a long filtered holder.

"How can we keep from handing over all of our atomics?" The President stubs out his cigarette, blows through the holder, lights another.

"All right," the Chairman says. "He has a list of our holdings, which he admits is incomplete." Ticks off on his fingers. "He will get a similar list from China: locations, method of delivery, yield. Chinese espionage has been pretty efficient. Another list from Russia. Between the three, that is among the three I guess—" Secretary of Defense makes a noise. "—he will probably be able to disarm us completely."

He makes a tent of his fingers. "You've thought of making a deal, I suppose. Partial lists from—"

"Yes. China's willing, Russia isn't. And Ramo is also getting lists from England, France, and Germany. Fairly complete, if I know our allies."

"Wait," says the Secretary, "France has bombs too—"

"Halfway to Reykjavik already."

"What the hell are we going to do?"

Similar queries about the same time, in Moscow and Peking.

NINETEEN: MORNING

Telegrams and cables have been arriving by the truck-load. The President's staff abstracted them into a nine-page report. Most of them say "don't do anything rash." About one in ten says "call his bluff," most of them mentioning a Communist plot. One of these even came from Akron.

It didn't take them long to find Ramo. Luckily, he had dismissed the bodyguard after returning safely to the Beachcomber, so there was no bloodshed. Right now he is in a condition something between house arrest and protective custody, half of Miami's police force and large contingents from the FBI and CIA surrounding him and his very important phone.

He talks to Reykjavik and Day tells him that all of the experts have arrived: 239 atomic scientists and specialists in nuclear warfare, a staff of technical translators and a planeload of observers from the UN's International Atomic Energy Agency.

Except for the few from France, no weapons have arrived. Day is not surprised and neither is Ramo.

Ramo is saddened to hear that several hundred people were killed in panicky evacuations in Tokyo, Bombay, and Khartoum. Evacuation of London is proceeding in an orderly manner. Washington is under martial law. In New York and Paris a few rushed out and most people are just sitting tight. A lot of people in Akron have decided to see what's happening in Cleveland.

TWENTY: NOON

President's intercom buzzes. "We found Ramo's man, sir."

"I suppose you searched him. Send him in."

A man in shirtsleeves walks in between two uniformed MP's. He is a hawk-faced man with a sardonic expression.

"This is rather premature, Mr. President. I was supposed to—"

"Sit down."

He flops into an easy chair. "—supposed to call on you at 3:30 this afternoon."

"You no doubt have some sort of a deal to offer."

The man looks at his watch. "You must be hungry, Mr. President. Take a long lunch hour, maybe a nap. I'll have plenty to say at—"

"You—"

"Don't worry about me, I've already eaten. I'll wait here."

"We can be very hard on you."

He rolls up his left sleeve. Two small boxes and some wiring are taped securely to his forearm. "No, you can't. Not for three days—you can't kill me or even cause me a lot of pain. You can't drug me or hypnotize me." (This last a lie.) "Even if you could, it wouldn't bring any good to you."

"I believe it would."

"We can discuss that at 3:30." He leans back and closes his eyes.

"What *are* you?"

He opens one eye. "A professional gambler." That is also a lie. Back when he had to work for a living, he ran a curious kind of a lathe.

TWENTY-ONE: 3:30 P.M.

The President comes through a side door and sits at his desk. "All right, have your say."

The man nods and straightens up slowly. "First off, let me explain my function."

"Reasonable."

"I am a gadfly, a source of tension."

"That is obvious."

"I can also answer certain questions about that bomb in your backyard."

"Here's one: How can we disarm it?"

"That I can't tell you."

"I believe we can convince you—"

"No, you don't understand. I don't know *how* to turn it off. That's some-body else's job." Third lie. "I do know how to blow it up—hurt me or kill me or move me more than ten miles from ground zero. Or I can just pull this little wire." He touches a wire and the President flinches.

"All right. What else are you here for?"

"That's all. Keep an eye on you, I guess."

"You don't have any sort of… message, any—"

"Oh, no. You've already got the message. Through the Polish embassy, I think."

"Come on now. I'm not naive."

The man looks at him curiously. "Maybe that's your problem. Mr. Ramo's demands are not negotiable—he really is doing what he says; taking the atomic weapons away from all of you… strange people.

"What sort of a deal do you think you could offer an eighty-year-old mil-lionaire? Ex-billionaire. How would you propose to threaten him?"

"We can kill him."

"That's right."

"In three days we can kill you."

The man laughs politely. "Now *you* are being naive."

The President flips a switch on his intercom. "Send in Carson and Major Anfel and the two MP's." The four men come in immediately.

"Take this man somewhere and talk to him. Don't hurt him."

"Not yet," the civilian Carson says.

"Come on," one MP says to the man.

"I don't think so," the man says. He stares at the President. "I'd like a glass of water."

TWENTY-TWO: 15 OCTOBER 1975

The only nuclear weapons in the United States are located in Colorado, Texas, Florida, and, of course, San Francisco, Washington D.C., and Akron, Ohio.

TWENTY-THREE: 16 OCTOBER 1975
2:30 A.M.

The only nuclear weapons in the United States are located in Colorado, Texas, Florida, San Francisco, and Washington, D.C. There is no Akron, Ohio.

Of the 139 who perished in the blast, 138 were very gutsy looters.

10:00 A.M.

Only San Francisco and Washington now. The others are on their way to Reykjavik.

The man who was named Andre Charvat walks down a deserted 14th Street with a 9-volt battery in his hand. A civilian and two volunteer MP's walk with him.

He walks straight up to the Econoline's rear bumper and touches the terminals of the battery to two inconspicuous rivets. There is a small spark and a click like the sound of a pinball machine, tilting.

"That's all. It's controlled by Reykjavik now."

"And Reykjavik is half-controlled by Communists. And worse, traitors," Carson said huskily.

He doesn't answer but walks on down the street, alone. Amnesty.

In a few minutes a heavy truck rumbles up and men in plain coveralls construct a box of boilerplate around the Econoline. People start coming back into Washington and a large crowd gathers, watching them as they cover the box with a marble facade and affix a bronze plaque to the front.

The man who owned the parking lot received a generous check from the Nuclear Arms Control Board, in kroner.

TWENTY-FOUR: QUOTE

"NUCLEAR WARFARE.... This article consists of the following sections:

I. Introduction

II. Basic Principles
    1. Fission Weapons
    2. Fusion Weapons

III. Destructive Effects
    1. Theoretical
    2. Hiroshima and Nagasaki
    3. Akron and Novosibirsk

IV. History
    1. World War II
    2. "Cold War"
    3. Treaty of Reykjavik

V. Conversion to Peaceful Uses
    1. Theory and Engineering
    2. Administration Under NACB
    3. Inspection Procedures

(For related articles see DAY, RONALD R.; EINSTEIN, ALBERT; ENERGY; FERMI, ENRICO; NUCLEAR SCIENCES (several articles); RAMO, HOWARD K.; VALE, PHILIP; WARFARE, HISTORY OF."
—Copyright © 2020 by Encyclopaedia Britannica, Inc.

THE MONSTER

Start at the beginning? Which beginning?

Okay, since you be from Outside, I give you the whole thing. Sit over there, be comfort. Smoke 'em if you got 'em.

They talk about these guys that come back from the Nam all fucked up and shit, and say they be like time bombs: they go along okay for years, then get a gun and just go crazy. But it don't go nothing like that for me. Even though there be the gun involved, this time. And an actual murder, this time.

First time I be in prison, after the court martial, I try to tell them what it be and what they get me? Social workers and shrinks. Guy to be a shrink in a prison ain't be no good shrink, what they can make Outside, is the way I figure it, so at first I don't give them shit, but then I always get Discipline, so I figure what the hell and make up a story. You watch any TV you can make up a Nam story too.

So some of them don't fall for it, they go along with it for a while because this is what crazy people do, is make up stories, then they give up and another one comes along and I start over with a different story. And sometime when I know for sure they don't believe, when they start to look at me like you look at a animal in the zoo, that's when I tell them the real true story. And that's when they smile, you know, and nod and the new guy come in next. Because if anybody would make up a story like that one he'd have to be crazy, right? But I swear to God it's true.

Right. The beginning.

I be a lurp in the Nam, which means Long Range Recon Patrol. You look in these magazines about the Nam and they make like the lurps be always heroes, brave boys go out and face Charlie alone, bring down the artillery on them and all, but it was not like that. You didn't want to be no lurp where we be, they make you be a fuckin lurp if they want to get rid of your ass, and that's the God's truth.

Now I can tell you right now that I don't give a flyin fuck for that U.S. Army and I don't like it even more when I be drafted, but I got to admit they be pretty smart, the way they do with us. Because we get off on that lurp shit. I mean we be one bunch of bad ass brothers and good old boys and we did love that rock an roll, and God they give us rock an roll—fuck your M-16, we get real tommy guns with 100-round drum, usually one guy get your automatic grenade launcher, one guy carry that starlite scope, another guy the full demo bag. I mean we could of taken on the whole fuckin North Vietnam Army. We could of killed fuckin Rambo. Now I like to talk strange, though any time I want, I can talk like other people. Even Jamaican like my mama ain't understand me if I try. I be born in New York City, but at that time my mama be only three months there—when she speak her English it be island music, but the guy she live with, bringing me up, he be from Taiwan, so in between them I learn shitty English, same-same shitty Chinese. And live in Cuban neighborhood, *por el español* shitty.

He was one mean mother fuckin Chinese cab driver, slap shit out of me for twelve year, and then I take a kitchen knife and slap him back. He never come back for the ear. I think maybe he go off someplace and die, I don't give a shit anymore, but when I be drafted they find out I speak Chinese, send me to language school in California, and I be so dumb I believe them when they say this means no Nam for the boy: I stay home and translate for them tapes from the radio.

So they send me to the Nam anyhow, and I go a little wild. I hit everybody that outranks me. They put me in the hospital and I hit the doctor. They put me in the stockade and I hit the guards, the guards hit back, some more hospital. I figure sooner or later they got to kill me or let me out. But then one day this strac dude come in and tell me about the lurp shit. It sound all right, even though the dude say if I fuck up they can waste me and it's legal. By now I know they can do that shit right there in LBJ, Long Binh Jail, so what the fuck? In two days I'm in the jungle with three real bad ass dudes with a map and a compass and enough shit we could start our own war.

They give us these maps that never have no words on them, like names of places, just "TOWN POP. 1000" and shit like that. They play it real cute, like we so dumb we don't know there be places outside of Vietnam, where no GIs can go. They keep all our ID in base camp, even the dog tags, and tell us not to be capture. Die first, they say, that shall be more pleasant. We laugh at that later, but I keep to myself the way I do feel. That the grave be one place we all be getting to, long road or short, and maybe the short road be less bumps, less trouble. Now I know from twenty years how true that be.

They don't tell us where the place be we leave from, after the slick drop us in, but we always sure as hell head west. Guy name Duke, mean honky but not dumb, he say all we be doin' is harassment, bustin' up supply lines comin' down the Ho Chi Minh Trail, in Cambodia. It do look like that, long lines of gooks carryin' ammo and shit, sometime on bicycles. We would set up some mine and some Claymores and wait till the middle of the line be there, then pop the shit, then maybe waste a few with the grenade launcher and tommy guns, not too long so they ain't regroup and get us. Duke be taking a couple Polaroids and we go four different ways, meet a couple miles away, then sneak back to the LZ and call the slick. We go out maybe six time a month, maybe lose one guy a month. Me and Duke make it through all the way to the last one, that last one.

That time no different from the other times except they tell us try to blow a bridge up, not a big bridge like the movies, but one that hang off a mountain side, be hard to fix afterward. It also be hard to get to.

We lose one guy, new guy name of Winter, just tryin' to get to the fuckin' bridge. That be bad in a special kind of way. You get used to guys gettin' shot or be wasted by frags and like that. But to fall like a hundred feet onto rocks be a different kind of bad. And it just break his back or something. He laying there and crying, tell all the world where we be, until Duke shut him up.

So it be just Duke and Cherry and me, the Chink. I am for goin' back, no fuckin' way they could blame us for that. But Duke crazy for action, always be crazy for killing, and Cherry would follow Duke anywhere, I think he a fag even then. Later I do know. When the Monster kill them.

This is where I usually feel the need to change. It's natural to adjust one's mode of discourse to a level appropriate to the subject at hand, is it not? To talk about this "Monster" requires addressing such concepts as disassociation and multiple personality, if only to discount them, and it would be awkward to speak of these things directly the way I normally speak, as Chink. This does not mean that there are two or several personalities resident within the sequestered hide of this disabled black veteran. It only means that I can speak in different ways. You could as well, if you grew up switching back and forth among Spanish, Chinese, and two flavors of English; chocolate and vanilla. It might also help if you had learned various Vietnamese dialects, and then spent the past twenty years in a succession of small rooms, mainly reading and writing. There still be the bad mother fucker in here. He simply uses appropriate language. The right tool for the job, or the right weapon.

Let me save us some time by demonstrating the logical weakness of some facile first-order rationalizations that always seem to come up. One: that this whole Monster business is a bizarre lie I concocted and have stubbornly held on to for twenty years—which requires that it never have occurred to me that recanting it would result in much better treatment and, possibly, release. Two: that the Monster is some sort of psychological shield, or barrier, that I have erected between my "self" and the enormity of the crime I committed. That hardly holds up to inspection, since my job and life at that time comprised little more than a succession of premeditated cold-blooded murders. I didn't kill the two men, but if I had, it wouldn't have bothered me enough to require elaborate psychological defenses. Three: that I murdered Duke and Cherry because I was… upset at discovering them engaged in a homosexual act. I am and was indifferent toward that aberration, or hobby. Growing up in the ghetto and going directly from there to an Army prison in Vietnam, I witnessed perversions for which you psychologists don't even have names.

Then of course there is the matter of the supposed eyewitness. It seemed particularly odious to me at the time that my government would prefer the testimony of an erstwhile enemy soldier over one of its own. I see the process more clearly now, and realize that I was convicted before the court-martial was even convened.

The details? You know what a *hoi chan* was? You're too young. Well, *chieu hoi* is Vietnamese for "open arms"; if an enemy soldier came up to the barbed wire with his hands up, shouting *chieu hoi,* then in theory he would be welcomed into our loving, also open, arms and rehabilitated. Unless he was killed before people could figure out what he was saying. The rehabilitated ones were called *hoi chans,* and sometimes were used as translators and so forth.

Anyhow, this Vietnamese deserter's story was that he had been following us all day, staying out of sight, waiting for an opportunity to surrender. I don't believe that for a second. Nobody moves that quietly, that fast, through unfamiliar jungle. Duke had been a professional hunting guide back in the World, and he would have heard any slightest movement.

What do I say happened? You must have read the transcript… I see. You want to check me for consistency.

I had sustained a small but deep wound in the calf, a fragment from a rifle grenade, I believe. I did elude capture, but the wound slowed me down.

We had blown the bridge at 1310, which was when the guards broke for lunch, and had agreed to rendezvous by 1430 near a large banyan tree about a mile from the base of the cliff. It was after 1500 when I got there, and I was worried. Winter had been carrying our only radio when he fell, and if I wasn't at the LZ with the other two, they would sensibly enough leave without me. I would be stranded, wounded, lost.

I was relieved to find them still waiting. In this sense I may *have* caused their deaths: if they had gone on, the Monster might have killed only me.

This is the only place where my story and that of the *hoi chan* are the same. They were indeed having sex. I waited under cover rather than interrupt them.

Yes, I know, this is where he testified I jumped them and did all those terrible things. Like *he* had been sitting off to one side, waiting for them to finish their business. What a bunch of bullshit.

What actually happened—what *actually* happened—was that I was hiding there behind some bamboo, waiting for them to finish so we could get on with it, when there was this sudden loud crashing in the woods on the other side of them, and bang. There was the Monster. It was bigger than any man, and black—not black like me, but glossy black, like shiny hair—and it just flat smashed into them, bashed them apart. Then it was on Cherry, I could hear bones crack like sticks. It bit him between the legs, and that was enough for me. I was gone. I heard a couple of short bursts from Duke's tommy gun, but I didn't go back to check it out. Just headed for the LZ as fast as my leg would let me.

So I made a big mistake. I lied. Wouldn't you? I'm supposed to tell them sorry, the rest of the squad got eaten by a werewolf? So while I'm waiting for the helicopter I make up this believable account of what happened at the bridge.

The slick comes and takes me back to the fire base, where the medics dress the wound and I debrief to the major there. They send me to Tuy Hoa, nice hospital on the beach, and I debrief again, to a bunch of captains and a bird colonel. They tell me I'm in for a Silver Star.

So I'm resting up there in the ward, reading a magazine, when in comes a couple of MPs and they grab me and haul me off to the stockade. Isn't that just like the Army, to have a stockade in a hospital?

What has happened is that this gook, honorable *hoi chan* Nguyen Van Trong, has come out of the woodwork with his much more believable story. So I get railroaded and wind up in jail.

Come on now, it's all in the transcript. I'm tired of telling it. It upsets me.

Oh, all right. This Nguyen claims he was a guard at the bridge we blew up, and he'd been wanting to escape—they don't say "desert"—ever since they'd left Hanoi a few months before. Walking down the Ho Chi Minh Trail. So in the confusion after the blast, he runs away; he hears Duke and Cherry and follows them. Waiting for the right opportunity to go *chieu hoi.* I've told you how improbable that actually is.

So he's waiting in the woods while they blow each other and up walks me. I get the drop on them with my Thompson. I make Cherry tie Duke to the tree. Then I tie Cherry up, facing him. Then I castrate Cherry—with my *teeth!* You believe that? And then with my teeth and fingernails, I flay Duke, skin him alive, from the neck down, while he's watching Cherry die. Then for dessert, I bite off his cock too. Then I cut them down and stroll away.

You got that? This Nguyen claims to have watched the whole thing, must have taken hours. Like he never had a chance to interrupt my little show. What, did I hang on to my weapon all the time I was nibbling away? Makes a lot of sense.

After I leave, he say he try to help the two men. Duke, he say, be still alive, but not worth much. Say he follow Duke's gestures and get the Polaroid out of his pack.

When those picture show up at the trial, I be a Had Daddy. Forget that his story ain't makin sense. Forget for Chris' sake that he be the fuckin *enemy!* Picture of Duke be still alive and his guts all hangin out, this godawful look on his face, I could of been fuckin Sister Teresa and they wouldn't of listen to me.

[At this point the respondent was silent for more than a minute, apparently controlling rage, perhaps tears. When he continued speaking, it was with the cultured white man's accent again.]

I know you are constrained not to believe me, but in order to understand what happened over the next few years, you must accept as tentatively true the fantastic premises of my delusional system. Mainly, that's the reasonable assertion that I didn't mutilate my friends, and the unreasonable one that the Cambodian jungle hides at least one glossy black humanoid over seven feet tall, with the disposition of a barracuda.

If you accept that this Monster exists, then where does that leave Mr. Nguyen Van Trong? One possibility is that he saw the same thing I did, and lied for the same reason I initially did—because no one in his right mind would believe the truth—but his lie implicated me, I suppose for verisimilitude.

A second possibility is the creepy one that Nguyen was somehow allied with the Monster; in league with him.

The third possibility… is that they were the same.

If the second or the third were true, it would probably be a good policy for me never to cross tracks with Nguyen again, or at least never to meet him unarmed. From that, it followed that it would be a good precaution for me to find out what had happened to him after the trial.

A maximum-security mental institution is far from an ideal place from which to conduct research. But I had several things going for me. The main thing was that I was not, despite all evidence to the contrary, actually crazy. Another was that I could take advantage of people's preconceptions, which is to say prejudices: I can tune my language from a mildly accented Jamaican dialect to the almost impenetrable patois that I hid behind while I was in the Army. Since white people assume that the smarter you are, the more like them you sound, and since most of my keepers were white, I could control their perception of me pretty well. I was a dumb nigger who with their help was getting a little smarter.

Finally I wangled a work detail in the library. Run by a white lady who thought she was hardass but had a heart of purest tapioca. Loved to see us goof off so long as we were reading.

I was gentle and helpful and appreciative of her guidance. She let me read more and more, and of course I could take books back to my cell. There was no record of many of the books I checked out: computer books.

She was a nice woman but fortunately not free of prejudice. It never occurred to her that it might not be a good idea to leave her pet darky alone with the computer terminal.

Once I could handle the library's computer system, my Nguyen project started in earnest. Information networks are wonderful, and computerized ordering and billing is, for a thief, the best tool since the credit card. I could order any book in print—after all, I opened the boxes, shelved the new volumes, and typed up the catalogue card for each book. If I wanted it to be catalogued.

Trying to find out what the Monster was, I read all I could find about extraterrestrials, werewolves, mutations; all that science fiction garbage. I read up on Southeast Asian religions and folk tales. Psychology books, because Occam's razor can cut the person who's using it, and maybe I was crazy after all.

Nothing conclusive came out of any of it. I had seen the Monster for only a couple of seconds, but the quick impression was, of course, branded on my memory. The face was intelligent, perhaps I should say "sentient," but it was not at all human. Two eyes, okay, but no obvious nose or ears. Mouth too big and lots of teeth like a shark's. Long fingers with too many joints, and claws. No mythology or pathology that I read about produced anything like it.

The other part of my Nguyen project was successful. I used the computer to track him down, through my own court records and various documents that had been declassified through the Freedom of Information Act.

Not surprisingly, he had emigrated to the United States just before the fall of Saigon. By 1986 he had his own fish market in San Francisco. Pillar of the community, the bastard.

Eighteen years of exemplary behavior and I worked my way down to minimum security. It was a more comfortable and freer life, but I didn't see any real chance of parole. I probably couldn't even be paroled if I'd been white and had bitten the cocks off two *black* men. I might get a medal, but not a parole.

So I had to escape. It wasn't hard.

I assumed that they would alert Nguyen, and perhaps watch him or even guard him for a while. So for two years I stayed away from San Francisco, burying myself in a dirt-poor black neighborhood in Washington. I saved my pennies and purchased or contrived the tools I would need when I eventually confronted him.

Finally I boarded a Greyhound, crawled to San Francisco, and rested up a couple of days. Then for another couple of days I kept an intermittent watch on the fish market, to satisfy myself that Nguyen wasn't under guard.

He lived in a two-room apartment in the rear of the store. I popped the back-door lock a half-hour before closing and hid in the bedroom. When I heard him lock the front door, I walked in and pointed a .44 Magnum at his face.

That was the most tense moment for me. I more than half-expected him to turn into the Monster. I had even gone to the trouble of casting my own bullets of silver, in case that superstition turned out to be true.

He asked me not to shoot and took out his wallet. Then he recognized me and clammed up.

I made him strip to his shorts and tied him down with duct tape to a wooden chair. I turned the television on fairly loud, since my homemade silencer was not perfect, and traded the Magnum for a .22 automatic. It made about as much noise as a flyswatter each time I shot.

There are places where you can shoot a person even with a .22 and he will die quickly and without too much pain. There are other sites that are quite the opposite. Of course I concentrated on those, trying to make him talk. Each time I shot him I dressed the wound, so there would be a minimum of blood loss.

I first shot him during the evening news, and he lasted well into Johnny Carson, with a new bullet each half-hour. He never said a word, or cried out. Just stared.

After he died, I waited a few hours, and nothing happened. So I walked to the police station and turned myself in. That's it.

So here we be now. I know it be life for me. Maybe it be that rubber room. I ain't care. This be the only place be safe. The Monster, he know. I can feel.

[This is the end of the transcript proper. The respondent did not seem agitated when the guards led him away. Consistent with his final words, he seemed relieved to be back in prison, which makes his subsequent suicide mystifying. The circumstances heighten the mystery, as the attached coroner's note indicates.]

State of California
Department of Corrections
Forensic Pathology Division
Glyn Malin, M.D., Ph.D.—Chief of Research

I have read about suicides that were characterized by sudden hysterical strength, including a man who had apparently choked himself to death by throttling (though I seem to recall that it was a heart attack that actually killed him). The case of Royce "Chink" Jackson is one

I would not have believed if I had not seen the body myself. The body is well muscled, but not unusually so; when I'd heard how he died I assumed he was a mesomorphic weight-lifter type. Bones are hard to break.

Also, his fingernails are cut to the quick. It must have taken a burst of superhuman strength, to tear his own flesh without being able to dig in.

My first specialty was thoracic surgery, so I well know how physically difficult it is to get to the heart. It's hard to believe that a person could tear out his own. It's doubly hard to believe that someone could do it after having brutally castrated himself.

I do have to confirm that that is what happened. The corridor leading to his solitary confinement cell is under constant video surveillance. No one came or went from the time the door was shut behind him until breakfast time, when the body was discovered.

He did it to himself, and in total silence.

GM:wr

GRAVES

I have this persistent sleep disorder that makes life difficult for me, but still I want to keep it. Boy, do I want to keep it. It goes back twenty years, to Vietnam. To Graves.

Dead bodies turn from bad to worse real fast in the jungle. You've got a few hours before rigor mortis makes them hard to handle, hard to stuff in a bag. By that time, they start to turn greenish, if they started out white or yellow, where you can see the skin. It's mostly bugs by then, usually ants. Then they go to black and start to smell.

They swell up and burst.

You'd think the ants and roaches and beetles and millipedes would make short work of them after that, but they don't. Just when they get to looking and smelling the worst, the bugs sort of lose interest, get fastidious, send out for pizza. Except for the flies. Laying eggs.

The funny thing is, unless some big animal got to it and tore it up, even after a week or so, you've still got something more than a skeleton, even a sort of a face. No eyes, though. Every now and then, we'd get one like that. Not too often, since soldiers usually don't die alone and sit there for that long, but sometimes. We called them "dry ones." Still damp underneath, of course, and inside, but kind of like a sunburned mummy otherwise.

You tell people what you do at Graves Registration, "Graves," and it sounds like about the worst job the army has to offer. It isn't. You just stand there all day and open body bags, figure out which parts maybe belong to which dog tag—not that it's usually that important—sew them up more or less with a big needle, account for all the wallets and jewelry, steal the dope out of their pockets, box them up, seal the casket, do the paperwork. When you have enough boxes, you truck them out to the airfield. The first week maybe is pretty bad. But after a hundred or so, after you get used to the smell and the godawful feel of them, you get to thinking that opening a body bag is a lot better than ending up inside one. They put Graves in safe places.

Since I'd had a couple of years of college, pre-med, I got some of the more interesting jobs. Captain French, who was the pathologist actually in charge of the outfit, always took me with him out into the field when he had to examine a corpse *in situ*, which happened only maybe once a month. I got to wear a .45 in a shoulder holster, tough guy. Never fired it, never got shot at, except the one time.

That was a hell of a time. It's funny what gets to you, stays with you.

Usually when we had an *in situ*, it was a forensic matter, like an officer they suspected had been fragged or otherwise terminated by his own men. We'd take pictures and interview some people, and then Frenchy would bring the stiff back for autopsy, see whether the bullets were American or Vietnamese. (Not that that would be conclusive either way. The Vietcong stole our weapons, and our guys used the North Vietnamese AK-47s, when we could get our hands on them. More reliable than the M-16, and a better cartridge for killing. Both sides proved that over and over.) Usually Frenchy would send a report up to Division, and that would be it. Once he had to testify at a court-martial. The kid was guilty, but just got life. The officer was a real prick.

Anyhow, we got the call to come look at this *in situ* corpse about five in the afternoon. Frenchy tried to put it off until the next day, since if it got dark, we'd have to spend the night. The guy he was talking to was a major, though, and obviously proud of it, so it was no use arguing. I threw some C's and beer and a couple canteens into two rucksacks that already had blankets and air mattresses tied on the bottom. Box of .45 ammo and a couple hand grenades. Went and got a jeep while Frenchy got his stuff together and made sure Doc Carter was sober enough to count the stiffs as they came in. (Doc Carter was the one supposed to be in charge, but he didn't much care for the work.)

Drove us out to the pad, and lo and behold, there was a chopper waiting, blades idling. Should've started to smell a rat then. We don't get real high priority, and it's not easy to get a chopper to go anywhere so close to sundown. They even helped us stow our gear. Up, up and away.

I never flew enough in helicopters to make it routine. Kontum looked almost pretty in the low sun, golden red. I had to sit between two flamethrowers, though, which didn't make me feel too secure. The door gunner was smoking. The flamethrower tanks were stenciled NO SMOKING.

We went fast and low out toward the mountains to the west. I was hoping we'd wind up at one of the big fire bases up there, figuring I'd sleep better with a few hundred men around. But no such luck. When the chopper started to slow down, the blades' whir deepening to a whuck-whuck-whuck, there was no clearing as far as the eye could see. Thick jungle canopy everywhere. Then a wisp of purple smoke showed us a helicopter-sized hole in the leaves. The pilot brought us down an inch at a time, nicking twigs.

I was very much aware of the flamethrowers. If he clipped a large branch, we'd be so much pot roast.

When we touched down, four guys in a big hurry unloaded our gear and the flamethrowers and a couple cases of ammo. They put two wounded guys and one client on board and shooed the helicopter away. Yeah, it would sort of broadcast your position. One of them told us to wait; he'd go get the major.

"I don't like this at all," Frenchy said.

"Me neither," I said. "Let's go home."

"Any outfit that's got a major and two flamethrowers is planning to fight a real war." He pulled his .45 out and looked at it as if he'd never seen one before. "Which end of this do you think the bullets come out of?"

"Shit," I advised, and rummaged through the rucksack for a beer. I gave Frenchy one, and he put it in his side pocket.

A machine gun opened up off to our right. Frenchy and I grabbed the dirt. Three grenade blasts. Somebody yelled for them to cut that out. Guy yelled back he thought he saw something. Machine gun started up again. We tried to get a little lower.

Up walks this old guy, thirties, looking annoyed. The major.

"You men get up. What's wrong with you?" He was playin' games.

Frenchy got up, dusting himself off. We had the only clean fatigues in twenty miles. "Captain French, Graves Registration."

"Oh," he said, not visibly impressed. "Secure your gear and follow me." He drifted off like a mighty ship of the jungle. Frenchy rolled his eyes, and we hoisted our rucksacks and followed him. I wasn't sure whether "secure your gear" meant bring your stuff or leave it behind, but Budweiser could get to be a real collector's item in the boonies, and there were a lot of collectors out here.

We walked too far. I mean a couple hundred yards. That meant they were really spread out thin. I didn't look forward to spending the night. The goddamned machine gun started up again. The major looked annoyed and shouted, "Sergeant, will you please control your men?" and the sergeant told the machine gunner to shut the fuck up, and the machine gunner told the sergeant there was a fuckin' gook out there, and then somebody popped a big one, like a Claymore, and then everybody was shooting every which way. Frenchy and I got real horizontal. I heard a bullet whip by over my head. The major was leaning against a tree, looking bored, shouting, "Cease firing, cease firing!" The shooting dwindled down like popcorn getting done. The major looked over at us and said, "Come on. While there's still light." He led us into a small clearing, elephant grass pretty well trampled down. I guess everybody had had his turn to look at the corpse.

It wasn't a real gruesome body, as bodies go, but it was odd-looking, even for a dry one. Moldy, like someone had dusted flour over it. Naked and probably male, though incomplete: all the soft parts were gone. Tall; one of our Montagnard allies rather than an ethnic Vietnamese. Emaciated, dry skin taut over ribs. Probably old, though it doesn't take long for these people to get old. Lying on its back, mouth wide open, a familiar posture. Empty eye sockets staring skyward. Arms flung out in supplication, loosely, long past rigor mortis.

Teeth chipped and filed to points, probably some Montagnard tribal custom. I'd never seen it before, but we didn't "do" many natives.

Frenchy knelt down and reached for it, then stopped. "Checked for booby traps?"

"No," the major said. "Figure that's your job." Frenchy looked at me with an expression that said it was my job.

Both officers stood back a respectful distance while I felt under the corpse. Sometimes they pull the pin on a hand grenade and slip it under the body so that the body's weight keeps the arming lever in place. You turn it over, and *Tomato Surprise!*

I always worry less about a hand grenade than about the various weird serpents and bugs that might enjoy living underneath a decomposing corpse. Vietnam has its share of snakes and scorpions and megapedes.

I was lucky this time; nothing but maggots. I flicked them off my hand and watched the major turn a little green. People are funny. What does he think is going to happen to him when he dies? Everything has to eat. And he was sure as hell going to die if he didn't start keeping his head down. I remember that thought, but didn't think of it then as a prophecy.

They came over. "What do you make of it, Doctor?"

"I don't think we can cure him." Frenchy was getting annoyed at this cherry bomb. "What else do you want to know?"

"Isn't it a little...*odd* to find something like this in the middle of nowhere?"

"Naw. Country's full of corpses." He knelt down and studied the face, wiggling the head by its chin. "We keep it up, you'll be able to walk from the Mekong to the DMZ without stepping on anything but corpses."

"But he's been castrated!"

"Birds." He toed the body over, busy white crawlers running from the light. "Just some old geezer who walked out into the woods naked and fell over dead. Could happen back in the World. Old people do funny things."

"I thought maybe he'd been tortured by the VC or something."

"God knows. It could happen." The body eased back into its original position with a creepy creaking sound, like leather. Its mouth had closed halfway. "If you want to put 'evidence of VC torture' in your report, your body count, I'll initial it."

"What do you mean by that, Captain?"

"Exactly what I said." He kept staring at the major while he flipped a cigarette into his mouth and fired it up. Non-filter Camels; you'd think a guy who worked with corpses all day long would be less anxious to turn into one. "I'm just trying to get along."

"You believe I want you to falsify—"

Now, "falsify" is a strange word for a last word. The enemy had set up a heavy machine gun on the other side of the clearing, and we were the closest targets. A round struck the major in the small of his back, we found on later examination. At the time, it was just an explosion of blood and guts, and he went down with his legs flopping every which way, barfing, then loud death rattle. Frenchy was on the ground in a ball, holding his left hand, going, "Shit shit shit." He'd lost the last joint of his little finger. Painful, but not serious enough, as it turned out, to get him back to the World.

I myself was horizontal and aspiring to be subterranean. I managed to get my pistol out and cocked, but realized I didn't want to do anything that might draw attention to us. The machine gun was spraying back and forth over us at about knee height. Maybe they couldn't see us; maybe they thought we were dead. I was scared shitless.

"Frenchy," I stage-whispered, "we've got to get outa here." He was trying to wrap his finger up in a standard first-aid-pack gauze bandage, much too large. "Get back to the trees."

"After you, asshole. We wouldn't get halfway." He worked his pistol out of the holster, but couldn't cock it, his left hand clamping the bandage and slippery with blood. I armed it for him and handed it back. "These are going to do a hell of a lot of good. How are you with grenades?"

"Shit. How you think I wound up in Graves?" In basic training, they'd put me on KP whenever they went out for live grenade practice. In school, I was always the last person when they chose up sides for baseball, for the same reason—though, to my knowledge, a baseball wouldn't kill you if you couldn't throw far enough. "I couldn't get one halfway there." The tree line was about sixty yards away.

"Neither could I, with this hand." He was a lefty.

Behind us came the "poink" sound of a sixty-millimeter mortar, and in a couple of seconds, there was a gray-smoke explosion between us and the tree line. The machine gun stopped, and somebody behind us yelled, "Add twenty!"

At the tree line, we could hear some shouting in Vietnamese, and a clanking of metal. "They're gonna bug out," Frenchy said. "Let's di-di."

We got up and ran, and somebody did fire a couple of bursts at us, probably an AK-47, but he missed, and then there were a series of poinks and a series of explosions pretty close to where the gun had been.

We rushed back to the LZ and found the command group, about the time the firing started up again. There was a first lieutenant in charge, and when things slowed down enough for us to tell him what had happened to the major, he expressed neither surprise nor grief. The man had been an observer from Battalion, and had assumed command when their captain was killed that morning. He'd take our word for it that the guy was dead—that was one thing we were trained observers in—and not send a squad out for him until the fighting had died down and it was light again.

We inherited the major's hole, which was nice and deep, and in his rucksack found a dozen cans and jars of real food and a flask of scotch. So, as the battle raged through the night, we munched pâté on Ritz crackers, pickled herring in sour-cream sauce, little Polish sausages on party rye with real French mustard. We drank all the scotch and saved the beer for breakfast.

For hours the lieutenant called in for artillery and air support, but to no avail. Later we found out that the enemy had launched coordinated attacks on all the local airfields and Special Forces camps, and every camp that held POWs. We were much lower priority.

Then, about three in the morning, Snoopy came over. Snoopy was a big C-130 cargo plane that carried nothing but ammunition and Gatling guns; they said it could fly over a football field and put a round into every square inch. Anyhow, it saturated the perimeter with fire, and the enemy stopped shooting. Frenchy and I went to sleep.

At first light, we went out to help round up the KIAs. There were only four dead, counting the major, but the major was an astounding sight, at least in context.

He looked sort of like a cadaver left over from a teaching autopsy. His shirt had been opened and his pants pulled down to his thighs, and the entire thoracic and abdominal cavities had been ripped open and emptied of everything soft, everything from esophagus to testicles, rib cage like blood-streaked fingers sticking rigid out of sagging skin, and there wasn't a sign of any of the guts anywhere, just a lot of dried blood.

Nobody had heard anything. There was a machine-gun position not twenty yards away, and they'd been straining their ears all night. All they'd heard was flies.

Maybe an animal feeding very quietly. The body hadn't been opened with a scalpel or a knife; the skin had been torn by teeth or claws—but seemingly systematically, throat to balls.

And the dry one was gone. Him with the pointed teeth.

There is one rational explanation. Modern warfare is partly mindfuck, and we aren't the only ones who do it, dropping unlucky cards, invoking magic and superstition. The Vietnamese knew how squeamish Americans were, and would mutilate bodies in clever ways. They could also move very quietly. The dry one? They might have spirited him away just to fuck with us. Show what they could do under our noses.

And as for the dry one's odd mummified appearance, the mold, there might be an explanation. I found out that the Montagnards in that area don't bury their dead; they put them in a coffin made from a hollowed-out log and leave them aboveground. So maybe he was just the victim of a grave robber. I thought the nearest village was miles away, like twenty miles, but I could have been wrong. Or the body could have been carried that distance for some obscure purpose—maybe the VC set it out on the trail to make the Americans stop in a good place to be ambushed.

That's probably it. But for twenty years now, several nights a week, I wake up sweating with a terrible image in my mind. I've gone out with a flashlight, and there it is, the dry one, scooping steaming entrails from the major's body, tearing them with its sharp teeth, staring into my light with black empty sockets, unconcerned. I reach for my pistol, and it's never there. The creature stands up, shiny with blood, and takes a step toward me—for a year or so, that was it; I would wake up. Then it was two steps, and then three. After twenty years it has covered half the distance and its dripping hands are rising from its sides.

The doctor gives me tranquilizers. I don't take them. They might help me stay asleep.

A SEPARATE WAR

Our wounds were horrible, but the army made us well and gave us Heaven, temporarily.

The most expensive and hard-to-replace component of a fighting suit is the soldier inside of it, so if she or he is crippled badly enough to be taken out of the fight, the suit tries to save what's left. In William's case, it automatically cut off his mangled leg and sealed the stump. In my case it was the right arm, just above the elbow. They say that for us women, losing an arm is easier than a leg. How did they come up with that?

But it was amazing luck that we should both get amputation wounds at the same time, which kept us together.

That was the Tet-2 campaign, which was a disaster, and William and I lay around doped to the gills with happyjuice while the others died their way through the disaster of Aleph-7. The score after the two battles was fifty-four dead, thirty-seven of us crips, two head cases, and only twelve more or less working soldiers, who were of course bristling with enthusiasm. Twelve is not enough to fight a battle with, unfortunately, so the *Sangre y Victoria* was rerouted to the hospital planet Heaven.

We took a long time, three collapsar jumps, getting to Heaven. The Taurans can chase you through one jump, if they're at the right place and the right time. But two would be almost impossible, and three just couldn't happen.

(But "couldn't happen" is probably a bad-luck charm. Because of the relativistic distortions associated with travel through collapsar jumps, you never know, when you greet the enemy, whether it comes from your own time, or centuries in your past or future. Maybe in a millennium or two, they'll be able to follow you through three collapsar jumps like following footprints. One of the first things they'd do is vaporize Heaven. Then Earth.)

Heaven is like an Earth untouched by human industry and avarice, pristine forests and fields and mountains—but it's also a monument to human industry, and avarice, too.

When you recover—and there's no "if"; you wouldn't be there if they didn't know they could fix you—you're still in the army, but you're also immensely wealthy. Even a private's pay rolls up a fortune, automatically invested during the centuries that creak by between battles. One of the functions of Heaven is to put all those millions back into the economy. So there's no end of things to do, all of them expensive.

When William and I recovered, we were given six months of "rest and recreation" on Heaven. I actually got out two days before him, but waited around, reading. They did still have books, for soldiers so old-fashioned they didn't want to plug themselves into adventures or ecstasies for thousands of dollars a minute. I did have $529,755,012 sitting around, so I could have dipped into tripping. But I'd heard I would have plenty of it, retraining before our next assignment. The ALSC, "accelerated life situation computer," which taught you things by making you do them in virtual reality. Over and over, until you got them right.

William had half again as much money as I did, since he had outranked me for centuries, but I didn't wait around just to get my hands on his fortune. I probably would have wanted his company even if I didn't love him. We were the only two people here born in the twentieth century, and there were only a handful from the twenty-first. Very few of them, off duty, spoke a language I understood, though all soldiers were taught "premodern" English as a sort of temporal *lingua franca*. Some of them claimed their native language was English, but it was extremely fast and seemed to have lost some vowels along the way. Four centuries. Would I have sounded as strange to a Pilgrim? I don't think so.

(It would be interesting to take one of those Pilgrim Fathers and show him what had evolved from a life of grim piety and industriousness. Religion on Earth is a curiosity, almost as rare as heterosex. Heaven has no God, either, and men and women in love or in sex with people not of their own gender are committing an anachronistic perversion.)

I'd already arranged for a sumptuous "honeymoon" suite on Skye, an airborne resort, before William got out, and we did spend five days there, amusing each other anachronistically. Then we rented a flyer and set out to see the world.

William humored my desire to explore the physical, wild aspects of the world first. We camped in desert, jungle, arctic waste, mountaintops, deserted islands. We had pressor fields that kept away dangerous animals, allowing us a good close look at them while they tried to figure out what was keeping them from lunch, and they were impressive—evolution here had not favored mammal over reptile, and both families had developed large swift predators in a variety of beautiful and ugly designs.

Then we toured the cities, in their finite variety. Some, like the sylvan

Threshold where we'd grown and trained our new limbs, blended in with their natural surroundings. This was a twenty-second-century esthetic, too bland and obvious for modern tastes. The newer cities, like Skye, flaunted their artificiality.

We were both nervous in Atlantis, under a crushing kilometer of water, with huge glowing beasts bumping against the pressors, dark day and dark night. Perhaps it was too exact a metaphor for our lives in the army, the thin skins of cruiser or fighting suit holding the dark nothingness of space at bay while monsters tried to destroy you.

Many of the cities had no function other than separating soldiers from their money, so in spite of their variety there was a sameness to them. Eat, drink, drug, trip, have or watch sex.

I found the sex shows more interesting than William did, but he was repelled by the men together. It didn't seem to me that what they did was all that different from what we did—and not nearly as alien as tripping for sex, plugging into a machine that delivered to you the image of an ideal mate and cleaned up afterwards.

He did go to a lesbian show with me, and made love with unusual energy that night. I thought there was something there besides titillation; that he was trying to prove something. We kidded each other about it—"Me Tarzan, you Jane," "Me Tarzan, you Heathcliff." Who on this world would know what we were laughing about?

Prostitution had a new wrinkle, with empathy drugs that joined the servicer and customer in a deep emotional bond that was real while it lasted, I suppose to keep in competition with the electronic fantasy. We told each other we weren't inclined to try it, though I was curious, and probably would have done it if I'd been alone. I don't think William would have, since the drugs don't work between men and women, or so one of them told us, giggling with wide-eyed embarrassment. The very idea.

We had six months of quiet communion and wild, desperate fun, and still had plenty of money left when it suddenly ended. We were having lunch in an elegant restaurant in Skye, watching the sun sparkle on the calm ocean a klick below, when a nervous private came up, saluted, and gave us our sealed orders.

They were for different places. William was going to Sade-138, a collapsar out in the Greater Magellanic Cloud. I was going to Aleph-10, in the Orion group.

He was a major, the Yod-4 Strike Force commander, and I was a captain, the executive officer for Aleph-10.

It was unbelievable, surreal; monumentally stupid and unfair. We'd been together since Basic—five years or half a millennium—and neither of us was leadership material. Neither of us was even a good *private*! The army had abundant evidence of that. Yet he was leaving in a week, for Stargate, to become a leader of men and women. My Strike Force was mustering here, in orbit around Heaven, in two days. Where I would somehow become a leader myself.

We flew back to Threshold, half the world away, and got there just as the administrative offices were opening. William fought and bought his way to the top, trying at the very least to have me reassigned as *his* XO. What difference could it make? Most of the people he'd muster with at Stargate hadn't even been born yet.

Of course it was not a matter of logic; it was a matter of protocol. And no army in history had ever been so locked in the ice of protocol. The person who *signed* those orders for the yet unborn was probably dead by now.

The remaining day and night we had together was not good. Naturally, we thought of running; we knew the planet well and had some resources left. But the planet belonged to the army. We wouldn't be safe in any city, and would be thoroughly conspicuous in the wild, since we wouldn't be able to survive without the pressor fields, easily detected.

Desertion would be punished by death, of course, and we discussed the possibility of dying together that way, in a final gesture of defiance. But that would have been passive, simply giving our lives to the army. Better to offer them one more time to the Taurans.

Finally, exhausted by talk and anger and grief, we just lay in each other's arms for the last night and early morning. I wish I could say we gave each other strength.

When he walked me to the isolation chamber three hours before launch, we were almost deferential with one another, perhaps the way you act in the presence of beloved dead. No poet who ever equated parting with death had ever had a door slam shut like that. Even if we had both been headed for Earth, a few days apart, the time-space geometry of the collapsar jump would guarantee that we arrived decades or even centuries apart from one another.

And this wasn't Earth. There were 150,000 light-years between Sade-138 and Aleph-10. Absolute distance means nothing in collapsar geometry, they say. But if William were to die in a nova bomb attack, the tiny spark of his passing would take 1500 centuries to crawl to Orion, or Earth. Time and distance beyond imagination.

The spaceport was on the equator, of course, on an island they called Pærw'l; Farewell. There was a high cliff, actually a flattened-off pinnacle, overlooking the bay to the east, where William and I had spent silent days fasting and meditating. He said he was going there to watch the launch. I hoped to get a window so that I could see the island, and I did push my way to one when we filed into the shuttle. But I couldn't see the pinnacle from sea level, and when the engines screamed and the invisible force pushed me back into the cushions, I looked but was blinded by tears, and couldn't raise a hand to wipe them away.

TWO

Fortunately, I had six hours' slack time after we docked at the space station Athene, before I had to report for ALSC training. Time to pull myself together, with the help of a couple of slowballs. I went to my small quarters and unpacked and took the pills, and lay on the bunk for awhile. Then I found my way to the lounge and watched the planet spin below, green and white and blue. There were eleven ships in orbit a few klicks away, one a large cruiser, presumably the *Bolívar*, which was going to take us to Aleph-10.

The lounge was huge and almost empty. Two other women in unfamiliar beige uniforms, I supposed Athene staff. They were talking in the strange fast Angel language, and I was listening with a rather slow brain.

While I was getting coffee, a man walked in wearing tan and green camouflage fatigues like mine. We weren't actually camouflaged as well as the ones in beige, in this room of comforting wood and earth tones.

He came over and got a cup. "You're Captain Potter, Marygay Potter."

"That's right," I said. "You're in Beta?"

"No, I'm stationed here, but I'm army." He offered his hand. "Michael Dobei, Mike. Colonel. I'm your Temporal Orientation Officer."

We carried our coffee to a table. "You're supposed to catch me up on this future, this present?"

He nodded. "Prepare you for dealing with the men and women under you. And the other officers."

"What I'm trying to deal with is this 'under you' part. I'm no soldier, Colonel."

"Mike. You're actually a better soldier than you know. I've seen your profile. You've been through a lot of combat, and it hasn't broken you. Not even the terrible experience on Earth."

William and I had been staying on my parents' farm when we were attacked by a band of looters; Mother and Dad were killed. "That's in my profile? I wasn't a soldier then. We'd quit."

"There's a lot of stuff in there." He raised his coffee and looked at me over the rim of the cup. "Want to know what your high school advisor thought of you?"

"You're a shrink."

"That used to be the word. Now we're 'skinks.'"

I laughed. "That used to be a lizard."

"Still is." He pulled a reader out of his pocket. "You were last on Earth in 2007. You liked it so little that you re-enlisted."

"Has it gotten better?"

"Better, then worse, then better. As ever. When I left, in 2318, things were at least peaceful."

"Drafted?"

"Not in the sense you were. I knew from age ten what I was going to be; everybody does."

"What? You knew you were going to be a Temporal Adjustment Officer?"

"Uh huh." He smiled. "I didn't know quite what that meant, but I sure as hell resented it. I had to go to a special school, to learn this language—SoldierSpeak—but I had to take four years of it, instead of the two that most soldiers do.

"I suppose we're more regimented on Earth now; créche to grave control, but also security. The crime and anarchy that characterized your Earth are ancient history. Most people live happy, fulfilling lives."

"Homosexual. No families."

"Oh, we have families, parents, but not random ones. To keep the population stable, one person is quickened whenever one dies. The new one goes to a couple that has grown up together in the knowledge that they have a talent for parenting; they'll be given, at most, four children to raise."

" 'Quickened'—test tube babies?"

"Incubators. No birth trauma. No real uncertainty about the future. You'll find your troops a pretty sane bunch of people."

"And what will they find me? They won't resent taking orders from a heterosexual throwback? A dinosaur?"

"They know history; they won't blame you for being what you are. If you tried to initiate sex with one of the men, there might be trouble."

I shook my head. "That won't happen. The only man I love is gone, forever."

He looked down at the floor and cleared his throat. Can you embarrass a professional skink? "William Mandella. I wish they hadn't done that. It seems… unnecessarily cruel."

"We tried to get me reassigned as his XO."

"That wouldn't have worked. That's the paradox." He moved the cup in circles on the table, watching the reflections dance. "You both have so much time in rank, objective and subjective, that they had to give you commissions. But they couldn't put you under William. The heterosex issue aside, he would be more concerned about your safety than about the mission. The troops would see that, and resent it."

"What, it never happens in your brave new world? You never have a commander falling in love with someone in his or her command?"

"Of course it happens; het or home, love happens. But they're separated and sometimes punished, or at least reprimanded." He waved that away. "In theory. If it's not blatant, who cares? But with you and William, it would be a constant irritant to the people underneath you."

"Most of them have never seen heterosexuals, I suppose."

"None of them. It's detected early and easy to cure."

"Wonderful. Maybe they can cure me."

"No. I'm afraid it has to be done before puberty." He laughed. "Sorry. You were kidding me."

"You don't think my being het is going to hurt my ability to command?"

"No, like I say, they know how people used to be—besides, privates aren't supposed to *empathize* with their officers; they're supposed to follow their orders. And they know about ALSC training; they'll know how well-prepared you are."

"I'll be out of the chain of command, anyhow, as Executive Officer."

"Unless everybody over you dies. It's happened."

"Then the army will find out what a mistake it made. A little too late."

"You might surprise yourself, after the ALSC training." He checked his watch. "Which is coming up in a couple of hours."

"Would you like to get together for lunch before that?"

"Um, no. I don't think you want to eat. They sort of clean you out beforehand. From both ends."

"Sounds… dramatic."

"Oh, it is, all of it. Some people enjoy it."

"You don't think I will."

He paused. "Let's talk about it afterwards."

THREE

The purging wasn't bad, since by that time I was limp and goofy with drugs. They shaved me clean as a baby, even my arms and cheeks, and were in the process of covering me with feedback sensors when I dozed off.

I woke up naked and running. A bunch of other naked people were running after me and my friends, throwing rocks at us. A heavy rock stung me under the shoulder blade, knocking my breath away and making me stumble. A chunky Neanderthal tackled me and whacked me on the head twice with something.

I knew this was a simulation, a dream, and here I was passing out in a dream. When I woke up a moment later, he had forced my legs apart and was about to rape me. I clawed at his eyes and rolled away. He came after me, intention still apparent, and my hand fell on his club. I swung it with both hands and cracked his head, spraying blood and brains. He ejaculated in shuddering spurts as he died, feet drumming the ground. God, it was supposed to be realistic, but couldn't they spare me a few details?

Then I was standing in a phalanx with a shield and a long spear. There were men in front of our line, crouching, with shorter spears. All of the weapons were braced at the same angle, presenting a wall of points to the horses that were charging toward us. This is not the hard part. You just stand firm, and live or not. I studied the light armor of the Persian enemy as they approached. There were three who might be in my area if we unhorsed them, or if their horses stopped.

The horse on my left crashed through. The one on the right reared up and tried to turn. The one charging straight at us took both spears in the breast, breaking the shaft of mine as it skidded, sprawling, spraying blood and screaming with an unearthly high whine, pinning the man in front of me. The unhorsed Persian crashed into my shield and knocked me down as I was drawing my short sword; the hilt of it dug in under my ribs and I almost slashed myself getting it free of the scabbard while I scrambled back to my feet.

The horseman had lost his little round shield but his sword was coming around in a flat arc. I just caught it on the edge of my shield and *as I had been taught* chopped down toward his unprotected forearm and wrist—he twisted away but I nicked him under the elbow, lucky shot that hit a tendon or something. He dropped his sword and as he reached for it with his other hand, I slashed at his face and opened a terrible wound across eye, cheek, and mouth. As he screamed a flap of skin fell away, exposing bloody bone and teeth, and I shifted my weight for a backhand, aiming for the unprotected throat, and then something slammed into my back and the bloody point of a spear broke the skin above my right nipple; I fell to my knees dying and realized I didn't have breasts; I was a man, a young boy.

It was dark and cold and the trench smelled of shit and rotting flesh. "Two minutes, boys," a sergeant said in a stage whisper. I heard a canteen gurgle twice and took it when it was passed to me—warm gin. I managed not to cough and passed it on down. I checked in the darkness and still didn't have breasts and touched between my legs and that was strange. I started to shake and heard the man next to me peeing, and I suddenly had to go, too. I fumbled with the buttons left-handed, holding onto my rifle, and barely managed to get the thing out in time, peeing hotly onto my hand. "Fix bayonets," the sergeant whispered while I was still going *and instinct took over* and I felt the locking port under the muzzle of my Enfield and held it with my left hand while my right went back and slid the bayonet from its sheath and clicked it into place.

"I shall see you in Hell, Sergeant Simmons," the man next to me said conversationally.

"Soon enough, Rez. Thirty seconds." There was a German machine-gun position about eighty yards ahead and to the right. They also had at least one very good sniper and, presumably, an artillery observer. We were hoping for some artillery support at 1:17, which would signal the beginning of our charge. If the artillery didn't come, which was likely, we were to charge anyhow, riflemen in two short squads in front of grenadiers. A suicide mission, perhaps, but certain death if your courage flags.

I wiped my hand on the greasy, filthy fatigues and thumbed the safety off the rifle. There was already a round chambered. I put my left foot on the improvised step and got a handhold with my left. My knees were water and my anus didn't want to stay closed. I felt tears and my throat went dry and metallic. *This is not real.* "Now," the sergeant said quietly, and I heaved myself up over the lip of the trench and fired one-handed in the general direction of the enemy, and started to run toward them, working the bolt, vaguely proud of not soiling myself. I flopped on the ground and took an aimed shot at the noise of the machine gun, no muzzle flash, and then held fire while squad two rushed by us. A grenadier skidded next to me and said, "Go!" It became "Oh!" when a bullet smacked into him, but I was up and running, another round chambered, four left. A bullet shattered my foot and I took one painful step and fell.

I pulled myself forward, trying to keep the muzzle out of the mud, and rolled into a shallow crater half-filled with water and parts of a swollen decaying body. I could hear another machine gun starting, but I couldn't breathe. I pushed up with both arms to gasp some air above the crater's miasma and a bullet crashed into my teeth.

It wasn't chronological. I went from there to the mist of Breed's Hill, on the British side of what the Americans would call the Battle of Bunker Hill. The deck of a ship, warding off pirates while sails burned; then another ship, deafened by cannon fire while I tried to keep a cool lead on the kamikaze Zero soaring into us.

I flew cloth-winged biplanes and supersonic fighters, used lasers and a bow and arrow, and leveled a city with the push of a button. I killed with bullets and bolos and binary-coded decimals. Every second, I was aware that it was a training exercise; I felt terror and sorrow and pain, but only for minutes or hours. And I slept at least as many hours as I was awake, but there was no rest—somehow while sleeping, my brain was filled with procedures, history, regulations.

When they unplugged me after three weeks I was literally catatonic. That was normal, though, and they had drugs that pulled you back into the world. They worked for more than 90 percent of the new officers. The others were allowed to drift away.

FOUR

We had two weeks of rest and rehabilitation—in orbit, unfortunately, not on Heaven—after the ALSC experience. While we were sweating it out in the officers' gym, I met the other line officers, who were as shaken and weak as I was, after three weeks' immersion in oxygenated fluorocarbon, mayhem, and book-learning.

We were also one mass of wrinkles from head to toe, the first day, when our exercises consisted of raising our arms above our heads, and trying to stand up and sit down without help. The wrinkles started to fade in the sauna, as we conversed in tired monosyllables. We looked like big muscular pink babies; they must have shaved or depilated us during the three weeks.

Three of us were male, which was interesting. I've seen lots of naked men, but never a hairless one. I guess we all looked kind of exposed and diagrammatic. Okayawa had an erection, and Morales kidded him about it, but to my relief it didn't go any further than that. It was a socially difficult situation anyhow.

The commander, Angela Garcia, was physically about ten years older than me, though of course by the calendar she was centuries younger. She was gruff and seemed to be holding a lot in. I knew her slightly, at least by sight; she'd been a platoon leader, not mine, in the Tet-2 disaster. Both her legs had the new-equipment look that my arm did. We'd come to Heaven together, but since her regrowth took three times as long as mine, we hadn't met there. William and I were gone before she was able to come into the common ward.

William had been in many of my ALSC dreams, a shadowy figure in some of the crowds. My father sometimes, too.

I liked Sharn Taylor, the medical officer, right off. She had a cheerful fatalism about the whole thing, and had lived life to the hilt while on Heaven, hiring a succession of beautiful women to help her spend her fortune. She'd run out of money a week early, and had to come back to Threshold and live on army rations and the low-power trips you could get for free. She herself was not beautiful; a terrible wound had ripped off her left arm and breast and the left side of her face. It had all been put back, but the new parts didn't match the old parts too well.

She had a doctor's objectivity about it, though, and professional admiration for the miracles they could accomplish—by the current calendar, she was more than 150 years out of medical school.

Her ALSC session had been totally different from ours, of course; an update of healing skills rather than killing ones. "Most of it is getting along with machines, though, rather than treating people," she told me while we nibbled at the foodlike substance that was supposed to help us recover. "I can treat wounds in the field, basically to keep someone alive until we can get to a machine. But most modern weapons don't leave enough to salvage." She had a silly smile.

"We don't know how modern the enemy is going to be," I said. "Though I guess they don't have to be all *that* modern to vaporize us." We both giggled and then stopped simultaneously.

"I wonder what they've got us on," she said. "It's not happyjuice; I can feel my fingertips and have all my peripheral vision."

"Temporary mood elevator?"

"I hope it's temporary. I'll talk to someone."

Sharn found out that it was just a euphoriant in the food; without it, ALSC withdrawal could bring on deep depression. I'd almost rather be depressed, I thought. We *were*, after all, facing almost certain doom. All but one of us had survived at least one battle in a war where the average survival rate was only 34 percent per battle. If you believed in luck, you might believe we'd used all of ours up.

We had the satellite to ourselves for eight days—ten officers waited on by a staff of thirty support personnel—while we got our strength back. Of course friendships formed. It was pretty obvious that it went beyond friendship with Chance Nguyen and Aurelio Morales; they stuck like glue from the first day.

Risa Danyi and Sharn and I made up a logical trio, the three officers out of the chain of command. Risa was the tech officer, a bit older than Sharn and me, with a Ph.D. in systems engineering. She seemed younger, though, born and raised on Heaven. Not actually born, I reminded myself. And never traumatized by combat.

Risa's ALSC had been the same as mine, but she had found it more fascinating than terrifying. She was apologetic about that. She had grown up tripping, and was accustomed to the immediacy and drama of it—and she didn't have any real-life experiences to relate to the dream combat.

Both Risa and Sharn were bawdy by nature and curious about my heterosex, and while we were silly with the euphoriants I didn't hold back anything. When I was first in the army, we'd had to obey a rotating "sleeping roster," so I slept with every male private in the company more than once, and although sleeping together didn't mean you had to have sex, it was considered unsporting to refuse. And of course men are men; most of them would have to go through the motions, literally, even if they didn't feel like it.

Even on board ship, when they got rid of the sleeping roster, there was still a lot of switching around. I was mainly with William, but neither of us was exclusive (which would have been considered odd, in our generation). Nobody was fertile, so there was no chance of accidental pregnancy.

That notion really threw Sharn and Risa. Pregnancy is something that happens to animals. Sharn had seen pictures of the process, medical history, and described it to us in horrifying detail. I had to remind them that I was born that way—I did *that* to my mother, and she somehow forgave me.

Risa primly pointed out that it was actually my father who did it to my mother, which for some reason we all thought was hilarious.

One morning when we were alone together, just looking down at the planet in the lounge, she brought up the obvious.

"You haven't said anything about it, so I guess you've never loved a woman." She cleared her throat, nervous. "I mean had sex. I know you loved your mother."

"No." I didn't know whether to elaborate. "It wasn't that common; I mean I *knew* girls and women who were together. That way."

"Well." She patted my elbow. "You know."

"Uh, yes. I mean yes, I understand. Thanks, but I…"

"I just meant, you know, we're the same rank. It's even legal." She laughed nervously; if all the regulations were broken that enthusiastically, we'd be an unruly mob, not an army.

I wasn't quite sure what to say. Until she actually asked, I hadn't thought about the possibility except as an abstraction. "I'm still grieving for William." She nodded and gave me another pat and left quietly.

But of course that wasn't all of it. I could visualize her and Sharn, for instance, having sex; I'd seen it on stage and cube often enough. But I couldn't put myself in their place. Not the way I could visualize myself being with one of the men, especially Sid, Isidro Zhulpa. He was quiet, introspective, darkly beautiful. But too well-balanced to contemplate a sexual perversion involving me.

I was still jangled about fantasy, imagination; real and artificial memories. I knew for certain that I had never killed anyone with a club or a knife, but my body seemed to have a memory of it, more real than the mental picture. I could still feel the ghost of a penis and balls, and breastlessness, since all of the ALSC combat templates were male. Surely that was more alien than lying down with another woman. When I was waiting for William to get out of his final range-and-motion stage, reading for two days, I'd had an impulse to try tripping, plugging into a lesbian sex simulation, the only kind that was available for women.

For a couple of reasons, I didn't do it. Now that it's too late—the only trips on Athene are ALSC ones—I wish I had. Because it's not as simple as "I accept this because it's the way they were brought up," with the implied condescension that my pedestal of normality entitles me.

Normality. I'm going to be locked up in a can with 130 other people for whom my most personal, private life is something as exotic as cannibalism. So rare they don't even have an epithet for it. I was sure they'd come up with one.

FIVE

TABLE OF ORGANIZATION
Strike Force Beta
Aleph-10 Campaign

1ECHN	MAJ Garcia		COMM Sidorenko
2ECHN	1LT Nguyen		
3ECHN	1LT Zhulpa		
4ECHN	CPT Potter	XO	
	2LT Danyi	TO	
	2LT Taylor, MD	MO	

	1	2	3	4
5ECHN	2LT Sadovyi	2LT Okayawa	2LT Mathes	2LT Morales
6ECHN	SSgt Baron	SSgt Troy	SSgt Tsuruta	SSgt Hencken
7ECHN	Sgt Naber	Sgt Kitamura	Sgt Yorzyk	Sgt Verdeur
8ECHN	Cpl Roth	Cpl Gross	Cpl Bruner	Cpl Graef
	Cpl Sieben	Cpl Simeony	Cpl Ritter	Cpl Henkel
	Cpl Korir	Cpl Sadovyi	Cpl Loader	Cpl Cather-wood
	Cpl Montgomery	Cpl Popov	Cpl Hajos	Cpl Hamay
	Cpl Daniels	Cpl Kahanamoku	Spl Miyzaki	Cpl Csik
	Cpl Son	Cpl Daniels	Cpl Taylor	Cpl Hopkins
	Cpl Devitt	Cpl Schollander	Cpl Winden	Cpl Spitz
	Cpl Gammoudi	Cpl Akii-Bua	Cpl Beiwat	Cpl Keino
	Cpl Armstrong	Cpl Kariuki	Cpl Brir	Cpl Keter
	Cpl Kostadinova	Cpl Ajunwa	Cpl Roba	Cpl Keimo
	Cpl McDonald	Cpl Balas	Cpl Reskova	Cpl Mayfair
	Cpl Zubero	Cpl Furniss	Cpl Kopilakov	Cpl Gross
	Cpl Myazaki	Cpl Roth	Cpl Pakratov	Cpl Lopez
	Cpl Ris	Cpl Scholes	Cpl Ris	Cpl Henricks
	Cpl Russell	Cpl Rozsa	Cpl Moorhouse	Cpl Lundquist
	Cpl Shiley	Cpl Csak	Cpl Coachman	Cpl Brand
	Cpl Ackerman	Cpl Pankritov	Cpl Nesty	Cpl O'Brien
	Pvt Darryl	Pvt Gyenji	Pvt Crapp	Pvt Hong
	Pvt Biondi	Pvt Stewart, M.	Pvt Baumann	Pvt Stewart, J.
		Pvt Engel-Kramer		Pvt Min Pvt Mingxia

Supporting: 1LT Otto (NAV), 2LTs Wennyl and Van Dykken (MED), Durack (PSY), Bleibkey (MAINT), Lackey (ORD), Obspowich (COMM), Madison (COMP);

1Sgts Mastenbroek (MED), Anderson(MED), Szoki (MED), Fraser (MED), Henne (PSY), Neelson (MAINT), Ender (ORD); SSgts Krause (MED), Steinseller (MED), Hogshead (MED), Otto (MED), Yong (MAINT), Jengyi (CK), Meyer (COMP); Sgts Gould (MED), Bonder (MAINT), Kraus (ORD), Waite (REC); Cpls Friedrich (MED), Haislett (MED), Poll (SEX), Norelius (SEX), Gyenge (ORD); Pvts Curtiss (MAINT), Senff (CK), Harup (ORD).

APPROVED STFCOM STARGATE 12 Mar 2458   FOR THE COMMANDER:

Olga Torischeva BGEN

STFCOM

The lounge was a so-called "plastic room"; it could reform itself into various modes, according to function. One of the Athene staff had handed over the control box to me—my first executive function as executive officer.

When the troop carriers lined up outside for docking, I pushed the button marked "auditorium," and the comfortable wood grain faded to a neutral ivory color as the furniture sank into the floor, and then rose up again, extruding three rows of seats on ascending tiers. The control box asked me how many seats to put on the stage in front. I said six and then corrected myself, to seven. The commodore would be here, for ceremony's sake.

As I watched the Strike Force file into the auditorium, I tried to separate the combat veterans from the Angels. There weren't too many of the latter; only fourteen out of the 130 were born on Heaven. For a good and unsettling reason.

Major Garcia waited until all the seats were filled, and then she waited a couple of minutes longer, studying the faces, maybe doing the same kind of sorting. Then she stood up and introduced the commodore and the other officers, down to my echelon, and got down to business.

"I'm certain that you have heard rumors. One of them is true." She took a single notecard from her tunic pocket and set it on the lectern. "One hundred sixteen of us have been in combat before. All wounded and brought here to Heaven. For repairs and then rest.

"You may know that this concentration of veterans is unusual. The army values experience, and spreads it around. A group this size would normally have about twenty combat veterans. Of course this implies that we face a difficult assignment.

"We are attacking the oldest known enemy base." She paused. "The Taurans established a presence on the portal planet of the collapsar Aleph-10 more than two hundred years ago. We've attacked them twice, to no effect."

She didn't say how many survivors there had been from those two attacks. I knew there had been none.

"If, as we hope, the Taurans have been out of contact with their home planet for the past two centuries, we have a huge technological advantage. The details of this advantage will not be discussed until we are under way." An absurd but standard security procedure. A spying Tauran could no more disguise itself and come aboard than a moose could. No one here could be in the pay of the Taurans. The two species had never exchanged anything but projectiles.

"We are three collapsar jumps away from Aleph-10, so we will have eleven months to train with the new weapon systems…with which we will defeat them." She allowed herself a bleak smile. "By the time we reach them, we may be coming from four hundred years in their future. That's the length of time that elapsed between the defeat of the Spanish Armada and the first nuclear war."

Of course relativity does not favor one species over the other. The Taurans on Aleph-10 might have had visitors from their own future, bearing gifts.

The troops were quiet and respectful, absorbing the fraction of information that Major Garcia portioned out. I supposed most of them knew that things were not so rosy, even the inexperienced Angels. She gave them a few more encouraging generalities and dismissed them to their temporary billets. We officers were to meet with her in two hours, for lunch.

I spent the intervening time visiting the platoon billets, talking with the sergeants who would actually be running the show, day by day. I'd seen their records but hadn't met any of them except Cat Verdeur, who had been in physical therapy with me. We both had right arm replacements, and as part of our routine we were required to arm-wrestle every day, apologetic about the pain we were causing each other. She was glad to see me, and said she would have let me win occasionally if she'd known I was going to outrank her.

The officers' lounge was also a plastic room, which I hadn't known. It had been a utilitarian meeting place before, with machines that dispensed simple food and drink. Now it was dark wood and intricate tile; linen napkins and crystal. Of course the wood felt like plastic and the linen, like paper, but you couldn't have everything.

Nine of us showed up on the hour, and the major came in two minutes later. She greeted everyone and pushed a button, and the cooks Jengyi and Senff appeared with real food and two carafes of wine. Aromatic stir-fried vegetables and zoni, which resembled large shrimp.

"Let's enjoy this while we can," she said. "We'll be back on recycled Class A's soon enough." Athene had room enough for the luxury of hydroponics and, apparently, fish tanks.

She asked us to introduce ourselves, going around the table's circle. I knew a little bit about everyone, since my XO file had basic information on the whole Strike Force, and extensive dossiers of the officers and noncoms. But there were surprises. I knew that the major had survived five battles, but didn't know she'd been to Heaven four times, which was a record. I knew her second-in-command, Chance Nguyen, came from Mars, but didn't know he was from the first generation born there, and was the first person drafted from his planet—there had been a huge argument over it, with separatists saying the Forever War was Earth's war. But at that time, Earth could still threaten to pull the plug on Mars. The red planet was self-sufficient now, Chance said, but he'd been away for a century, and didn't know what the situation was.

Lillian Mathes just came from Earth, with less than twenty years' collapsar lag, and she said they weren't drafting from Mars at that time; it was all tied up in court. So Chance might be the only Martian officer in service.

He had a strange way of carrying himself and moving, wary and careful, swimming through this unnaturally high gravity. He told me he'd trained for a Martian year, wearing heavier and heavier weights, before going to Stargate and his first assignment.

All of them were scholarly and athletic, but only Sid, Isidro Zhulpa, had actually been both a scholar and an athlete. He'd played professional baseball for a season, but quit to pursue his doctorate in sociology. He'd gotten his appointment as a junior professor the day before his draft notice. His skin was so black as to be almost blue; with his chiseled features and huge muscularity, he looked like some harsh African god. But he was quiet and modest, my favorite.

I mainly talked with him and Sharn through the meal, chatting about everything but our immediate future. When everything was done, the cooks came in with two carts and cleared the table, leaving tea and coffee. Garcia waited until all of us had been served and the privates were gone.

"Of course we don't have the faintest idea of what's waiting for us at Aleph-10," the major said. "One thing we have been able to find out, which I don't think any of you have been told, is that we know how the second Strike Force bought it."

That was something new. "It was like a mine field. A matrix of nova bombs in a belt around the portal planet's equator. We're assuming it's still there."

"They couldn't detect it and avoid it?" Risa asked.

"It was an active system. The bombs actually chased them down. They detonated four, coming closer and closer, until the fifth got them. The drone that was recording the action barely got away; one of the bombs managed to chase it through the first collapsar jump.

"We can counter the system. We're being preceded by an intelligent drone squad that should be able to detonate all of the ring of nova bombs simultaneously. It should make things pretty warm on the ground, as well as protecting our approach."

"We don't know what got the first Strike Force?" Sid asked.

Garcia shook her head. "The drone didn't return. All we can say for sure is that it wasn't the same thing."

"How so?" I asked.

"Aleph-10's easily visible from Earth; it's about eighty light-years away. They would have detected a nova bomb 120 years ago, if there'd been one. The assumption has to be that they attacked in a conventional way, as ordered, and were destroyed. Or had some accident on the way."

Of course they hadn't beamed any communication back to Earth or Stargate. We still didn't. The war was being fought on portal planets, near collapsars, which were usually desolate, disposable rocks. It would only take one nova bomb to vaporize the Stargate station; perhaps three to wipe out life on Earth.

So we didn't want to give them a roadmap back.

SIX

A lot of the training over the next eleven months had to do with primitive weapons, which explained why so much of my ALSC time had been spent practicing with bows and arrows, spears, knives, and so forth. We had a new thing called a "stasis field," which made a bubble inside which you *had* to use simple tools: no energy weapons worked.

In fact, physics itself didn't work too well inside a stasis field; chemistry, not at all. Nothing could move faster than 16.3 meters per second inside—including elementary particles and light. (You could see inside, but it wasn't light; it was some tachyon thing.) If you were exposed to the field unprotected, you'd die instantly of brain death—no electricity—and anyhow freeze solid in a few seconds. So we had suits made of stuff like tough crinkly aluminum foil, full of uncomfortable plumbing and gadgets so that everything recycled. You could live inside the stasis field, inside the suit, indefinitely. Until you went mad.

But one rip, even a pinprick, in the fabric of the suit, and you were instantly dead.

For that reason, we didn't practice with the primitive weapons inside the field. And if you had a training accident that caused the smallest scratch, · on yourself or anyone else, you got to meditate on it for a day in solitary confinement. Even officers; my carelessness with arrow points cost me a long anxious day in darkness.

Only one platoon could fit in the gym at a time, so at first I trained with whoever was using it when I got a few hours off from my other duties. After awhile I arranged my schedule so that it was always the fourth platoon. I liked both Aurelio Morales, the squad leader, and his staff sergeant, Karl

Hencken. But mainly I liked Cat Verdeur.

I don't remember a particular time when the chumminess suddenly turned into sex; there was nothing like a proposition and a mad fling. We were physically close from the beginning, because of our shared experience at Threshold. Then we were natural partners for hand-to-hand combat practice, being about the same physical age and condition. That was a rough kind of intimacy, and the fact that officers and noncoms had a shower separate from the other men and women gave us another kind. Aurelio and Karl took one side, and Cat and I took the other. We sort of soaped each other's backs, and eventually fronts.

Being a sergeant, Cat didn't have her own billet; she slept in a wing with the other women in her platoon. But one night she showed up at my door on the verge of tears, with a mysterious problem we'd both been dealing with: sometimes the new arm just doesn't feel like it belongs. It obeys your commands, but it's like a separate creature, grafted on, and the feeling of its separateness can take over everything. I let her cry on my shoulder, the good one, and then we shared my narrow bed for the night. We didn't do anything that we hadn't done many times in the shower, but it wasn't playful. I lay awake thinking, long after she fell asleep with her cheek on my breast.

I still loved William, but barring a miracle I would never see him again. What I felt for Cat was more than just friendship, and by her standards and everyone else's there was nothing odd about it. And there was no way I could have had a future with Sid or any of the other men.

When I was young there'd been a sarcastic song that went something like "If I can't be with the one I love, I'll love the one I'm with." I guess that sort of sums it up.

I went to Elise Durack, the Strike Force psychologist, and she helped me through some twists and turns. Then Cat and I went together to Octavia Poll, the female sex counselor, which wound up being a strange and funny four-way consultation with Dante Norelius, the male counselor. That resulted in a mechanical contrivance that we giggled about but occasionally used, which made it more like sex with a man. Cat sympathized with my need to hold on to my past, and said she didn't mind that I was remembering William when I was with her. She thought it was romantic, if perverse.

I started to bring the subject up with the major, and she brushed it off with a laugh. Everyone who cared aboard ship knew about it, and it was a good thing; it made me seem less strange to them. If I had been in Cat's platoon, above her in the direct chain of command, she would be routinely assigned to another platoon, which had been done several times.

(The logic of that is clear, but it made me wonder about Garcia herself. If she became in love with another woman, there wouldn't be any way to put that woman someplace outside of her command. But as far as I knew, she didn't have anybody.)

Cat more or less moved in with me. If some people in her platoon resented it, more were just as glad not to have their sergeant watching over
them every hour of the day. She usually stayed with them until first lights
out, and then walked down the corridor to my billet—often passing other
people on similar missions. Hard to keep secrets of that sort in a spaceship,
and not many tried.

There was an element of desperation in our relationship, doomed souls
sharing a last few months, but that was true of everybody's love unless they
were absolutely myopic one-day-at-a-timers. If the numbers held, only 34
percent of us had any future beyond Elephant, which is what everybody
called Aleph-10 by the time we angled in for our second collapsar jump.

William had tried in a resigned way to explain the physics of it all, the
first time we did a jump, but math had defeated me in college long before
calculus kicked me permanently into majoring in English. It has to do with
acceleration. If you just fell toward a collapsar, the way normal matter does,
you would be doomed. For some reason you and the people around you
would seem to be falling forever, but to the outside world, you would be
snuffed out instantly.

Well, sure. Obviously nobody ever did the experiment.

Anyhow, you accelerate toward the collapsar's "event horizon," which is
what it has instead of a surface, at a pre-calculated speed and angle, and you
pop out of another collapsar umpty light-years away—maybe five, maybe
five million. You better get the angle right, because you can't always just
reverse things and come back.

(Which we hoped was all that happened to the first Elephant Strike Force.
They might be on the other side of the Galaxy, colonizing some nice quiet
world. Every cruiser did carry a set of wombs and a créche, against that
possibility, though the major rolled her eyes when she described it. Purely
a morale device, she said; they probably didn't work. I wondered whether,
in that case, people might be able to grit their teeth and try to make babies
the old-fashioned way.)

Since we were leaving from Heaven, we were required to make at least two
collapsar jumps before "acquiring" Elephant. That soaked up two centuries
of objective time, if such a thing exists. To us it was eleven fairly stressful
months. Besides the training with the old-fashioned weapons, the troops
had to drill with their fighting suits and whatever specialized weapon system they were assigned to, in case the stasis field didn't work or had been
rendered useless by some enemy development.

Meanwhile, I did my Executive Officer work. It was partly bookkeeping,
which is almost trivial aboard ship, since nothing comes in and nothing
goes out. The larger part was a vague standing assignment to keep up the

troops' morale.

I was not well qualified for that; perhaps less qualified than anybody else aboard. Their music didn't sound like music to me. Their games seemed pointless, even after they'd been relentlessly explained. The movies were interesting, at least as anthropology, and the pleasures of food and drink hadn't changed much, but their sex lives were still pretty mysterious to me, in spite of my affection for Cat and the orgasms we exchanged. If a man and a woman walked by, I was still more interested in the man. So I did love a woman, but as an actual lesbian I was not a great success.

Sometimes that gave me comfort, a connection to William and my past. More often it made me feel estranged, helpless.

I did have eight part-time volunteers, and one full-time subordinate, Sergeant Cody Waite. He was not an asset. I think the draft laws on Earth, the Elite Conscription Act, were ignored on Heaven. In fact, I would go even further (to make a reference that nobody on the ship would understand) and claim that there was a Miltonian aspect to his arrival. He had been expelled from Heaven, for overweening pride. But he had nothing to be proud of, except his face and muscles. He had the intelligence of a hamster. He did look like a Greek god, but for me what that meant was that every time I needed him to do something, he was down in the gym working out on the machines. Or off getting his rectum reamed by some adoring guy who didn't have to talk with him. He could read and write, though, so eventually I found I could keep him out of the way by having him elaborate on my weekly reports. He could take "This week was the same as last week," and turn it into an epic of relentless tedium.

I was glad to be out of the chain of command. You train people intensively for combat and then put them into a box for eleven months of what? More training for combat. Nobody's happy and some people snap.

The men are usually worse than the women—or, at least, when the women lose control it tends to be a shouting match rather than fists and feet. Cat had a pair who were an exception, though, and it escalated to attempted murder in the mess hall.

This was ten days before the last collapsar jump—everybody on the ragged edge—between Lain Mayfair and "Tiny" Keimo, who was big enough to take on most of the men. Lain tried to cut her throat, from behind, and Tiny broke her arm at the elbow while everybody else was diving for cover, and was seriously strangling her—trying to kill her before she herself bled to death—when the cook J. J. ran over and brained the big woman with a frying pan.

While they were still in the infirmary there was a summary court martial. With the consistent testimony of forty witnesses, Major Garcia didn't have any choice: she sentenced Lain Mayfair to death for attempted murder. She administered the lethal injection herself.

I was required to be a witness, and more, and it was not the high point of my day. Mayfair was bedridden and, I think, slightly sedated. Garcia explained the reason for the verdict and asked Mayfair whether she would prefer the dignity of taking the poison herself. She didn't say anything, just cried and shook her head. Two privates held her down by the shoulders while Garcia took her arm and administered the popper. Mayfair turned pale and her eyes rolled up. She shook convulsively for a few seconds and was dead.

Garcia didn't show any emotion during the ordeal. She whispered to me that she would be in her quarters if anybody really needed her, and left quickly.

I had to supervise the disposal of the body. I had two medics wrap her tightly in a sheet and put her on a gurney. We had to roll it down the main corridor, everybody watching. I helped the two of them carry her into the airlock. She was starting to stiffen, but her body wasn't even cold.

I had a friend read a prayer in Mayfair's language, and asked the engineer for maximum pressure in the airlock, and then popped it. Her body spun out into its lonely, infinite grave.

I went back to the infirmary and found Tiny inconsolable. She and Mayfair had been lovers back on Stargate. Everything had gone wrong, nothing made sense, why why why why? My answer was to have Sharn give her a tranquilizer. I took one myself.

SEVEN

We came tearing out of the Elephant's collapsar about one minute after the defense phalanx, the ten high-speed intelligent drones that had multiple warheads, programmed to take out the portal planet's nova-bomb minefield.

The first surprise was that the minefield wasn't there. The second surprise was that the Taurans weren't, either. Their base seemed intact but long deserted, cold.

We would destroy it with a nova bomb, but first sent a platoon down to investigate it. Garcia asked that I go along with them. It was Cat's platoon. It would be an interesting experience to share, so long as a booby trap didn't blow us off the planet. The deserted base could be bait.

We would have a nova bomb with us. Either Morales or I could detonate it, if we got into a situation that looked hopeless. Or Garcia could do it from orbit. I was sure Garcia could do it. Not so sure about me or Aurelio.

But while we were down in the prep bay getting into our fighting suits, there came the third surprise, the big one. I later saw the recording. The main cube in the control room lit up with a two-dimensional picture of a young man in an ancient uniform. He popped in and out of three dimensions while he spoke: "Hello, Earth ship. Do you still use this frequency? Do you still use this language?"

He smiled placidly. "Of course you won't respond at first; neither would I. This could be a trap. Feel free to investigate at long range. I am calling from a different portal planet. I'm currently 12.23 million kilometers from you, on the plane of the ecliptic, on an angle of 0.54 radians with respect to the collapsar. As you probably know by now.

"I am a descendant of the first Strike Force, nearly half a millennium ago. I await your questions." He sat back in his chair, in a featureless room. He crossed his legs and picked up a notebook and began flipping through it.

We immediately got a high-resolution image of the portal planet. It was small, as they usually are; cold and airless except for the base. It was actually more like a town than a base, and it was as obvious as a beacon. It wasn't enclosed; air was evidently held in by some sort of force field. It was lit up by an artificial sun that floated a few kilometers above the surface.

There was an ancient cruiser in orbit, its dramatic sweeping streamlined grace putting our functional clunkiness to shame. There were also two Tauran vessels. None of them was obviously damaged.

All of us 5-and-above officers were on the bridge when we contacted the planet. Commodore Sidorenko sat up front with Garcia; he technically outranked her in this room, but it was her show, since the actual business was planetside.

I felt a little self-conscious, having come straight from the prep bay. Everyone else was in uniform; I was just wearing the contact net for the fighting suit. Like a layer of silver paint.

Garcia addressed the man in the chair. "Do you have a name and a rank?"

It took about forty seconds for the message to get to him, and another forty for his response: "My name is Man. We don't have ranks; I'm here because I can speak Old Standard. English."

You could play a slow chess game during this conversation, and not miss anything. "But your ancestors defeated the Taurans, somehow."

"No. The Taurans took them prisoner and set them up here. Then there was another battle, generations ago. We never heard from them again."

"But we lost that battle. Our cruiser was destroyed with all hands aboard."

"I don't know anything about that. Their planet was on the other side of the collapsar when the battle happened. The people here saw a lot of light, distorted by gravitational lensing. We always assumed it was some robotic assault, since we didn't hear anything from either side, afterwards. I'm sorry so many people died."

"What about the Taurans who were with you? Are there Taurans there now?"

"No; there weren't any then, and there aren't any now. Before the battle they showed up now and then."

"But there are—" she began.

"Oh, you mean the Tauran ships in orbit. They've been there for hundreds of years. So has our cruiser. We have no way to get to them. This place is self-sufficient, but a prison."

"I'll contact you again after I've spoken to my officers." The cube went dark.

Garcia swiveled around, and so did Sidorenko, who spoke for the first time: "I don't like it. He could be a simulation."

Garcia nodded. "That assumes a lot, though. And it would mean they know a hell of a lot more about us than we do about them."

"That's demonstrable. Four hundred years ago, they were supposedly able to build a place for the captives to stay. I don't believe we would have any trouble simulating a Tauran, given a couple of hundred captives and that much time for research."

"I suppose. Potter," she said to me, "go down and tell the fourth platoon there's a slight change of plans, but we're still going in ready for anything. I think the best thing we can do is get over there and make physical contact as soon as possible."

"Right," Sidorenko said. "We don't have the element of surprise anymore, but there's no percentage in sitting here and feeding them data, giving them time to revise their strategy. If there *are* Taurans there."

"Have your people prepped for five gees," Garcia said to me. "Get you there in a few hours."

"Eight," Sidorenko said. "We'll be about ten hours behind you."

"Wait in orbit?" I said, knowing the answer.

"You wish. Let's go down to the bay."

We had a holo of the base projected down there and worked out a simple strategy. Twenty-two of us in fighting suits, armed to the teeth, carrying a nova bomb and a stasis field, surround the place and politely knock on the door. Depending on the response, we either walk in for tea or level the place.

Getting there would not be so bad. Nobody could endure four hours of five-gee acceleration, then flip for four hours of deceleration, unprotected. So we'd be clamshelled in the fighting suits, knocked out and superhydrated. Eight hours of deep sleep and then maybe an hour to shake it off and go be a soldier. Or a guest for tea.

Cat and I made the rounds in the cramped fighter, seeing that everybody was in place, suit fittings and readouts in order. Then we shared a minute of private embrace and took our own places.

I jacked the fluid exchange into my hip fitting and all of the fear went away. My body sagged with sweet lassitude and I let the soft nozzle clasp my face. I was still aware enough to know that it was sucking all of the air out of my lungs and then blowing in a dense replacement fluid, but all I felt was a long, low-key orgasm. I knew that this was the last thing a lot of people felt, the fighter blown to bits moments or hours later. But the war offered us many worse ways to die. I was sound asleep before the acceleration blasted us into space. Dreaming of being a fish in a warm and heavy sea.

EIGHT

The chemicals won't let you remember coming out of it, which is probably good. My diaphragm and esophagus were sore and tired from getting rid of all the fluid. Cat looked like hell and I stayed away from mirrors, while we toweled off and put on the contact nets and got back into the fighting suits for the landing.

Our strategy, such as it was, seemed even less appealing, this close to the portal planet. The two Tauran cruisers were old models, but they were a hundred times the size of our fighter, and since they were in synchronous orbit over the base, there was no way to avoid coming into range. But they did let us slide under them without blowing us out of the sky, which made Man's story more believable.

It was pretty obvious, though, that our primary job was to be a target, for those ships and the base. If we were annihilated, the *Bolívar* would modify its strategy.

When Morales said we were going to just go straight in and land on the strip beside the base, I muttered, "Might as well be hung for a sheep as a goat," and Cat, who was on my line, asked why anyone would hang a sheep. I told her it was hard to explain. In fact, it was just something my father used to say, and if he'd ever explained it, I'd forgotten.

The landing was loud but feather-light. We unclamped our fighting suits from their transport positions and practiced walking in the one-third gee of the small planet. "They should've sent Goy," Cat said, which is what we called Chance Nguyen, the Martian. "He'd be right at home."

We moved out fast, people sprinting to their attack positions. Cat went off to the other side of the base. I was going with Morales, to knock on the door. Rank hath its privileges. The first to die, or be offered tea.

The buildings on the base looked like they'd been designed by a careful child. Windowless blocks laid out on a grid. All but one were sand-colored. We walked to the silver cube of headquarters. At least it had "HQ" in big letters over the airlock.

The shiny front door snicked up like a guillotine in reverse. We went through with dignified haste, and it slammed back down. The blade, or door, was pretty massive, for us to "hear" it in a vacuum; vibration through our boots.

Air hissed in—that we *did* hear—and after a minute a door swung open. We had to sidle through it sideways, because of the size of our fighting suits. I suppose we could have just walked straight through, enlarging it in the process, and in fact I considered that as I sidled. It would prevent them from using the airlock, until they could fix it.

Then another door, a metal blast door half a meter thick, slid open. Seated at a plain round table were Man and a woman who looked like his twin sister. They wore identical sky-blue tunics.

"Welcome to Alcatraz," Man said. "The name is an old joke." He gestured at the four empty chairs. "Why not get out of your suits and relax?"

"That would be unwise," Morales said.

"You have us surrounded, outside. Even if I were inclined to do you harm, I wouldn't be that foolish."

"It's for your own protection," I extemporized. "Viruses can mutate a lot in four hundred years. You don't want us sharing your air."

"That's not a problem," the woman said. "Believe me. My bodies are very much more efficient than yours."

" 'My bodies'?" I said.

"Oh, well." She made a gesture that was meaningless to me, and two side doors opened. From her side a line of women walked in, all exact copies of her. From his side, copies of him.

There were about twenty of each. They stared at us with identical bland expressions, and then said in unison, "I have been waiting for you."

"As have I." A pair of naked Taurans stepped into the room.

Both our laserfingers came up at once. Nothing happened. I snatched the utility knife from my waist and threw it, and Morales did the same. Both creatures dodged the weapons easily, moving with inhuman swiftness.

I braced myself to die. I hadn't seen a live Tauran since the Yod-4 campaign, but I'd fought hundreds of them in the ALSC. They didn't care whether they lived or died, so long as they died killing a human. But these two didn't attack.

"There is much to be explained," the Tauran said in a thin, wavering voice, its mouth-hole flexing and contracting. Its body was covered with a loose tunic like the humans', hiding most of the wrinkled orange hide and strange limbs, and the pinched, antlike thorax.

The two of them blinked slowly in unison, in what might have been a social or emotional gesture, a translucent membrane sliding wetly down over the compound eyes. The tassels of soft flesh where their noses should have been stopped quivering while they blinked. "The war is over. In most places."

The man spoke. "Human and Tauran share Stargate now. There is Tauran on Earth and human on its home planet, J'sardlkuh."

"Humans like you?" Morales said. "Stamped out of a machine?"

"I come from a kind of machine, but it is living, a womb. Until I was truly *one*, there could be no peace. When there were billions of us, all different, we couldn't understand peace."

"Everyone on Earth is the same?" I said. "There's only one kind of human?"

"There are still survivors of the Forever War, like yourselves," the female said. "Otherwise, there is only one human. As there is only one Tauran. I was patterned after an individual named Khan. I call myself Man."

There were sounds to my left and right, like distant thunder. Nothing in my communicator.

"Your people are attacking," the male said, "even though I have told them it is useless."

"Let me talk to them!" Morales said.

"You can't," the female said. "They all assembled under the stasis field, when they saw the Taurans through your eyes. Now their programmed weapons attack. When those weapons fail, they will try to walk in with the stasis field."

"This has happened before?" I said.

"Not here, but other places. The outcome varies."

"Your stasis field," a Tauran said, "has been old to us for more than a century. We used a refined version of it to keep you from shooting us a minute ago."

"You say the outcome varies," Morales said to the female, "so sometimes we win?"

"Even if you killed me, you wouldn't 'win'; there's nothing to win anymore. But no, the only thing that varies is how many of you survive."

"Your cruiser *Bolívar* may have to be destroyed," a Tauran said. "I assume they are monitoring this conversation. Of course they are still several light-minutes away. But if they do not respond in a spirit of cooperation, we will have no choice."

Garcia did respond in less than a minute, her image materializing behind the Taurans. "Why don't we invite *you* to act in a spirit of cooperation," she said. "If none of our people are hurt, none of yours will be."

"That's beyond my control," the male said. "Your programmed weapons are attacking; mine are defending. I think that neither is programmed for mercy."

The female continued. "That they still survive is evidence of our good intentions. We could deactivate their stasis field from outside." There was a huge *thump* and Man's table jumped up an inch. "Most of them would be destroyed in seconds if we did that."

Garcia paused. "Then explain why you haven't."

"One of my directives," the male said, "is to minimize casualties among you. There is a genetic diversity program, which will be explained to you at Stargate."

"All right," Garcia said. "Since I can't communicate with them otherwise, I'll let you deactivate the stasis field—but at the same time, of course, you have to turn off your automatic defenses. Otherwise they'd be slaughtered."

"So you invite us to be slaughtered instead," he said. "Me and your two representatives here."

"I'll tell them to cease fire immediately."

All this conversation was going on with a twenty-second time lag. So "immediately" would be a while in coming.

Without comment, the two Taurans disappeared, and the forty duplicate humans filed back through the dome.

"All right," the male Man said, "perhaps there is a way around this time lag. Which of you is the ranking officer here?"

"I am," I said.

"Most of my individuals have returned to an underground shelter. I will turn off your stasis field and our defenses simultaneously.

"Tell them they must stop firing immediately. If we die, our defenses resume, and they won't have the protection of the stasis field."

I chinned the command frequency, which would put me in contact with Cat and Sergeant Hencken as soon as the field disappeared.

"I don't like this," Morales said. "You can turn your weapons on and off with a thought?"

"That's correct."

"We can't. When Captain Potter gives them the order, they have to understand and react."

"But it's just turning off a switch, is it not?" There was another huge bang, and a web of cracks appeared in the wall to my left. Man looked at it without emotion.

"First a half-dozen people have to understand the order and decide to obey it!"

The male and female smiled and nodded in unison. "Now."

Thumbnail pictures of Karl and Cat appeared next to Morales. "Cat! Karl! Have the weapons units cease fire immediately!"

"What's going on?" Karl said. "Where's the stasis field?"

"They turned it off. Battle's over."

"That's right," Morales said. "Cease fire."

Cat started talking to the squads. Karl stared for a second and started to do the same.

Not fast enough. The left wall exploded in a hurricane of masonry and chunks of metal. The two Men were suddenly bloody rags of shredded flesh. Morales and I were knocked over by the storm of rubble. My armor was breached in one place; there was a ten-second beep while it repaired itself.

Then vacuum silence. The one light on the opposite wall dimmed and went out. Through the hole our cannon had made, the size of a large window, the starlit wasteland strobed in silent battle.

The three thumbnails were gone. I chinned down again for command freek. "Cat? Morales? Karl?"

Then I turned on a headlight and saw Morales was dead, his suit peeled open at the chest, lungs and heart in tatters under ribs black with dried blood.

I chinned sideways for the general freek and heard a dozen voices shouting and screaming in confusion.

So Cat was probably dead, and Karl too. Or maybe their communications had been knocked out.

I thought about that possibility for a few moments, hoping and rejecting hope, listening to the babble. Then I realized that if I could hear all those privates, corporals, they could hear me.

"This is Potter," I said. "*Captain* Potter," I yelled.

I stayed on the general freek and tried to explain the strange situation. Five did opt to stay outside. The others met me under the yellow light, which framed the top of a square, black blast door that rose out of the ground at a forty-five-degree angle, like our tornado shelter at home, thousands of years ago, hundreds of light-years away. It slid open and we went in, carrying four fighting suits whose occupants weren't responding but weren't obviously dead.

One of those was Cat, I saw as we came into the light when the airlock door closed. The back of the helmet had a blast burn, but I could make out VERDEUR.

She looked bad. A leg and an arm were missing at shoulder and thigh. But they had been snipped off by the suit itself, the way my arm had been at Tet-2.

There was no way to tell whether she was alive, since the telltale on the back of the helmet was destroyed. The suit had a biometric readout, but only a medic could access it directly, and the medic and his suit had been vaporized.

Man led us into a large room with a row of bunks and a row of chairs. There were three other Men there, but no Taurans, which was probably wise.

I popped out of my suit and didn't die, so the others did the same, one by one. The amputees we left sealed in their suits, and Man agreed that it was probably best. They were either dead or safely unconscious: if the former, they'd been dead for too long to bring back; if the latter, it would be better to wake them up in the *Bolívar*'s surgery. The ship was only two hours away, but it was a long two hours for me.

As it turned out, she lived, but I lost her anyhow, to relativity. She and the other amputees were loaded, still asleep, onto the extra cruiser, and sent straight to Heaven.

They did it in one jump, no need for secrecy anymore, and we went to Stargate in one jump aboard *Bolívar*.

When I'd last been to Stargate it had been a huge space station; now it was easily a hundred times as large, a man-made planetoid. Tauran-made, and Man-made.

We learned to say it differently: *Man*, not man.

Inside, Stargate was a city that dwarfed any city on the Earth I remembered—though they said now there were cities on Earth with a billion Men, humans, and Taurans.

We spent weeks considering and deciding on which of many options we could choose to set the course of the rest of our lives. The first thing I did was check on William, and no miracle had happened; his Strike Force had not returned from Sade-138. But neither had the Tauran force sent to annihilate them.

I didn't have the option of hanging around Stargate, waiting for him to show up; the shortest scenario had his outfit arriving in over three hundred years. I couldn't really wait for Cat, either; at best she would get to Stargate in thirty-five years. Still young, and me in my sixties. If, in fact, she chose to come to Stargate; she would have the option of staying on Heaven.

I could chase her to Heaven, but then *she* would be thirty-five years older than me. If we didn't pass one another in transit.

But I did have one chance. One way to outwit relativity.

Among the options available to veterans was Middle Finger, a planet circling Mizar. It was a nominally heterosexual planet—het or home was now completely a matter of choice; Man could switch you one way or the other in an hour.

I toyed with the idea of "going home," becoming lesbian by inclination as well as definition. But men still appealed to me—men not Man—and Middle Finger offered me an outside chance at the one man I still truly loved.

Five veterans had just bought an old cruiser and were using it as a time machine—a "time shuttle," they called it, zipping back and forth between Mizar and Alcor at relativistic speed, more than two objective years passing every week. I could buy my way onto it by using my back pay to purchase antimatter fuel. I could get there in one collapsar jump, having left word for William, and if he lived, could rejoin him in a matter of months or years.

The decision was so easy it was not a decision; it was as automatic as being born. I left him a note:

11 Oct 2878

William —

All this is in your personnel file. But knowing you, you might just chuck it. So I made sure you'd get this note.

Obviously, I lived. Maybe you will, too. Join me.

I know from the records that you're out at Sade-138 and won't be back for a couple of centuries. No problem.

I'm going to a planet they call Middle Finger, the fifth planet out from Mizar. It's two collapsar jumps, ten months subjective. Middle Finger is a kind of Coventry for heterosexuals. They call it a "eugenic control baseline."

No matter. It took all of my money, and all the money of five other old-timers, but we bought a cruiser from UNEF. And we're using it as a time machine.

So I'm on a relativistic shuttle, waiting for you. All it does is go out five light-years and come back to Middle Finger, very fast. Every ten years I age about a month. So if you're on schedule and still alive, I'll only be twenty-eight when you get here. Hurry!

I never found anybody else and I don't want anybody else. I don't care whether you're ninety years old or thirty. If I can't be your lover, I'll be your nurse.

— Marygay

NINE

FROM *THE NEW VOICE*, PAXTON, MIDDLE FINGER 24-6
14/2/3143
OLD-TIMER HAS FIRST BOY

Marygay Potter-Mandella (24 Post Road, Paxton) gave birth Friday last to a fine baby boy, 3.1 kilos.

Marygay lays claim to being the second-"oldest" resident of Middle Finger, having been born in 1977. She fought through most of the Forever War and then waited for her mate on the time shuttle, 261 years.

The baby, not yet named, was delivered at home with the help of a friend of the family, Dr. Diana Alsever-Moore.

GIZA

I hope you already know all this. I hope it's nothing but a redundant, overly dramatic gesture. But in case there's nothing left tomorrow, in case the ones in orbit don't survive, there will at least be this record, buried beneath the rubble, sending out radio beeps for about a million years, until the power source decays away.

This is how it came about.

When we bred the first ghosts—giza, as they came to call themselves—there was a predictable outcry from conservative folk all over the world. Playing God, making monsters, yammer yammer. They do seem to have turned into monsters, after all, of a certain kind. Though they started out fairly human.

Nobody could argue with the practical aspect then, almost eighty years ago. If we were going to proceed with space industrialization, we needed people in space—lots of people, even though the physical work was done by machines.

Back then, you didn't normally keep people in orbit for more than eighteen months at a time. Even with mandatory exercise and diet supplements, most started to weaken and waste away before a year had gone by. But when we started mining the Earth-grazing asteroids, the most accessible source of metals for space manufacturing, a merely year-long tour was out of the question. The rocks do come close to the Earth's orbit, by definition, but they spend most of their orbits far away, and distance means time, and money.

We needed people who could live in space permanently. So we made some.

Biological engineering was perfectly legal and routine by 2050. Almost nobody in the most prosperous half of the world was born without some degree of intervention. Who would take a chance on having children mentally or physically crippled from birth? There were limits, in most of the world—you couldn't have a child born with four arms, in hopes of selling him to the circus, any more than you could today.

155

Unless you lived in Spain. Their starting-from-scratch revolution in 2042 left a huge loophole in local laws controlling how profoundly parents could manipulate the genetic makeup of their potential children. The Basques, forever proud of their difference from the rest of the world, took advantage of the law with a vengeance, first with children capable of superhuman athletic prowess, and then stranger talents. By the time the loophole was forced shut in 2063, there were Basques with wings and gills and tentacles, who could breed true if they could find mates. Most of them did.

Though banned from professional sports, there were other niches where the engineered Basques had no competition. Barrel-chested giants with uncanny balance carried girders in high steel. Thousands of arrain, the fat gilled ones, took over sectors of marine engineering and the fishing industries. And of course the ghosts took over space.

A normal human of average size needs 1800 kilocalories of energy every day just to lie in bed. That's about a loaf of bread. If you're up and working all day, you need twice as much. Working in null-gee, inside an asteroid, doesn't take as much energy as working on Earth, but you can't get over that 1800 k-calorie minimum. Unless you're very small.

The giza were not just bred small; they were bred weak. Spindly muscle and porous bone, so they needed only meager amounts of protein and calcium and phosphorous. They look like translucent skinny six-year-olds with adult faces on adult-sized heads, but ten of them use the same mass of food and water and air as one of you.

The first ghosts had mothers born on Earth, of course, but the first generation was born in low Earth orbit, in a small hospital-and-nursery satellite run by Hispania Interspacial. For consenting to such extreme genetic engineering, the families were paid 100,000 eurams per child, half in cash and half in a trust fund in the child's name.

It was not a lot of money at the time, in prosperous Spain—a down payment on a decent city flat—but the Basques didn't do it for the money, and they didn't want the city. They did want space, to conquer space, and they almost succeeded.

H.I. guaranteed each child a technical education, at their orbital university, if they qualified. If they didn't, or flunked out, there was room in orbit for people to do other kinds of work. The only thing they couldn't do was go back to Earth, against whose gravity they could hardly breathe, let alone walk. Even lunar gravity would be dangerous to their flimsy bones.

They lived fairly well, though, in the hive they carved inside the ferrous asteroid Quetzalcoatl. A small city was in place when the first ones arrived, and it expanded naturally, as the mining machines ground their automatic way through the iron and nickel.

It was spartan in many ways, but the Earth sent much of their required carbon, hydrogen, and oxygen in the form of food. They ate well. When it costs a thousand eurams to send a kilo of food, it might as well be caviar as beans. They had closed-cycle agriculture, too, so those kilos of caviar and pâté and artichoke hearts became soil for less exotic fare.

The ghosts were able to bear children at the age of ten, and large families were rewarded, since H.I. needed workers, and it was expensive to orbit pregnant women from Earth. Their population doubled and redoubled. They doubled and quadrupled the number of machines, though, and honeycombed the asteroid, making interior real estate as well as profit for H.I.

Giza culture diverged from Earth's, most strikingly in religion: their terrestrial parents had mostly been agnostic or Nuevo Catolico, but the giza regressed to (or rediscovered) the Neolithic Basque worship of the Goddess, Mari, who, like them, lived in caves.

The discovery of warm fusion revolutionized ghost society; cheap space flight brought tourism into their otherwise closed economy. Earthling tourists brought money, of course, but they were also required to bring food, water, and air enough to support them during their stay—which resources of course remained within the asteroid's recirculating biome.

The stranger the ghosts appeared, the more interesting they were to tourists, and what started as a more or less cynical exploitation of this became a jarringly swift transformation of their culture into a kind of juvenile primitivism. A female could have six or seven children before she was eighteen, and many did. So you had children being led and taught by children, more or less supervised by a small core of technologically elite, who prospered from the display of the children's charming and strange naiveté, set against their high-tech environment.

And then it stopped. The ninth generation was sterile. Every single one of them.

To the giza, it was obvious that the whole thing had been set up from the time the first one of them had been delivered custom-made into space. They bred true down to the very last manufactured gene, and that last gene was a time bomb that doomed them as a species.

They had been invented, they said, to spend a century setting up a comfortable civilization in space. And then die off and get out of your way. You have always hated the Basques, anyway.

Ridiculous, the Spanish authorities said. Nobody could be so malicious and heartless. It had been an extreme experiment in an inexact science, and a mistake was made.

The ghosts didn't answer. The only communication Earth got from them was a continuous loop of a long prayer to Mari in an obscure Basque dialect. None of the tourists there got through to Earth, either, and none returned. We've just learned, in a final message, that they were all told to leave at once, and crowded into airlocks. When the warning bell rang and the airlocks opened, there was nothing on the other side but vacuum. They may have gotten off easy.

For months, we heard nothing from Quetzalcoatl but recorded prayer. Then we saw that it was being moved, the giza using warm-fusion steering rockets to bend its orbit. When it became obvious that it was aiming toward Earth collision, we started to take measures.

Ghost psychology was not necessarily the same as human psychology, but the planners had known enough about human nature to allow for extremes. H.I. had a huge bomb capable of diverting the asteroid, in case a maniac got ahold of it and decided humans should go the way of the dinosaurs. The diversion would destroy the asteroid and all its inhabitants, of course; still, the decision to launch was no decision.

But the giza either knew about the defense or had deduced it. When the bomb-carrying missile was halfway there, they sent a vicious farewell message and committed suicide, blowing themselves up.

It was a careful, calculated act. They had prepared the asteroid with their burrows so that rather than blowing apart into random fragments, it cracked into twenty-one pieces, any one of them large enough to doom life on Earth, all continuing along roughly the same path. Our bomb pulverized one piece.

The fragment blew up at nighttime here, and it was quite a sight, as bright as the full moon for some seconds. We can't see its dark companions yet. I suppose the first and last thing people will see of them will be the bright flash of impact.

I'm going down into the basement of this building, turn on the beacon, and lock this record in its safe. Then I'll come back up and wait for the light.

SAUL'S DEATH

One

I used to be a monk, but gave it over
Before books and prayer and studies cooled my blood,
And joined with Richard as a mercenary soldier.
(No Richard that you've heard of, just
A man who'd bought a title for his name.)
And it was in his service I met Saul.

The first day of my service I liked Saul;
His easy humor quickly won me over.
He confided Saul was not his name;
He'd taken up another name for blood.
(So had I—my fighting name was just
A word we use at home for private soldier.)

I felt at home as mercenary soldier
I liked the company of men like Saul.
(Though most of Richard's men were just
Fighting for the bounty when it's over.)
I loved the clash of weapons, splashing blood—
I lived the meager promise of my name.

Saul promised that he'd tell me his real name
When he was through with playing as a soldier.
(I said the same; we took an oath in blood.)
But I would never know him but as Saul;
He'd die before the long campaign was over,
Dying for a cause that was not just.

Only fools require a cause that's just.
Fools, and children out to make a name.
Now I've had sixty years to think it over
(Sixty years of being no one's soldier).
Sixty years since broadsword opened Saul
And splashed my body with his precious blood.

But damn! we lived for bodies and for blood.
The reek of dead men rotting, it was just
A sweet perfume for those like me and Saul.
(My peaceful language doesn't have a name
For lewd delight in going off to soldier.)
It hurts my heart sometimes to know it's over.

My heart was hard as stone when it was over;
When finally I'd had my fill of blood.
(And knew I was too old to be a soldier.)
Nothing left for me to do but just
Go back home and make myself a name
In ways of peace, forgetting war and Saul.

In ways of blood he made himself a name
(Though he was just a mercenary soldier)—
I loved Saul before it was all over.

Two

A mercenary soldier has no future;
Some say his way of life is hardly human.
And yet, we had our own small bloody world
(Part aches and sores and wrappings soaking blood,
Partly fear and glory grown familiar)
Confined within a shiny fence of swords.

But how I learned to love to fence with swords!
Another world, my homely past and future—
Once steel and eye and wrist became familiar
With each other, then that steel was almost human
(With an altogether human taste for blood).
I felt that sword and I could take the world.

I felt that Saul and I could take the world:
Take the whole world hostage with our swords.

The bond we felt was stronger than mere blood
(Though I can see with hindsight in the future
The bond we felt was something only human:
A need for love when death becomes familiar).

We were wizards, and death was our familiar;
Our swords held all the magic in the world.
(Richard thought it almost wasn't human,
The speed with which we parried others' swords,
Forever end another's petty future.)
Never scratched, though always steeped in blood.

Ambushed in a tavern, splashing ankle-deep in blood;
Fighting back-to-back in ways familiar.
Saul slipped: lost his footing and our future.
Broad blade hammered down and sent him from this world.
In angry grief I killed that one, then all the other swords;
Then locked the doors and murdered every human.

No choice, but to murder every human.
No one in that tavern was a stranger to blood.
(To those who live with pikes and slashing swords,
The inner parts of men become familiar.)
Saul's vitals looked like nothing in this world:
I had to kill them all to save my future.

Saul's vitals were not human, but familiar:
He never told me he was from another world:
I never told him I was from his future.

DX

So every night
you build a little house

You dig a hole
and cover it with logs

Cover the logs
with sandbags
against the
shrapnel weather

A house you
sleep beside
and hope not
to enter

Some nights you wake
to noise and light
and metal singing

Roll out of the bag
and into the house
  with all the scorpions
  centipedes   roaches
but no bullets flying inside it

Most nights
you just sleep
deep sleep
and dreamless
mostly
from labor

This night was just sleep.

In the morning
you unbuild the house

hours of work
again
for nothing

Kick the logs away
pour out the sandbags
into the hole

Roll up the sandbags
for the next night's bit
of rural urban renewal

Eat some cold bad food
Clean your weapon
Drink instant coffee
from a can

Check the tape on
the grenades,
check the pins.
Inspect ammo clips

Most carefully
repack the demolition
bag: blasting caps
TNT plastic timefuse
det cord—

(Clean the top
rounds with
illegal gasoline.)

ten kilograms of fragile
most instant
death

Then shoulder the heavy rucksack
Secure your weapons and tools
and follow the other primates
into the jungle

watching the trees

walk silently
as possible
through the green

watching the ground

Don't get too close
to the man in front of you

This is good advice:
don't let the enemy
have two targets.

Remember that: don't get too close to any man.

Only a fool, or an officer,
doesn't grab the ground   high pitched
at the first shot   rattle
                                     of M-16s
            even if it's rather distant
                               louder
                               Russian rifles
                               answer
       even if it's
       a couple of klicks away   manly chug
                               of heavy
God knows which way they're shooting   machineguns

                             grenade's
                             flat
                             bang

Like fools, or officers,
we get up off the ground and move

                               All that metal
                               flying through
                               the air—
                     and do we move away from it?

                               no

We make haste   like fools or officers
in the wrong direction   we head for the action

making lots of noise now
who cares now

     but careful not to bunch up

Remember: Don't get too close to any man.

It's over before we get there.
The enemy, not fools
(perhaps lacking officers)
went in the proper direction.

As we approach   "You wanna get some
the abandoned enemy camp   X-Rays down here?
a bit of impolite and   Charlie left
(perhaps to you)   a motherfuckin'
incomprehensible   DX pile
dialogue greets us: behind."

TERMS:

X-Rays are engineers,   Charlie is the enemy.
demolition men,
us.

                    "DX" means destroy;
                    a DX pile is a collection
                    of explosives that are no longer
                    trustworthy. When you leave
                    the camp finally, you
                    put a long fuse on the DX pile, and
                                        blow it up.

(Both "motherfucker" and "DX"
are technical terms that can serve
as polite euphemisms:
        "Private,   "Private,
        you wanna   instead   kill
        DX that   of   that
        motherfucker?"   man.")

We'd been lucky.
No shooting.
Just a pile of
explosive

leftovers
to dispose of.

        And we'd done it before.

It was quite a pile,   artillery shells
though,   mortar rounds
taller than a man   satchel charges
enough to kill   rifle grenades
        all
everybody   festooned with chains of
with some left over   fifty-caliber ammunition

The major wouldn't let us
evacuate his troops
    then put a long fuse on
        the pile

We had to stand there
nervous   no
and guard it

They'd been working hard
first they get lunch and a nap
then we can move them out
and we can blow it.

(we liked his "we")

We didn't know
it was wired for sound

    it was booby-trapped

    Remember: Don't get too close to any man:

Don't know that Farmer
has an actual farm waiting   and   Don't know that Crowder
back in Alabama   has new grandbabies
    and is headed
    for retirement
and   don't know that Doc   when he gets home
    was a basketball champ
    in his black high school
    and really did want

to be a doctor

Because they all are
one short beep
of a radio detonator
                    away
                    from

                              a sound
                              so loud   gray smoke
                              you don't
                              hear it   blood
                              really

                    It just hits you like a car.

                              everywhere blood
                              and screaming

Doc
both his long legs
blown off   Sergeant Crowder
dies quickly   ·   separated from one
                                   foot is unconscious
                                   or stoic

Farmer had his belly spilled
but lived long enough to
shout

        "Professor?
        Where'd they get   and   since I didn't have
        you?"   enough breath
                                           for a complete
                                          catalogue

                                          (foot shins knees
                                          thigh groin genitals
                                          arm ear scalp and
                                          disposition)

                                          I settled for "the balls."

Oh my God
Farmer said
then he died

        Two days later
        I woke up in a dirty hospital
        (sewed up like Frankenstein's charge)
        woke up in time
        to see Crowder leave
        with a sheet   over his eyes
and so it was over

        in a way

                the whole squad DX
                but me

        there is nothing for it
        there is nothing you can take for it
        they are names on a wall now
        they are compost in Arlington
        and somehow   I am not

        but give me this

There are three other universes, like this:

In one,   Farmer curses the rain
        wrestles his tractor through the mud
        curses the bank that owns it
        and sometimes remembers
        that he alone survived

        In another   Crowder tells grown
                            grandchildren
                            for the hundredth time
                            over a late-night whiskey
                            his one war story that
                            beats the others all to hell

    In the third   Doc stands over a bloody patient
                steady hand   healing knife

and sometimes he recalls
blood years past   and sometimes
remembers   to be glad to be alive;

in these worlds
I am dead

and at peace.

INTRODUCTION: A TANGLED WEB

I started writing *1968* in 1974, while I was a student at the Iowa Writers' Workshop. My professor that semester was the sly and sardonic Stanley Elkin, who forbade me to write science fiction, which he despised. So I wrote the first twenty or so pages of a novel I was calling *Spider's Web*, plus the battle scene that wound up being the book's turning point.

Elkin liked the work, but I found it just too hard to write. I was too close to it — I'd left Vietnam only five years before — and I'd wake up with nightmares, revisiting combat, something my PTSD didn't need. So I tabled it for sixteen years. About ten other books, all of them (sorry, Stan) science fiction.

I'm 62 as I write this, and can do the math even though I don't believe it — exactly half of my life has gone by since I wrote those first pages in Iowa. It was about a year before I won the Nebula and Hugo Awards for *The Forever War*, permanently warping my career away from mainstream "literary" fiction. Except for this one detour, to revisit that fascinating and terrible time. It's my longest book, and took the longest time to write, about two and a half years.

People ask me whether *1968* is autobiographical, and the usual answer — if you don't want to sit for an hour and talk about the necessary connection between autobiography and fiction — is no, the main character is based on a guy I liked who died there, plus a man I saw on a plane. Plus some of what I've observed about fellow combat veterans. Plus the stuff I did as a young man somewhat touched by the counter-culture both before and after being drafted. The other main character is less specific, sort of an amalgam of many women and girls I liked and loved, and tried to understand, back then.

The book is an exploration of a year I felt I missed, which became a pivotal year in American culture. I spent all of it either sequestered in Basic Training or trying to cope with combat and subsequent hospitalization in Vietnam. We didn't have transistor radios in my unit — I think they were forbidden because of "sound discipline" on patrol — and we rarely got news from home. Or if we did, it seemed far away and trivial compared to the business of daily avoiding and dealing death. I do remember the unreal feeling of opening a letter in the jungle and unfolding the front page of the Washington *Post*, with a picture of Washington in flames, in the riot that followed Martin Luther King's assassination. Maybe there *were* more important things going on back in the World.

Yes and no, it says here.

1968

FIRST WEEK

A WORLD OF DIRT

Spider was on a planet far away, a world better than this one. There was a beautiful princess involved, and a reluctant hero, and dragons and swords, but it was science fiction, not fantasy. A big book called *Glory Road*, by Robert Heinlein.

"You still readin' that flyin' saucer crap?" Batman dropped two heavy boxes of C-rations, raising a cloud of red dust.

Spider didn't look up. "Bite my crank."

"Whip it out." Batman's face was a big black moon. He wiped it carefully with a green bandanna. "Let me see your sixteen."

Spider started to frame a smartass reply, but let it go. "I'll do it." He unfolded his six-foot-two skinny frame, stretched and yawned, stuffed the fat book into a side pocket. Spider was white, nominally; like all the other white boys and men at the fire base, he was actually red, his unwashed skin deeply stained with ground-in laterite dirt.

Spider retrieved his M16, which he had never fired, from where it was propped up against a low bunker. The flash suppressor on the end of the barrel had three prongs that served as an adequate wire-cutter for the baling wire that bound the boxes C-rations came in: you slip the prongs around the taut wire and give the rifle a quick twist; the wire gives way with a satisfying snap.

What Spider didn't know was that if you do this often enough, with enough force, you will begin to unscrew the barrel. Then you can squeeze off a round and have the receiver explode in your face. This would happen to a lot of soldiers before the Army changed the design of the flash suppressor. But it's not what happened to Spider.

Batman shouted, "Chow!" while Spider snapped open the boxes.

"Happy fucking New Year," Spider said. "Get laid?"

"Sure I got laid. Didn't get off the fuckin' base." The boxes were deliberately upside down. Batman kneeled and opened them. Inside each were twelve meals in light brown cartons. If you exposed them label-side-up, nobody would take Scrambled Eggs (which the Army called Ham & Eggs, Chopped) or Ham & Lima Beans (which the soldiers called Ham and Motherfuckers). This way, choosing your meal was pot luck, often the most exciting event of the day. "Didn't even get any beer. Had to pull fuckin' guard while the clerks an' jerks partied."

Spider felt ambiguous about that term. He had been a certain kind of clerk for his first two weeks in Vietnam. He hated the job, and lost it by shouting at a sergeant, and attempting to land a punch. In his new position, Combat Engineer (Pioneer), he got to work with more congenial men, but other than that it was dirt everywhere, unrelenting heat, hard labor, bad food, and the possibility of people shooting at you. He didn't yet realize how dangerous it could become. Not many did. It was 29 days before Tet, 1968.

RELIGIOUS HOLIDAYS

CHRISTIANITY

The week before, the fire base had been temporarily transformed with red and green bunting and a plastic Christmas tree. Doughnut Dollies, Red Cross workers, came out in a helicopter with a carefully wrapped and perfectly random gift for each soldier. Spider got a 250-piece jigsaw puzzle of a snow scene in Vermont.

A Methodist chaplain in clean starched fatigues offered some prayers and a sermon that put Spider to sleep. He woke up when the Doughnut Dollies turned on a tape recorder, loud and tinny, and led the boys in a ragged half-hour of Christmas carols. The man whose code name was Moses knew all the words and sang with a clear, strong voice. Nobody else was very good, and the excruciation was cut short when the 8-incher behind the Dollies started a sudden fire mission, the shells about as loud as Hiroshima, blasting every twenty seconds or so.

Spider was deeply depressed by the travesty; Christmas had always been the big family get-together, a warm and loving time. He would have cried if he could have had some privacy. Some men and boys did, the tears making temporary mud streaks on their permanently dirty faces.

(Spider had opened his presents from home early. A book of poetry, *Palgrave's Golden Treasury*, from Beverly; a cross on a chain and a tin box of moldy Rice Krispies cookies from his mother, and from his father, a Swiss Army knife that had everything, including a magnifying glass and a toothpick.)

JUDAISM

Moses had grown up Reform, and hadn't been noticeably devout since he started high school. But like a lot of men, he suddenly became Orthodox when he arrived in Vietnam. Every Jewish holiday, the Army sent out a helicopter to take him to the nearest synagogue, 150 miles away. He would come back with a bag of Hebrew National salamis and Mogen David wine from the Kosher PX, and share them with his less fortunate gentile brethren.

BUDDHISM

The Vietnamese lunar holiday of Tet was sort of a combination of Christmas and New Year's, and throughout the war it was customary to declare a cease-fire for that day. 1968 was no exception.

WHYS AND WHEREFORES

"Flat ... *busted* that mother." Spider rocked the little P-38 can opener around the soft-metal lip of the green can, Peaches, Cling. Aggressively.

"Stupid asshole thing to do." The other guy, Tonto, was half writing a letter, half listening to Spider. He'd heard the story before, second-hand, slightly different.

Spider drank off part of the juice and crumbled a piece of pound cake into the peaches. "Oh, man. You shoulda been there. Take just so much shit off a lifer."

Tonto set down his pencil and looked at Spider. "I could take a lot."

"You don't know, man. Drive you outa your fuckin' gourd."

"I was a clerk stateside. Wasn't so bad."

"Shit, stateside." Spider slurped at his peaches-and-pound-cake mixture. "It's another world over here. Screw up one form, they put a pack on your back. Wise-ass lifers. They're safe."

Spider had attempted to strike his company's First Sergeant and, rather than go through the formality of a court martial, they had taken away his typewriter, given him a rucksack and a rifle that didn't work, and put him on a helicopter. All this was subsequent to the First Sergeant having given him two black eyes, a split lip, and several loosened teeth. Spider was impressed by the asymmetry of the exchange (see "Entropy"). All he had done was misspell a name in a signature block.

ENTROPY

Entropy was a buzzword in 1968, a perfectly good thermodynamic term captured and put in thrall by those who traffic in metaphor. When something changes the entropy of a system, that change is, innocently enough, the heat absorbed in the process, divided by the system's temperature. The entropy of a system measures the availability of energy in it; energy to do work. The more entropy, the less useful energy available.

What makes this concept dramatic and literary and symbolic of futility, perversity, *anomie*, is that any change in a real system results in an increase of entropy. When the dust settles, you have less to work with than when you started.

So the entropy of a system is said to be an indicator of the degree of disorder in that system. In any change worked upon a closed system, entropy, thus disorder, must either (trivially) remain constant or increase.

One familiar secular statement of this basic thermodynamic principle is Murphy's Law: if anything can go wrong, it will. That was one of the things Spider had written on the camouflage cover of his helmet.

NAMES (1)

Spider was named Darcy after a rich uncle who unfortunately left all his money to other people.

He got the name Spider partly because of the abnormal length of his arms and legs. He'd had the name since the seventh grade, and was very good at drawing spiders. He drew a large black one on the top of the camouflage net of his helmet.

The Army let him use Spider as his code name (see "Names (2)").

HUMAN RELATIONS

"I can get along with most anybody," Spider said. He tossed the can away and sat down in the inch-thick dust. He lit up a Lucky Strike. "I mean that sergeant had to *go* some."

"I know what you mean." Tonto was writing again, trying to describe his surroundings to his wife:

Were in a clearing about the size of a football feild. There's a old stone farmhouse in the middle, all bombed out. We got six 155s and a 8-incher and four or five tanks and three compnies of infantry. No way in Hell Charlys gonna mess with us.

"Spelled the fuckin' sergeant's name wrong at the bottom of a letter. I woulda typed it over. But he started hollerin' and callin' me names. I don't have to take that kind of shit."

"Damn straight." *Theres a rubber plantation all around us. I guess were at one end of it. You can see the jungle off to the west. We got patrols out all day and ambushes all night. We got 3 layers of barbed wire and 50s all around the permeter. This place has been here for a year and never got hit. So you dont have to worry.*

"Better out here anyhow. Nobody fucks with you."

"Nobody but Charlie."

"Ah, shit. What do you know about it?" The other man had only been in Vietnam for one month.

"Just what I hear. Same as you."

DUST

Laterite is a ferruginous mineral, brick-red in color, that makes up much of the soil of the Central Highlands of Vietnam. If the brush is cleared from an area during the dry season, this laterite manifests itself as a fine red dust, like gritty talcum powder, that gets on and into everything.

In semi-permanent installations, the dust is often several inches deep, piling up in drifts like hot dry snow. It's constantly airborne; making breathing difficult, dyeing the skin, fouling machinery, giving food an interesting texture.

FIRST BLOOD

That night a squad of enemy sappers cut their way through the barbed wire and set a satchel charge under the 8-inch howitzer. Returning through the hole in the barbed wire, one tripped over a string that set off a magnesium flare. All six of them were slaughtered by a .50-caliber machinegun, operated by the guard whose drowsiness had let them through the perimeter in the first place. Their return fire was valiant but only succeeded in amputating a cook's earlobe. The satchel charge went off but it was too small, and only knocked a wheel off the howitzer. The NVA squad that had been waiting for the sappers' return fired five hasty mortar rounds toward the American camp. All five rounds fell short (see "Entropy").

ATTITUDES

"God, you see them dead gooks?" The man who said this, grinning, had earned his nickname "Killer" by single-handedly zapping an unarmed North Vietnamese soldier who'd come crashing through the woods, shouting deliriously, a few months before. The first round, a head wound, had probably been sufficient, but Killer had walked over to him, switched the M16's selector to FULL AUTO, and put seventeen more rounds in a line across the man's back, point blank, almost cutting him in two. He'd never killed anyone before or since.

"Yeah." Spider had seen them from a distance. "Big shit. I seen worse."

(Spider wasn't lying. When he'd tried to slug the sergeant he had been employed as a clerk at "Graves Registration" in Kontum. Besides typing and filing, he had tagged the bodies of American soldiers, inventoried their personal possessions, and sent them along to Cam Ranh Bay inside a plastic bag inside an aluminum casket. He hadn't liked the job and after two weeks it had driven him a little crazy.)

"Monday." The medic Doc, walking by, gave Spider and Killer each their weekly malaria pill, an orange disc just smaller than a cookie. This was in addition to their daily Chloroquine.

"God." Killer made a face and, gagging, washed the thing down with half a canteen of water. Spider belonged to the other school of thought: he broke it into four more-or-less equal pieces with his Swiss Army knife, and took each piece separately. Killer watched him with the righteous contempt of a man who has seen a physical challenge and faced it directly.

"Yer gun clean?" Killer asked. His was immaculate, always.

"All I ever do is clean my fuckin' gun." He knew it was probably pretty dusty, but he hadn't checked it this morning. "What's it to you?"

"Gonna saddle up. Search an' destroy."

" 'Saddle up,' " Spider mocked him. "Will you get off that shit?" Every morning of the week Spider had been at the fire base, somebody said they were going to be moving out.

"No shit. Captain's been in the command tent all morning."

"Playin' cards."

"Uh uh, Miller says it's for real this time." Miller was their platoon sergeant, a graybeard of forty who had actually fought in Korea.

"Well." Spider got up and brushed the dust from the seat of his pants, a futile instinctive gesture. "Maybe I'll go get my shit straight."

"Maybe you better." Spider really hated the guy when he was on that hard-core kick. When he wasn't playing John Wayne he was all right. He read books, even science fiction sometimes.

Spider went to the fuel dump and sloshed a couple of inches of gasoline into his helmet. He carried it back to his hooch and picked up his M16 and sat down cross-legged on a sandbag.

THE BLACK DEATH (1)

Soldiers in Vietnam were told that the enemy, primitive superstitious devils, called our M16 "the Black Death." It did appear menacing: sleek, dull black, efficient-looking, modernistic. A great deal of thought had gone into the visual aspect of its design. But it had its drawbacks.

For some reason, the magazine only held twenty rounds. The weapon's cyclic rate of fire was such that if you held the trigger down for three-fourths of a second, you'd be suddenly out of ammunition. Also, the spring-feed would jam if you tried to fill the magazine completely; most people carried only eighteen rounds per magazine.

It was mechanically as cantankerous as a cheap watch. If there was any dirt or rust inside the receiver, it just wouldn't work. And it was too light to make a good club.

It fired tiny bullets whose effect on the human body was inconsistent.

If you cocked it too fast you'd lose a fingernail.

The rear peep-sight kept filling up with crud.

The sling was useless.

When you tried to sneak through the jungle, the hollow stock made loud clacks and scrapes against the brush. The sling swivels (unless you'd taped them or taken them off) made jolly little squeaking, snickering sounds.

It was very disconcerting to American soldiers when, after a battle, they would collect enemy ordnance and find that the primitive superstitious devils had been returning fire enthusiastically with weapons that were dirty, rusty, and held together with wire and friction tape. Whereas GIs often had to scrunch down behind a tree in the middle of a battle, and take their beautiful weapon apart and try to figure out why it had stopped working.

A graffito often found scratched on the stocks of M16s was "Made by Mattel, it's Swell."

HYGIENE (1)

Scratched on the stock of Spider's M16 was the disconcerting legend "This machine doesn't work." The supply sergeant who had issued him the weapon said not to worry about it.

Spider cleaned his hands with a little bit of the gas, then worked over the external metal parts of the gun with a piece of toilet paper moistened with gas.

"Good morning, Mr. Spider." Wilkes, buck sergeant, Spider's squad leader.

"Pull up a chair." Spider worked the little toggle free and the gun swung open. He dropped the slide, bolt, and trigger assembly into the helmet to soak.

"Know you're not supposed to use gasoline." Wilkes sat down across from him. "Fire hazard."

"That a fact." Spider threaded a patch of cotton the size of his thumbnail through the eye of a cleaning rod. He soaked the patch with gas and ran it through the barrel.

"Yep. If you try to shoot the gun when it's full of gasoline vapor, it'll blow up in your face."

Spider showed him what was written on his stock.

"Guess you're safe." Wilkes broke open his rifle. Can I bum some?"

"Go ahead." Spider ran the cleaning rod through again, this time with a few drops of LSU light grease. He took the soaking parts out of the gasoline and lined them up on a strip of clean toilet paper on his knee, then offered the helmet to Wilkes. "Save me some for my ammo."

He didn't want to go through the hassle of taking apart the bolt and trigger assembly. They looked clean enough, so he just wiped them off and gave them a thin coat of LSU. "True we're goin' out today?"

"Shit, I hope not. I had early guard last night. Didn't get two hours' sleep." The fire base had gone on "100 percent alert" after the abortive sabotage: everybody up and standing guard in bunkers around the perimeter, until dawn. If you were already up, you had to stay up.

Spider started to put the thing back together, which always took as long as all the rest of the cleaning operation. It was like assembling one of those carved-wood Chinese puzzles.

He got it back together, carefully propped it against his rucksack, out of the dust, and then stepped away from the gas to light up a cigarette.

"It won't be so bad, though, if we do go out. Right?"

"Depends." Wilkes was ostentatiously taking apart his bolt assembly. "All we ever do is walk, practically. Walk all day, dig a hole at night. Fill up the hole in the morning and start walkin' again." He made a face, concentrating so as not to lose the little spring when it popped out. "Some guys like it better. You know that. No dust, no officers to speak of."

"No dinks."

"Not in over a month. And the last one wasn't even a firefight, just a little argument. One casualty."

"Yeah, I heard —"

"Poor ol' Smiley. Got it right here." He indicated a point midway between his own sternum and navel. "Haven't heard anything since we put him on the medevac, guess he's dead." He got the spring out, without its flying into the dust. "Ah. Son of a bitch owed me almost a hundred bucks."

"You and everybody else."

Wilkes laughed. "We oughta get together and hit up his ol' lady for it. Hire a bill collector or somethin', shit, *he* was such a hard ass..." The trigger assembly came apart more easily. He swished them around in the gasoline.

"I like fire base better. Like right here, three hots a day, beer, sleep on a cot—"

"You've got a cot?"

"Hell, yes. Don't seem so safe since last night, though, shit. Fuckin' gooks just walked in, all it takes is one asshole asleep at the switch."

"They find out who?"

"Nah. Prob'ly Bravo, if they went out the same way they came in." He dipped a toothbrush into the gasoline and worked over the outside, all around the receiver. "Trouble with a fire base is that you're a bigger target. Liable to get a whole fuckin' regiment attack at once. Human wave, man, bad shit."

"Like a *banzai*—"

"I guess. Never been in one myself, but God… bloodbath, that's all. They just keep comin'. Happened down Plei Djarang, was it? Couple of months ago, two and a half." He shook his head and started fishing pieces out of Spider's helmet.

"Heard about it. Said we had a lot of work at Graves."

THE ENEMIES

Spider soon learned that the GI had four enemies in Vietnam. They had four distinct ways of killing him.

The NVA were green-uniformed North Vietnamese Regular Army troops. They were the GIs' counterparts, a mixture of career soldiers and draftees. They moved in relatively large units through the jungle and engaged the Americans with "conventional" weapons: rifles, grenades, machineguns, artillery, and sometimes even tanks. They occasionally employed small airplanes for reconnaissance, but didn't have jet fighters in the south.

Most GIs had some sympathy for the NVA. From policing up bodies after a battle, or taking an occasional prisoner, a composite picture emerged of the NVA private as young, scared, ill-equipped, and undersupplied. A sixteen-year-old drafted out of high school would walk a thousand miles and go into battle with a taped-together rifle older than his father, a cloth sack with a couple of dozen loose cartridges, and a plastic bag of rice and dried fish heads. He could kill you with one of those two dozen bullets, but it would take a lot of bad luck on your part.

There were two varieties of Viet Cong. The ones you encountered in the boonies were guerilla fighters who set ambushes, littered the landscape with boobytraps, harassed you with hit-and-run mortar and rocket engagements, and sometimes came charging out of the night bent on suicidal mayhem. They tortured prisoners and mutilated the dead. If a village tried to resist them, the village chiefs would be found castrated and/or disemboweled and/or beheaded. The GIs saw them as dangerous maniacs, and so did some of the Vietnamese.

The other VC were civilians, women and children and old men, who would walk up to you smiling with a basket of soft drinks or a sexual proposition or a hand out, begging. Inside the basket or under the clothing would be a hand grenade or satchel charge or just a loaded pistol. When the smoke cleared and the bodies were tallied, the GIs would shake their heads in wonder. How could they hate us so much? How could they value their own lives so little?

And the lesson constantly fed back was this: Every slope is an enemy; they don't care whether they live or die; they don't see you as a human being at all. Never turn your back on one.

The fourth enemy was the Army, the lunatics that had sent you to Vietnam in the first place, the ones that ordered you out of the relative safety of base camp or bunker to go produce a body count. This implacable enemy was personified by officers and noncoms, who sometimes perished from a perceived lack of empathy with those beneath them. Vietnam was not the first American war where a significant number of officers were killed by their own men, but it was the only war that produced a verb describing the action: to "frag," because the preferred weapon for assassination was the fragmentation grenade, ubiquitous and impossible to trace.

LOVE LETTER

January 3, 1968
Dear Spider,

Happy birthday to me! There's not much happening here. I hope you can say the same!

We're just hanging around, waiting for the new semester to start. Still just working afternoons. We went down to the Roma for pizza last night, and I got served without using my ID. They've got a really awful band. So we went down to the Zebra and watched Tommy Cole and the Belvederes, we went there with the St. Andrews crowd before you got drafted, remember? They're funny. "Passengers will please refrain from using toilets while the train is in the station Darling I love you." We sang it all the way home. Guy asked for my ID but didn't really look at it, good thing.

There's not much on the TV about Vietnam, so I guess things are pretty quiet. Hang in there.
Love,
Beverly

EXCREMENT (1)

When he was working at Graves Registration, Spider was twice punished by being assigned the shit-burning detail. This was the lowest-caste job in the Army, and Spider pretended outrage and disgust when it fell to him. Actually, he rather enjoyed it.

The latrines at his base camp were four-holer outhouses. Instead of emptying into a pit, though, the droppings dropped into old fuel containers, 55-gallon drums, with their top thirds cut off. Every couple of days they would fill up, and whichever enlisted man was in least favor would be assigned shit-burning detail.

You were given a pair of gloves reserved for the purpose. You locked the latrine and propped up the swinging door at the rear that allowed access to the 55-gallon drums. The smell was Olympian in the tropical heat. You dragged the heavy drums to the side of the road and sat upwind, if there was wind, which was rare.

In a few minutes or hours, a fuel truck would come by, and top off the drums with diesel. You would float a gasoline-soaked crumpled piece of paper on top of the noisome mess and light it, and with luck, that would coax the diluted diesel fuel alight, and soon you would have four festive bonfires pouring forth choking black smoke with an aroma that is difficult to describe. They would burn for a couple of hours; your job was to watch them.

As unpleasant as the detail sounds, it did give you lots of time to read. And it wasn't unreasonable for Spider to enjoy it, at least on those days when his normal employment would have entailed the manipulation of decomposed bodies and fractions of bodies.

While he was hauling the barrels of shit, Spider would sing, at the top of his lungs, "Passengers will please refrain/from using toilets while the train/is in the station Darling I love you," to the tune of "Funiculi, Funicula."

LIFE IS BUT A DREAM (1)

It's a place that Spider visits almost every night. It is very cold and smells bad, bad like a butcher shop with roadkill inside. Grace notes of Lysol and body wastes. The lights are bright and blue. There are three barber chairs and in one of them a naked man sits dead and white, his hide sewn together in big clumsy stitches that close his half-emptied body. One eye is a fish eye and one eye is gone.

The skinny black man who is Spider's guide stops at the corpse and shakes its hand. "Good evening, Major." He giggles and moves the hand down, forcing against rigor mortis, so it modestly covers shrunken genitals. "An officer and a gentleman."

Six dark green body bags are lined up next to a white porcelain-clad table with blood gutters. "Every day is just like Christmas," the black man says. "Give me a hand here."

Spider helps him wrestle a heavy, lumpy body bag up onto the table. The black man undoes the clamp and cable that holds the bag closed, and starts to skin the plastic back. A head rolls out and falls on the floor with a wet smack.

"Ah, shit." He picks up the head by the hair and sets it on the table facing Spider. A man or beast has flayed the skin off the face; it looks like a grinning anatomy illustration crusted with clotted blood. The eye sockets are dark holes. A shiny black millipede scurries out of one of them. Spider screams and wakes up.

SECOND WEEK

"Everybody humps three meals and at least two gallons of water." Wilkes had popped four boxes of C's with the flash suppressor of his M16 "They got some pogeybait and weeds down at the LZ; get your ammo there too. Everybody humps four hundred rounds and three grenades."

"Heavy shit," Killer said. Wilkes shrugged.

"Goin' out on slicks?" Spaz asked. The LZ was the helicopter pad, landing zone; slicks were the standard UH-1 utility helicopters, also called Hueys. (They were originally HU-1's, for "Helicopter, Utility." The Army changed its nomenclature but the old name stuck.)

"Not this time. Humpin'. Meet back here when you got your shit together, ten minutes. I'll go get some plastic and stuff."

The squad headed down toward the LZ, the more experienced ones moving faster than the new guys. Candy and cigarettes were in limited supply; if you wanted your favorite brand you had to be there first. They came in boxes called SP packs, which also had a few cigars and packs of pipe tobacco and things like razor blades and shaving soap.

There were never enough Winstons and Marlboros and always two cartons of Salems that nobody wanted. Spider liked nonfilters, Luckies or Camels or in a pinch Pall Malls, so he didn't have much competition.

They also had "fours and fives" at the LZ; four beers and five sodas apiece. There was some on-the-spot horse-trading; Spider, like most of the guys, would rather have had warm Coke than warm beer. Killer took his four Buds in exchange for a Coke and an orange soda.

Their rucksacks about fifteen pounds heavier, they returned to the engineer bunker. Wilkes passed out C-4 plastic explosive, two one-kilogram blocks per man, and three bricks of TNT apiece. Moses got the demo bag, a canvas sack with fuses, an extra load of detonation cord, and blasting caps, which you didn't want to treat too roughly. Everyone else carried a tool—shovel, axe, or pick mattock—for making bunkers each night, one for each two or three men.

Everyone carried an M16, including Doc, who swore he would never use it. Wilkes also carried a .45 automatic, carefully wrapped in plastic to save him the labor of cleaning it, or firing it, for that matter. Killer had managed to score a civilian .44 Magnum revolver with a shoulder holster, although he only had six rounds for it.

"So how long we gonna be out?" Killer asked.

"Two days, anyhow," Wilkes said. " 'Course, last time they said that it was, what, two weeks."

"More like three," Spaz said. "Fuckin' uniform was rotting off my back."

"Jus' that powerful BO," Doc drawled.

Two whistle blasts echoed from the other side of the camp. "No rest for the weary," Wilkes said. "Saddle up."

SEARCH AND DESTROY

The infantry company to which Spider's engineering squad was attached was about to embark upon a "search-and-destroy" mission, a term both inaccurate and unfortunate. It was unfortunate because it sounded brutal, vaguely un-American, and did not help the image of the war at home. It was inaccurate because the company did not so much search for the enemy as expose itself to them. It was sort of like trolling. When they made contact with the enemy they would take cover and shoot back, and call in artillery and air support, a deadly rain of high·explosives and white phosphorus and napalm, which could come in minutes or hours or not at all. Usually it *was* minutes, and the enemy knew this, so most contacts were brief and furious.

The company would walk through the jungle in three lines, roughly parallel, making as little noise as possible, which was usually quite a lot. If they were lucky, they wouldn't make contact with the enemy, and in late afternoon would settle down and dig in for the night.

The two outside lines were infantry platoons, carrying along with their M16s an assortment of M79 grenade launchers, M60 machineguns, and two "light" 60mm mortars, which actually weighed almost fifty pounds each, with baseplates. Two people carried LAWs, M72 Light Antitank Weapons. (There weren't any tanks here in the mountains, but they were handy against bunkers, or just to point and shoot at wherever the bullets were coming from.) The infantrymen also had a wide assortment of nonstandard weapons, such as captured Chinese AK47s, civilian pistols like Killer's, and old-fashioned Thompson submachine guns and grease guns, both of which fired the fat slow .45 ACP slug, much better suited for jungle warfare than the M16's light 5.56mm round (see "The Black Death (2)").

Spider's engineers were in the middle line, the "command group." Protected by the two flanking platoons, this group also contained the captain who was in charge of the operation, the top sergeant who actually knew what was going on, the FAO (forward artillery observer), the RTO radioman, a squad of riflemen, and the head medic. Sometimes, not this time, there were temporary people like observing officers and official photographers.

The command group carried weapons but would not normally fire them, since they would be shooting through their own lines. If the company made contact with the enemy, the captain and sergeant would figure out what to do and pass orders to the platoon sergeants, who might obey them. With the help of the FAO and radioman, they would attempt to call in artillery or air strikes onto the enemy's position. The engineers, protected by the squad of riflemen, would go back down the trail and try to find a place to make an LZ, blasting away a circle of trees with C-4 and TNT, so that helicopters could land to evacuate the wounded and resupply the company. It was not as dangerous a job as the infantrymen's, but it sometimes had its moments.

HAPPY TRAILS

The company formed three ragged lines in the dust, smoking and trading comments with the artillery crews. The top sergeant stomped through, yelling, "Spread 'em out, spread 'em out, you know the drill," in a hoarse but penetrating voice. The soldiers picked up their gear and shuffled around until no one was closer than six to nine feet from anyone else, so that not too many people could be wiped out by a single grenade or mortar round.

Wilkes walked back to where the engineers were standing. "Killer, Spider, come on up. You got point." Killer looked happy at the prospect, but Spider felt his knees go weak. The guy who walked point was likely to be the first one to meet the enemy.

"This should be an easy one," Wilkes said to Spider. "Killer'll have it for the first hour or so; just watch what he does. Mainly you keep tabs on the point men on your right and left, stay even with them. Watch the ground for tripwires or any sign that somebody's been digging."

"And look up in the trees for snipers?"

"Yeah, but you won't see 'em. They don't shoot the point man, anyhow. They wait for the RTO. They bust the radio, we're in deep shit.

"If you do spot a mine or a tripwire, do like this." He dropped to one knee and raised a fist. "Batman will bring Moses up and figure out what to do."

"Disarm it?" Killer said eagerly.

"Jesus, no. They just do that in the movies. Blow it in place. Maybe mark it and have everybody walk around it, if they don't want to make noise. Batman's done it a couple of times."

"You're not comin'?" Spider said.

"Huh uh. I'm staying here with Chevy and Spaz and Tonto and Doc. We'll join you if something interesting happens."

"We're goin' out without a *medic?*" Killer said.

"Infantry's got medics. Don't worry; it's gonna be a walk in the park."

"You sure?" Spider said. "Lotta people."

"Just a feeling, talkin' to Top. Somebody at Brigade got a hair up his ass about those sappers. So you get to walk around for a couple days, report you didn't find anything, come back to the fire base." They got to the front of the line. "Okay. Here and here." Killer and Spider took their positions.

Like a lot of people, Killer took the weight off his shoulders by standing up his M16 and propping the packframe of his rucksack on its muzzle, leaning back slightly against it. It looked dangerous, but of course the weapon wouldn't go off unless there were a round in the chamber. If it did go off, the bullet would enter in the small of his back and come out somewhere between his scalp and his navel (see "The Black Death (2)").

He lifted the heavy Magnum from its shoulder holster and clicked the cylinder around, checking it. It was a mannerism that annoyed Spider as much as anything Killer did. "Still have six?" he said.

"All six." He dropped the pistol back in and snapped the retaining strap over its hammer. "You done with that Heinlein yet?"

"Hundred pages to go. You think we'll have time to read?"

"Oh, yeah. We usually got an hour or so of light after we get the bunker dug. Depends on the ground. Let me see the first part. Trade you *Man in the High Castle* or *Pawns of Null-A*."

"I read *Null-A*. That's some weird shit." He took the Heinlein book out of his side pocket and tore out the first half and gave it to Killer. It made him wince inwardly to damage books, because he had a rather large collection of paperbacks at home, and he took care of them. But everybody did it, and it wasn't as if he were planning to carry the Heinlein around for the next ten months. He took *The Man in the High Castle* in exchange.

A sergeant from the right flank came over with a complex topographic map and a simple diagram. He showed Killer and Spider where they were headed. They were going roughly east along a game trail that had been scouted out by a team of lurps, Long Range Reconnaissance Patrol.

Whistle blast and the top sergeant shouted, "Move 'em out." They started toward the woods.

The fire base was protected by three coils—"strands"—of concertina barbed wire, like heavy Slinkies with spikes. The coils were temporarily opened, tripwires disabled, in a space large enough for the three columns to pass through. Two men stood on either side, waiting to close it up again. Spider thought they looked a little too happy about staying behind.

The hill was cleared down to stubble for about a hundred yards. Beyond that the rain forest loomed. It had seemed calm and beautiful from the air, when Spider flew into the fire base. But as they moved toward it, it grew taller and darker and more foreboding. Even the slight coolness that breathed out from it, the loamy woodland smell, seemed threatening.

Once they were in it, the rain forest was neither dark nor cool. Large trees formed a thick canopy of leaves dozens of yards up, but dappled sky or sunshine broke through here and there. The going was all downhill, sometimes steep, but it looked as if the central file, the command group, would have a comparatively easy time of it, since they did have a trail to follow. The two flanks had to pick their way through a tangle of vines and small saplings.

Spider watched the ground and trees, just in case Killer missed anything, and he tried to maintain the requisite three yards' separation. They kept colliding anyhow, Killer stopping to let the flanks catch up and Spider intent on looking for boobytraps. The third time they collided, Killer whispered, "If I wanted a fuckin' date I'd give you my fuckin' phone number!"

Spider caught the fear in Killer's voice. "You walk point a lot?"

He looked at him for a second and shook his head in a little jerk. "Once."

Both flanks were making what seemed like too much noise, their point men crashing through the brush, cursing the come-along vines. It occurred to Spider that they must still be in a pretty secure area. That's why the more experienced troops were casual about noise; that's why he and Killer were given point. Or maybe it was all a horrible mistake and they were going to run into an ambush and die.

He resumed his study of the ground.

MINES AND BOOBYTRAPS

Boobytraps would eventually account for eleven percent of American deaths in Vietnam (as opposed to three percent in World War II). They would account for seventeen percent of wounds, and many of the wounds were terrible.

American soldiers were cautioned against littering in the field, because rubbish could come back in fatal form. The largest C-ration can—the type that held Frankfurters and Beans or Spaghetti with Meat Sauce—was just the right size to hold a Mark 2 hand grenade, restraining the safety lever from popping away. So an enemy soldier could attach a thin wire to the grenade, slip it into the can, pull the pin, and then carefully arrange the assembly so the can—conveniently dark green—was hidden from view and the just-taut wire crossed a trail at ankle height. A careless American would snag the wire and pull the grenade out of the can. He would certainly hear the safety lever pop away, even if he hadn't noticed the tripwire, but he might not react in time to save his life or limbs. The person behind him might be killed or mutilated as well, or even someone much farther away. The base plug of an M2, a solid chunk of metal, could be flung as far as 200 yards.

The Vietnamese made boobytraps out of all kinds of salvaged and stolen ordnance, from single rifle rounds to dud 500-pound bombs. The most dangerous and effective ones were "command-detonated," an observer watching from a safe distance with an electrical switch or a radio-frequency detonator. That way he could wait and pop the boobytrap when the RTO walked over it, or blow a specific vehicle off the road.

The enemy also employed non-explosive boobytraps, which were effective both as psychological and tactical weapons. The most common was the punji stake, a spike of hardened bamboo smeared with human excrement and buried in a shallow hole, pointing up at a slight angle, camouflaged with brush. If a soldier put his weight on it, the spike could punch through the sole of his boot, penetrate the entire foot, and come out the top. The pain was indescribable. Even with quick evacuation, the infection spread by the excrement could lead to amputation or death. The weapon didn't cost a nickel and it would stop a column just as surely as a frontal assault.

There were also tiger pits, deep holes filled with punji stakes and camouflaged. The most bizarre use of the punji stake, though, was a device called the killerball. This was a ball of hardened clay or concrete, bristling with punji stakes, suspended at the end of a rope tied to a stout tree branch. The heavy ball was pulled back like a swing or suspended pendulum, and released at the proper moment, to whip down a jungle trail at waist level and impale one or several Americans. Killerballs were rarely seen but often discussed.

WALKING POINT

After an hour or so of walking, the word came up to shift positions. Killer stood aside to wait for the end of the line, Spider moving up to point.

Killer removed the magazine from his rifle, jacked the round out of the chamber and slid it into the top of the magazine. Only the point men were supposed to carry a round in the chamber. "Lock and load," he said to Spider, clicking the magazine back into place. "Keep it on safety."

Spider's rifle had never been off safety. He pulled the cocking lever back and let it slap forward. He hit it once sharply with the heel of his hand, as he'd seen other men do, to make sure the cartridge was properly seated. It ripped a piece of skin off his palm.

Sweat trickled down his ribs as he waited for the flanks to start moving. He clicked the selector switch off SAFE to SEMI and FULL—single-shot and fully automatic—then back to SAFE again. It made the back of his head prickle.

He might actually have to kill someone in the next hour. His mouth went dry and he tasted bile in the back of his throat. He unscrewed a canteen and swallowed a mouthful of tepid water, flavored with metal and plastic. Really and truly kill someone forever.

"Move it," the man behind him muttered. Spider hustled forward five or six steps and then slowed down, carefully scanning the trail in front of him.

The trail was well defined, soil showing through the beaten-down underbrush here and there. But it wouldn't be difficult to conceal a mine or boobytrap in the trampled weeds. Spider recalled the one day of schooling he'd had about mines in engineer training—he'd been assigned KP the second day—and remembered how hard it was to see the little pin that would detonate the mine if you stepped on it. And that demonstration mine had been buried in soft dirt, with no obscuring grass.

Something crashed through the branches overhead and Spider tilted his weapon up at it, heart hammering. "Just a monkey," the guy behind him said. His bored tone was reassuring. He was one of the riflemen assigned to the command group. Spider didn't know him, but he'd assumed the officers would pick the most experienced men.

But then he thought about it: no, they'd put the experienced men on the flanks, since they were the ones who actually shot at the enemy. This guy might not know any more than Killer or even Spider himself.

For a moment Spider was actually paralyzed. He couldn't move; he couldn't even feel his arms and legs. It was as if his body had realized *one step and you could die*, and decided not to take that step. Then he went forward, catching up with the man on his left, but his guts churned, audibly.

This is just great, he thought, a great time to get the shits. He clenched it back and was rewarded with a sharp cramp. Sweat broke out cold on his face. What do you do? Raise your hand and get a hall pass from the teacher?

"Got to take a crap," he whispered to the man behind him.

"No you don't. You gotta hold it."

Spider glanced at his watch and realized he hadn't checked the time when he'd rotated to point. Did they shift every hour, or just odd times now and then? It was 10:15. Maybe at eleven they'd rotate, and he could duck behind a bush and let fly. He could hold on for forty-five minutes. He wouldn't look at his watch.

He really wanted a cigarette. Nobody'd said anything, but Killer hadn't smoked while he was on point. As if to give permission, the man behind him lit up. Spider juggled rifle and axe and managed to shake out a Lucky and locate his Zippo, which worked on the third try.

Meanwhile he had walked several yards without looking down. The thought galvanized him even as the nicotine relaxed him. He studied the ground and trees through a cloud of smoke as he inhaled two deep drags.

Just hang in there. You can make it through forty-five minutes, more like forty now, don't look at the watch. He swallowed hard and spent an uncomfortable minute wondering whether it would be worse to vomit or to lose control of one's bowels. Either end seemed possible. But you couldn't, you *couldn't*! It would be better to step on a mine and be vaporized. Or step on a punji stick. Nobody would blame you if you lost control. *Poor old Spider God I'd shit too,* they'd say.

The cramp subsided and Spider was able to relax at least one part of his body. Then he clenched up again when the man behind him whispered "Snake!"

A huge snake, as big around as a man's thigh, was coiled up in the crotch of a fat tree between him and the right flank. It seemed to be sleeping; he couldn't see its head. "Reticulate python," he said automatically, recalling the one in the Snake House at the Washington Zoo. (It was actually an Indian python, but he was close enough.)

"Big motherfucker," the other guy said in agreement. Spider thought of the sergeant who had given the orientation lecture, the first day in Vietnam. There are a hundred different kinds of snakes in Vietnam, he said, and ninety-nine of them are poisonous. The other one eats you whole.

But Spider knew that pythons didn't eat people. Maybe babies. He stared at it, fascinated and unafraid. He loved exotic animals; dragged Beverly to the zoo more often than she wanted to go. He'd never seen anything in the woods bigger than a garter snake.

He had to move on, catch up with the flanks. Another twinge, don't look at the watch, maybe thirty minutes, thirty-five tops.

Suddenly there was a distant rattle of machinegun fire. Spider dropped to one knee. He looked around and saw the flanks had disappeared, flopping out of sight into the brush. The man behind him had flattened out, too, lying on his side, listening. Spider imitated him.

There was another short burst of machinegun fire and a pop that was probably a grenade. Spider thought it had to be at least a mile away, behind them, but he didn't really know. He could hear the captain talking on the radio to someone.

After a couple of minutes a message was passed whispering up the line. "Cap says they had movement back at the fire base, one of the OP's. We're supposed to wait." OP's were outposts, teams of two or three men hiding in four or five places near the base, listening and watching for enemy movement.

Spider knew the OP's weren't supposed to shoot. Just report by radio and then tiptoe back to the base.

"Shit," the man behind him said. "If that's for real they prob'ly make us go back and play soldier."

There was no more machinegun fire, but less than a minute later there were five faint pops from the opposite direction, and a salvo of artillery rounds went overhead with a sound like ripping cloth. Then five overlapping, echoing explosions from the fire base. Spider was about to ask why they didn't use their own artillery, but he figured it out: the OP was too close to the fire base. To reach it with their own guns, they'd have to shoot almost straight up, and that would be wildly inaccurate. (He'd paid close attention during the artillery demonstration in Basic. A lot of it reminded him of science fiction.)

An older man Spider didn't recognize moved quickly up the right flank, speaking urgently to a few people. A few of them followed him back. There was a similar shifting around on the left.

"Bet they're settin' up ambushes," the man behind him said. "Figure the gooks'll run from the artillery, come down the trail here."

Batman and Moses hurried up the trail, slightly crouched. "We gotta find a place to blow an LZ," Batman said. "You Murphy?"

The rifleman nodded. "You're all X-Ray?" That was the code name for the engineers.

"Right. You get to be our support."

"Jesus fucking Christ. Just me?"

"For now." Batman studied the terrain ahead. "Looks lighter over there." He pointed to a place a couple of hundred yards to the right and started off the trail.

Murphy cocked his M16. "Better lock an' load." Batman and Moses did. They picked their way down a slight defile, come-along vines pulling at their pants legs, and then back up again. The land leveled off and there was a partial clearing.

In the middle of it was a rubber tree with a trunk about a foot and a half thick. Batman patted it. "Five pounds for this one. Maybe half a stick for that one and that one. That one, too. A third stick each." He pointed at other trees nearby, smaller.

"You're not gonna blow any LZ now," Murphy said.

"Huh uh. Not unless they make contact."

"They set up an ambush?"

"God, who knows. They just told me to find a place." Three more artillery rounds ripped overhead. "I don't think it's nothin'. You hear any return fire?"

"Nah. Prob'ly just some fuckin' dinks walkin' through the woods."

"Well, let's hope so. Lay it out anyhow. Take Spider through the drill," he said to Moses. They were both the same rank, Spec-4, but Batman had been in-country twice as long, and automatically took charge.

"Wait, man," Spider said in a voice that was almost squeaky with strain.

"I got to take a shit in the worst way."

"Do it in your pants; that's the worst way." Batman handed him his shovel. "Go behind a bush and dig thyself a hole."

Spider shrugged out of his rucksack, rushed to the nearest bush and scooped up one shovelful of dirt. He dropped his pants and backed squatting over the hole and evacuated, liquid and embarrassingly loud, and managed to pee all over his trousers in the process. C-ration meals each had one small roll of toilet paper in a brown wrapper; he used all of one and half of another. He pulled up his damp pants and slid the divot back over the hole.

He returned to the others and Batman handed him his M16. "Always take a weapon. Never can tell." That would be a hell of a way to die, caught with your pants down.

Moses laid out the proper amounts of C-4 by each tree. The five-pounder was two of the packages, which looked like vanilla salt-water taffy. Then he tore open a package and broke the stick into thirds, saving the plastic wrapper. The broken C-4 had a sweet chemical smell. He set the chunks of explosive next to the three smaller trees and then paced around from one to the other, unrolling det cord from a reel. Detonation cord was just plastic tubing filled with an explosive similar to C-4. Once properly connected, all four trees would blow up simultaneously.

Murphy watched them with growing nervousness. "This sucks, man. You want to hurry up with the fuckin' lesson?"

"He's right," Batman said. "We're pretty exposed."

Moses finished explaining about the blasting caps, where and how to put them, and all four retired out of the clearing, back into the relative safety of the bush. At Murphy's suggestion, they went far enough back so that he could see a couple of the right-flank riflemen. Batman stayed within sight of the clearing. Spider and Moses took up intermediate positions, hiding behind trees.

Spider tried to relax. The worst thing that could happen would be that the gooks come running down the trail and hit the ambush. That was hundreds of yards away. He looked around at the quietly rustling rain forest. No, the worst that could happen would be a thousand VC popping out from behind all those trees and killing everybody. Spider scrunched down a little more and waited, smoking, trying to look at everything at once.

Murphy was studying a book titled *Thongs*, whose cover featured a naked women tied spread-eagled to an old-fashioned brass bed. He moved his lips while he read. Spider took out his Heinlein book and tried to read it. He couldn't concentrate. He could feel a thousand eyes on him, aiming. He put it away.

"That your real name, Spider?" Murphy asked.

"No, Speidel. Not supposed to use our real names."

"Oh yeah. Buncha happy horseshit."

NAMES (2)

Every person was given a code name for use in radio transmissions. The medic was always Doc. A person with a college degree was usually Professor. (Spider's platoon had had a Prof until a couple of weeks before Spider arrived. He'd gotten his educated kneecap ruined in a chainsaw accident.)

Sometimes, as in Spider's case, they asked you what code name you wanted. Sometimes you were given one based on appearance or ethnicity: Ears, Moses, and Tonto. Sometimes circumstances prompted the platoon sergeant to change your name. Spaz had been named Frosty at first, since he came from Alaska. Then one day he stepped out of a helicopter carrying a flat of two and a half-dozen very precious fresh eggs, and dropped them.

In some outfits, like Spider's, you were encouraged to forget your comrades' actual names, and only use code names even in everyday conversation. Then you couldn't slip up and use a person's real name in radio communication, which was usually monitored by the enemy. Once the enemy knew where you were at a given time and day, they could send a bogus telegram from Washington, through the Polish embassy, supposedly from the Army, regretting to inform your parents or wife that you had been killed in action there and then. Thus undermining morale on the home front.

Spider went along with it, but he did notice that sergeants Miller (code name Papa) and Wilkes (code name Sarge) used their actual names. He assumed it was just another one of those things the Army did to take control of your life.

A WALK IN THE PARK (1)

No more artillery rounds came over and there was no more gunfire from the fire base. After about an hour, somebody whistled and waved them back. Spider and Moses retrieved the demolition stuff, repacking the three broken chunks of C-4 into their plastic wrapper and rolling the det cord back onto its spool.

Murphy was moving into point. He reminded Spider to "safe" his weapon before going back to the end of the line: take the round out of the chamber and replace it in the magazine. Spider pulled back the arming lever and the round didn't eject.

"Murphy. Look at this." Spider showed him the ejection port. The cartridge was stuck in the chamber at an odd angle.

"Son of a bitch." Murphy wiggled the cartridge out and cocked the weapon, then slid the arming lever back again. Same thing. He handed it back. "This piece of shit don't work. Better get it replaced when we get back. Tell the RTO to call the armorer."

Spider went back down the column and found the radioman squatting on his haunches, smoking intently. He explained the problem and the man nodded wordlessly over and over, then spun the generator on the Prick-25 and told Ivy Four-niner Bravo that an X-Ray Echo Mike name Spider wanted to DX a Mike One Six and trade up. He listened for a moment and then nodded at Spider.

"What they say?"

"They said 'That's a rodge, out.'"

"Do I get a new gun?"

He shrugged. "I guess if they got enough." Spider started to walk away. "Hold it; let me see that thing." He cocked it and pried open the ejection port with his fingernail. The round was at the same useless angle. "Be damned." He jiggled it out and reseated it, straight, then removed the magazine and cocked it again. This time it worked. "That's what you gotta do. Seat the round manually. Give you at least one shot."

"But then won't the second round jam it up again?"

"Prob'ly. One round's better than none."

"Yeah. Thanks." Spider walked on back to the rear and took up his position. After a few minutes the column started moving.

He felt just as exposed here as he had walking point. He'd heard that in a box ambush, they hold their fire until the last man comes through. And he knew there were enemies behind him, unless the OP had been shooting at ghosts.

Of course they were always behind you in this country. And in front of you and on both sides, and up in the trees and even underground. And he had a weapon that fired one round at a time and had to be reloaded manually.

THE BLACK DEATH (2)

The M16 that Spider carried in 1968 was the retarded child of an elegant parent, the ArmaLite AR15, designed by weapons genius Eugene Stoner. The AR15 was an ideal weapon for jungle warfare—lightweight, reliable, deadly. Its tiny 5.56mm bullet was more lethal than the 7.62mm one it was designed to replace, because it tumbled end over end inside the victim's body, tearing a wide swath of destruction rather than punching a neat hole straight through. If it hit a bone, it could glance off at any angle; there were stories of bullets that would hit a man in the leg and rip all the way through the body to exit through the top of his head.

But the U.S. Army did not accept the AR15 without modifications. The bullet tended to wobble at minus 65 degrees Fahrenheit, which could be a real disadvantage if we declared war on Antarctica, so they increased the "degree of twist" in the rifling, which stabilized the round in frigid weather, but also reduced the amount of tumbling inside the victim, and thus the weapon's lethality.

Another problem was lubrication: the technical manuals that accompanied the M16 recommended the same lubrication procedures as its predecessor, the M14, but the two weapons are as dissimilar as a sports car and a pickup truck. The conventional lubricant, VV-L-800, decomposed in Vietnam's humidity.

What really destroyed the M16's efficiency, though, was a change in its propellant powder, from IMR ("improved military rifle") to slower-burning conventional "ball" powder. This increased the cyclic rate of fire from 700 to 1000 rounds per minute, which caused the weapon to jam. It left a residue that gummed up the barrel and the action. When Colt tested M16s in 1965, it found that none of its samples failed if they used IMR, but half of them did on ball powder.

At first the military denied that this was the *real* problem. The real problem was that soldiers were being lazy, not cleaning their weapons properly. The U.S. Congress didn't think much of this attitude when one of their number read them a letter a wounded marine wrote home to his mother:

"We've been on an operation since the 21st of last month... We left with close to 1,400 men in our battalion and came back with half. We left with 250 men in our company and came back with 107. We left with 73 men in our platoon and came back with 19...

"You know what killed most of us? Our own rifle... the M16. Practically every one of our dead was found with his rifle torn down next to him where he had been trying to fix it."

After some years, too late to help Spider and his contemporaries, the M16 was retrofitted with a chrome-lined chamber and a buffer modification to slow down the cyclic rate of fire, which made it a little more reliable—though still not as good as the original, using IMR. Why did they continue to use ball powder? It was a complicated skein of interservice rivalry, bureaucratic inertia, and pork-barrel politics that has never been unravelled, and never will be. A pity, since it would be nice to be able to point a finger: this man's inefficiency, or ego, or avarice, killed more American GIs than any division of Vietnamese.

FOREIGN INFLUENCES

After an hour or so the word came back to Spider to take ten, scarf some chow. He dropped the rucksack with relief and flopped to the ground. His neck and shoulders and back and thighs ached. He was in prime shape—he'd worked out every day from the time he got his draft notice until he left for Basic Training, and Basic had been a constant aerobic hell of running and cal-isthenics—but this would take some getting used to. It wasn't just the weight of the burden, but also the stop-and-go shuffling. And his muscles couldn't relax, shift the burden around, any more than his brain could relax.

He rubbed his neck and looked around uneasily. He couldn't see either of the flanks. The only person visible was Killer, about ten feet up the trail, looking through his rucksack.

He was hungry but didn't feel like challenging his nervous stomach with a can of cold greasy food. He rummaged through two boxes of C's and took out their jungle chocolate and cookies. The jungle chocolate didn't melt in the heat, but it didn't taste like chocolate, either. It wasn't too bad with a cookie and warm Coke. His mother used to give him warm Coke to settle his stomach; the association was comforting.

Murphy came quietly down the trail to take up the rear position. He sat down next to Spider and slipped out of his rucksack. "Havin' fun?"

"Tired."

"You get used to it." He frowned into the pack and pulled out a C-ration box. "Can't eat the eggs unless I'm fuckin' starvin'."

"You short?"

"Hundred and two days. Guess in three days I'll call myself short. You got a while?"

"I'm not even countin' yet. November 29th."

"Jesus." He opened a can of beans and franks and popped a beer. "This your first hump?"

"Yeah. I was a clerk for a couple weeks."

"Quartermaster?"

"Naw, Graves. Over in Kontum."

"Shit, I'd get out of that, too. Gotta be a fuckin' bummer." He spooned a piece of fat out of the beans and threw it away. "But you got a X-Ray MOS?"

A man's Military Occupational Specialty was determined by stateside training. "Oh yeah," Spider said. "Did Basic and AIT at Fort Leonard Wood, that's all engineers. But I got in-country and they asked if anyone could type. I was the only one who raised my hand, wound up in Graves."

"Go to college?"

"One year. Learned to type in junior high."

"Flunk out? College, I mean."

"Yeah, yes and no. Got shafted. Filed an appeal but then I got my draft notice. I think the fuckin' college got in touch with the draft board." Spider did have a legitimate grievance. He flunked out of college because of an F in a five-hour chemistry course. He'd been getting B's all along and studied hard for the final, and in fact breezed through it with no effort. He was the first person to hand in his blue book, which turned out to be a fatal error: the graduate assistant left it lying on the table when he collected all the others, and, not knowing one student from the other, assumed Spider had not been there and recorded his grade as a zero. When Spider got his F, it was his word against the graduate assistant's. By the time his appeal was processed, the graduate assistant had gone home to Iran. Ten years later he would die, defending the Shah. Spider would have cheerfully killed him now. "You go to college?"

"Shit, no. Got a wife and kid, kept me outa the draft for awhile. They're gettin' hard up. Be draftin' college guys before long, don't even *have* to flunk out."

Spider was tempted to tell him the whole story, the fuckin' towelhead grad assistant who lied, but he'd told it too often and sometimes people didn't believe him, especially if they hadn't gone to school. "How're they gettin' along? She got a job?"

"No, she went back with her folks. She could get her old job back, waitin' tables, but you know. Fuckin' Jody." "Jody" was the archetypal civilian, probably a draft-dodger, who had an insatiable appetite for soldiers' wives and girlfriends.

"Get to see her at R&R?"

"Naw, no way we could afford Hawaii. I just went to Bangkok, try some of that slope pussy."

"How was it?"

"Out... standing." He closed his eyes. "I couldn't fuckin' walk for a week."

"Sounds great." Actually, Spider didn't have much information to go on (see "Spider's Sex Life (1)"), other than pictures. Everyone who went to Bangkok brought back Polaroids.

He didn't think he would go to Bangkok if he were married to Beverly.

But he wasn't sure, of that or a lot of other things.

LOVE LETTER

January 6th, 1968
Dear Spider,

Thanks for the long letter. I'm sorry you aren't safe in an office anymore, but it must have been awful, working with all those dead boys. It made me want to cry and throw up at the same time, you know what I mean, the way you wrote about them.

You know there was that red dust all over your letter, inside and out. I can't imagine, it must be like flour.

I went with some friends down to a demonstration at the White House last week. Nobody got hurt, though there were a lot of police, riot police. A band started playing but they confiscated all the amplifier stuff. So we sang anyhow.

I'm getting to be a real peacenik. I hope you still feel the same way. I don't want you over there, I don't want anybody over there. Except maybe Lyndon Johnson and his gang.

It was exciting, with all the singing and chanting. Some of the cops, the young ones, looked like they wanted to be on our side. Some of them looked like they wanted us to drop dead. Everybody looked cold!

Afterwards we went back to College Park where a church had hot cider and cookies for those of us who were there. One guy could do great Phil Ochs songs, even the fancy guitar playing. He was SO cool.

After the church thing shut down we went down to the Starlight, but they were checking IDs. I wonder how many kids get killed because they can't get served near the University and so they drive into the District and get loaded, then try to drive home. That must seem pretty remote to you. I wish I could send you a cold beer.

Better hit the books. Keep your head down and your chin up, as they say.
Love,
Beverly

LOVE LETTER

10 Jan 68
Dear Beverly,

It's funny how sometimes your letters get here in a couple of days and some-times it takes a couple of weeks. We're out in the boonies now, the boondocks, and I didn't think I'd hear from you until we got back to the fire base. But a helicopter came in with mail and hot food! (Never thought I'd love spaghetti and meatballs and wilted salad.)

This morning we went out to "hump the boonies" or what the newspapers call a search & destroy mission. We didn't find or destroy anything, we just walked around as quiet as possible. I had to walk point for an hour, which was pretty scary until I got used to it. Walking point is when you're in the front of the line.

We stopped once in the morning when we heard a machinegun. Turned out to be nothing but some triggerhappy grunts back at the fire base, but we had to put out ambushes and sit around. Us X-Rays had to find a place to blow an LZ in case of a firefight, so we were out in the jungle by ourselves for awhile. That was not cool. But Moses showed me how to set the charges to blow down the trees but we didn't do it, we just gathered up all the stuff and went back to humping again.

I met a grunt named Murphy who walked behind me most of the time. Other outfits, people don't have to call each other by their code names.

About 3:00 we stopped near the top of a hill and dug in. I went out to chop down some trees while Moses and Killer dug a hole. You cut down a few trees about four inches in diameter and then cut them into two short logs and a bunch of long ones. Gave me two good blisters on my palms.

We took the logs back to the hole, which looked a lot like a grave! About three feet by six feet by five feet deep. There was a sandbag for each corner; we put the short logs on the three-foot sides and then laid the long ones out in a roof. Then we filled more sandbags with the dirt out of the hole and put them on top. They say four layers of sandbags will stop a mortar round. We did five.

You don't sleep in the bunker. It's just in case of an attack during the night. We sleep outside on our air mattresses, just like at the fire base. It won't rain at night until monsoon season, and then it won't stop. Sounds pretty awful. Sure wish I was with you in all the snow and cold. I'd go down to the White House and give them hell too.

Could you send me a newspaper, or at least some clippings you think I might be interested in? Back at Graves I at least got Stars & Stripes *and sometimes* Time *or* Newsweek. *Out here we don't git nuthin'.*

Mother sent me some Christmas cookies but they were all moldy. Don't tell her! I'm going to write how good they were.
Love,
Spider John

P.S. My gun doesn't work. But I never wanted to shoot anybody anyhow. (They're getting me a new one, they say.)

BEVERLY'S SEX LIFE (1)

The "SO cool" guitar player who had impressed Beverly at the peace rally and the church-sponsored afterglow was Lee Madden, a house-painter and sometimes hippy who lived in San Francisco. He'd left after the Summer of Love and come to Washington for the march on the Pentagon in October, '67, and had been staying with local people in the Movement since. He got along with odd jobs and by retailing a little marijuana every now and then. A friend with a farm outside of Berkeley sent him a coffee-canfull about every two weeks, on consignment; Lee sent back a scrupulous 50 percent of the money he got, after holding back a few Baggies for smoking and barter.

He liked Beverly immediately, but then he tended to like every potential sexual partner immediately, occasionally boys as well as girls. (He stayed away from boys on the East Coast, though; too many people were uptight

about it.) He walked her back to her dorm after they'd been rebuffed at the
Starlight Lounge. She gave him her phone number and a goodnight kiss
and politely avoided his hands.

Her roommate Sherry had been watching from the window. "So who's
your new hippy hunk?"

"He's just a guy I met at the rally, Lee. He's a folksinger from San Francisco."

Sherry watched him through the window, walking away. "He give you a
wide-on?"

"*Sherry!*"

"I mean like really. You said you don't love Spider anymore. It's not healthy
to suppress your sex drive."

"You must be a regular Charles Atlas, then." Sherry was always full of lurid
details about what she had done with her dates. Beverly was still a virgin,
though she'd never said so. She and Spider had progressed as far as "heavy
petting," fast and furtive mutual masturbation. That was about as much fun
as she wanted to contend with for the time being.

She looked at Spider's dust-stained letter on her desk. "I never said I
didn't love him."

"Yes, you di-i-id. Night before last."

"What I meant was like he's so far away, and I haven't seen him since before
Thanksgiving, and before that he was away at Basic for four months and I
just, I just don't know *how* to feel. He's not even the same *guy* anymore. God,
they fired him from his clerk job and they've got him out in the jungle, in
a firing base, whatever that is."

"You just don't want to send him a Dear John letter."

"I don't know. That would be pretty shitty, wouldn't it?"

Sherry pulled down the blind and started undressing. "Well . . . maybe
it might be the best thing. What if you keep leading him on, and when he
comes back, you're doing it every night with the San Francisco Kid?"

"Sure, fat chance." She went over to look at Spider's letter. Sherry's casual
attitude toward nakedness made Beverly uncomfortable. Bad enough that
you had to do it in gym. Beverly took her shower at night and changed into
pajamas in the relative privacy there.

"I saw you give him like your phone number, didn't you?"

"You aren't nosy or anything."

"So you're gonna see him again."

"Sure, maybe." In another week, Lee was going to see more of her than
Spider ever had.

FIRST CONTACT

After he finished his letter to Beverly he wrote a short, neutral one to his mother. Her letter had been a long and scrawled ramble. One or two highballs too many. Dear old Dad had done $300 damage to the car in a "parking accident," sure. One of those high-speed parking accidents you're always hearing about.

He'd been stopped for drunk driving two times that Spider knew of. How could he make a living if they took his license away?

Spider sealed both letters into dusty envelopes and franked them, writing "free" where the stamp would normally go. Other than lots of fresh air and exercise, that was the only advantage Spider had found to living in Vietnam.

He heard a helicopter coming in and he and Killer went around the hill to meet it. There was a "natural LZ" there, a clearing large enough for the chopper.

All the helicopter brought were two old guys, a major and a bird colonel. It waited on the LZ, blades idling, while they walked around in a kind of surprise inspection. Spider put his letter in a mailbag made of fluorescent-pink polyester—for easier spotting in case it fell out of the helicopter—and then followed Killer back to their hole.

The officers walked by their bunker without looking at it or them, which disappointed Spider, since he was rather proud of their handiwork. The colonel walked with his hands in his pockets, frowning, while the major whispered importantly and sliced diagrams in the air.

The chopper left and Batman came by with the good news that since they hadn't brought any extra C's, the company wasn't going to hump more than another day, back to the fire base.

While he was talking, another chopper came, loaded down with C-rations. The engineers split two boxes; six meals each.

"Shit," Spider said. "Does this mean we'll be humpin' for two more days?"

Batman shrugged. "Don't mean nothin'. Still might go back tomorrow; might be out for a month. Bet the captain don't know any more than we do. Give me one of them Luckies." He took a cigarette from Spider, lit it up and coughed. "Jesus. You gonna *die* with this shit, man."

"So smoke your own."

Batman waved at a tall black man approaching, a buck sergeant who'd been on the left flank during the morning walk. "Hey, fool. What's happenin'?"

"Hey, nigger." They slapped palms and he looked at Killer. "You the fuckin' new guy?"

"That's me," Spider said as Killer pointed.

"Oh." He hunkered down in what Spider recognized as a Vietnamese squatting position, feet and knees together, shoulders thrust forward. It took hours of practice, but definitely proved you weren't an FNG, fuckin' new guy. "Just makin' sure you don't kill none of us, okay?"

"Don't shoot at me," Spider said.

"Ha ha. Look. My guys gonna be right down the hill in front of you here, in a LP, listening post. You don't shoot or throw no grenade till they come back here, no matter what kinda shit's goin' on."

"Okay. My sixteen doesn't work anyhow."

"Oh. That's good." He pointed in a line. "Gonna have a tripwire all along there. You get up to take a leak in the middle of the night, don' trip it. Magnesium flare, somebody shoot you."

"They'd think I was a gook?"

"Shoot you for bein' *dumb*."

"Yeah, yeah." Batman said, "You pop a flare by accident, yell 'friendly!' loud as you can, wave your arms. You can put it out by beatin' it with a shovel. Ambushes out yet?"

"They got two, Bravo and Charlie. Bravo's coverin' that little stream we crossed; Charlie's someplace on the other side of the hill, down past the LZ someplace."

"They really think we're gonna get some action?" Killer said.

"Naw, just Big Bird come out, we gotta act strac for a day or two." He straightened up and cracked his knuckles loudly. "Go an' get my shit together. Be cool, fool."

"You be cool." Batman watched him go. "Funny thing, we knew each other back in the World."

"Before Basic?" Spider said.

"Way before, junior high."

"Never heard of that," Killer said. "Maybe guys from the same city."

"Me neither. I wouldn't've known him, but I saw the name on a TO before I came out from base camp, Abraham Q. Westlake. Can't be too many of *them*. He was a year in front of me but we both played baseball, he must've pitched to me a hundred times. He was a long tall motherfucker even then."

There was a tearing sound of artillery coming in and Killer and Spider hit the dirt. The shell made a relatively quiet pop sound. "Just a smoke round," Batman said. "Be another one in a minute."

"They're laying down a smoke screen?" Spider said.

"No, they just do that to check our position, calibrate the guns. We get hit tonight, they can respond real fast." Another round popped on the other side of the hill. "If they do respond."

"What do you mean?"

"Sometimes we won't have priority. Sometimes the VC and NVA get cute, set it up so they hit several places at once. If the airfield at Pleiku is gettin' hit, they probably can't spare anything for us."

"Same with air support," Killer said. "We don't get artillery and air support, we might could get overrun."

"People talk about that," Batman said, "but I ain't never seen it. Never talked to anybody that went through it."

"Maybe they don't talk because they're all dead," Spider said.

"All you guys from Graves so cheerful?" Killer said.

"We're more cheerful when we have nice fresh meat." Spider licked his lips and stared at Killer. "Napalm especially. Crispy Critters."

"Anybody ever tell you you're one weird motherfucker?"

From the jungle below them came a muffled *bang*. "Oh, shit," Batman said. "Grenade." He picked up his rifle and put the steel pot on his head. Spider followed suit; Killer was already wearing his.

"That the LP?" Killer said.

"Maybe the ambush. I don' know. Maybe somebody's fuckin' around, or had an accident." Then there was a sustained burst of automatic-rifle fire. "No, that's an AK47. We've got contact."

Somebody started screaming, an eerie wavering ululation. There were several bursts of M16 return fire and another grenade blast, then two more. The screaming man stopped, and then started again.

"What're we supposed to do?" Spider said.

"Keep down," Batman said. "Wait an' see."

Four artillery rounds rushed in, spaced about two seconds apart. Then three came in almost simultaneously. "Quick work," Killer said.

"Still zeroed from the smoke rounds," Batman said. "Just drop it a cunt hair and fire for effect."

Moses came scrambling up the hill. "Know anything?" Batman shook his head.

An M60 machinegun started up, a constant manic chatter to accompany the screaming. When the machinegun stopped, the screaming stopped, too. "Wonder if that's one of us who got hurt," Moses said.

"Oh yeah," Batman said. "Charlie don't scream." In the distance they could hear the thumping blades of a helicopter approaching. "Medevac already."

For a minute there was no sound except the helicopter, louder and louder. Then four men struggled up the hill by their bunker, carrying a casualty by the armpits and ankles. The wounded man had his pants pulled down to his knees and clutched a bloody pile of bandages over his crotch. His eyes were clenched shut and he kept repeating, "Oh. Oh. Oh. Oh."

One of the carriers was a short black man whose skin was gray with shock or fear or empathy. He recognized Batman. "Fuckin' dick shot off, Jesus. Shot clean off." He held out his hand, displaying a small scrap of bloody meat. "Jesus."

"Anybody else?"

"Huh uh. Dead gook."

They watched them stagger toward the LZ. "Might as well throw it away," Spider said. "No way they can sew it back on."

"What makes you an expert?" Killer said. "You sew on a lot of dicks?"

Spider grabbed his crotch. "Sew this, motherfucker."

"Let's get down to the LZ, assholes," Batman said, moving. "Might have to offload some stuff." Medevacs weren't always done by medical helicopters. If someone was in the air nearby and not on a fire mission, he'd drop in for a pickup if that would move the casualty to help a little faster.

This time it was a medevac chopper, a red cross in a white square painted on the nose. There was one other wounded man aboard, his arm in a makeshift sling and his hand bandaged. He looked annoyed at the interruption.

They watched the helicopter leave. "That's gotta be about the worst," Killer said. "I'd rather lose both legs. Both arms."

"You lose both arms, you wouldn't have any sex life anyhow," Spider said.

"Don't be such a fuckin' hard case, okay?" Killer said. "That guy just had his *dick* blown off!"

Spider reddened and looked at the ground. "Yeah, it's really bad. I guess I'd rather get killed." He kicked twice at a rock that stayed embedded in the ground. "I'll try to watch my mouth. It's Graves, you know? You had to joke about everything."

"Guess so," Batman said. "Drive you fuckin' nuts if you couldn't."

Three men came down to the LZ dragging a poncho with a dead body. Another man carried a bloody field pack. "Top said somebody wanted this," one of them said. "Another slick comin' in?"

Batman shrugged. "We just work here. That's the slope?"

"Yeah." He flopped the poncho open. It looked like a boy of fifteen or sixteen, wearing the standard black pajamas, with a bolt-action rifle lying next to him on the plastic. There were blood-slick patches on his abdomen and chest, from bullet or fragment wounds, and an ugly exit wound through his mouth. The bullet had blown out his upper teeth and split his nose. His mouth was a big red hole full of splintered bone and brains, his bottom row of teeth intact, white and small. His eyes were open, slightly rolled back. The shape of his face had been deformed by the force of the bullet, but his hair was neatly combed.

"He hardly looks real," Moses said.

One of the men who'd been carrying the corpse kicked it hard in the side. "Bitch!" He kicked it again. "Fuckin' *bitch!*"

"That does a lot of good, Chap," the first man said quietly.

"Does *me* some fuckin' good." He kicked the corpse again and stalked away.

"Just got the one?" Batman asked.

"I don't know. We hit another one; there's a pretty clear blood trail." He looked at the setting sun. "No way we're gonna go after him this late. Let the motherfucker bleed to death."

Spider was still staring at the corpse. He'd never seen a dead Vietnamese before. "Top say why they want this guy?"

"I don' know. Stuff him and mount him. Put 'im in the officers' club."

"Couple of months ago they collected a bunch of them," Batman said. "Never did say what they did with 'em."

"Cut their assholes out and ship 'em to Lyndon," Killer said. "He likes rim jobs."

"That must be it," Batman said. "Not like they have enough assholes in Washington."

They went back to their bunker and got ready for the night, giving their weapons a once-over and blowing up air mattresses. They used C-4 to heat up some C-rations—it burns with a bright yellow flame; a piece the size of a walnut will heat a whole can—but nobody had much appetite, even before Moses ate half a can of Ham & Limas and barfed. He joked about it not being kosher.

SPIDER'S SEX LIFE (1)

It was not going to be a good night for sleeping, or for anything. After all the artillery had come and gone, a Vietnamese sniper fired one round into the camp, just to prove he'd survived. The bullet grazed a man on the cheek, a superficial wound only a little more serious than a shaving cut, except that no shaving cut would ever come so close to causing cardiac arrest.

That twenty-five-cent bullet precipitated several hundred thousand dollars worth of response. The 155mm cannons at the fire base blasted a widening circle around their search-and-destroy camp as darkness fell. Then the 8-incher threw in a few rounds for dramatic effect. Then a jet flew over and dumped two canisters of napalm, and then made a U-turn and dropped a few cluster bombs for good measure. Then a four-deuce platoon, 4.2-inch mortars, decided they could use some practice, too, and did a firing exercise that tore the hell out of the jungle about 200 yards to the north of where the LP had reported the sniper. If their mistake had been 200 yards south, instead, it would have vaporized Spider and the other engineers, and they knew it. That would not have made for good sleep even if you *could* sleep, with illumination rounds popping every couple of minutes. They floated down on parachutes, and they didn't turn night into day, actually; it was more like night-into-a-dim-black-and-white-TV-picture. But it was bright enough to give you exactly no privacy.

Spider had been looking forward to night. There had been no privacy at the fire base, either, and he had gone far too long without jerking off. His testicles ached and he kept having spontaneous erections, to no end.

Early in the evening he wasn't thinking about sex because he was more worried about survival, with all the explosions marching around the camp and the jet dropping fiery hell. But after a couple of hours it settled down to the random "pop!" of the illumination rounds. They were fiendishly timed. Sometimes there would be fifteen or twenty minutes of darkness, and he would start to think about Beverly, her humid slickness and the musky smell of her sex in the car when he made her come, and her shy stroking of him afterwards, and the one time she'd licked him, and Spider would just start to reach for his aching dick and pop!—you're on *Candid Camera*. Around midnight he invented a no-hands technique, lying on his stomach in such a way that the sensitive frenum of his penis lay against the rough texture of the inside of his fly. By rhythmically clenching and unclenching his anus, he could make the delicate bit of flesh move back and forth about a millimeter each second, and in a surprisingly short time he was rewarded with a mild but prolonged orgasm. There seemed to be an embarrassingly copious flood of semen, but he was long past caring about appearances. He closed his eyes and slept like a dead man.

He anxiously checked in the morning and realized that his fatigues were so profoundly besmirched, anyway, that the stain from a tablespoon or three of ejaculate would escape notice. The other men's uniforms looked about the same.

Spider and the other men didn't know about the Viking bands who had begun their voyages into battle by standing on the beach in a line as the sun came up and pumping together, spending a sacrifice into the sea. Perhaps it's just as well.

MOVING ON

A small patrol of seasoned veterans crept out as soon as it was light enough to follow the blood trail. They found the body about a hundred yards away, untouched by the fortune spent on artillery and air support. The Viet Cong guerilla had quietly bled to death from a bullet wound in his side, having propped himself into a firing position behind a fallen log. His rifle magazines and four grenades were in a neat row in front of him. The soldiers took the AK47 and the ammunition and grenades and searched the body for identification, but he wasn't carrying anything except a plastic bag of fish heads and rice, and a small image of Buddha on a golden chain in his pocket. They left the body in place. Back inside the perimeter, they reported to the captain and then disarmed and buried the grenades. They kept the rifle and ammunition for the point man to carry, and cut a deck for the Buddhist good luck charm.

By then it was time to move out, but there was still one extra Vietnamese corpse, waiting patiently beside the LZ. Nobody was able to contact the major in G-2, Intelligence, who had requested that they hold on to it, and no helicopter was going to come out and take it off their hands without a direct order. Spider wondered if they were going to have to drag it along with them.

It didn't take long to break camp. They built a fire in one of the holes, into which went all the C-ration detritus: loose paper and plastic and cardboard and stamped-flat cans. Some joker tossed a rifle round in just to watch everybody hit the dirt. They refilled all the bunker holes and rolled up the emptied sandbags for reuse, and scattered the logs. Wouldn't do to leave ready-made bunkers for Charlie.

Spider was comfortably leaning back against his rucksack, reading the Heinlein novel while most of the other X-Rays shot craps. Batman walked over from the command group, looking disgusted.

"Come on, guys. We gotta bury the stiff."

"Jesus," Killer said. "Why don't we just leave him there?"

"That's what I said. What difference does it make? But the captain says we gotta do it, so we gotta do it."

Spider looked around for a shovel. "He would have to wait until the holes were all filled."

"Natch. You okay, Mose?"

Moses had sat down suddenly, white under dirt. "I don't . . . can't I maybe . . ."

"Freaks you out?" Killer said with a grin.

"Y-yes it does." He was trying to control the quaver in his voice. "Bad enough to sit here and smell it."

"Look, I'm used to it," Spider said. "You just hang loose and I'll—"

Batman shook his head. "You know you gotta do it, Mose. It gets a lot worse, and you gotta be ready for whatever."

"I know, shit." He got back to his feet, using his rifle for support. "So I'm a pussy."

It was easier to dig the soil back out of a bunker than to start a fresh hole, of course. The nearest position to the LZ was an M60 perimeter point. The machinegun crew watched them work without comment.

"Deep enough," Batman said when they'd dug down a yard. "Don't have to go to fuckin' China." Spider laughed nervously at that, wondering what country they would actually reach, Canada? Batman took his shovel and gave him a hand out of the hole. "You and me drag him over."

"Oh, I'll come too," Moses said. "Might as well."

The corpse looked pretty bad even to Spider. It was spread-eagled with rigor mortis and the body had swelled enough in decomposition so that buttons had started to pop off the shirt, which the night before had been pajama-loose. The mouth and eyes were black, crawling with ants. The smell was so strong it was choking. Moses dropped to his hands and knees and vomited onto the ground.

Spider and Batman took opposite sides of the poncho and half carried, half dragged the stiff body. They dumped it in the hole and everybody shoveled furiously to cover it up. The M60 crew even helped. They left one puffy hand protruding from the dirt, a Marlboro jaunty between its fingers.

Spider knew his pack was only a few cans of food heavier, but it felt like twice the previous day's load. There was a knotted cramp between his shoulder blades and a fiery ache in the small of his back. Just not used to it, obviously; the infantry carried more and they just saddled up and walked off grumbling. Spider's walk was more of a stagger, sometimes leaning on the shovel as a crutch.

At dawn the jungle had resounded with a cacophony of bird calls and monkey howls and a kind of lizard that shrieked "Fuck you!" The animals were silent now, but the people were not. The company didn't have a trail to follow this time. They just toiled through the underbrush in pursuit of a compass point. The noise of their struggling and muttering made Spider nervous; he thought it sounded like the clumsy advance of a large beast that didn't have any natural enemies in the jungle. If only they didn't!

They came to a sudden stop after forty-five minutes because Moses had fainted, weakened and dehydrated from vomiting. The medic revived him with ammonia and water, but said there was no way he could hump a full pack. The engineers split up his load. Spider got the demolition bag and an extra box of C's.

Moses was apologetic and embarrassed. "It's not supposed to happen this way," he said to Spider in a feeble croak that was scary. "In every war movie there's one Jew in the platoon, and he always dies. But not like this."

"Not gonna die," Batman said. "That's always a New York Jew. You from Idaho."

"Ohio, damn it."

"Same, same. Think you can get up?"

He nodded and managed to stand without help. He wobbled a bit, then stabilized. "Whew. Let's get to wherever we're goin'." Batman passed up the word and the three twisting columns started forward again, Moses lurching like a man constantly moving forward to keep from falling on his face. But at least he was moving.

They only humped for three hours, though the last hour was all uphill.

They wound up on the crown of a hill that overlooked Route 14, the road between Kontum and Dak To. A small campfire site indicated Charlie had probably been there not too long ago. The brush was trampled down, too.

That was why they'd come to this location. A few nights before, Charlie had dropped mortar rounds on a convoy from somewhere up here.

He might have left some surprises. The three columns formed in one shoulder-to-shoulder line and swept the hilltop for mines or boobytraps, at first inching along and studying the ground with intense concentration. After they'd covered about half of the hill with no discoveries, inspection of the second half became progressively more desultory. Spider continued inspecting just as slowly and carefully, waiting for the loud bang when somebody else stepped on a mine. But it didn't come.

Before the engineers could start on their bunkers, they had to clear an LZ, and they weren't allowed explosives, because of "sound discipline." There were a lot of large evergreens covering the top of the hill, but down the side away from the road there was an area that was mostly saplings. They hacked away with machetes and axes for an hour, and wound up with an area of stubble slightly larger than a helicopter. The captain took a look at it and said to make it half again as big.

When they eventually did get around to digging their hole, they found that it was not as easy a proposition as last time, since the hill was mostly granite. So on top of his axe blisters and machete blisters, Spider got to add some pick mattock blisters. They all tore the skin off at a slightly different place. Before the hole was half deep enough, Spider had bandannas tightly bound around both palms, and they were both soaked with blood.

Moses had tried to help but he had collapsed a few minutes after they started working on the LZ. The medic said he had a temperature of 102 degrees, and probably ought to be evac'ed if a chopper came in. They weren't expecting any resupply, though, and he didn't think it was serious enough to call in a medevac. Just stay in the shade and take water and salt pills.

Moses said he didn't want to be evac'ed as long as he could keep up with everybody. It was one thing to get slack time because of Army policy about religion—that was just FTA, fuck the Army, and nobody in his right mind could disapprove of that—but getting out of humping because you couldn't look at a dead body without throwing up, that was a lot less cool. He tried to explain this in a garbled way to the medic, but the medic said bullshit; it could be malaria or some infectious disease you could pass on to the others. Don't try to be so fuckin' hard-core.

The sound discipline must have applied only to engineers. The fire base dropped in four smoke rounds, zeroing in on the top of the hill. That would give Charlie a nice surprise the next time he used it.

Of course there wouldn't be a next time. They were being watched, and their actions correctly interpreted. The 82mm mortar that had been there a few nights before was now being carried to an adjacent hill. It wouldn't have a clear shot at the road, but tonight it wasn't the road they would be interested in.

BEVERLY'S SEX LIFE (2)

Our activist house-painter, folksinger, and purveyor of homegrown hemp, Lee Madden, thought love was the most powerful force in the universe, and sex was the most direct and dramatic manifestation of it. He also knew there was *mana*, spiritual power, associated with the sex act, and the more you did it the more *mana* you had. There seemed to be objective evidence for that: the more fucking you did, the easier it was to find willing partners. (His philosophical readings were largely confined to the Eastern religions; he had neglected logic.)

Lee would have bristled if you called him a lady-killer, but his persona was as smooth and effective as any pseudo-Bogart lounge lizard's would have been for a previous generation of women. He was scruffy but not unwashed, cynical but compassionate, experienced but childlike. Loud in denunciation of wrongdoing, his voice was intimate and husky one on one. He had long blond hair and a California tan on a lean body hard with muscle from honest labor and surfing.

Beverly had never met anybody like Lee, and when he turned his focused searchlight of attention in her direction she was more than flattered, she was literally captivated: trapped. After she said goodnight to him she couldn't get him out of her mind. When her roommate Sherry was asleep, she squeezed a pillow hard between her legs and pretended it was him.

Their next date, their first actual "date," was takeout pizza and cheap wine at the house Lee was using as a crashpad. There were always ten or twenty people hanging around listening to music, smoking dope, trying to study, making out on the sofa, or whatever. The couple who rented the house had real jobs and soft hearts, and never turned anyone away. Lee was a semipermanent fixture, though; he even had his own bedroom upstairs, since he chipped in a little on the rent and always had good grass.

Beverly was intoxicated by the bohemian atmosphere—not the psychedelic posters and peace slogans on the walls, not the hippy outfits and attitudes, but the combination of easy acceptance, good humor, and earnest commitment. She was not stupid but she *was* innocent, and at first she didn't see that for many of these people, sincerity was something they practiced the way some children practice the piano: a chore you had to do if you wanted to go out and play.

Lee wasn't that way. He was honestly committed to both the civil rights and peace movements; he'd been jailed twice for the latter and cracked over the head with a nightstick for the former. He was brave on the barricades and modest afterwards. He was fiercely honest about most things, though he lied a little about his draft deferment. He said he was 4-F from ulcers. It had actually been a psychiatric deferment for homosexuality, buttressed by letters from a psychiatrist and two dear friends.

No one would have guessed that who saw him with Beverly. It was a big chaotic party, the arguers in the kitchen, the singers in the study, the people who were listening to Hendrix and smoking dope in the living room. Lee propelled Beverly from one aspect of the party to another, his arm always around her waist or shoulders, feeding her pizza, passing the bottle of wine back and forth. At first she refused marijuana—she'd tried it once before and hadn't liked it—but eventually she took a couple of puffs, and got a little giddy and silly. Her indulging in the wine and the dope were both at least partly out of nervousness. She was sure that Lee was going to ask her to spend the night, and she was building up the courage to say yes.

In fact, it was she who asked him, in a moment of relative isolation in the hall between the study and the living room. He answered with a pointed squeeze, the first time he'd touched her intimately that night, which made her squeal and then giggle again.

So Lee was in for a surprise an hour later, when it was a squeal of real pain and then blood on his sheets. He hadn't known; he didn't think; he never would have done anything to hurt her. She said and did the right things, though, instinct sometimes working better than experience, and by morning Lee found himself both physically exhausted and emotionally in unfamiliar territory: for the first time in years, he was falling in love.

Later the next day, after some of the fog had dissipated from his brain, he told himself this was stupid. There was no room or time in his life for romance. Romance was just a shackle, anyhow, a device through which men declared ownership of women and chained them to the kitchen and the cradle. Besides, he was busy; the world needed changing. His emotions had been subverted by guilt over having taken her virginity—but hell, she was the one who set it up! He ought to feel resentment, not this sentimental puppydog shit.

But when she came through the front door that afternoon, he ran to her from the kitchen and almost broke his neck, slipping on the hall rug. She moved to help him up and they started wrestling playfully, then earnestly, and barely made it to the bedroom—almost literally, barely.

INCOMING

The six-man Viet Cong mortar team waited until it was nearly dark to move their two weapons into place. They did have a clear line of sight to the top of the other hill through some light brush, and didn't want a sudden motion or stray reflection to give them away. They were less than a mile from the Americans, as a bird flies.

Initial calibration of the larger mortar, a Soviet M36 82mm, was not difficult, because they had fired three test rounds from the target hill to here, earlier. Since the hills were the same elevation, the same angle of fire would be effective. The small mortar was an antique, a 50mm Japanese leftover that was considerably older than the boys who carried it. The twenty-four shells that went with it had come from a falling-apart box stencilled 1942; each round had been carefully cleaned and wrapped in oiled cloth. The one test round had worked, and the weapon had demonstrated sufficient range for this job. It could not be particularly accurate, though the two boys manning it were certain they would at least hit the hill with most of their twenty-four rounds. Their orders were to start firing when the others did; to fire as fast as possible and then run like sudden wind, abandoning the old thing.

The other four men had a more demanding job, since of course the new Russian mortar could not be abandoned. They would wait until the American fire base to the south was engaged in a fire mission elsewhere, which could gain them a few valuable minutes. Then a man with night glasses, 7 x 50 binoculars, would look at the target while they fired one round. If he saw where it fell, he would call out traversing instructions; if they missed the hilltop, they'd have to guess on the next round, and maybe the next. But they were confident they wouldn't miss.

They carried forty rounds, and once they had the hilltop targeted, they would fire them all as fast as possible, once every three or four seconds. Then they would disassemble the machine into its three parts—asbestos gloves for the man with the barrel—and run down into the valley.

That is, if everything went well. The enemy seemed perilously close. As they worked on their bunkers you could hear the pickaxes clinking against rock, and occasionally snatches of their guttural unmodulated speech. If the Americans were able to zero in on the sound of the mortars, it could be swift death. The VC squad was just within range of their M60 machineguns, and they also were carrying two light mortars. The moonlight that made spotting easy would fall on both hills.

The lieutenant in charge was tempted to open fire now, while the Americans were out in the open. But it would be suicide. In the light, their position would be obvious. After sundown they would have a good chance to fire all of their rounds and escape.

Spider and his squad were still digging at sundown. Out of necessity, they quit before the bunker was quite as deep as might be desirable; about an axe-handle. Four guys could squeeze in there if they had to. They only had three layers of sandbags, and those were pretty lumpy, filled mostly with rocks. That was definitely not recommended, since there would be occasions when you were outside the bunker, firing from behind the sandbags. An enemy bullet could strike a rock and explode it into hundreds of fast-flying fragments. The argument articulated by Batman was that they would only be firing their rifles if the enemy overran the camp, in which case they were dead meat anyway. And three layers filled with rocks was better than one layer filled with pristine earth.

Spider hardly had the strength to open a can of food. He decided the world owed him a treat, though, so he did a can of chili and mixed in the little can of cheese sauce. He bummed a splash of Tabasco from Murphy and heated it all to bubbling with C-4. (This was one thing the engineers had over the infantry: the grunts had to heat their food with regulation heating tabs, which gave off a faint blue flame that took forever to warm up a can.) Murphy had noticed his bloody hands and sent the medic over; he gave him a Darvon for pain and washed the wounds with hydrogen peroxide and bandaged them with gauze. He said he would do the same tomorrow, gotta watch out for jungle rot.

It made Spider feel better to look slightly heroic, bandaged. The meal was good, and he drank half a Budweiser that Moses gave him. He was so tired he could barely blow up the air mattress.

He lay back and sipped the beer, looking at the patches of sky that were visible through the trees. It got dark really fast here. On a moonless night the sky became remarkably black and deep, the Milky Way a billowing cloud. Spider had been an amateur astronomer as a kid, and still had taken his telescope out occasionally in high school and weekends home from college. The southern skies were fascinating and mysterious, all kinds of stars he could never see from Washington's latitude. He'd asked his mother to send a southern star chart, but either she hadn't done it or it had been lost in the mail. He would have to ask her again, or maybe Beverly.

The winter stars were impossibly high, Orion almost overhead. He knew the constellation under Orion was Lepus, the Hare, but there was a whole bunch of stuff under that one that he didn't have the faintest idea about.

The fire base started a mission, at least two guns, a faraway "bang-bang... bang-bang." Spider shifted around to look in that direction. Sometimes you could see the artillery rounds fly overhead, swift, dull-red meteors.

There was a faint sound like a champagne cork popping in the distance. Someone shouted, "Incoming!" and for a moment Spider was puzzled. Our own artillery? Then other people picked up the cry and suddenly there were people running every which way. Someone tripped over Spider's leg in the dark and went sprawling in a clatter of rifle and helmet, cursed, kept running. Spider got to one knee and tried to orient himself, which way was the bunker, where's my M16? He put his helmet on just as the first round hit, off to the left about fifty yards, a smoky orange flash and a sharp loud bang and shrapnel hissing and whirring through the air. Spider dropped to the ground and crawled very fast toward the bunker, fuck the M16, let's just get under something. He found the shelter just as the second round hit, much closer, and toppled into a tangle of arms and legs. The other three shifted around so there was room for all of them to keep their heads below ground level.

Behind them came a *spat* sound, not as loud. "They got two," Batman said. "A light mortar and a medium one."

"Are we okay down here?" Spider asked. Another *spat*, below and to the right, by the LZ.

"Oh yeah we strac." Spider translated Batman's monotone into "Boy, I wish we had another layer of sandbags," and agreed heartily. His mouth was cotton, his knees were water, he desperately wanted to pee, and his asshole was doing a dangerous flutter. Do people actually shit themselves if they get scared enough?

In the bunker next to them the artillery forward observer was shouting into the radio. He wasn't sure where the mortar was, he said, but take the last coordinates, drop a thousand, fire one HE, see what happens. Spider knew enough of the jargon to translate: he wanted a single high-explosive round put a thousand meters from our position, in the direction of the fire base.

Two people who seemed to be in the same place were yelling for a medic. The heavy rounds started coming in like clockwork, every four seconds, walking across the camp from left to right. The light ones popped all around, sporadically, in syncopation.

Then somebody yelled, "Pig's got 'em!" and an M60 started chattering, spraying a red-orange arc across the valley—every third round a tracer—at first playing it like a hose, and then settling down in a steady stream. An artillery round, one of ours, shrieked in and exploded in the valley. The forward observer yelled "Drop four hundred left two hundred fire for effect!"

The enemy mortars stopped. The medic sprinted across to where one person was still crying out. Another machinegun joined the first and the light mortar squad sent a round over there, *poink*. It turned out to be an illumination round, crackling and sizzling under its parachute. There was no obvious movement on the hill, but they kept up the machinegun fire.

The fusillade had been fairly effective on the VC position. The children who had been firing the small antique mortar had probably escaped, but the other four men were caught in a rain of machinegun fire while frantically disassembling the big Russian weapon. The lieutenant had been hit in the throat; another man had a shattered elbow.

It was obvious that they would not be able to take the mortar with them.

The lieutenant, coughing blood, unable to speak, was suddenly visible in the bobbing stroboscopic light from the illumination round. He made a waving motion, releasing the other three men: get down the hill while you can. Then, bullets spattering around him, blood streaming, he stood and took careful aim with his AK47.

It looked kind of pathetic from Spider's bunker, the constant rain of orange fire being answered by a little line of green tracers. It must have looked more serious from the American target's point of view, though; one of the M60's stopped.

Then a salvo of artillery rounds came in right under the bobbing light: four, five, six, seven orange flashes and puffs of gray smoke. The forward observer confirmed that they were on target and asked for two wooly peter. Thirty seconds later, two white phosphorus shells crashed in, making impressive sprays of white smoke and fire just before the illumination round sputtered out. Then another three HE rounds, and another two, and silence.

"We got 'em," Batman said. "Can't be nobody alive up there."

At that moment, he was wrong. The lieutenant, blood still pulsing from his throat, his eardrums shattered by the artillery blasts, his body torn by more than a dozen shrapnel wounds, was patiently trying to fit a fresh magazine into his AK47. He was choking on blood and phosphorus fumes and two particles of phosphorus were burning their way into arm and forehead. He knew he had only seconds to live and was trying with every molecule of his will not to cry out, to die well. As he raised the rifle toward the American hill he felt no anger, but only immense, hopeless sadness. He thought a prayer for his wife and children and pulled the trigger.

From the American side it looked like a gesture of defiance, the green tracers flying every which way, to no effect. The action did bring in another five artillery rounds, but by the time they hit, there was no one left on the enemy hill alive.

The VC would have been better off if they had fired one round and split. The first round caused the only serious casualty. A later round did score a direct hit on a bunker, but the structure held, and the men inside only suffered ringing in the ears and temporary incontinence. The earlier casualty was very serious, though: right leg blown off at the knee, left leg mangled, genitals history. He'd lost quarts of blood and was in deep shock. The medic said he needed a dustoff ASAP or the guy was meat.

The captain was doubtful, nighttime and hostile fire, but said he'd try. He ordered the X-Rays down to the LZ with blinkers and purple smoke.

CHOPPERS

No American who fought in Vietnam would ever be able to hear the sound of a helicopter throbbing without a sudden rush of remembered emotion, a compound of relief and anxiety. Usually helicopters came to save you. Sometimes they came to carry you to places you would rather leave alone.

The time and place where Spider was fighting, most of the helicopters were UH-1 Hueys, "slicks." These were general-purpose machines that ferried people and supplies around, and evacuated the wounded and dead. Some of them were turned into gunships, by adding on machineguns and rocket launchers, but the main gunship was the sleekly streamlined Cobra, with its Gatling-style minigun and automatic 40mm grenade launcher and wing-pods full of rockets. The other common helicopter was the fat ponderous Chinook, inevitably called a "shit-hook," a flying boxcar that could deliver a whole company of men at once, albeit slowly and with a lot of noise. They were heavily armored on the bottom, out of necessity, because they drew a lot of attention and were easy to hit.

Most of the men who flew Hueys loved them. They were nimble and fast as a sports car, if also as cantankerous. Some pilots developed a scary don't-give-a-shit hotrod attitude—either confident of their immortality or certain they were going to die no matter what—and jumped at any mission, the hairier the better. One such cowboy was available in Kontum when the call came from Spider's captain. He hauled his door gunner and another pilot—"crew chief"— out of the EM club, beers in hand, and within five minutes they were sailing up into the hills, into the darkness.

CHILL

Dear Spider,

Here's the map of the southern constellations that you wanted. Boy, I had to Xerox it three times before it came out, all that black.

It must be really neat to see stars you've never seen before. Does anybody in your platoon have binoculars you can use? I remember all the great stuff you showed me with your telescope that night last year, Jupiter and the O'Brien Nebula.

I hope all that bullshit with the chemistry department didn't put you off science when you come back to college. You really ought to be an astronomer. Maybe an astronaut! I read in the paper the other day that NASA is taking guys with PhDs and teaching them how to be test pilots, so they can fly on the Apollo missions.

Funny to think about you in the jungle this morning. I got caught down-town yesterday in a sudden blizzard and had to just leave my car and walk to a friend's house. Nobody in Washington knows how to drive in the snow! It's like it was a southern city that gets surprised every year. Anyhow I better close this and trudge back and see if the snow plow buried my car. Brrr! I'm gonna

put some boots in the car for the next time this happens!
Love,
Beverly

ROAD RACE

The pilot's name was Smeeps, but he wanted people to call him Fangio, after a racing-car driver he admired. They usually called him Fang. He had an overbite.

Fang was in Operations, drinking coffee and trying to learn whist, when the dustoff call came in from Spider's hill. No one would be ordered to fly a mission like that, but you could volunteer, and it was uncool not to. Fang tossed his cards in, wrote down the coordinates in his notebook, and checked the wall map. No sweat in this moonlight, he said; just follow Route 17 about fifteen miles south, then have them pop a flare. He went next door to the EM Club and asked Willy Joe if he'd like to go scrag some gooks. The door gunner put a couple of beers in his side pockets and followed him down to the pad. His crew chief Monsoon, actually a copilot, shrugged and came along, too. They'd left the slick set up, ready to crank; they had it in the air in less than a minute, flying at treetop level with no lights.

Fang was among the best, but this mission was not quite the milk run he'd pretended it to be in Ops. The people in Ops knew that, of course, and so did Monsoon and Willy Joe, who leaned out the door with studied nonchalance, sober enough to be terrified. He sipped the warm beer while he scrutinized the flickering darkness of the treeline, waiting for the stream of tracers that would give him something to aim at: bright red or green balls that floated toward you with deceptive slowness. He'd seen them a few times, and twice the slick he was in had been hit, both times without doing major damage. It bothered him that he hadn't known they'd been hit, either time, until they landed. But the rotor blades and his M60 made a lot of noise; more noise than a bullet popping through soft aluminum.

Fang kept one eye on the elapsed time; when it looked like they'd gone about fifteen miles, he radioed the LZ for a flare to guide him in. They rogered that, but said they couldn't hear the slick. That was weird. A few seconds later, Monsoon yelled, "Shit!" loud in his earphones and punched him twice on the shoulder. Fang craned around and saw a dim flare hanging maybe ten miles away, behind and to the right.

In the thin wash of moonlight, he'd picked up the wrong road. Cursing monotonously, he circled the machine around, climbing, and took a bearing on the flare as it faded. He stayed fairly high and told them he'd be about five minutes; pop another flare when they heard him approach. Then he muttered a line that Monsoon would make famous: "If that motherfucker bleeds to death I'll kill him."

LUNACY

Spider sat on the ground in the semi-darkness, M16 in his lap, turning the blinker over and over in his hands, looking up at the moon's face, remembering the names of some dark areas: Oceanus Procellarum, Mare Tranquillitatus, the man-in-the-moon-eye of Mare Crisium and tiny Sinus Iridium. He could barely make out the ray system radiating from the crater Tycho, or maybe he just thought he could, since he remembered how it looked in a telescope. He was staring at the moon, naming its parts, in an unsuccessful attempt to take his mind off the shattered sobbing wreck of a man behind him, flanked by medics who murmured at him while he mourned his legs, his balls, his cock, no no no no no no. He was quiet for a minute and then said in a strangled whisper, "Just shoot me. Please just shoot me. Once in the head."

Where was the fucking helicopter? That flare a minute ago had to have been to guide it in. Maybe it got shot down. That would be a bitch; this guy's gonna die anyhow, or wish he was dead. Maybe somebody *should* just shoot him; maybe the medics ought to keep popping him morphine until he dies.

Graves was bad enough, but all those dead bodies were just like cartoons of dying, compared to this. The real thing, real pain, a real person. Spider knew the guy from fire base, although he didn't know his name. He was one of the guys with Bangkok pictures. Bang cock, Jesus. Two guys' dicks blown off in two days.

Oceanus Procellarum, sounds good, but what the hell does it mean? Ocean of Procells. Mare Serenitatis, the Sea of Serenity. Spider wondered whether he was going crazy. Anybody who didn't go crazy with this shit going on must have been crazy before it started. So everybody is crazy and nobody can tell.

One of the medics lit a joint and offered it to the wounded man. He didn't pay any attention. He passed it to the other medic, who passed it to Spider. Spider took two big tokes, holding the second one in for as long as he could.

He declined a third hit. The dope made him feel dizzy and even more tired. He chugged a Coke and ate a piece of jungle chocolate, which gave him a little bit of a compensating buzz.

Finally, the faint throb of a helicopter beating its way over. After a minute, the mortar team popped an illumination round and the RTO shouted, "Blinkers on."

The engineers and three other guys were positioned around the inside of the LZ with blinkers, small but powerful red lights that were shielded so as to be visible only from overhead. Shadows danced crazily as the illumination-round flare bobbed under its parachute.

The helicopter got louder and the blades changed pitch. Moses yelled, "Pop smoke on the LZ?" The RTO shouted back, "No, he's got you." The flare sputtered out.

Then there was a swirling gale and the dark bulk of the helicopter slid in front of the moon, louder and larger than any slick had ever seemed in the daytime. For a few seconds, hovering, it shined down a dazzling spotlight—Spider incongruously thought of the Lucas Lasers he'd installed in his Chevy's brights—and, satisfied that the way was clear, dropped swiftly.

The helicopter didn't even land. It bobbed a foot off the ground, a few inches, while the two medics hoisted the wounded man aboard. He was struggling and screaming something, unintelligible over the whack-whack-whack of the blades. One of the medics got aboard, hauled into the red-lit darkness by the door gunner, and the slick shot straight up and banked away.

As the sound faded, Spider reached down and tugged at his scrotum, an unconscious magical gesture that most of the other men were conjuring as well.

THIRD WEEK

Two weeks with Lee, and Beverly had done things the bare mention of which would have made her mother faint. Everything was equally new and different, and she was willing to try almost anything. She knew he would never hurt her on purpose, though sometimes her own inexperience, her tightness, caused pain. She was uncomfortable for a couple of days after the first time they enjoyed anal intercourse, the sphincter bruised and some pain deeper within, but in a way even that was nice; she could sit in class and take notes automatically while feeling the ghost of him hard inside her, plumbing, probing. He showed her how to practice for oral sex with a banana, to subvert the gag reflex, saying he'd learned it from a Berkeley student, a co-ed who was a part-time prostitute, which was mostly true, except for the co-ed part. The prostitute was male and had skipped college.

In the dialectic of a slightly later period, people would say he was exploiting her mercilessly for sex, but in his own mind he was patiently, lovingly, initiating her into the mysteries of a sacred order.

No one would deny that he had a lot of energy; most would give him credit for more positive qualities. He had actually gotten a job, three weeks of inside painting in an office building downtown. On weekends, he and Beverly put in ten- or twelve-hour days doing volunteer work for Martin Luther King's upcoming Poor People's March on Washington. They ran a hand-cranked mimeograph together, slipsheeting and collating, dead on their feet and feeling good about it.

Police cars cruised slowly by the small shopfront, and at one time, for several days, a conspicuous white man in a suit walked by and peered in every couple of hours. Finally, they all waved at him. He never came back. They knew that a lot of powerful people didn't want a hundred thousand poor blacks descending on the Mall. "Martin better watch his ass," Lee said once. "The pigs are gonna get him. If they want him dead, he's dead. Just like they got JFK."

Lee was always saying things like that. It upset Beverly that he could be so cynical and nihilistic. But other times he was upbeat and almost childlike, exuberantly playful. His orthodontist father diagnosed him as a manic-depressive and had tried to get him into therapy, which was one reason he left California.

Beverly and Lee felt especially virtuous, working on the 6th of January, most of Washington paralyzed by an eleven-degree cold snap. That same day, five people, including Benjamin Spock, were indicted for "conspiracy to block the draft," and, in a better part of town, the Reagan For President office quietly opened.

LOVE LETTER

Beverly didn't want to tell the truth to Spider, and she didn't want to lie.

January 6th
Dear Spider,

Just a short note, I'm beat. Spent all day cranking a mimeograph. My new roommate Lee and I are working down at Martin Luther King's Poor People's March office downtown. Lee's pretty, has long hair, plays the guitar, kind of a hippy. I think you'll like Lee.

The paper today says that an average of 26 GIs died every day last year in Vietnam, and 170 were wounded. Do you think that's the truth? I mean, you had so many GIs coming in when you worked at that awful place, and that was just one little part of the country, right? I think they're lying. But then I'm turning into a radical. Mother would just shit. (She doesn't know I'm going down into Southeast every weekend to work with Negroes. Please don't mention it to your Mother either, I know they talk.)

Hanoi sent another peace feeler out, I don't know whether they tell you about things like that. Some people are saying it's just a bluff, and Ho Chi Minh just wants to stop the bombing for awhile. Well, who wouldn't? Bobby Kennedy says that if negotiations don't work we can always go back to killing each other. I'm sort of caught in the middle myself. I like Bobby Kennedy, and I don't like anybody being bombed, but he doesn't have a boyfriend in Vietnam, and I know that at least some of the bombs are to keep the enemy out of the south. Keep them from getting even stronger. (Lee doesn't like to hear me talk like that, but then Lee doesn't have a boyfriend in Vietnam either.)

Another cold snap. Got down to 11 last night. (Bet you'd trade!) I'm getting around okay now on snow tires with chains.

Well, I can't keep my eyes open, I'm going to bed.
Love,
Beverly

P.S. Look at this new stamp—can you believe 10 cents for airmail?

• • •

Spider didn't want to tell the truth to Beverly, and he didn't want to lie:

6 Jan 68
Dear Bev,
  God am I bushed. We had a little mortar attack last night after we were dug in. Nobody killed, one guy wounded, just in the legs. They sent a medevac to get him in the middle of the night, which is more than I would expect from the FA. But everybody had to stay up all night, on guard.
  Since the sun came up we've been on "two on, two off," that is, sleep two hours and be on guard two hours. I was up for the first two, and managed to keep my eyes open. (It's not too hard to stay awake in the dark, especially after an attack like that. But once it gets light you stop seeing ghosts.) (Actually I shouldn't say that—a guy on guard in the position next to me fell asleep last night about three and started to snore. Somebody kicked him.)
  Smoked some dope that might have had something else in it. Kept me pretty jumpy all night, which I guess was a good thing.
  Anyhow I better get some sleep. Will write more later on.
  (Later) Chopper coming in, they say with mail. Better put this in an envelope and send it off, don't know how long it'll be before the next mailbag goes out.
Love,
Spider

EDGED WEAPONS

The mailbag brought Spider a late Christmas present from his Uncle Terry: an impossibly shiny, impossibly keen Randall Made Fighting Knife, in a leather sheath that smelled like new shoes, like civilization.

The message inside was not too civilized, because Uncle Terry wasn't: "Wish I could have sent you my old Randall from Korea, but I left it in a gook." Spider wondered whether they actually called the enemy gooks back then, or was that just Uncle Terry trying to be cool?

(It was kind of sad. Spider's father told him that everybody knew Uncle Terry never saw actual combat in Korea; he served six weeks in the Quartermaster Corps and then broke both legs in a traffic accident. He had all kinds of vivid stories that weren't true.)

He did need a sheath knife. The M7 bayonet that was issued with the M16 was useless as a cutting tool, having a blade about as sharp as a butter knife's, made of metal so soft a fairly strong man could bend it without its breaking. The design was visually impressive, a sleek black dagger to match the sleek blackness of the rifle. It spoiled the balance of the rifle, though, and nobody expected ever to be in a situation where he would have to fix bayonets and charge. So most of them were thrown away. Some came back.

A lot of grunts carried some version of the Marine's kabar, a no-nonsense sturdy utility knife. They weren't issued to Army personnel, but you could buy one at the PX for $7.50, and what else was there to spend money on? (A very few old hands had kabars actually made by Ka-Bar, the original factory, that stopped manufacturing them after World War II.)

The Gerber Mark 2 Combat Knife was a big number, and Bucks were also popular. Handmade knives were the ultimate cachet, though. Probably nine out of ten of them came from the Randall factory in Orlando, Florida (which in pre-Disney 1968 was a small town with no other claim to fame). General Westmoreland carried an ivory-handled Randall Model No. 1 on his belt.

It made Spider feel a little silly. As much as he needed a sheath knife, and he couldn't have asked for a better one, but God, Randalls were for *lifers*!

He tried wearing it tucked inside his boot, but that was uncomfortable. The sheath wouldn't fit on the wide canvas web belt that held his first-aid kit and ammo pouches and two canteens, and he didn't have a regular belt. So he put it inside his rucksack. If an enemy ever got close enough to stab with a knife, Spider could fire his one bullet at him.

LUCK OF THE DRAW

Batman and Moses walked over to Spider's perimeter bunker, looking unhappy. Batman waved for Killer to join them. "Look," Batman said, "they're gonna send a patrol over to that mortar position. They need a X-Ray volunteer. Anybody want to do it?"

"Shit," Killer and Spider said simultaneously. Moses had already testified.

"Draw straws," Batman said, and stooped to pick some grass. He arranged the stems with his back to them, then turned around and offered them to Moses. The one he chose was obviously long, and he breathed relief. Killer's was also long.

Spider stared at the two bits of grass protruding from the black man's fist, trying to see some sign but convinced he would draw the short one. He did.

All four were silent for a moment. "Shouldn't be much," Batman said. "Carry the demo bag; we already got our LZ."

Spider was about to protest that he'd never blown an LZ, but a more pressing objection came to mind: "But my M16 doesn't work. Somebody trade?"

Everybody looked at each other. "Here," Killer said, shrugging out of the shoulder harness. He handed Spider his precious Magnum. "It's single action. You got to pull the hammer back."

Spider hefted it. The weight was reassuring. He laughed nervously. "Like in a cowboy movie?"

"Right. Here." Spider helped him thread the harness over his shoulders and adjust it. "Just bring it back clean, okay? And remember you just got six shots?"

"Uh, yeah." Spider felt lightheaded, almost to the point of fainting. He realized Batman was holding out the demo bag, and took it.

"So saddle up and get over to the RTO's position," Batman said, looking at the watch pinned to his shirt pocket. "You got five minutes."

"Saddle up? Got to carry C's and everything?"

"Sure." Batman slapped him on the back, not hard. "Just 'case you get lost." Moses agreed to take over the perimeter guard. Spider shuffled back toward his own bunker. How many people were in a patrol? What was he walking into? Get *lost*?

Spider stacked the stuff in his rucksack as efficiently as possible; searching, he found that the Randall knife fit into a side pocket on the left, where he could reach it if he stretched. Then he went back to the LZ to top off the canteen he'd been drinking from (he'd already filled three canteens and a gallon plastic sack from the water cans the slick had brought in) and pick up a carton of Camels.

He carried his burden over to where the RTO was sitting in dappled shade, drinking coffee with about fifteen men. The slick had brought coffee in, too, in a large insulated container, and it smelled good. White paper cups looked incongruous in the scruffy setting; every one that had been touched by a soldier was fingerprinted brown.

"You the X-Xay?" said a man Spider didn't recognize, reclining with stiff casualness on his clean rucksack. His fatigues were clean.

"That's right, sir."

"Don't-call-me-sir-I-work-for-a-living"; a sergeant's stock reply upon being mistaken for an officer. Both men were following ritual. No one wore rank insignia in combat, and when you came upon a stranger in his late twenties or thirties, it was a lot safer to "mistake" a sergeant for an officer than the other way around. "You're new; you got a name?"

"John Speidel, Sergeant. They call me Spider." He took the cup the RTO offered him and tipped some coffee into it.

"I'm Sarge. Don't they give you guys M16s anymore?"

"Mine's busted, Sarge." He patted the butt of the Magnum. "Bummed this from a friend."

"It's really fucked up," the RTO said. "Won't chamber. I looked at it yesterday."

Sarge nodded, staring intently at the space between the two men. He was a formidable and strange-looking man, very black but with pale gray eyes, head completely shaved, long weight-lifter's body. He moved slowly and carefully, as if coiled to spring. "Homer, you go over to Pig and get that spare AK." To Spider: "Have you ever fired an AK47?"

"Uh, no." In fact, Spider had only fired thirty-six rounds through an M16, in training, and although not many of them hit the target, he was rated Expert. Someone Stateside had declared that no one should be sent into combat in Vietnam unless he had attained an Expert rating on the M16. So no one came to Vietnam without an Expert rating, whether or not he had ever seen an M16. "Is it a lot different?"

"Somewhat, yes." He picked up his own M16 by the barrel and pointed it at Spider. "Here, I'll take the AK. You didn't *break* your 16, did you?"

Spider gingerly took the weapon. "No, Sarge. It came that way."

"Fuckin' army," he said with no inflection. Homer brought the AK with two banana clips. Sarge slid a magazine into place and jacked a round into the chamber. Satisfied, he cleared the weapon and snapped the round back into the top of the magazine. He peered around, counting heads. "Missing one."

"Freeling," the RTO said without looking. "Went to take a crap."

"Of course." He turned to Spider. "I'm usually Bravo's platoon sergeant. Been on R&R."

"Pussy patrol," a white boy with a southern accent sang out.

"Gone to see you' momma," he growled, scowling.

"You like my momma?"

"She one ugly piece a ass, man, wonder how you ever got born."

"Daddy always put a bag over her head."

"Me too." He gave the guy a gleaming smile. "But first I cuts a hole in de bag. I lo-o-oves dem white mommas wit' no teef."

Some of the laughter was nervous. The white guy tried to mimic Sarge's accent: "Someday I'm gonna find *you'* momma."

"Oh, you've found her." He plucked at his uniform. "You already married her ass. Two years, anyhow." He grinned. "She fuckin' you all day and night."

A man who was evidently Freeling came out of the woods, carrying an M16 and a shovel, looking agitated. "Sarge?" He swiveled to stare at him. "Look, I don't wanta be chickenshit. But I'm, I'm too short for this fuckin' detail."

"How short is that?"

"Twelve . . . fuckin' . . . days."

"Hmm." Sarge squeezed his eyes shut and kneaded his forehead, as if trying to imagine such a state. "We don't expect any contact. But okay. You go help X-Ray, you know Batman?" The man nodded. "Tell him I detailed you over. They're puttin' out wire today."

"Wire?" Homer said. "We're gonna stay in this goddamn place?"

"Think they tell me anything? I just heard a confirm on four strands of concertina." He took a pair of reading glasses out of a plastic bag and unfolded a topographical map. "Gather round if you want to see where you're goin'."

He tapped two places that had X's pencilled in. "This is us and this is where the mortar position was. Bearing's 142 degrees, but we won't hardly need a compass. We just go downhill until we cross the little stream, and then go uphill until we get to the mortar position. Shouldn't take but two hours, maybe three."

"It's pretty thick," the RTO said. "No trails?"

"Huh uh." His finger traced a pencil line halfway around the other hill. "This here's a game trail some lurps found a couple of months ago. "We could follow the stream around until we find it. But that wouldn't be too smart."

"Is this just a fuckin' body count?" someone asked.

"Yeah, and 'confiscate or DX enemy ordnance.' Plus we're humpin' three AP mines to put up there in case Charles comes back." He folded up the map and checked his watch. "Let's saddle up. We hustle, maybe we get back by 1500." He put his arms through the straps and kneeled forward to lift the rucksack onto his back. Something heavy inside clanked; the anti-personnel mines. He stood gracefully. "Single file, I'll take point. Everybody lock an' load when you pass the perimeter."

"Shit," Homer said. "Charlie's Country."

"Nah. A walk in the park," the sergeant said, and ambled off on a bearing of 142 degrees. Spider checked the time: exactly ten.

ALL YOU NEED IS LOVE

The clock downstairs chimed ten. Beverly looked at Lee's handsome features, silhouetted against the nightlight. He took a drag on the joint and his face glowed orange.

"I wonder what Spider's doing," she whispered. "It's ten in the morning there."

He paused. "I wonder," he said. "Nothing much fun."

"I don't know what to do."

"Take a toke." He held the joint out.

"Not now." Her throat was sore. The banana was easier, symmetrical; Lee's penis hooked to the left. She took another sip of water. "I can't send him a Dear John letter. He's too depressed already."

"That's true. But writing him's not the problem."

"No . . . it's if he—it's *when* . . ." She sobbed once and tears ran down her cheeks. She groped for a tissue and couldn't find a dry one; blew her nose into semen musk.

"You can say 'if.' If he comes back."

"Oh, yuck." She wiped her chin and mouth with the back of her hand. "I don't want to say it. Seems like bad luck."

"You got freaked out by that fucking bulletin."

"Didn't you?"

"Yeah." An American company had been boxed in by an NVA division. After fighting all night, all but 24 of the 103 GIs had been killed, wounded, or captured. "If they tell us about that, God knows what worse things are going on."

"Oh, don't start. Sometimes they must tell the truth."

"When it suits them or when they get caught," he said harshly. "Sorry. I shouldn't bring politics into bed with me."

"That's all right; I shouldn't bring another man. But you're right. That film got to me." She knuckled her eyes. "I don't even *love* him. Or I do, but like a brother-sister thing, y'know?"

"You can't tell him that, though."

"No."

Lee took a deep drag and held it in, thinking. There was no doubt in his mind that Spider was going to die in Vietnam. Karma, kismet. "Look, he comes back, *when* he comes back, I just fade for a couple of months. You make sure he meets lots of girls, let him down easy."

"You . . . you'd wait for me?"

"You have to ask?" He barely got the joint out of the way as she enveloped him in a crushing desperate hug.

Her warm tears trickled down his neck. "You're the most loving man," she said, muffled.

"Where it's at, baby," he said, not consciously mocking himself. He stared at the glowing ember. "Love is all we have."

A WALK IN THE PARK (2)

Spider tried to be conscientious about not bunching up; he tried to keep at least three meters between him and Homer, the grenadier in front of him. The rationale was inarguable. The first enemy grenade or mortar round or spray of machinegun fire ought not to kill more than one person. Still, he could usually see only one person beyond Homer, and if he fell back and lost both of them, he wouldn't have any idea of which way to go, except downhill, and he might lead the five or six people behind him straight into doom. He tried to fight rising panic, tried not to make noise, strained to hear the noise from the people behind him.

Every now and then, he thought of the phrase "a walk in the park." Under other circumstances, this could be a lot of fun. He had sort of liked Boy Scouts, enjoyed hiking and camping, and could remember a time when being allowed to carry a gun while hiking would have been the ultimate in cool. (His parents hadn't even let him own an air rifle.) But none of the scenarios he'd acted out in his childhood had covered the situations of gagging over rotting flesh, screaming with indescribable pain, having your pecker shot off.

He tried not to make any noise but felt like a walking symphony of clanks, snaps, and scrapes. The guys behind and in front of him seemed to be moving as silently as Indian scouts. Guess who the enemy would zero in on. His skin was cold and greasy in the jungle heat.

They made it down to the stream without being blown to bits. Spider checked his watch and was surprised to read 10:44. He visualized the map and revised his estimate of the scale. It might not be too bad.

The stream was about two meters of black water, too wide to jump. The water was tepid and came up to his knees. When he got out, he'd added the sound of socks squishing to his repertoire.

He realized he had it pretty easy, being about tenth in line. The other guys had worn down a temporary path by the time he came along. Sarge was probably making more noise than anybody, breaking trail. But then of course they don't shoot the point man. He studied the thick forest around him and remembered the camouflage demonstration at Fort Leonard Wood. That had been familiar scrub pine and berry bushes, but the trainees had all walked right by a machinegun position with two men. It opened up on them with blanks, enough to kill everybody, and then they were marched back by it again. Knowing where to look, you could see the two men. But you could have walked by them a dozen times. What could be hiding in this thick welter of vines and brambles? A tank, if they could get it down here.

The going was easier at first, uphill, because it was easier to keep your balance, leaning slightly forward with the pack on your back. But it got steeper. Spider had to use his free hand sometimes to haul himself up, trying to grab a root or vine rather than a venomous snake.

The extra physical effort was distracting, though, and after an hour or so Spider was less nervous, even though they were working ever deeper into Charlie's Country. There were occasional sparkles of blue sky in the canopy overhead, so they must be getting close.

Then suddenly Homer flopped to the ground and stared silently back at Spider, making a patting motion: get down! Spider repeated the actions.

God, his body was making a racket. Breath rasping, heart hammering.

He strained to hear what was going on up ahead, but knew that was futile. Anything important that happened would be plenty loud.

He felt a bug on his calf, under the pants leg, and quietly flicked it. It wiggled but didn't move away. He carefully raised up the loose fabric and sickened when he saw a leech, gorged with black blood, the size of his finger. He must have picked it up in the water.

He'd heard that you were supposed to apply the end of a cigarette to the thing's head, to make it let go, but nobody'd been smoking. He eased the Zippo out of his pocket and spun up a flame and held it to the creature, which slid off with no agility and tried to wiggle into the brush. Spider crushed it with his boot heel. Blood trickled from where it had been attached.

Homer was whispering, "Cool it! Cool it, asshole," and Spider realized how much noise he'd been making in his panic. Just a bloodsucking worm, nothing to get all dramatic about. He looked down for the thing's squashed remains and was not happy to see that it wasn't there anymore.

Homer eased to his feet and Spider followed suit. The blood was still trickling but he didn't feel the wound. The thing must inject some sort of anesthetic before it bites.

After a couple of minutes the compost-rot smell of the forest took on a new component, sickening, that Spider recognized immediately. Add a little Lysol and you'd have the holding room at Graves. Homer stopped as the man in front of him worked his way back and whispered in his ear. Then Homer backed down and transferred the message: "We're gonna move into a circle around this clearing. Watch out for boobytraps." Spider passed it on down. Homer was clambering off to the left, so he did too, trying to maintain an interval and study every square inch of ground at the same time. He passed by two shell holes, raw craters of fresh dirt.

He heard it before he saw it, flies buzzing. The roadkill stench was suffocating in the still air. He moved toward the light.

The clearing was like something out of a gruesome fifties EC comic, the kind he'd hid from his parents. The bottom part of a man's body lay next to a rifle. Animals had been disputing over it, and intestines were strung all over the clearing. Spider's practiced eye identified a gnawed liver and heart. He could only locate one arm, fingers chewed off. A head with the cheeks torn out stared at the sky, eyes clotted with insects. He heard two people retching and had to swallow hard himself. Pretty fucking gross.

The sergeant broke into the clearing, looking at the ground, and lit a cigarette. "Smoke 'em if you got 'em," he said. Spider fumbled for a Camel.

"RTO?" The radioman came up behind him, pale. "Tell 'em we got two November Victor Alfa Kappa India Alfa." Two NVA killed in action. "Enough blood an' guts for two, anyhow." He looked around, picked up the dead man's AK47, tossed it to the ground, and inspected the mortar tube, which was still standing but was full of holes. "Tell 'em we got a mortar, I guess 82 Mike Mike Sov or Chicom, and a Alfa Kappa Four Seven, both inoperable." He took a deep drag, looking around. When the RTO stopped transmitting, he said, "Request permission to place mines and withdraw. Let's get outa this fuckin' place."

The rush of nicotine, combined with everything else, almost made Spider faint. The clearing glowed and shimmered. The revolting smell changed, still a little sickening but sort of like food, like pork chops frying. The sergeant did a remarkable thing: unbuttoning his fly, he walked over to the corpse's head; he pulled out a big stiff black dick and picked up the head, rotated it, and found the mouth . . . Spider clenched his eyes shut and shook his head violently.

When he opened his eyes, the sergeant was toeing the head, hands in his pockets. "Poor bastard," he said.

Shit, I'm losing it, Spider thought. A couple of puffs of marijuana could do that? Better stay away from it.

"Sarge, they say we gotta DX the enemy ordnance, or hump it back."

"Sure, we're gonna hump this shit back." The mortar with its plate weighed more than a hundred pounds. "X-Ray? Get your ass up here."

Spider moved into the clearing, stepping carefully over dirt-crusted intestines.

"You wanna blow this shit? Give it about a two-minute fuse." He threw down his cigarette after using it to light another one. "Homer and Stick, get a couple shovels and get up here." To Spider: "You set up the plastic and I'll check it out after we do the mines."

Spider slid out of his rucksack and opened the demo bag. He had only a vague idea of what to do, but he supposed a stick of C-4, one kilogram, would be enough. No way they could reuse that mortar anyhow. He jammed the top end full of the white stuff.

He took the coil of red time fuse out of the demo bag, measured off two feet, and cut it. Then he took a deep breath and opened the green cardboard box of blasting caps.

Blasting caps made him nervous. The one part of his demolition training that really stuck with him was the pictures they passed around of hands with freshly missing fingers and one guy with his jaw and nose blown off from crimping a cap with his teeth.

The box was full. He had to pick one out with his fingernails. The cold touch of the clean metal was electric. He had a vision of his hands as bloody stumps, and almost dropped the box. That would be cool. He folded the box closed and returned it to the bag.

He tried to remember the ritual. Inspect the open end of the cap, tap it over your wrist, blow into it *gently*, slip the fuse into it *gently*, make sure it's all the way in, and *gently* squeeze it closed with the crimpers. Then poke a hole in the plastic explosive with the pointy end of the crimpers and slide the cap in.

The AK47 was covered with blood and had most of a lung sticking to the stock. He picked it up by the magazine, which was reasonably clean, scraped the lung tissue off with his foot, and was able to balance it on top of the muzzle of the mortar. That would surely blow it in two.

He looked around. Sarge and the other two had buried their mines and were camouflaging them. The RTO was over at the corpse's head, sawing an ear off with his knife. He put it in his pocket. Then the second ear, which he licked and put into his mouth.

Spider sat down hard, his face in his hands. Cold sweat trickled down his ribs. He looked at the RTO again and he was just pushing the head around with a stick. It still had both its ears.

"Pretty tough shit for a new guy," Sarge said, inspecting Spider's handiwork. "Funny arrangement, but I guess it'll work. Why don't you go on down and get in line. I'll light the fuse when we get clearance."

"Thanks." Spider saddled up and headed for the treeline, not looking back. God knows what he'd see.

The men had lined up in the same order as before, facing downhill. Spider found his place behind Homer and sat down, leaning back against the rucksack in a half-comfortable position, and lit a fresh cigarette off his old one. He opened a Coke to help settle his stomach. Only one left now. He'd heard two slicks come in to the LZ while they were humping, though; maybe they brought fours and fives.

Was he going nuts? There wasn't anybody he dared talk to about it. The sergeant fucking that head and the RTO eating the ear were just as real-looking as anything around him now. Maybe all this would go away, too, if he could close his eyes long enough.

Sarge hustled down the line saying laconically, "Fire in the hole, fire in the hole, fire in the hole. Let's get the fuck outa here." Everybody got to their feet and followed him fast.

After a couple of minutes a loud *bang* echoed through the valley, along with a whirring sound that must have been the AK, or part of it, trying for orbit. They worked their way downhill for about ten minutes more and then the word came up to stop, take a five-minute break in place. Spider could hear four or five people working out to the right and left, he supposed as listening posts.

He gratefully slumped to the ground and sorted through his rucksack. Beans & franks would be okay cold. He opened the can and mixed in some Tabasco sauce.

"God, you can eat after that?" Homer whispered.

"Hungry."

"Yeah, you're the guy from Graves. That must do something to ya."

"I guess it does." He looked straight at Homer because he didn't like what he'd glanced in the can. Shit and crawling worms. "You gotta eat, though." He took a bite and it tasted like beans & franks.

"Not as bad as that up there," Spider continued, nodding in the direction they were headed. "You can get used to almost anything, I guess. But we never had anybody get his dick shot off or lose both legs."

"Yeah, well, those are the first two casualties we've had in weeks. I guess the law of averages ought to keep us safe for a while."

Spider knew from reading *Analog* that there was no such thing as a "law of averages"; that the probability of one independent event didn't affect the probability of another. If they had killed a few thousand enemy soldiers, that would reduce the probability of an attack tonight. Killing one, and making as much noise as the bombing of London, might have the opposite effect. It could draw attention to them.

But he didn't say anything. Nobody likes a smartass.

Someday he ought to make a list of the valuable things he'd learned in the army. Nobody likes a smartass. How to use a floor waxer. How to break an egg with one hand. How to burn shit; just knowing that you *could* burn shit. Hospital corners on a tight bunk. How to roll socks. All that stuff about guns and knives was interesting, but wouldn't be very useful in civilian life, unless you took a job with the Mafia.

The humping back to camp was more relaxed, though Spider had a feeling it shouldn't have been. If the enemy hadn't heard them crashing through the woods, he certainly would have heard the C-4 blowing up. Of course, Charlie didn't usually come out during the day. Sneaky little bastards. *Smart* little bastards!

All the way down one hill and up the next, Spider intermittently felt a sniper's sights on his back. But at least he didn't see anything else interesting.

SCHIZOPHRENIA (1)

Nineteen sixty-eight was not a simple time for people to be seeing things that weren't there. There were legions of people going out of their way, breaking laws while building bridges, or walls, seeking out constructive, revealing hallucinations—but others who were just plain nuts. Or mentally ill. Or temporarily unable to cope with stress in a socially acceptable way.

The medic who gave Spider a couple of tokes from his joint may or may not have been smoking straight marijuana; he may or may not have known exactly what he was smoking. A lot of dope in Vietnam was seasoned with opium, horse tranquilizer, speed, or heroin, any of which might cause one to see odd things. Twelve hours later? Who knows? Every body's different.

Schizophrenia. An ordinary Joe who was walking down the street and saw a man eating eyeballs out of his hand or heard voices telling him to jump naked from the Empire State Building would probably seek medical help. He would be diagnosed as schizophrenic.

But Spider, like most laymen at that time, would never have applied the term "schizophrenia" to those symptoms, or his. He thought it meant "split personality," but it never had. Schizophrenia was a term applied to people who exhibited some of a cluster of related symptoms, including visual and auditory hallucinations—and olfactory ones, like smelling pork chops when there aren't any around. Not all schizophrenics had dramatic symptoms, though; some just acted foolish or stopped acting at all; withdrew, became lumps.

It was hard to get two scientists to agree on what caused schizophrenia. Some thought it was strictly biochemical. Others blamed the genes or the environment. The diet or gross brain malformation or a bad child/mother relationship. A few said that schizophrenia was not a disease or even a mal-adaptation, but simply a reasonable response to an insane world.

One minor school of thought related schizophrenia to body shape. They would have loved Spider, because he was a perfect asthenic: lean with long limbs, long face, narrow trunk. You did see more asthenics than roly-poly types in the schizo wards.

Spider's hallucinations of corpse sodomy and cannibalism might not have put him in that ward, though, depending on the clinician who examined him. Hallucinations can be precipitated by fatigue and emotional stress, both of which he had in abundance, even without having smoked marijuana of unknown provenance. If he kept seeing such things "back in the World," he would be in trouble.

He didn't feel he had to worry about that, though. Unwittingly agreeing with his replacement Lee, Spider was absolutely convinced that he would never leave Vietnam alive.

WIRED

When the patrol had worked up to the top of the hill, they found their way blocked by Slinkies from Hell. Two strands of concertina barbed wire, like the fire base had. Concertina gave a quick way of putting up temporary barbed-wire entanglements to slow down an enemy charge. Each strand was a more or less taut spiral of metal, covered with rusty spikes, encircling the camp, a sadistic giant version of the child's toy. The two strands together made, effectively, a metal bramble bush about six feet thick.

Its springiness was its strength. A direct hit from a mortar round or grenade wouldn't break it; it would just bounce. If the enemy snuck up in the middle of the night and snipped it with wire cutters, it would embarrass him with a loud *sproing*! You couldn't charge through it or over it—not until bodies piled up deeply enough to weigh it down and make a bridge, which was uncommon.

There was a gate of sorts around on the other side of the hill, the place where the two ends of the coils had been joined together. A man with pliers and heavy gloves opened the circle so they could come in, and closed it back up behind them.

Spider trudged back to his area. The other engineers and Freeling, the rifleman Sarge had excused, were relaxing with beer and soft drinks. Spider's fours and fives were stacked on top of the bunker. He dumped his pack and opened a beer.

"You were the lucky one," Killer said, holding up both hands wrapped in bandages. "That concertina's a bitch."

"Yeah; looka me." Batman held up uninjured hands. "Gloves."

"Too hot," Killer groused.

"Heard you found a couple bodies," Freeling said.

"Just one." Spider flopped down and leaned against the bunker. "Enough blood an' guts for two, but I think it was just one, got blown to pieces by artillery."

"Take any pictures?" Killer said.

"Didn't think of it." Spider had an Instamatic that Beverly had sent him.

"Guess you've seen worse," Freeling said. "Guys say you come from Graves."

"I don' know." Spider sipped the beer. "Maybe this was about the worst. I guess it's easier when they bring 'em to you in bags. And it was an old guy. It got to my head."

"Your head?" Moses said.

"Hard to explain." Sure, tell them about the guys fucking and eating the corpse. "Some animals had got to him. Also I was feelin' kinda nauseous from last night, smoked some kinda shit with the medics, that didn't help much."

"You're not used to it?" Batman said.

"Huh uh. Couple of times." Once, actually, at a party with Beverly. He hadn't liked it, which was why he hadn't smoked at Graves. Almost everyone else did. "It's not my bag. Oh." He unbuckled the shoulder harness and handed the Magnum to Killer. "Thanks."

"Sure." Killer set it carefully on top of his pack. "No new rifles came in. I was on the LZ for both of the slicks."

"Well, shit. I wonder how long it takes."

Freeling stood up and brushed himself off, to no visible effect. "Don't hold your breath. If I was you I'd stock up on grenades." He found his weapon and helmet. "Better get back. See you guys."

"Not for long, asshole," Batman said.

"Short!" Freeling squawked, high-pitched like a big bird. "Short! Short!"

"Twelve days, they ought to just send him back," Moses said. "How long does it take to outprocess?"

"I don't know," Batman said. "Tell you in eighty-nine days."

Killer lit a cigarette off his old one. "He was really blown apart?"

"Yeah, really. We don't have to talk about it, do we?"

"Musta been somethin' *else*," Batman said, "gross out the Spider."

"Like I say, different." Spider upended the can, drained the beer in two gulps, and then stretched out with the rucksack as a pillow, steel helmet tipped over his eyes. "Wake me up for the next truce."

TRUCES

The next truce was going to be for the Tet holiday, three weeks away, and Spider would be awake.

The previous truce, the New Year's one a week before, hadn't been all that peaceful. The Americans recorded eighty-two Viet Cong violations of the thirty-six-hour "stand-down," the most impressive of which was a human wave attack on a Tay Ninh camp on January 3rd, where twenty-seven Americans were killed and over two hundred wounded, in an action that began six hours before the end of the truce—or eighty minutes before the end, according to the Viet Cong. The two sides never agreed on much.

After Tet, that violation would be an obscure footnote.

SPIDER'S SEX LIFE (2)

Spider was having an ugly dream. They were back in the reek of the clearing, but it was he who unbuttoned his fly and picked up the rotting mutilated head, turned the cold slimy thing around so that its open mouth—

"Wake up! Get up, you lucky asshole!" Killer was shaking his arm. It was late afternoon; Spider had slept for a couple of hours.

He levered himself over onto one elbow, bones creaking. "So what's going on?" He had a painful erection that was wilting fast. A fragment of the dream stayed with him and he was horrified, confused.

"You guys who were on the recon get a one-day pass into Pleiku, God knows why. But you gotta be down on the pad in a couple minutes."

"Pleiku?"

"Pussy!" He punched him hard on the shoulder. "It's one ... big ... whorehouse!"

Spider got up and brushed himself off. He could hear a helicopter in the distance, more than one. "So do I leave my shit here?"

"Shit, no, take it all along. Think *I'm* gonna hump it if we move out while you're gettin' your rocks off?"

"Yeah, yeah, I'm not thinkin' yet." He kneeled, leaned back into his ruck-sack straps, and hoisted the pack up onto his back, then picked up his steel pot and rifle. "Maybe trade this sucker in while I'm in there."

"Yeah, rotsa ruck." Killer extricated his wallet from three layers of dirty plastic bag. He handed Spider a ten-dollar Military Payment Certificate. "Look, if you think of it, get me a bottle of booze, some kinda whiskey."

"They take MPCs in Pleiku?"

"Shit yes, good as money." Merchants with Viet Cong sympathies especially liked MPCs. They sold them back to GIs for greenbacks at $1.25 to the dollar, and the American dollars wound up in North Vietnam, which desperately needed hard currency. The GIs got twenty-five percent more to spend at the PX and the massage parlor and Ho Chi Minh got surface-to-air missiles.

Killer walked down to the LZ with Spider. "So you've been into town?"

"Mmm, yes." He closed his eyes. "Yes!"

"So where should I go? What's a good place?"

"Ain't no *bad* place with pussy, is there?" He shrugged and resorted to the truth. "I don't know the name of the place we went to; I've only been in once. Just went with some other guys who knew where they were goin'."

"Sounds like a good idea. How much you pay?"

"Twenty bucks for boom-boom, ten for a blowjob. Maybe you can cut a deal for both."

Both, Spider thought. How long would it take you to get it up again; what would you do with her in the meantime?

Would he even know what to do at all? His total practical sex education comprised four handjobs in parked cars and one grainy black-and-white porno movie the sergeant at Graves showed on a sheet tacked up to the billet wall. What if you got it in the wrong hole?

Well, animals did it without any instruction. The whore presumably would have had experience with virgins before. As the slicks came in Spider was getting his hard-on back.

"A penny for your thoughts," Killer shouted as they crouched into the swirling storm kicked up by the blades.

Six scared-looking men in clean creased fatigues got out of the helicopter, FNGs. Spider was momentarily confused by the way they looked at him, trading places, and then realized that he looked like an old hand—cruddy and unshaven, equipment beat-up and dirty. He laughed out loud as the helicopter surged up into the sky.

• • •

It took a couple of hours before all of them were choppered into Camp Enari and trucked to a transient billet. By that time it was almost dark. They wouldn't be going into town until the next morning; meanwhile, it was clean fatigues, a shower, a hot meal, and a movie, all of which were exotic novelties that would have been appreciated more under other circumstances. A gruff sergeant changed some of their money into Vietnamese piastres and read them a lecture about not hurting the local economy by using MPCs or dollars, and then gave each of them six condoms and an imaginative lecture about venereal disease. If you caught Brand X, for which there was no cure, you would spend the rest of your life quarantined on a little island in the Pacific. Use a rubber even for a blowjob.

At least the outdoor movie was hilarious—John Wayne in *The Green Berets*. People laughed and passed joints around and threw empty beer cans at the Duke. Spider declined the marijuana and left the movie halfway through, to sit in the din of the EM club and drink cold beer and read the Heinlein novel.

His dreams were gentler that night, sexual but romantic, and after an amazing breakfast of bacon and eggs, he caught the second jeep into town. The RTO Morrison and three other guys were stuffed into the jeep; Morrison recommended Suzy Wong's Massage Parlor for a start. The driver nodded wordlessly and drove them through the heavily guarded gate.

The half-hour ride into town was interesting, a kind of scenery Spider had never seen at ground level. A dry grassy plain surrounded by the low mountains they'd been clambering around on the day before. Every couple of miles there was a cluster of shacks with walls that seemed to be constructed from flattened-out soft drink cans, fronted by children in rags standing beside the road with their hands out. Scrawny dogs, chickens, pigs. Sometimes green lawns decorated with piles of human-looking shit. Morrison confirmed that that's what it was—all the fertilizer the poor bastards could afford.

The town was dusty and dirty, littered with garbage. Faded signs advertised Winstons and Cokes in incomprehensible language. Old men and women and children stared at them with pleading or hostility. Some of the buildings were piles of charred rubble, a lot of them pocked with bullet and shrapnel scars. A new-looking Mercedes-Benz sat on flat tires, its doors stitched by machinegun fire, the bullet holes fresh enough to show bright metal.

The jeep stopped in front of a building with a weirdly lettered cardboard sign in the window: SUZY WONG'S MASSAGE PARLOR AND BAR—AMERICAN FOOD AND BEER. The driver, a buck sergeant who'd been silent all the way in, gave his speech. "I'll be back here at 1430 sharp.

Anybody's not here has to find his own way back. Cab ride's fifty bucks and you might get rolled. Or killed. If you're not back at Enari by sundown, it's a general court martial and LBJ." Long Binh Jail, a place of legendary cruelty; it made Marine boot camp look like the Campfire Girls. "Don't lock and load unless you're fired upon. Don't kill any fucking women or children unless they're shooting at you. And keep your fucking ammo secure. The little gooks'll pick your pockets and take the ammo to Papasan; you'll be eatin' it up in the hills next week. Any questions?" They murmured no and started to get out of the jeep. "And use those fucking rubbers! Otherwise you'll be pickin' your pecker up off the floor."

The jeep peeled out. "Fuck that shit," Morrison said, and threw his rubbers into the gutter.

Spider was properly shocked. "You're not afraid of the clap?"

"Shit, you get the clap, you go to the hospital. You rather be in a hospital or out in the boonies?" He coughed and spit. "Besides, I got 237 fuckin' days. No way I'm gonna make it. I'm gonna leave this fuckin' place in a body bag and so are you." One of the other guys said, "Damn straight," and tossed his rubbers away, too.

They trooped into Suzy Wong's, but rather than a seductive temptress in a slit skirt, they ran into a hard-eyed old gent who bore a striking resemblance to Ho Chi Minh, standing in front of an empty rifle rack. "Give him your gun but keep the magazine and the bolt," Morrison said.

Spider had a hard time getting the bolt out, because his hands were shaking and slippery with sweat. His mouth was dry and he felt dizzy and he could taste bacon and eggs and bile at the back of his throat. He hadn't known exactly what it was going to be like, but he hadn't foreseen anything quite like this. The old man locked their M16s in the rack and gave Morrison a key on a loop of string. "If the shit hits the fan," Morrison said, "get on down here and I'll hand out the rifles. Make sure you get your own." As if anyone else would want it.

They walked up a dusty flight of stairs; when Spider was halfway up, a tinny speaker started playing "I Wanna Hold Your Hand." The room they walked into was pleasant but disorienting, too American: jukebox, red vinyl booths with Formica tables. The walls were decorated with posters from stateside—the Beatles and the Doors and a peace symbol with the slogan WHAT IF THEY GAVE A WAR AND NOBODY CAME? One corner of that one was charred. The air smelled of stale hamburger grease and oriental perfume.

Eleven small women sat in the booths, one per booth, wearing low-cut silk dresses or shorts. They smiled what looked like sincere smiles of welcome. Spider thought they all looked uniformly impossibly desirable, and just went to the closest one.

He started to slide in across from her, but she said, "No, ovah heah, GI," and giggled, patting the seat next to her. He got in, unsure of what to do or say next; she slid over so that their thighs were in contact and caressed his bicep. "Big muscle." Her breast brushed his elbow and jasmine perfume made him dizzy. "What's you' name?"

"Spider." He looked down and saw an absolutely perfect pair of breasts, nipples and all, no bra, nestled in rustling silk.

"Nice name, Spida'," she said, and made a spidery walk with her sharp nails down his arm. She saw the activity in his lap and dropped her hand for a friendly squeeze, perhaps unaware of how close she had come to giving him a freebie. He made a noise between a sigh and a groan.

"My name's Li. You buy me some tea, Spida'?"

"Uh ... couldn't we just ... "

"Sure thing, GI. You buy me tea later." She bumped his hip with hers. "Upstairs, numbah five." They got out of the booth and she led him by the hand. Some of the other guys hooted and made sarcastic comments, but Spider couldn't hear them for the blood roaring in his ears.

Number five was just a swinging door; the room was a small area set off by plywood partitions, furnished with a rickety sagging bed and a screen and a stand with a water basin and a rag. She pointed to the bed. "You get undress. You got rubbers?"

"Uh, sure." Spider dropped a handful of condoms on the bed and started unbuttoning his shirt. He didn't do too good a job because he was hypnotized: the screen was in front of a bright window; when she went behind it to undress, it was a slow seductive shadow show. He only had the shirt halfway done when she came back out.

She laughed. "You hurry, now."

Spider had never seen a naked woman before. He had felt Beverly's sex, but always under layers of clothing. Li's was a plain frank slit, shaved, an indescribable miracle of flesh that she carried over to the basin and washed. Spider tried to undo one button and failed.

Her back to him, Li replaced the rag and bent over in a gymnast's pose, her pretty face in syzygy with the delicate petals of her labia and clenched pink anus dot. "How much you want?" she said, upside down. "Blowjob fifteen doll', boom-boom twenty-five, 'roun' the worl', fifty. Massage free."

Spider had no idea what "around the world" might be, but he had over a hundred dollars as well as two thousand piastres. "Everything," he said.

"Okay." She glided over to him and nimbly unbuttoned his shirt and slipped it off. She rubbed his neck and stood on tiptoe to kiss him, and then unfastened his belt and worked slowly down the buttons of his fly. Fortunately, Spider wasn't encumbered by underwear. She looked at his erection and said, "Pretty," and touched it lightly as she reached for a condom. It was more than Spider could take. He shot a string of ejaculate over her shoulder. With the speed of commerce she took him between her soft lips and sucked, cradling his testicles with one hand, gently stroking the shaft of his penis with the other, draining him as expertly and dispassionately as a milking machine. When he started to soften, she licked him down and up and then slowly took all of his average-sized dick into her mouth and throat. There was not even a term for this practice yet in America, not for another four years, and it was not something Spider would have thought physically possible. He stood in the presence of a miracle, raunchy but transfigured.

She slowly released herself from him and had him sit down while she removed his boots and socks and trousers. "You lie down now." He started to recline on his back. "The other way. I give massage now."

First she rubbed him all over, shoulders, back, and buttocks, soft circular motions with fingertips and teasing nails. Then she got up on the bed with her knees on either side of him and dug into the tense ropy neck and shoulder muscles that yesterday had complained so much about the rucksack. She was surprisingly strong, strong enough to hurt, but it drew out the deeper pain. Then she rubbed his scalp vigorously and did something strange with his ears. She sat back on him to rub his ribs and lower back, making playful circular motions around his tailbone with her wet vagina; he had to raise up to make room for a fresh erection.

Then she stood up on the bed and carefully stepped onto his back, all eighty pounds of her, and walked up toward his head, her toes massaging his backbone. She turned around and walked back and stepped off, straddling him. "Okay, now you turn over."

The massage was evidently over. She kneeled and scooted back, taking him in her mouth again while presenting a view of her private parts so close up that Spider's eyes crossed painfully, focusing, memorizing. Then he buried his face in the musky wetness—dismissing one flickering worry about venereal and other diseases — and licked and sucked with enthusiasm and curiosity. Then she slipped her finger past his mouth, slowly up into her vagina and back, and then slid it up his rectum and touched him inside and he exploded again, an almost painful and desperate kind of orgasm, trying to discharge after there was nothing left. When she slid her finger out he bucked so hard he almost threw her off the bed.

She slithered around to lie with her chin on his shoulder. She was quiet, almost motionless, for more than a minute. "I wash up now," she said softly. "You buy me tea now?" She slipped off the bed and padded to the basin.

"Yeah, tea. Me, too." So that was "around the world." He wondered how long it would be before he could get another pass. "Thank you, Li. That was, it was, it was great."

She was scrubbing her finger with soap. She smiled and blushed. "You numbah one GI, Spida'. " She shrugged into a kimono not quite long enough to cover her ass and stepped into slippers and was gone.

Spider thought about Beverly for the first time. They hadn't discussed his staying true to her, because the possibility of his being tempted by a prostitute had never come up. Well, they could talk about it later. Much later, after they were married. If he lived through the year. He was only human, he thought, getting a little angry at Beverly, in advance, for not understanding. Who could resist a woman like Li? (A moral man could, he scolded himself; a man with self-control; a man truly in love.) Well, he would use a rubber from now on.

Li backed through the swinging door and abstractions evaporated. She had a small tray with two glasses of tea and a pastry on a saucer. She slid the tray under the bed and handed Spider a glass of tea. It was cool and mint-flavored. He watched her hang up the kimono and step out of the slippers. Was there more to come?

She crouched at his feet and drank about half of her tea in two unfeminine gulps. Then she fed him the pastry one delicate bit at a time. It was sweet and rich. "What do you call this, Li?"

"Petty four," she said. "Numbah one Bit-nam pastry. You lie down now." She put his glass back on the floor and guided him down with one palm on his chest and the other pulling on his dick. So there would be more.

She worked on him gently with both hands and her mouth. He was a little sore but surprisingly eager. When he was stiff, she scrambled up on the bed to straddle him, unrolled a condom over his penis, and with a series of little thrusts and sideways wiggles, impaled herself on him to the hilt, and then rose up to his tip and waited. She passively let him push into her a few times, arching his back, penetrating as deeply as possible, and then she began a complex rhythm of partial retreats and sudden downward plunges, digging into his waist with her sharp nails, completely in control, watching his face with no expression, her own face and body misting with sweat.

It was almost more than he could bear: this was the real thing, the complicated insides of her rubbing up and down on him, a tiny round muscle grasping him as tightly as her lips had (he didn't realize that not all women had that talent), and the sight of her beautiful body straining above him—

But then she took him out, holding him firmly by the dick. "Now you stand."

"What?"

"On de floor, you stand. Now!" While he was untangling his legs to obey the order, she produced a blue glass jar with a white cream. She rubbed the stuff around her anus and, biting her lower lip, pushed some inside and moved it around with her finger. Then she covered most of Spider's condom with it and leaned forward with her head on her arms, eyes closed. "You go ahead now. Roun' de worl'." Spider tentatively touched her between the buttocks with the tip of his penis and she surged back, enveloping him suddenly, weirdly tight and hot. He thrust deeply three times and came so fast he hardly had time to enjoy it. Li eased forward, panting, and his dick popped out. He was surprised that the rubber looked clean, but stripped it off carefully, holding it by the end that hadn't been inside. "Where should I put this?"

Li opened one eye and shrugged. "Flo." Then she stretched like a cat, sighing, and sat up. "You like that okay, Spida'?"

"It was real nice. It was wonderful."

"You ask for Li next time you come. We do more nex' time." She slid off the bed and repeated the washing ritual. Spider watched her while he dressed. He couldn't believe it had happened.

"I pay you, or the guy downstairs?"

"Pay Li. Fifty dolla' plus five fo' tea plus tip."

"How much is that in piastres?"

She gave him a look. "You know we no take pee. Fifty-five dolla' MPC, same-same fifty dolla' American."

Spider counted out sixty-five in MPCs and left them on the bed. He lit up a cigarette. "Thanks, Li. You're really nice." He knew he had been dismissed but couldn't take his eyes off her.

"Here." She smiled and took the cigarette from him. She stuck it into her vagina and half squatted, tensing, then removed it and produced an impressive stream of smoke. She handed the cigarette back. "Bet no round-eye girl do that." She pushed him out through the swinging door.

He looked at the cigarette and put its wetness to his lips. Then he stubbed it out and carefully put the butt in his shirt pocket. Back at the base, he would find a plastic bag. For three weeks he would take it out now and then and kiss it, a charm against her countrymen. After that he would need luck of a different kind.

• • •

Spider retrieved his M16 and left Suzy Wong's. He drifted up and down the main drag, half asleep in the warm afterglow but not worried about pickpockets, since he'd managed to find a belt and so kept his wallet cinched up tight against his abdomen. It would be a while before he realized that children, presumably, had stolen two magazines of ammunition from his pockets while he ambled from window to window.

They were everywhere, from little knee-high tykes to wary, serious boys around ten or eleven. Some of them offered to sell drugs or Numbah One boom-boom; one even offered the sexual services of his grandfather, whom he claimed had no teeth.

Spider amiably refused all of the offers. He wasn't surprised that there were so many children. If the average Vietnamese woman was a tenth as sexy as Li, she'd be pregnant all the time.

He came to an alley and his reverie was suddenly broken. In the corner of his eye he saw a VC in black pajamas raise an AK47. He hit the dirt—children scattering like panicked chickens—cocked his ineffective weapon and brought it up to aim, but just before he could yank the trigger his target grinned and disappeared. Its lipless smile was from the face of the decapitated corpse.

Spider stood up slowly, brushed himself off, and ostentatiously cleared the round from the chamber. It was in there at the expected angle, harmless to any VC, real or imaginary.

An Army MP came running up, brandishing his .45. Spider waved him off. "Nothin'. Just a ghost."

The MP peered down the dark alley. "You guys and your fuckin' ghosts. Just leave 'em back in the fuckin' boonies, okay?" He replaced the pistol in its holster with a loud snap and strode away, erect.

Spider studied the shadowy passage. Random garbage, nothing that bore the remotest resemblance to a man in black pajamas. Nothing big enough to hide behind. "I'm crackin' up," he whispered to himself. "I am losing . . . my fucking . . . mind." He leaned against the dusty stucco and tried to force a laugh.

SHOWDOWN

Beverly did not especially like her twice-monthly Thursday night trips home for dinner. This one was especially tense. She knew her parents knew something, and had discussed it, and were waiting for the proper time to dump it on her.

"Did you catch the moon lander on TV?" she asked, making conversation. "The Surveyor?"

Her mother reached for seconds of spaghetti. "Your John would have liked that."

"Spider? Oh, yeah, I'm going to write him about it."

"That's nice. He's such a nice boy."

Actually, Mom, he's a helpless pawn in a cynical . . . oh, well. She didn't know what to say, so she tossed the salad in front of her and served herself some lettuce.

"Beverly," her father said with a tone of finality, and patted his mouth with a napkin. She looked at him.

"Dolores Hopkins says she saw you down in the Negro part of town Saturday."

"That's right." Her insides were fluttering but she knew she had to be firm now. "I told you I was doing volunteer work weekends."

"You said it was the Red Cross," her mother said plaintively.

"No, I didn't say what it was. I said I was still doing volunteer work, and you assumed that since it was the Red Cross last summer, it's still—"

"Don't get smart with your mother, young lady."

"I'm working for Martin Luther King—"

"Oh, *God*!" her father said.

"—and he doesn't have any offices out in the suburbs. Don't you believe in Negro equality?"

"Of course we do, dear, but—"

"He's just a goddamned rabble-rouser! Those people are too impatient already, and he's firin' 'em up to march on Washington."

"Someone has to get Johnson's attention."

"Those niggers are gonna get more attention than they want."

"Murray, don't—"

"Negroes, then. Nee-groes. It's like nobody remembers the Veterans' march. Those guys were real heroes, with real grievances, and they got nothin' but lumps."

"You don't think the Negroes have real grievances?"

"Don't you twist my words around, young lady. She saw you with a boy."

"What?"

"Dolores Hopkins," her mother translated. "When she saw you, you were with a boy."

"Well? Was *he* a Negro?"

"No, thank God. But he was a hippy; hair as long as a girl's. Is he who you're shackin' up with?"

"Murray!"

"Well, I call a spade a spade."

"Or a *nigger*!" Beverly said.

There was a heavy, crawling silence. "You are living with him," her father said. "Or with somebody."

"I went by your dorm three times last week," her mother said, "and you weren't there. Finally I asked one of the girls, and she said you're living out in Chillum with this, this, man with the long hair."

"Chillum Heights," Beverly said. "It's not Chillum."

Her mother started crying. "And you feel good about this?" her father said. She just looked at him, nostrils flaring.

"Do you . . . love him?"

"Maybe I do, Mother, I—"

"Maybe?"

"Murray! Let her *talk!*" The novelty of her mother raising her voice stunned her father into silence.

"Mother, I'm not sure of anything. He's a good man; he's very kind and gentle, and when I'm around him I just feel like, I feel like nothing I've ever felt before. Maybe it's love."

"Maybe," her father said.

Her mother dabbed at her eyes. "Have you told John?"

"No. I feel bad about him. I didn't—"

"You should feel bad, God damn it. He's man enough to serve his country—"

"He was *drafted!*" Beverly threw down her napkin and spoke right into her father's face, almost shouting. "He didn't want to go! When they wouldn't take him for the Peace Corps he talked about shooting his toe off so they'd turn him down! Did you know that?"

"Don't give me any of your—"

"I won't give you anything. And you don't give me anything either." She turned and ran out of the dining room, knocking her chair over in the process. While she was gathering her clothes and books, her father ranted about Don't set foot inside this house until you're ready to straighten up, and her mother was saying We have to talk, we have to talk, and even as she slammed the door behind her she realized she had left behind her only hat and gloves. She slid into the frigid car and ground the engine into life, shouted Fuck! six times and popped the clutch, laying ten feet of rubber in front of her parents' house, pointing toward Chillum Heights, where Negroes lived.

LOVE LETTER

January 11th

Dear Spider,

I just had a real knock-down drag-out fight with Dad. He found out that I'm doing volunteer work for Martin Luther King—the Poor People's March I told you about—and boy did he blow his stack! His little girl working in the same room as NIGGERS! I couldn't reason with him, I just walked out.

You remember Peggy Radnor, who was my roommate first semester last year? She's preggers! She doesn't want to say who the guy is. (I bet she doesn't know. Let's see, was it the football team or the soccer team or the Glee Club?)

Bobby Kennedy says he's not going to run this time. I'm disappointed, but I guess it's a smart move. No matter what any candidate says about the war, whichever side he's on, there's a million people waiting to jump down his throat.

Well, no. I guess I'd be happier if he went ahead and put his money where his mouth is. God, I sound like my Father!

I watched the Surveyor 10 land on the moon, which was exciting. It landed near Tycho—when they showed a picture of it from space, I remembered it from looking through your telescope. They call it tee-ko, though, not tie-ko like we did. It sure looks weird from ground level. I'll find the picture that was in the paper yesterday.

Bottom of the page and I better study for Botany. But I'm still so pissed off at Dad I don't know if I can think straight.

Love,

Beverly

THE ARMY AND THE WHORES

If Spider had come to Vietnam a year or so earlier, he wouldn't have had to go all the way into Pleiku for sex. At that time there was a village, or at least a ramshackle assemblage of huts, on the other side of the barbed wire from Camp Enari, called Sin City. It was mostly whorehouses and bars, with a couple of souvenir shops thrown in just in case the soldiers had some money left over.

It was a dump, inarguably, but it was also a safe place for the boys to get laid, on two counts.

One was venereal disease: the girls were regularly inspected and certified by Army doctors. Of course if the fellow who came before you, so to speak, had clap or gleets, you were liable to come down with a dose, but it was safer than the city.

Likewise with murder. There certainly were Viet Cong sympathizers in Sin City—they probably outnumbered the ones who approved of the American "presence"—but at least they weren't heavily armed.

Sin City got bulldozed to the ground, so the story goes, because of mothers. The upper-case Army loves mothers, the flag, and apple pie, but the lower-case army thinks that mothers are a hindrance. In the case of Sin City, somebody wrote his mother about the goings-on there, and she wrote angry letters to a bunch of politicians, who leaned on the generals, who leaned on the colonels, who leaned on the majors, who ordered the sergeants-major to have their boys fire up the bulldozers. So the women and girls who worked Sin City moved back into town, where they didn't have to put up with the doctors' probings. They had fewer customers, but charged more.

Toward the end of January, Spider would develop syphilis chancres on his lip and anus, both of them courtesy of the *Treponema pallidum* that thrived in Li's vaginal mucosa. They would be the least of his worries.

DIFFERENT KINDS OF CRAZINESS

Spider had no luck with the supply sergeant back at Camp Enari. Standing in front of a full rack of presumably functional M16s, he told Spider that he couldn't spare one. Spider's request for a new weapon was "in the hopper," and when a new weapon came in from Cam Ranh Bay, he would send it out to the field with the proper paperwork. When Spider asked whether he could just loan him one that worked, he patiently, sarcastically, explained how supply channels worked.

Translated, the message was that Spider had made extra work for the sergeant, and Spider would get no favors. Meanwhile, since he was back early from his pass, he automatically went on the duty roster. So for the next two hours he shoveled gravel out of a wheelbarrow onto walkways defined by staked one-by-fours. That tore open his old blisters and made him some new ones.

At six, they knocked off for chow, a stew made of beef or water buffalo—one never knew—ladled over lumpy mashed potatoes. It was ambrosia, compared to C-rations, but Spider had difficulty getting it to his mouth, his hand splayed like a claw, the spoon's handle awkwardly inserted between his first and second fingers. The claw fit more naturally around a can of cold beer, he found, so he sat in the EM Club for about twelve of them, feeding quarter slugs to the jukebox, playing Beatles tunes. He wound up drinking with Morrison, who had been smart enough to stay downtown and take a cab back, getting in too late to go on duty.

It's a good thing they were together, because it was unlikely that either one of them could have found his way back to the strange billet alone. A combination of remembered landmarks and dumb luck got them back to their hard bunks, where they crashed so solidly they slept through a general alarm and some light incoming, two rockets and ten mortars; hardly enough to stop dreaming for.

The next morning, Spider followed Morrison's lead and feigned indifference about the attack, but privately vowed that he would never drink that much again, even in the supposed safety of base camp. It's like they said. There were no front lines in this war. Charlie was everywhere.

They walked to the helipad pretty well loaded down, each of them with two chain saws and a can of gasoline as well as their normal load and stuff from Pleiku. The powers that be had decided that the Army needed a fire base on the hill they had left a couple of days before. Morrison said it was stupid; they obviously had all the area covered anyhow. There was probably an extra artillery unit embarrassing everybody by standing around with no work to do.

...

The next week was uneventful except for hard labor, which was a pleasant alternative to walking around the jungle being a target. The engineers dug a semipermanent bunker, deep enough to stand up in, the top insulated with eight layers of sandbags. They dug shelves in the underground walls, long enough for their air mattresses. Most people preferred to sleep out in the open, near the entrance to the bunker, but when the monsoon season started it would rain day and night for weeks on end, and their roof would be a coveted luxury.

Spider found that he enjoyed lumberjacking. He learned how to predict where a tree wanted to fall by the distribution of mass in its limbs, and how to aim it by proper placement of the initial cut. They used explosives to bring down the largest trees, several at a time, which was good clean destructive fun.

Charlie pretty much left them alone, though they assumed they were being watched all the time. One night a sniper fired a dozen blind rounds at them. It was over in less than a minute; no one could tell where the sniper had been or where the bullets had hit. The engineers were drafted into a "sweep" the next morning, along with a rifle platoon, searching the ground outside the perimeter for brass. They didn't find any, which was a relief. Nobody knew what they'd be ordered to do if they had found the guy's position, but it probably wouldn't have been a matter of "Okay, come on back."

Spider got mail from home and had time to write long letters to Beverly and his parents. It felt strange not to be able to write about the thing uppermost in his mind. He thought about Li day and night; on the edge of sleep she would come and clasp him with her legs or mouth. She stalked his dreams and even appeared sometimes during the day, a more pleasant apparition than the other ones, who also made regular appearances.

He wondered whether to tell a doctor about the hallucinations, which often seemed as real as the people and things around him. They would probably accuse him of shamming and put him on a lurp team. That was LRRP, for Long Range Reconnaissance Patrol, people who went out in groups of four and five, looking for trouble and usually finding it. In some divisions these were all-volunteer, made up of gung-ho types who loved action. In Spider's, being assigned to a LRRP team was punishment, sometimes capital, for cowardice, insubordination, or laziness.

Spider decided he could live with the hallucinations for the time being. The one of Li was pleasant, and the others were just startling, now. He'd always had an overactive imagination, according to his parents, and he reasoned that this was just his brain's way of dealing with a difficult situation. There were probably lots of guys with the same problem, who didn't want to say anything about it because they didn't want people to think they were crazy.

But what if they, and he, actually were?

Spider suspected that wondering whether you were crazy was a pretty good indicator that you weren't. He hadn't read much about psychology, which he now regretted, but he was pretty sure that crazy people thought they were sane.

FOURTH WEEK

January 21st

Dear Mom and Dad,

Well, I never thought I'd be glad to be out in the field rather than in base camp. But nothing's been happening out here at all, and the base camps are getting kicked. Pleiku was hit last night, the airfield and the hospital. We could barely see the light, over the horizon from the hill here. Lotsa fireworks. Too far away to hear anything.

I think maybe the last letter you got from me was when I was in Pleiku. Camp Enari, which is where the hospital is that got hit. Don't worry, in case you read about this attack in the papers. I'm not there anymore. But I guess you'll read about it before you get this letter, duh.

I finished the Heinlein book you sent. It was really fine. Any other Heinlein would be appreciated, even if I've read it before. I traded it for a Philip K. Dick book, which is also science fiction but pretty weird.

Also, could you try to find a paperback introduction to psychology? Think I'll take a few courses in it when I go back to school.

Lumberjacking is the first thing I've learned in the army that's actually kind of fun. These rubber trees, you really have to work on them. Even with a chain saw it can take an hour to drop one. It's a real feeling of power. But I don't think it's something I would want to go into, peacetime. They say the pay's pretty high, but chain saws aren't the safest things to work with. And I almost got hit by a tree yesterday. Moses was working uphill from me, he yelled TIMBER! but I couldn't hear him because I had a chain saw roaring in front of me, natch. So this big rubber tree comes crashing down about ten feet away, scared the beJesus out of me!

So maybe I should look for a line of work where you use a pencil instead of a chain saw.

You know what the lumberjack stuff reminds me of, though? Pancakes. One of the first books I can remember Mom reading to me from was about lumberjacks and the big stacks of pancakes they ate. Then she taught me how to make pancakes on the griddle. I remember standing on the piano bench, turning them.

I think about food alot for some reason…

Linda wrote me about Uncle Terry killing himself. That's awful. But I guess he's always been a little crazy, even before Aunt Phyllis left. The note he sent with the Christmas present knife was about how he'd left his own knife in a Korean "gook." From what Dad said that couldn't be true, he was never actually in the war zone. But he was crazy by the time he got out of the army anyhow. (That goes along with what people here say, though, and my own impressions, too. The guys back in base camp are alot crazier than us out here.)

Beverly's writing me almost every day. I miss her so much.

Love,

John

P.S. Supposed to be a big truce next week, for the Vietnamese Tet holiday. I'll believe it when I see it.

•••

January 24th

Dear Spider,

I'm sorry it's been so long since I last wrote you. Beginning of school and all. Every professor piles on the reading like you didn't have any other courses.

God, the world is going crazy! You don't get any news, you say, so maybe you don't know about the H-Bombs and the Pueblo.

The H-Bombs were yesterday. A B-52 bomber crashed in the ocean off Greenland yesterday with four live H-Bombs aboard! What was it doing over Greenland anyhow?

The Pueblo was this morning. That's the name of a Navy ship, evidently a spy ship, that cruised into North Korean territory and the Communists seized it. The government says it was in neutral territory, and they want to send troops in to get it back. My friend Lee says it was a setup, an excuse to broaden the war. I usually think stuff like that is paranoid, but this time maybe it's true.

I wonder whether your mail gets opened, speaking of paranoid. In WWII they censored mail with a razor blade. If you don't get this letter, write and tell me!

Let's see, what other subversive stuff in the paper. Lyndon Johnson is as good an art collector as he is a president. One of the paintings he brought to the White House has been hanging upside down all this time.

I'm glad you're not farther north. It looks like the Marines are in for a hard time up by the DMZ, in a place called Khe Sanh. They're surrounded by

11,000 NVA soldiers. It's just a few days till the New Year's truce, but someone on TV said that the NVA would probably use that time to sneak more people and supplies in.

I guess the only good news is that they orbited that lunar module, the thing that the astronauts are going to use to go back and forth between the moon and their capsule. That's going to be exciting!

I'd better get back to my exciting history. It's so revelant ...
Love,
Beverly

TET 1968

The 1968 Tet Offensive had a lot in common with Japan's World War II surprise attack on Pearl Harbor. Both attacks were expected by the Americans, sooner or later, but nevertheless caught the Americans unprepared; both were the most significant turning points of their wars. But Pearl Harbor was an unqualified success for the Japanese, which ultimately led to their defeat; Tet was a total disaster for the Vietnamese, which ultimately led to their victory.

In both cases, this was because of changing civilian attitudes rather than strictly military factors. Pearl Harbor galvanized an America most of whom were already spoiling for a fight. Tet further demoralized an America that was getting ready to quit.

You couldn't ignore the pictures. Pearl Harbor's mighty ships helplessly sinking in billows of smoke; the Army Air Corps destroyed on the tarmac while Jap Zeros buzzed at treetop level, strafing civilians and military alike. American MPs cowering inside Saigon's American Embassy, American boys dead at their feet; the televised offhand execution of a handcuffed prisoner—by *our side*! The real-time interviews with confused, dog-tired GIs. All the American blood, in living color.

Tet became a symbol, in some quarters, for the hopelessness of continuing the war. But the NVA and Viet Cong had been soundly defeated in a desperate all-out attack, with 33,000 dead before the campaign slowly fizzled out. The 1500 American dead would have a greater political impact.

STRATEGY

"What you *mean*," Batman said, "is that we get to spend this truce settin' in some ambush out in the boonies." Spider had the sinking feeling that he would be part of the "we."

Sarge had come over to collect three engineers. "No, not really, not all of us. We just quietly set up a position and if Charles breaks the truce, we send out two squads to watch over the trails headed here." He sat down on the edge of the engineers' bunker and opened a beer. "I volunteered for it, Home," he said softly.

Batman squinted at him. "No shit."

"Look around." He gestured with the can. "This place ain't got shit. We got no fifties, no recoilless, and you know we been watched from day one. Charlie wants to break the truce, he gonna hit here first, take out the one-five-fives. He gonna wipe our ass."

"Jus' hold it," Batman said. "Don't Charlie have to come by your ambush on the way up? I mean, he wipe your ass *first*. Then he come up here and finish the job."

"You ain't thinkin' it through, bro." He took a drink and displayed about a hundred white teeth. "They ain't gonna fuck with no little ambush. Gonna know where we are and *avoid* us!"

Moses was sitting next to Spider. "Sounds screwy to me, Sarge. What you're saying is you make a lot of noise setting up the ambush—"

"A little more than usual, maybe."

"Okay. Why doesn't he hit you then, though?"

"We set it up early, before it gets dark. Charlie ain't gonna fuck with us in the daytime." He pointed at the ground. "Gonna hit here after midnight. Midnight tomorrow."

"During the truce?"

"Fuckin' A. Truce don't mean shit to Charlie."

"I don't know," Batman said. "I guess one place just as bad as the other, Charlie decide to fight."

"Up here, they'd give you more air support," Spider said. "Wouldn't they? Protect the guns."

"Of course they would, my man," Sarge said. "And more artillery support. But that's what I'm sayin'. I don't wanta be here when they need all that shit! Be in some little pissant ambush a couple miles away."

"But if they hit the ambush—"

"They got no reason to, like I say."

"Ah, you fulla shit, Sarge," Batman said good-naturedly. "I'll go along with it, though."

"What, you fulla shit, too?"

"Yeah. This place too quiet, been too quiet too long. 'Bout time it got hit."

"I'll go along with you too," Moses said. They all looked at Spider.

He had a bad feeling about it. The eight layers of sandbags on top of that bunker felt like a secure investment. "Think I'll wait till Killer gets back." He was on a sump detail on the other side of the hill, digging a garbage pit. "Flip him for it."

Sarge looked at his watch. "Better go settle with him now. Wanta hump in about an hour."

Spider considered it for a second. "Aw hell. Count me in." He figured he'd just lose the toss anyhow.

LOVE LETTER

Beverly and Lee came back from their volunteer work exhausted but happy. They'd been called in early that Sunday morning, the 28th of January, because of King's "go for broke" speech in Atlanta. He said he intended for the April Drive for the Poor to "escalate nonviolence to the level of civil disobedience." Poor people camping on the Mall, on the White House lawn unless Johnson kicked them off. The office wanted all hands on deck to deal with the press. Lee's strong and undeniably Caucasian telephone voice was an asset with certain kinds of callers.

Her old roommate Sherry had come by earlier but couldn't stay. She left behind a stack of mail, mostly junk but also a dirt-stained letter from Spider. The last one, from Pleiku, had been clean. "Well, he's out in the boonies again," she said. He'd known he would only be in base camp for a couple of days, though.

They said hello to a foursome of people they vaguely knew, who were sitting on the couch smoking dope, and went into the kitchen for a snack. They were alone with a half-eaten pizza. Lee picked up a guitar and strummed quietly.

She opened the letter and read some of it to Lee, interesting stuff about lumberjacking and the various kinds of ants and mantises he'd observed. She didn't read him romantic or horny parts, by prior agreement.

"He seems pretty up," she said after the first page. "Maybe it's time I told him about us. At least start hinting."

Lee munched on cold pizza. "I wouldn't. By the time he gets the letter, who knows how he'll feel?"

She scanned the second page. "Oh shit."

"Oh?" He set the pizza down and wiped his fingers. "Bad news."

"He wants me to meet him for R&R. 'Rest and Recreation,' in Hawaii, this spring. For a week."

"Well, hell. What's that, five hundred bucks?" He struggled with the cork in a wine bottle, but his fingers were too slippery. "You and I together couldn't buy a ticket to Philadelphia."

"Shit. Oh, shit."

"What?"

"He wrote to dear old Dad. *My* father! He says he'd be *glad* to pay my way. A no-interest loan until he gets out."

"Oh, now, that's cool. That really sucks." He used a paper napkin for traction and the cork came out with a loud pop. He got up to rinse out a couple of glasses. "Forces the issue."

"He asked his own family, but they don't have any money. He apologizes for not clearing it with me first. 'But your Dad and I always got along so well.' Jesus! I wonder what the old bastard told him."

"Probably nothing. What's he gonna say? 'Your girlfriend's fucking a hippy and I think you ought to try to talk her out of it'?"

She took the tumbler of wine he handed her. "I do have to write him. Write my father, too, about what a big help he is to our boys overseas."

They both watched silently as one of the dopers shuffled, lost in thought, through the kitchen and out the back door, which led to nothing but a fenced-in yard of junk. Probably wanted to take a leak in the rain. Organic.

"Don't be too quick to tell Spider everything. Blow his mind."

"So what should I tell him?" She set the glass down without tasting it. "Say I'm having an argument with Dad; you can't borrow money from him? What should I tell him we're arguing about?"

"You could just tell him it sounds like a great idea."

"Go to Hawaii?"

"Tell him that, yeah."

"Maybe I should just go and give him a good *fuck*ing," she said, voice rising, as the doper returned through the door. He looked at them both and walked seriously back into the living room.

"If that's what you want."

"Want? What do you mean by that?"

"I don't own you."

"You mean you don't *love* me."

"I mean it's your body. You have to make your own decisions."

She stood up, gripping the edge of the table. "And what would you decide to do with your body, while I was away? Hmm?" He didn't reply; didn't change expression.

"Jesus!" She yanked her coat off the back of the chair and rushed out of the kitchen, through the sweet smoke, out into the cold drizzle. She walked hatless the mile into town, at first crying and then just furious. She stopped at a drug store for a box of stationery, and took it into the all-night doughnut shop.

With every version of the letter she bought a cup of coffee and a different kind of doughnut. Cream-filled, jelly-filled, glazed, dusted.

Cream-filled: everything, the awful truth. The sex, the lies.

Jelly-filled: Yes, I'll come to Hawaii, I can't wait to see you again.

Glazed: I need time to think; things have become complicated.

Dusted: Only if I can raise the money myself; I can't take money from

Dad; don't ask me why.

She had a mad impulse to put each letter in an envelope and mail one at random, and then open the others to see what her future would be. Instead, she got a glass of milk and a fried apple pie and wrote this one:

Dear, dear Spider,

Your letter about Hawaii comes at a difficult time for me, and for us. I'm not speaking to my father, because of an argument a few weeks ago, and he didn't consult me about his offer.

The argument was over a man I'm seeing, who Dad calls a "hippy." I thought I was falling in love with him, but now I don't know. I'm confused by everything.

So I don't know how I'll feel when your R&R comes. I would love to see you then, but it might be just as a friend rather than your girlfriend.

I would rather raise the money myself, too. I don't want to cost you extra and I don't want anything from my father.

I'm sorry. I've been wanting to write you about this for awhile, but I guess it was just easier to lie a little bit and keep from hurting you, and me. But I don't want you to build up hopes and then have a big disaster happen in Hawaii. Your very best friend,
Beverly

She read it over several times and then sealed it and stamped it. She hurried outside, suddenly afraid she was going to throw up, but getting out of the stuffy, smoky atmosphere into the clean cold settled her stomach.

It settled her mind, too. She had thought hard about going back to the dorm. Instead, she would go back to Lee and have it out with him.

So it was with mixed feelings — regret but determination — that she opened the mouth of the mailbox, set the letter inside, and let it slam shut. She had never written a letter before that she knew would actually change her life.

It wouldn't change Spider's life, though. He would never see it.

MISCALCULATIONS

Spider's rucksack was too heavy. Ten C-ration meals, five extra hand grenades and a smoke grenade, two extra sticks of C-4 besides the demo bag. Ten cans of beer and soda and three books. An extra gallon of water clipped to the packframe with a D-ring. Three M16 magazines, besides the two taped back-to-back that the rifle already carried, and three hundred more rounds in cardboard boxes. At least they were for Sarge's M16, which presumably worked. He'd be leaving his own behind. Killer would DX it if they had to evacuate the hill.

In which case, Spider would be stranded out in the boonies with Sarge and his gang, with no fire base to go back to. It was not something you wanted to dwell on.

He sat in the heat smoking, making a list of all this extra stuff as part of a letter to Beverly. Hurry up and wait. Sarge had said they were leaving in an hour. That was three hours ago. The spaghetti he'd had for lunch grumbled in his stomach; made him queasy in the heat. He opened a warm Coke to quiet it down.

Sarge came down the hill from the shade of the Command Group bunkers. "Fuckin' shit," he said, "go on back to your areas. They want us stayin' here tonight, four-on-four-off. Hump out tomorrow."

"Think we'll get hit tonight?" Spider said.

"Guess that's what they think. Ain't nothin' gonna happen." He stretched and yawned. "Bet your ass they turn it into full alert, though. Gonna catch some Z's."

"Good idea." Spider dragged his junk back up to the bunker and collapsed.

• • •

On the other side of the world, Beverly's morning paper was being delivered, with the secondary headline SAIGON TAKES ON HOLIDAY AIR AS TET ARRIVES.

American intelligence was pretty sure something was about to happen, possibly right after Tet. Enemy troops were massing around the Marine base at Khe Sanh, and on the eve of the truce they struck hard at support bases that supplied Khe Sanh and served to protect it with artillery crossfire.

Lyndon Johnson was worried—some say obsessed—by the potential similarity of Khe Sanh to Dien Bien Phu thirteen years before. At that time it was the French who had faced the Vietnamese across a conference table, both sides needing a decisive military victory for political leverage. The Communists laid siege to Dien Bien Phu and crushed the French, winning independence and undermining French influence all over the world. Could it happen again, with Americans across the conference table?

Lyndon Johnson had been a member of the Senate Armed Services Committee, and had advised against helping the French save the beleaguered base. That was 1954. In 1968, he vowed that Khe Sanh was not going to be "no goddamned Dien Bien Phu," and went so far as to secure a written guarantee from the Joint Chiefs of Staff that the base would not be abandoned.

On January 20th, one Lieutenant La Than Tonc defected from the enemy with detailed information about their plans for Khe Sanh. He said, accurately, that the attack was going to begin that night, and was going to build up to an all-out assault during Tet—turning the base into a second Dien Bien Phu, a final humiliating defeat for the Americans.

The Americans responded by throwing everything they had at the enemy besiegers, committing 2000 fixed-wing aircraft and 3000 helicopters to the defense of the base. B-52s dropped 75,000 tons of bombs, turning the surrounding territory into a lunar wasteland.

But when Tet came around, the enemy ignored Khe Sanh. It had evidently been a feint intended to draw American forces away from the cities to the south. Instead, a combined force of 100,000 NVA and VC troops infiltrated over a hundred cities and towns, cleverly using the holiday confusion as a cover, and attacked more or less simultaneously. People in Saigon and Hue and Long Binh thought they were listening to fireworks. Then they saw the muzzle flashes.

It was all very dramatic and bloody, and would ultimately lead to the curious combination of crippling military defeat and ambiguous political victory described earlier. American television would be full of compelling pictures of Saigon in flames, of panicked civilians fleeing Hue as determined Marines marched in. For Stateside newswatchers, it was not evident that the regular war was still going on. But there were still small units out in the bush, waiting to engage other small units.

As the sun came up on January 30th, while anxious Marines scanned the perimeter at Khe Sanh, while a hundred thousand enemy troops studied their infiltration routes, Spider shouldered his heavy pack after a sleepless night—not only full alert, but the 155s booming constantly a couple of hours before dawn—and followed Sarge down the trail that led to the little creek.

•••

Spider didn't have enough hands, or enough shoulders. The M16 was slung so that it rested pointing forward at elbow level, so you could snatch it and fire. You kept one hand on it. He had an axe in the other hand. The awkward demolition bag was slung over that shoulder, and it would beat against his ribs as he walked, unless he steadied it with the hand holding the axe. So he had a sort of stooped-over, old-man way of walking. He had enough firepower to knock out a phalanx of Roman centurions, but he didn't feel very dangerous. He felt sorry for himself.

It was easier going once they got to the stream. Rather than ascending the hill where Spider had started to see things that weren't there, they turned right and followed the meandering streambed, roughly in the direction of the road that connected Kontum and Dak To. Spider knew they wouldn't go as far as the road, though. They'd be cutting northwest for about a mile to a hillock where they'd establish a patrol base. From there they'd set out two ambush teams, which would presumably have nothing to do but wait out the truce. Maybe watch the fire base get hit.

It made Spider nervous to leave behind the security of the bunker, but Sarge was right about the fire base being underdefended. Half the infantry there were FNGs, unblooded, sent in a bunch from Kontum to give the fire base the regulation number of support troops.

After about an hour, they stopped to rotate positions. Sarge wanted to stay on point in the center column, so Spider walked back to take up the rear. Better than walking point, he supposed, but only just. At least he was able to pass the demo bag to Moses, which lightened his step. It was only about twelve pounds, but the box of blasting caps inside carried a lot of psychic weight.

They started moving forward again. They'd gone less than a hundred yards when Spider heard something behind him. He twirled, and there was a man not twenty feet away—but he was the death's-head ghost, grinning.

What would happen if he fired at it? Maybe it would go away forever. Spider thumbed the selector switch past SEMI to AUTO. The apparition disappeared.

"What is it?" a guy to his left whispered. "See something?"

"Thought I heard something," Spider said, and turned around to continue walking. He swore that nothing would make him look back.

A NEW DAY DAWNS

Beverly almost slept through the alarm. Seven o'clock. Monday was a bad day, an 8:00 math class to pay for the sins of the weekend. She hit the plastic bar that gave her a ten-minute "snooze" delay, knowing that it probably meant another parking ticket. Her sticker spot, Lot EE, was out somewhere in Carroll County—since of course she supposedly lived in a dorm and walked to class—so she had to park illegally or hike a mile to the math building. But if she didn't get an extra ten minutes now, she'd get it during the algebra lecture.

Lee got out of bed quietly and went downstairs to put on the water, as he did every Monday, Wednesday, and Friday. It had been a long night of whispered argument, recrimination, tears. The fact that it had ended with love-making didn't mean that it was resolved.

What did she want from him? Did she really *know* what she wanted? Was he really any less confused than she was?

She wanted him to demonstrate his love for her by "staying true," but not because sexual fidelity was morally right. She agreed that it was bourgeois ownership of women, a shackle. It was a sacrifice she wanted him to make for the time being, until she got her head straight.

But how long would that be? Besides, it was almost a non-issue; he *had* been true to her ever since they first made love—except for one little blow-job, which didn't really count; he hadn't even known her name. (Beverly did, unfortunately.)

Part of it was obviously her distress over having to make a decision about Spider. She said she didn't love him anymore, except like a brother. Lee told her that she was still confused by the illusions of romance, that only allowed her to admit erotic love for one person at a time. But that was his rational side speaking, and it didn't seem as strong an argument as it used to. He was in some version of love, too.

He heard the upstairs toilet flush and checked his watch. She'd have to run to make class. He found her large Redskins mug and made her a double coffee with milk and sugar, feeling expertly domestic (she only used milk in the first cup of the morning), and put some bread in the toaster. It popped up just as she came running down the stairs, pulling on her coat.

She looked pretty awful, puffy eyes, no makeup except a slash of lipstick, hair hurriedly tucked into a cap. She thanked him for the coffee and slice of toast and gave him a little peck, and then a hug and a sloppy kiss. Juggling bookbag and toast and coffee, she opened the front door and slid the morning paper inside with her toe. She looked down at the headline.

"Tet," she said. "Maybe at least Spider will get some rest."

THE FIRST VERSION

This is what Spider would say:

After we turned north the going got easier. We were temporarily out of the hills, in some kind of a wooded basin. It felt safer. I guess we got careless. We shouldn't have followed the trail. They were waiting for us.

First there was a single shot, a loud *crack* like a stick breaking. It was still echoing by the time I hit the dirt. Then someone's M16 emptied a full magazine—a half-second rip of pop-pop-pops—and a heavy machinegun, theirs, started to chatter. Short bursts from AK47s both left and right. Then grenades every couple of seconds. We started shooting back. It was obscenely, impossibly loud, an unrelenting terrifying racket, but I could still hear the soft hum and whisper of bullets and shrapnel flying over my head.

I slid out of the pack and got behind it, pissing in spasms. The M16 was useless; I had jammed the muzzle into the dirt on the way down. I slid the cleaning rod out but my hands were shaking so hard I couldn't find the button to break the weapon open.

But I wasn't supposed to shoot anyhow. Not until I saw the whites of their eyes. That meant something now. I dug down into the pack and found two grenades and put them in front of me.

It got louder somehow. Sarge was yelling for the A team to fall back, fall back. Two people were screaming for medics. I found the button on the M16 but nothing happened when I pushed it. It wouldn't go down. I tried pushing hard on it with the bottom rim of a grenade; it wouldn't pop.

I saw the RTO Morrison get hit. A bullet or something hit his steel pot and knocked it off. He put his hand up to his head and it came back bloody and stringy. He fell over sideways, I suppose dead. Sarge lowcrawled back to shout into the radio. He had been hit in the butt and was bleeding pretty hard. He kept twirling the little generator handle on the radio. I don't think it was working.

A black guy I didn't know came squirming by on his back, no weapon or helmet, screaming for a medic. He was holding up his right arm, broken in two below the wrist, blood fountaining out of an artery.

But I didn't really lose it until I saw Moses explode. Moses and another guy were running back toward me—or sort of running, scrunched down—when something must have hit the demo bag. There was a yellow flash and a dull *whack* sound, and then just gray smoke and red mist. His legs were intact, and they rolled off to the left and right.

I threw the rifle down and got up and ran away. Actually, I ran about three steps and smacked my forehead into a low-hanging tree limb. The universe went all ink and stars and I fell over backwards.

A CALCULUS OF DEATH (1)

The day that Spider ran in panic and knocked himself out on a tree limb was, Stateside, a day of bizarre harmony: the U.S. Army and the Association of University Professors agreed on something.

The year before, the Selective Service had democratically decreed that being admitted to graduate school was no longer adequate grounds for draft deferment. They hadn't thought it through.

With only women and physically handicapped males to draw from, the population of graduate programs was dropping precipitously all over the country. Many schools would not survive the loss of tuition income. Many academic departments would die for lack of junior members. It was a disaster.

It was also shaping up to be a disaster for the Army. They needed under-educated nineteen-year-olds. You could slap them around for a few weeks in Basic Training, then hand them a gun and say Go Kill People, and most of them would do it. College graduates were "harder to handle; more resentful." They also tended to upset the illiterate nineteen-year-olds by discussing options that were incompatible with the Army's plans for them, like desertion.

When Spider was drafted, only five percent of draftees had been college graduates. That was already too many. Next year, the percentage might be as high as sixty-seven percent—recalcitrant, sarcastic, conniving readers and thinkers, whose presence would destroy the Army's infrastructure, even while their absence was destroying the university's infrastructure.

The problem was all of those voters who saw the lopsided deferment system in terms of wealth and privilege, rather than the pragmatic business of trainability that it actually was. So the politicians wrapped themselves, collectively, in a fresh flag and appealed to old-fashioned American values of fairness and instituted the draft lottery, which brought the proportion of disgruntled college graduates back down to a manageable level.

Spider would have liked a lottery, but it came about a year too late.

RUDE AWAKENING

He had never had a headache like this one. It sang through his eyes and all the way to the base of his skull. The skin on his forehead stung and it felt like there was blood crusted there. He started to raise his hand to touch it but heard a noise. Pop. Then another pop.

He opened his eyes to slits and turned his head microscopically in the direction of the noise. About twenty yards away, a tall Vietnamese in black pajamas was walking around with a rifle, studying the ground. When he came to a body, pop. He shot it in the head. Just making sure. The one Spider watched was alive enough to raise one arm in feeble protest. Then pop, and the Vietnamese chattered angrily at the man he'd killed.

Spider closed his eyes and lay still. Maybe he wouldn't see him over here. Running was out of the question.

The rifle shots grew louder. Maybe he could actually run. There was only one of them. Maybe he would miss, maybe he would run out of ammunition. But Spider probably couldn't even stand up and walk.

Just stick it out. Maybe he's not shooting everyone. If you look real dead, he might walk by.

His urethral and anal sphincters were fluttering, threatening to make his last act an embarrassing one.

An ant crawled up on his neck and stung him.

He heard the footsteps. He tried not to breathe.

The muzzle of the rifle was hot on his forehead. He opened his eyes to look at his executioner.

He was neither young nor old. He looked Chinese. There was an abrasion on one high cheekbone. His eyes were red, and deeply sunk in lines of worry or fatigue.

He tilted his head to an odd angle, and blinked. Spider squeezed his eyes shut, waiting to die. The man said nine odd syllables, as if he were counting, and then lifted the muzzle and stepped away.

PERCHANCE TO DREAM

Beverly could not concentrate on matrices. Determinants. You had one that was just a bunch of random numbers, and so you multiplied it by another, that had ones all down the diagonal. She stared at it and nothing happened. Nothing got into her brain.

She was mad and confused about Lee and her crotch hurt, her labia, because he had been too forceful last night, this morning, and her body had listened to her heart and withheld lubrication. She was about two days away from her period, and that didn't help anything. She tended to feel grouchy and helpless this time of the month, and being able to predict it made it worse.

She remembered the ignorant pawings with Spider. He was so clumsy and sweet. They hadn't known anything except "you rub this long enough and she starts to moan; you rub this long enough and he spurts." But it had been exciting to discover stuff that way, to piece together a sexual self-awareness partly out of what other people said, partly from the veiled descriptions in books, partly from the shy fumblings with one another. She didn't feel guilty about Lee, not really, but it was sad that she'd learned so much so fast. It might have been nicer to work it out slowly with Spider.

She felt a cold prickling of sweat on the small of her back, from guilt? Poor Spider. That letter he'd written about never having any privacy, he obviously meant masturbation. She'd never talked to him about it, and couldn't visualize him doing it to himself, even though she'd watched Lee do it, and Lee said men would do it every day if they didn't have anything else. Well, she liked a little time to herself every now and then, even with all the sex she had with Lee. And Spider had always seemed so desperate; so impatient to come. It must be awful for him.

She crossed her legs surreptitiously and squeezed, thinking about Spider, trying to project the feeling ten thousand miles. Unfortunately, she closed her eyes.

"Beverly?" the graduate assistant said. "Would you please come to the board?"

DULCE ET DECORUM EST

Spider lay with his eyes tightly shut, listening to the man rummage through his rucksack, muttering in Vietnamese. Apparently he was alone; maybe the others had moved out because reinforcements, Americans, were coming.

Why weren't they here yet? How long had he been unconscious?

Even with the radio not working, the people at the fire base would have known they were in trouble. Or had they gone so far that the sound of gunfire wouldn't carry?

The noises stopped. Spider could visualize the man looking at him, thinking. Why hadn't he pulled the trigger; was he changing his mind? After a minute the man walked off, his footsteps growing fainter and disappearing.

Spider decided to continue playing dead. The jungle sounds returned, muted this time of day. A few birds. Wind rustling the canopy.

Tiny ants stung him on the arm and neck. He tried to ignore them by cataloguing all of his other pains. The forehead was the worst, but he had also done something to his leg, to the back of his thigh. Couldn't be a bullet wound; that would hurt more. His back ached, as always, and he had small sores in his mouth and anus that he didn't associate with Li. A persistent rash of jungle rot on the back of one hand, which didn't hurt much but looked awful, a running sore. And now a prickly kind of diaper rash from peeing on himself.

He remembered Morrison looking at a handful of his brains and dying. Moses exploding. You could see the bone in the top of his leg as the leg flew away, charred meat. Never knew what hit him, as they say. Or maybe he had known. One awful microsecond of agony as his body blew into a million pieces. Maybe he'd have to feel that for all eternity. No. That would be too awful.

Footsteps again, light, walking toward him. Don't open your eyes this time. Just let him do what he's going to do.

The footsteps stopped. There was a long minute of silence, Spider trying not to breathe. Then a sudden sharp stab of pain in his infected hand. He rolled away instinctively and looked up. A huge vulture flapped its wings and screeched at him.

The big birds were all around, six of them feeding on the bodies of his comrades. They all looked up at the sudden motion.

Kill the bastards. He looked around for his rifle, but it was gone. There was his rucksack, but no rifle, no grenades. He crawled over to it and fished around inside. The grenades and ammunition were gone, and his Randall Made Fighting Knife, but there were still some cans of pop and beer and two boxes of C-rations.

He stood up and slung the rucksack over one shoulder, staggering. The birds hopped nervously. He could see ten or twelve bodies lying around with the strange random postures dead people take. One man was sitting up, slumped over, his hands still clasped under the pile of bluish intestines he'd been holding in.

Their heads were all shattered, except for one who had no head. There was one lone leg that probably belonged to Moses. Smell of raw meat starting to spoil.

Sarge was lying on his back, the front of his shirt slick with blood, completely saturated. He had also been shot in the mouth. A man next to him was curled up in a ball with no apparent wound except for the one that had sheared off the top of his head and sprayed his brains all over the grass.

Spider vomited over and over, until nothing came out but acid mucus. Then he limped away, anywhere, just away. He knew he should look around for a weapon, but he didn't care. He didn't expect to live. He just wanted to die someplace else.

He staggered a couple of hundred yards down the trail, collapsing three times. The third time, he didn't stand up, but just dragged the rucksack and himself over to a big rubber tree. He leaned up against the tree and unclipped the water bag from the packframe. He washed his mouth out and drank some and it stayed down. Then he drank three beers in rapid succession and passed out as night began to fall. He didn't hear the rolling thunder of artillery that proclaimed the official beginning of the Tet Offensive.

Spider had always remembered two dreams from childhood, from second or third grade. In one of them, he was exploring through some woods and cautiously peeked from behind a bush and saw a glade full of prehistoric monsters. In the other, he was a soldier dying unattended on a muddy battlefield, probably Korea. Life was ebbing from him as wakefulness slips from a tired child. It felt noble and correct and terribly alone and sad.

RESCUE

The Tet Offensive started prematurely in Spider's area. The original plan had been for the nationwide attack to begin in the early morning hours of January 30th, but the powers-that-were in Hanoi called for a twenty-four-hour postponement at the last minute. A lot of the Viet Cong and NVA troops in what America called II Corps didn't get the word in time, so six cities, including Pleiku and Kontum, were infiltrated and attacked a day early, just after four in the morning, precipitating the artillery response that had helped Spider stay awake on guard duty.

That should have let the cat out of the bag, but it didn't.

The Americans declared the truce abrogated and the Army put all its troops on full alert. Most of the troops treated the alert with their usual cynicism; "maximum alert" came more often than mail. The ones in Saigon were going to be spectacularly unprepared.

The people around Pleiku and Kontum, though, did have their hands full—including, emphatically, the new fire base that covered the road between Kontum and Dak To, full of scared green troops and rattled by conflicting fire orders. Nobody was especially concerned about not having heard from Sarge's patrol.

Two days later, a very nervous squad, mostly FNGs, set off down along the streambed to find out why Sarge's patrol didn't respond to repeated radio hailing. If their radio had stopped functioning, they should at least have sent a squad back for a replacement.

They found Spider first, lying almost catatonic under the tree, whimpering. Even Killer didn't recognize him at first sight: wild-eyed, befouled, smeared all over with dried blood. He had ripped off his shirt and torn with his nails at the skin of his chest and abdomen. When they tried to help him he fought them off like a wild man and then collapsed.

From where Spider was, they could smell the rotting remains of the rest of the men. Killer blew an LZ upwind from them and a helicopter came out with two enlisted men from Graves and a stack of body bags.

At first there were two men unaccounted for. Eventually they found Moses's head in a tree about forty yards from where he had exploded. The other missing man, a rifleman who was on his second tour in Vietnam, walked into Kontum two days later. He said he'd been following orders to retreat back down the path and had gotten separated from his squad and hopelessly lost. He wandered till he found the road. He eventually went before a court martial, accused of desertion under fire, but was not convicted. The only other living witness to the action did not respond well to questioning.

To get Spider to stay on the stretcher, they'd had to bind his wrists and ankles with tape and strap him down. When he was medevac'ed he tried to throw himself from the helicopter.

The hospital in Pleiku was very busy, more civilian casualties than military, but they were able to shoot Spider full of Thorazine and clean him up enough to assess his condition. Small shrapnel wound in the left leg, superficial scratches on thorax, self-inflicted; bruise and laceration on forehead, mild concussion. The diagnosis was paranoid schizophrenia. The treatment was drugs and a straitjacket and a ticket to Walter Reed.

FEBRUARY

Walter Reed Army Medical Hospital
Psychiatric Division (Inpatient)
Preliminary Patient Assessment

Date: *2 Feb 68*
Physician in Charge: *CPT Michael Folsom for MAJ G. B. Tolliver, MD*
Patient: *E3 John Darcy Speidel US 334789213*

JDS was a combat engineer in Vietnam, one of two survivors of an ambush of a small patrol in II Corps. He was injured only slightly but the experience seems to have exacerbated a previously existing psychotic condition.

His first assignment in RVN was a clerical position in Graves Registration, Kontum. He assaulted the NCO in charge of his office and was reassigned to a field position in lieu of Article 15 proceedings or a summary court martial.

(Statements from other EMs and NCOs who knew him: "He was weird but a nice guy." "He always did what you told him to do but never seemed quite 'with it.'" "He sat around and read science fiction all the time. He was really serious about it." "He seemed all right to me but I know I'm crazy. I signed up for another year in this shit hole." These are quotes from radio interviews requested by a staff psychiatrist, handwritten on a yellow sheet appended to the patient's file from 121st Evac in Pleiku, RVN.)

The patient arrived in a comatose state, heavily sedated with Thorazine. Wounds from enemy action included a small shrapnel wound in the l. thigh, rear; fragment extracted and wound debrided and closed with five stitches, and a laceration to the forehead which required three stitches. Patient claims he was shot in the head, but that is inconsistent with the nature of the wound.

The patient also denies homosexual orientation, but presents syphilis chancres in both mouth and anus (not penis).

Self-inflicted scratches on the chest and abdomen have become infected; three stitches were necessary to close a tear to r. nipple, which has developed a local fungus infection ("jungle rot"). There is a similar fungus infection, well developed, on back of l. hand.

The patient is not yet communicating well. He was acutely agitated initially, and is alternately combative and reticent now. His medication, which on admission was 400mg Thorazine I.M. q4-6h., now stands at 500mg a day, administered orally.

JDS's file had an FBI flag. The Bureau's Military Liaison Office sent over some information that might be useful. His family and friends live in the Washington D.C. area; the flag is there because his girlfriend is involved in questionable activities related to draft resistance and Martin Luther King.

When asked whether he wanted his family to visit, JDS responded firmly in the negative. Asked about his girlfriend, he said he did want to see her "when he was better," but he called her "Lee." His girlfriend's name is Beverly, but the man she lives with is Lee Atwood, an anti-war activist who was granted a draft exemption because of well-documented homosexuality. So there may be a complex relationship involved.

THE SECOND VERSION

We were on a small patrol headed out a few miles from fire base to set up two ambush points in case Charlie violated the truce. We might just be doing recon, though. If the force was too big for us to engage, we'd let them go by and then radio their position in for artillery and air strikes. Then the idea was we were supposed to attack them on their way back, but Sarge thought it might be more sensible to first let them go on by a ways, and call in the first artillery *between* us and them, so as to have them running away from us instead.

We never got to try out that strategy, though. They were waiting for us. It was a good ambush. We walked into this clearing and they must have had us completely covered.

I was walking point when the ambush started, and one of the first rounds hit me. It must have gone through my helmet, which slowed it down enough so it knocked me out but didn't kill me. Anyhow I don't remember seeing any of the battle until it was over.

Then a gook was walking around with an AK47, that's when I woke up, he was shooting everybody left alive, or anybody who looked like he might be alive. So I closed my eyes and played dead, and he walked right up to me and then went on by. I mean I could feel the muzzle of the AK47 on my forehead, hot, but I guess he figured I was dead, so why waste a bullet?

After that, I don't know. I guess I went a little crazy.

THREE CONTRIBUTIONS TO THE THEORY OF SEX

Through a predictable bureaucratic screwup, Spider's parents thought he was still in Vietnam, when in fact he was only twelve miles away, in the "Looney Tunes ward" at Walter Reed.

When he'd gotten to Vietnam, Spider, like most soldiers, had signed a document asking that the Army not notify his parents in the event of his being "lightly wounded." So if they got a telegram, it meant they would see him soon, in a bed or in a box.

Someplace in the 121st Evacuation Hospital there were two file trays for the records of incoming patients—"Telegram" and "No Telegram." Spider's physical wounds were superficial, so his records were tossed on the "No Telegram" pile. Under normal circumstances, somebody would certainly have checked before he left the hospital for Cam Ranh Bay and home. But with Tet going on, things were far from normal.

Tet worried Ray and Carrie Speidel. They hadn't heard from John in weeks. They called Beverly's dorm and left a message; she called back saying she hadn't had a letter in twelve days. But she thought that the Tet confusion probably had slowed the mail to a standstill.

So when Captain Folsom called from Walter Reed, they were relieved as much as worried. Folsom said that John had been through a terrible experience, and although his physical wounds were superficial, the psychological wounds were profound. No, it would not be a good idea to come see him, not yet, but Captain Folsom would appreciate it very much if they would come in for a talk with people involved with John's case.

That turned out to be an interview with Captain Folsom alone, who admitted he wasn't a doctor. He had a master's degree in psychology, specializing in abnormal psychology. Faced with being drafted, he had joined up, and his useful specialty kept him off the battlefield.

This is not to say his job was easy. He'd belatedly found out that he really hated crazy people, and now he had to spend almost all day with them.

•••

Cpt. Folsom: Thank you for coming to see me so quickly. Sometimes people are reluctant.

Mrs. Speidel: When their sons are involved?

Cpt. Folsom: People are afraid of mental illness. And ashamed. It's not a clean heroic thing like a bullet wound… but it can be just as serious; more serious.

Mr. Speidel: John had a bullet wound, too.

Cpt. Folsom: Yes, shrapnel, anyhow, and other… light injuries associated with the ambush that put him here. But if it were only those injuries, he could go straight home. Or would've been sent back into combat; never left Vietnam.

But the psychiatric wounds are so severe he may be under treatment for a long time, though I hope he can be an outpatient soon.

Mrs. Speidel: Live at home?

Cpt. Folsom: Or by himself, if that's what he wants. I would feel more comfortable if he went back to a family environment.

Mr. Speidel: What actually happened?

Cpt. Folsom: Well, it's hard to say, exactly. There was only one other survivor to the ambush, and he ran away, didn't see anything. And John seems confused about it, understandably. He was unconscious for most of it.

All we know for sure is that John's platoon was attacked by an overwhelmingly large force. The battle was probably over in a few minutes; there wasn't even time for them to call for help.

Mrs. Speidel (dabbing at her eyes): How terrible.

Cpt. Folsom: Yes. Evidently the enemy forces then went through and shot all the wounded. They passed over John because he was unconscious, and they took him for dead.

MR. SPEIDEL: Bastards.

CPT. FOLSOM: The Viet Cong are a cruel, implacable enemy. Your son is very brave. (He shifts and clears his throat.) He saw things that no one should have to see.

MR. SPEIDEL: I suppose that could drive anyone crazy.

CPT. FOLSOM: Well, of course we don't like to call people crazy. But yes, an extremely terrifying or gruesome experience can cause a person who previously was acting normally to... exhibit symptoms of mental illness.
    Is there any history of mental illness in the family?

MRS. SPEIDEL: Terry.

MR. SPEIDEL: Uh huh, yeah. My brother Terry, his uncle, shot himself last month. He locked himself in the garage and sat in the car with the motor running. Then he drank a whole bottle of gin and shot himself. In the head with a shotgun.
    He hadn't been right since Korea. He was really gung ho, joined the Marines and all, but he was in a car accident, a jeep, before he could see much action. Came back with two gimpy legs but no medals or anything.
    See, he'd missed out on the war, World War II, on account of flat feet. He got them fixed up, though, and was just barely young enough to get into the Marines when Korea rolled around. And then he didn't get to be a hero anyhow.
    After awhile, a couple of years, he began telling people he'd stepped on a land mine, up in Inchon. He could tell you anything about that battle, and a couple of others. He even had a bunch of medals, bronze cross or something—

CPT. FOLSOM: Bronze Star.

MR. SPEIDEL: Yeah. He must have picked them up in a pawn shop somewhere. He had a rifle and a Marine uniform that he kept in a case in the living room with the medals. Drove his wife crazy; she left him. Couldn't hold onto a job. He got by on his disability payment and handyman stuff, carpentry.
    I didn't talk to him much after a couple of years. I guess he could tell I was disgusted with him. He'd come by after school, before I got home from

work, and play ball with Spider. They got along all right.

CPT. FOLSOM: That's John?

MR. SPEIDEL: Yeah, that's what he liked to be called.

MRS. SPEIDEL: The kids in grade school teased him about his long arms and legs, and called him Spider because of our name. He got back at them by taking it as a nickname.

MR. SPEIDEL: He even had a pet spider, a tarantula. It died while he was in Basic Training.

CPT. FOLSOM: Mrs. Speidel, has there been any mental illness on your side of the family?

MRS. SPEIDEL: (Thinks for a minute) No… what about your father, Ray?

CPT. FOLSOM: Your father?

MR. SPEIDEL: Oh, yeah. I never met him. Mother had Terry when she was eighteen. I guess they had to get married. Then she got pregnant with me and the guy just walked out. Nobody ever heard from him again.
    I don't know. Is that mental illness or is it being a jerk?

CPT. FOLSOM: Impossible to say, of course. Did she ever tell you anything about him that would make you think he was strange?

MR. SPEIDEL: She won't talk about him at all. I don't even know his name.

CPT. FOLSOM: Hmm. That's extreme.
    The pet tarantula is fairly odd. Did Spider have any other unusual hobbies?

MR. SPEIDEL: Science and science fiction. He made a telescope, ground his own lens, I mean mirror. Has a big rock collection in the garage, even some pretty expensive fossils and meteorites he bought with paper-route money. I got him a microscope when he got out of junior high school.

CPT. FOLSOM: He wasn't successful at it in college, though?

MR. SPEIDEL: Well, he's smart, but he never learned how to study. He kind of drifted through high school and then college hit him like a ton of bricks. He'll do better when he goes back, like I did. If he goes back.

CPT. FOLSOM: Oh, he will. It's just a matter of time. What about the science fiction?

MRS. SPEIDEL: He's such a nut about it. (She pauses and looks at her husband.) I don't mean a *nut* nut, I mean he's really serious about his collection. He goes down to the used bookstores around Ninth Street at least once a month, buying and trading.

He has hundreds of books, all alphabetized and cross-referenced. I mean he has a 5 x 7 card made up for each one, where he typed out a summary of each book and what he thought about it, and there are holes punched along the side of the card that classify the book as to what it's about, whether he gives it an A, B, or whatever. What year it came out...

CPT. FOLSOM: Punched holes? Like an IBM card?

MR. SPEIDEL: No, the holes are just along the margin. It's a system he made up himself. He can stick a long knitting needle through the hole, say, for time travel, and give the stack a shake, and all the time travel books fall out of the stack. Pretty ingenious.

CPT. FOLSOM: Does he collect other books?

MRS. SPEIDEL: Science. He used to collect comics, but he sold and traded those away when he got so involved with science fiction. Oh, I brought him some. (She rummages through her bag and brings out three shiny garish paperbacks. Cpt. Folsom takes them and studies them for a moment.)

CPT. FOLSOM: I'll keep them for him. Right now I don't think it would be a good idea to encourage, ah, fantasy.

Is there anything you can tell me about... Spider's childhood that might have disturbed you at the time? Ways he was different from other boys?

MR. SPEIDEL: Maybe he was more moody than other boys, more quiet. He didn't go out for sports a lot, except Little League. He was a pretty good outfielder, but he lost interest in baseball when he was around twelve.

CPT. FOLSOM: Hmm, puberty. Tell me... did he ever show any interest in boys?

Mrs. Speidel: Boys?

Cpt. Folsom: I mean a homosexual interest.

Mr. Speidel: What, *queer*? (He looks at Mrs. Speidel and they both laugh.) Spider's absolutely girl crazy. He couldn't keep his eyes or his hands off them. If he's queer he hides it pretty well.

Cpt. Folsom: I see. (He writes a lengthy note.) Other than quietness, what would you say made him different from other boys? Special?

Mrs. Speidel: Well, we didn't have any other boys to compare him to. Everything he did was pretty special.

Cpt. Folsom: Does he have any sisters?

Mr. Speidel: No. We had a daughter who died at the age of two.

Cpt. Folsom: Ah. Was he extremely upset?

Mr. Speidel: We all were.

Cpt. Folsom: How old was he then?

Mr. Speidel: Nine.

Cpt. Folsom: Did he do anything unusual afterwards? Like claiming to have seen her ghost. Hearing her talking to him?

Mrs. Speidel: She couldn't talk much. She was just two.

Cpt. Folsom: I know, I know. (Takes off glasses and rubs eyes.) Mrs. Speidel, I'm trying to find out whether John had some mental problem as a child. In the movies, somebody sees or does something traumatic and goes insane, but it's not that simple in real life. Usually it's a pre-existing condition. A person starts to exhibit schizophrenic symptoms and the people around him will say, "Oh, he just broke up with his fiancée," or "It must have been his war experiences"—but he was actually ill all along. A lot of schizophrenics start to present symptoms at John's age.

Mr. Speidel: Schizophrenic? John doesn't have a split personality or anything like that.

CPT. FOLSOM: Oh, that's not schizophrenia. It's a totally unrelated neurosis. Common mistake.

MRS. SPEIDEL: I want to see him. Why can't we see him? (She is destroying her only tissue, twisting and tearing it; the captain slides a box across the desk.)

CPT. FOLSOM: I do sympathize, Mrs. Speidel. But John is very confused. He doesn't really know where he is —

MRS. SPEIDEL: So why don't you *tell* him!

CPT. FOLSOM: We have.

MR. SPEIDEL: Honey, he's right. We'd just make things more complicated.

CPT. FOLSOM: I'm afraid so. Besides, the ward he's in is closed to visitors. There are other patients who would be upset if unfamiliar people came in. (Hastily) It's not a "loony bin." It's just a controlled environment.

MR. SPEIDEL: I don't think he did anything really crazy as a kid.

CPT. FOLSOM: Was he ever in trouble with the law?

MR. SPEIDEL: Broke a window with a rock. (Laughs) It was two in the morning. He snuck out and went over to a girl's house. Tried to wake her up by throwing pebbles at her window, on the second floor. Got caught by the girl's father, who called the police. No big deal, really.

MRS. SPEIDEL: You thought it was at the time.

MR. SPEIDEL: I was pretty damn annoyed. We were on vacation. He met this fast girl and tried to get a little premature sex education.

CPT. FOLSOM: Did he?

MR. SPEIDEL: I don't think so. That was back when he was fifteen, sixteen. I think he's still a virgin.

MRS. SPEIDEL: Beverly's such a nice girl.

CPT. FOLSOM: (Pauses) I'm sure. Of course the army changes people. Your son may be more sophisticated now. More experienced.

MR. SPEIDEL: Well, there sure weren't any girls out in the boonies where he was.

CPT. FOLSOM: No. No girls.

The captain gave Ray Speidel a knowing look, and held it. For a moment he was puzzled. Then his jaw dropped.

DANGLING CONVERSATION

For a long time Lee couldn't get Beverly to talk. When he came into the bedroom she was sitting up in bed, rocking, sobbing, the covers pulled up to her shoulders.

He stopped asking questions and sat quietly with his arm around her. She was fully clothed and shivering, stiff. Finally she leaned into him.

"Could you get me a drink? I don't want to go downstairs, I might meet somebody."

"Coffee, tea, or me?" That was the title of a silly book they'd read about stewardesses. She gave him a weak smile.

"See if there's some of that rum left. Or anything with alcohol."

He came back up with half a pint bottle of Bacardi and some root beer. "No Coke," he said, and mixed her a drink. He poured himself an inch of straight rum and waited for her to talk.

"Spider's ... he's ..."

"Dead? He's not dead?"

"No, he's ... he's here. In Walter Reed."

"Wounded!"

"No. Well, yes." She took a long drink. "I talked to his father. He's ... he says Spider's in a 'rubber room.' He's gone insane."

"My God."

"The Army wouldn't let him see him. His dad ... I've never heard a man so freaked out. All I could get out of him was it's something awful and he can't talk about it." She sobbed once and wiped her face with a corner of the sheet. "I should never have sent him the letter."

Lee shook his head. "What letter?"

"I didn't tell you. I told him, I wrote him—I told him all about us."

He swirled the rum around and sipped it. "Everything."

"Oh, you know. Not the nitty-gritty. Just that we were together, living together. You know, I told you I wrote him about Hawaii."

"You said you told him you couldn't come. You couldn't let your father pay for it."

"Yeah, well, that was part of it. I also said that if somehow I could come, it would be just as a friend, a good friend. Because I, you…"

"You told him you loved me?"

She looked at him. "Something like that, yeah."

"What does that mean?"

"I was really pissed off at you. You may remember."

"Because I said you could go fuck him?" He shrugged, slowly. "I still say that's your own business."

"Yeah, you're such a fucking romantic fool. I think what I told him was I wasn't sure where we were headed, you and me. I just couldn't be his girl-friend anymore, his virgin."

"Okay. You were going to have to do that sooner or later."

"But now he's, he's " She started to cry again.

"It's not your fault." He stroked her arm. "Even if he did read the letter. Which he probably didn't."

"The timing's right. And he didn't write back."

"Maybe he didn't write back because he didn't get the letter. He was out in the field, that can mean an extra week or two. And there was all that Tet bullshit."

"I guess. I don't know." She set the glass on the floor and started unbut-toning her flannel shirt. "Feel like shit. Could we just lie here a while?"

"Sure." He lit the candle on the nightstand and turned out the light and watched her undress. "You don't want to, uh…"

"No. Not now."

"Sure." He took off his boots and slid under the covers next to her, rough denim pressed to her skin. She sighed and put an arm around him, and in a few minutes was asleep, snoring softly while he stared at the candle flame.

THE THIRD VERSION

It was too late in the day to start a patrol. They sent us out even though they knew we wouldn't have time to make any kind of bunkers for the night. Just scrape out a little hole and hope nobody comes along.

It was tough going, prickly come-along vines up to your knees and thick stands of bamboo to chop through with machetes. We made enough noise to wake up the dead.

Wake up the dead. We came to a Montagnard cemetery just as night was falling. There were two artillery craters in it, and one had dug up a bunch of bones and old gray rotten cloth, maybe skin. Creepy.

Sarge knew it was on the map as an artillery reference point, so we went on past it into the jungle about two hundred yards straight north. We dug our holes, one for each two guys, and did perimeter guard four-on-four-off.

The moon was full and it was godawful bright. In a way, that was worse than pitch darkness. The jungle looked like a washed-out black-and-white photograph of snarled and shifting lines and curves. It could have hidden anything.

My buddy Moses had the first watch. I couldn't sleep, though; I was spooked. I kept hearing things—I mean, you always hear little stuff all night in the jungle; the wind moves the tops of the trees around, critters jump from limb to limb and scurry through the brush—but I was hearing things I never heard before, like voices whispering, just loud enough so you could tell it wasn't English. Sometimes I'd hear something like heavy breathing right behind me, but I'd turn around quick and there was nothing there.

So after four hours of this, Moses gets out of the hole and racks out on his air mattress. *He* isn't scared; he's been sucking cold C-ration coffee to stay awake. I'm still scared, though, even though I'm sure it's my imagination, just got a little freaked by the cemetery. I secure my grenades and magazines and get into the hole, which is about waist-deep. We'd cut a little shelf to sit on.

I swear I couldn't have fallen asleep. Just not possible. Some kind of trance or something. I blink and suddenly it's like the moon has moved about thirty degrees. I mean you can't *see* the moon but you can tell where the light's coming from.

I check my watch and it's 3:30, past time for shift change. But then I look over at the air mattress and see that Moses isn't there. But then I see that part of him *is* there, his legs. Bones sticking out, jagged and slick in the moonlight, and this dark shiny shit sprayed all over in front of the position, like Moses just exploded or something.

I look out and there are dead people all around, some just wounded but not moving much. I think it must be a dream but you can smell it and I look down and I'm covered with blood, too, from Moses.

There's someone walking around out there. I scrunch down and peer out over the edge of the hole. At first it just looks like a head floating, but then I see that he's dressed all in black, in black pajamas. His skin is gray and rotting; you can see his teeth all the way back where there should be cheeks. His eyes are round black holes with a dim point of light inside each one.

He stops over one guy who's moving a little bit. He kneels down and grabs him by the throat with one hand, and with the other hand he sticks his finger right on the guy's forehead and pushes down. The skull cracks like a teacup and you can hear his finger mushing around inside. The guy's legs and arms flail around for a second and then he falls limp.

The man in black stands up and wipes the brains off his finger and moves on to the next one. This guy's dead already but he pops his skull anyhow.

I don't want to see any more. I curl up in a ball in the bottom of the hole and wait.

He never comes for me. It gets light and I get out of the hole and on the ground there's nothing but dead people, rotting guts and brains everywhere, flies and buzzards. Worms. I guess I went a little crazy. I ran like hell.

SCHIZO (1)

If Spider had been diagnosed as schizophrenic twenty years before 1968, he might have been treated with an ice pick thrust through the eye socket into the brain: transorbital lobotomy. About a third of the 5000 lobotomies performed annually at that time were transorbital, which was an inexpen sive office procedure. All the doctor has to do is knock the patient out with electroshock, saving the expense of an anesthesiologist; lift up the eyelid and insert the ice pick (sometimes a "transorbital leucotome," which is an ice pick with centimeter markings) and pound on it until the orbital plate fractures and the point jabs through into the brain. Then stir left and right, up and down, randomizing the information in the frontal lobe. Then withdraw the point carefully, applying pressure to the eyelid so blood and cerebrospinal fluid don't leak out into the eye socket, which could upset the patient. Then go to the other eye.

A fast worker could do three or four patients in an hour.

Lobotomy had fallen out of favor by 1968. Psychoactive drugs like chlor-promazine and reserpine were just as effective in calming down mental pa-tients, and although the drugs didn't cure people of schizophrenia, it wasn't clear that lobotomy worked too well, either. Lobotomized people, perhaps unsurprisingly, showed a marked decrease in intellectual ability, and many of them relapsed into schizophrenia or depression or committed suicide.

Captain Folsom regretted the absence of lobotomy from his repertoire. He felt that people's rejection of it was due more to squeamishness than anything else. It certainly had a better cure rate than any school of psychotherapy.

He had other tools.

MINDS MEETING

This was Folsom's second year at Walter Reed, so he knew that February was the worst month on the wards, in terms of smell. In March, they could start opening up the windows in the day rooms. The window fans would draw fresh air down the corridors and attenuate the smell of urine and vomit. In February it was ghastly.

He was aware that his sensitivity to smell was abnormal. He knew that he was too sensitive in many ways, for this job.

He always spent as much time as possible loitering at the nurses' station at the north end of Ward A. The smell was least strong there, but it was strong enough for his olfactory receptors to begin to adapt. If he tried to walk straight from the brisk clean outdoor air into the middle of the ward, he would probably lose his breakfast.

The only nurse at the station was Leticia Washington, a young black woman from Georgia whom Folsom had difficulty understanding. She was pretty, though, and more important, she seemed somewhat afraid of Folsom. Most of the nurses treated him with good-natured contempt. Head Nurse Charton was openly sarcastic, and unfortunately outranked him.

He leaned into the service window, inhaling Washington's wildflower perfume. "Let me have Private Speidel's folder, please."

"Yes, sir," she said with three musical Savannah syllables, and produced a gray file with only four pages. "Dr. Yarrow drop his Thorazine down to twenty-five milligram last night."

"Did he sleep all right?" Folsom snapped the report into place under the jaws of an all-metal clipboard.

"Far as I know, sir."

"No morning meds yet?"

"No, sir. Specialist Knox don't come in until nine."

"Good. That should make him more, uh, verbal." He studied the four pages intently, although he had written three of them himself and was probably the world's only expert on the mental state of Pvt. John Speidel. He really didn't want to walk down that corridor. "Interviewed his parents yesterday."

"He say they live 'round here."

Folsom looked up. "When did he say that?"

"Last night. I go in to check those stitches and he ask 'Where am I?' When I tol' him Walter Reed, he say that his parents live in, where, Bethesda?"

"Right, right." He rubbed his chin. "That's good. Did he say anything about wanting to see them, or anything?"

"No, sir. He was half asleep." She looked thoughtful. "He did say, he say some nonsense. Bathsheba, like in the Bible, mother to Solomon? And then cheese. 'Bathsheba cheddar cheese.' Funny thing to say."

"Nothing else?"

"No, sir. Just 'Bathsheba cheddar cheese' two, three times."

Folsom took a 3 x 5 card out of his shirt pocket and wrote the phrase down. "I guess Bathsheba comes from Bethesda; that's simple paronomasia. No telling where the cheese comes from. Did Bathsheba have anything to do with cheese in the Bible?"

"No, sir, not that I know. But she did be connected to the army, to sol-dierin'—she's Uriah's wife, Uriah the Hittite; old David sees her takin' a bath, he lusts after her and orders her to, uh, to get to his bed. She get pregnant and David get rid of Uriah by tellin' his commander, Joab, to put him up front where he be killed."

"That's interesting. Speidel was sent to the front, so to speak, as punishment."

"What he do? Sir."

"Oh, he flew off the handle, attacked a sergeant. He was probably starting to present symptoms then, but there was nobody around to properly interpret them."

"Maybe he should be restrain', sir?"

"Oh, I don't think that's necessary; it was a one-time thing." He shuffled through the pages. "He isn't otherwise violent. If he becomes agitated, you can tell me or Captain Yarrow. We can adjust his Thorazine."

"I keep an eye on him. He probably a nice enough boy, religious."

"Probably. Let's hope we can help him." He put the clipboard under his arm and looked down the corridor. "I'd like to see him in the consultation room. Would you have an orderly bring him over?"

"See can I find one, sir. Might be a while."

"That's all right. I'll wait in there." Folsom could have interviewed Spider by his bedside, but he decided the patient would be more comfortable talking to him in the neutral, nonmedical surroundings of the consultation room. It smelled better, too.

At least this wasn't Ward C, the Vegetable Garden. That was all catatonia and gibberish, the air thick with urine and soil and disinfectant. He had only been there once; its inhabitants had no use for his talents. He hoped Speidel wouldn't wind up there.

He held his breath most of the way to the consultation room, covering the last ten yards with two shallow inhalations. He closed the door behind him and crossed the small room to sit in the swivel chair under the only decoration, a black-and-white portrait of Lyndon Johnson. The walls were the same depressing green as the walls outside. He pulled a fresh 3 x 5 card from his pocket and wrote "paint & pictures in CR?" The old oak table could use refinishing, too; the other side, where patients sat, was an intaglio jungle of names and doodles and graffiti.

The table had a stained blotter, a brass ashtray, and an intercom that looked like someone had used it for batting practice. He pushed the button. "Corporal Washington ... do you hear me?" She answered yes, sir.

He leaned back, withdrew a fat leather tobacco pouch from his back pocket, and unzipped one side to extract the day's pipe, a natty Kaywoodie white briar, Yacht shape. He allowed himself three bowlsful a day; perhaps more on a stressful day. Most work days were stressful.

He unzipped the other side and deeply inhaled the reassuring fragrance of his special mixture. He packed the pipe scientifically—"first with a child's hand, then with a woman's hand, then with a man's hand"—and struck a wooden match, waited for the sulfur and phosphorus to burn down, and lit the tobacco carefully all around the perimeter of the bowl. Then he took a pewter tool from his pocket and tamped the coals down evenly, and relit it. He leaned back and savored the exotic smoke: perique, Latakia, and Turkish, flavoring a base of the finest Virginia.

He knew that most of the people he worked with thought it smelled like compost burning. But he outranked most of the people he worked with.

There was one perfunctory knock and the door swung open. Phillips, a Spec 6 lifer, stuck his neckless head in and made a slight grimace at the smoke. "In here," he said, and steered Spider in.

Spider shuffled in with a crutch, staring at the floor, slightly limping. Folsom noticed he was using the crutch wrong, putting it down in time with his injured leg, rather than using it to take the weight off his bad leg, working in parallel with the good one. He wore faded blue pajamas a couple of sizes too large and garish homemade orange-and-red slippers donated by the Red Cross.

"Sit." Phillips helped him into the straight chair with surprising gentleness. Folsom's main impression of Phillips lingered from his second day on duty: a patient more than a head taller than the stocky little aide had screamed and jumped him; Phillips took expert hold of his wrist and shoulder and folded him like a piece of origami. He wasn't respectful, though. "Just give me a call when you need him taken back, Doc." He called every man "Doc" and every woman "Sweets."

Folsom nodded and turned his attention to Spider. "Do you remember me, Private Speidel?"

Spider raised his head a little bit and looked at him with hooded eyes. "Prison."

"No, this isn't prison. This is—"

"You. Prison. Fulsom Prison."

"I see." He leaned back and puffed. "A play on words."

"Got a cigarette?"

Folsom carried a pack for patients. He didn't have to buy them; other patients left them lying around, and he had a drawer full in his office, more or less stale. He flipped the half-pack out on the table between them.

"Newports." Spider shook one out and carefully tore off the filter. Folsom struck him a light and he inhaled deeply.

"Take the pack. I've got more."

Spider considered that for a moment. "Okay." He picked up the pack by one corner and dropped it into his large shirt pocket.

Folsom took out one of the cards. "You said something about Bathsheba to the night nurse."

"Huh uh." He shook his head several times.

"You don't remember 'Bathsheba cheddar cheese'?"

"*Beth*sheba Cheddar Cheese. You a Baron?"

"Am I barren?"

"Yah, Baron Fon Rick-stoffen, nish var." He reversed the cigarette and held it between thumb and forefinger, European style. "You haff relatiffs in Chermany." He French-inhaled and pronounced carefully: "Nicht wahr?"

"Sorry. I don't get it."

"The Barons of B-CC. Bethsheba Cheddar Cheese."

"Hmm. Okay." He made a note of that on the card. There was something familiar about it. "I saw your parents yesterday."

Spider stared at the cigarette end and blew gently on it.

"They're worried about you."

He started rocking, a short, jerky motion, about two times a second. "*I'm* worried about me."

"Would you like to see them?"

"No," he said quickly. "Not now, not now. Not now, no."

"What about your girlfriend?"

"Li?"

"Beverly, not Lee. Or is that what you call her?"

Spider broke into a laugh that became a giggle. "Beverly not Li. No way, GI." He giggled again. "Beverly would never let me cornhole her."

"Really—"

"Li would, though." He closed his eyes in ecstasy. "First me, then Li. Around the world, it's really great, really great."

"Yes, but, uh…" Folsom puffed so furiously he was burning his tongue. Spider's growing erection was obvious even in the loose pajamas. Folsom had had patients start masturbating in front of him, and that was difficult enough to deal with when they were heterosexual.

"I thought it was just something guys talked about; I didn't know you could really *do* it!" His tongue rubbed along the syphilis chancre on his lip.

"Forget about Lee for just a minute. Please!"

He leaned forward, elbows on the table. "Easy for you to say, white man. Me think about Li alla time. Numbah One boom-boom."

"Boom boom." He nodded slowly and looked at the top page on the clipboard, Spider's high school transcript. "Look, uh, you got straight A's in English all through high school."

"College, too, one semester. Read an' write, big deal."

"But you didn't major in English."

He started rocking even faster. "Astronomy. *Ad astra per aspera.*"

"Pardon?"

"Up your ass-tra with your aspirin. Latin." He stopped. "Ooday ooyay eakspay igPay atinLay?"

"Uh, yes, when I was—"

"Önnenkay eesay rechenspay igPay atinLay *auf eutschday*?"

"Uh, hmm." Folsom concentrated on tapping the top ash off his pipe and tamping down the dottle. "Yeah, what I meant was, maybe we could communicate better if you expressed yourself in writing. You know, writing in English?"

"*Ja, auf englisch.*" He reversed the cigarette again and took a huge drag, bringing the ember down to within a fraction of an inch of his fingers. He put it out with exaggerated care. "Meestair Bond. You bring me ze fountain pen and ze stack of papair, and I will write anyzang you want."

"Good. Good, I'll get right on it." He stabbed the intercom. "Phillips. Are you there?"

He was about two seconds away. Again, a single rap on the door, and he slid in. "Trouble, Doc?"

"Oh, no. No, we're done." He made a shooing motion with his left hand. Phillips helped Spider stand and move dragging toward the door. "I'll get you that pen and paper right away."

Spider stopped in the doorway and looked at him with a haughty air. "*Bond* papair, if you please." Then he looked at the floor again and shuffled off.

Folsom watched the door glide shut. "Bethsheba cheddar cheese," he said under his breath, and sighed. "Queers."

He stared at the transcript for the tenth time, without the name of the school registering: Bethesda-Chevy Chase, it said. "Home of the Barons."

GIRL TALK

Beverly was at the doughnut shop having coffee with her ex-roommate Peggy, who looked deceptively wholesome in a starchy new maternity dress. Beverly had never seen her in anything but faded jeans or skin.

"So Soldier Boy's in the hospital." Beverly was clasping and unclasping her hands, staring at the newspaper between them. She nodded. "At least he's alive." They both looked at the headlines. Tet was still crackling along, hard fighting in Hue. But the main headlines were about the crippled Paris peace talks—the U.S. accusing North Vietnam of answering our restraint with a vicious sneak attack—and the *Pueblo*, with the U.S. conceding the ship may have strayed into foreign waters; let's put our nukes away for the time being.

"Yeah, but a *mental* hospital."

"Bev, look. He was always kinda weird."

"Well, he was eccentric." She sipped thoughtfully. "He might've gone to

Canada if I'd gone with him."

"Really? You told me about the Peace Corps. I didn't know he'd talked about actually dodging."

"It doesn't seem like draft-dodging to me anymore. It's asking another country for political asylum."

Peggy laughed. "I know who *you've* been hanging around with." Stage whisper: "You talk politics in bed?"

"No, we talk about you." She flicked her tongue out. "Spider never seriously suggested it, I guess. I just remember he talked about other guys doing it. His family would've disowned him. But he might have gone if I went along. Then *my* old man would track him down with a shotgun."

"Your old man is a fucking lunatic, you don't mind me saying."

"Tell me about it." Beverly was cutting her pie into neat pieces, not eating it. "I remember once he did say, Spider, that if he went to Canada or Sweden he'd never know how much of it was principle and how much was fear. Cowardice."

"Things have changed a lot in the last year or two. I'd go to Canada if I was a boy and got drafted."

"You really would?"

"No doubt about it. And maybe some of it would be fear, so what? It's not exactly World War II. We don't belong over there."

"You wouldn't've said that last year."

"Yeah, well, part of it's people like Spider. And I got a cousin, step-cousin or whatever, he got shot by a piece of shrapnel and they just patched him up and sent him back out. We got a picture of him with this big fucking bandage on his arm, in a sling, out in the jungle looking scared shitless. I mean, really."

Beverly nodded with a faraway expression. "I think I'd go to jail. If I were a boy."

"Canada's nicer."

"But at least you'd be doing something. If everybody said 'send me to jail instead' the war'd be over in a few months."

"Dream on. They'd build more jails. Or put 'em in camps—how long do you think it took 'em to build those concentration camps for the Japanese Americans in World War Two? They'd find a place to put everybody."

Beverly smiled at her friend. "Being pregnant has made you into a radical."

"Yeah, maybe. In between learning how to puke politely and knitting little booties, I guess you think about the future."

"Really."

"Yeah. Every morning I run into the john and hope there's a stall so I don't have to barf in the sink. Gross everybody out. Must be nice to have your own bathroom."

"Sure. Me and six or seven other people and whatever strangers decide to have sex in the bathtub."

"That *happens*?" She giggled at the thought.

"Yesterday morning. I'd never seen them before in my life. They didn't even lock the door."

"So what were they doing?"

"Having *sex*."

"No, I mean *what*?"

"Oh, I don't know." She was blushing. "Just the regular."

"Was the guy good-looking?"

"Peggy! I didn't stand around and stare."

"I would, if it was my bathroom."

"If it were your bathroom, you'd get in there with them."

"Maybe I would." Whispering: "Did he have a really big one?" Beverly looked up at the ceiling and got even redder. "Come on, you looked. How big was it?"

"Oh, I couldn't see from the door. He had a nice behind, though. Lots of muscles on his back. Want me to get his phone number?"

"Yeah, tell him you've got a girlfriend who's absolutely sure she won't get knocked up. Doesn't care if he uses a rubber. Doesn't *want* him to."

"You ought to just put up little cards on all the bulletin boards."

"Nah, I already did that. You meet a really cruddy class of boys."

They laughed so hard together the owner of the shop glared and told them to keep it down. Peggy answered with "I *can't*," and a loud belch, and they staggered out the door on the edge of hysteria.

SCHIZO (2)

If Spider had exhibited symptoms of schizophrenia twenty years after 1968, he probably would have been stabilized with drugs and sent home with a prescription.

Chlorpromazine seemed to be the magic bullet for most schizophrenics. Developed in the 1940s as an antihistamine, French doctors used it in a "lytic cocktail" that swiftly knocked out agitated patients. A French psychiatrist, Pierre Deniker, became curious about the compound and used it by itself on some psychotic patients. It was strikingly effective in reducing the severity of schizophrenic symptoms. Although nobody was sure how it worked, by the 1950s chlorpromazine (usually known by the brand name Thorazine) was the drug of choice for controlling schizophrenia.

Research in the sixties produced an explanation for chlorpromazine's action in terms of brain chemistry. Dopamine is a neurotransmitter associated with schizophrenic symptoms. It's picked up by "dopamine receptors" in the brain. Chlorpromazine and other antipsychotic drugs seem to block off the dopamine receptors selectively; that is, they don't affect the receptors of other neurotransmitters. Clinical observation showed that the effectiveness of any drug in preventing schizophrenic behavior depended on how effectively it blocked dopamine receptors.

(There was supporting evidence in the behavior of "speed freaks"; abusers of amphetamines. Amphetamine increases the production of dopamine, and people who overdose on it will temporarily show symptoms indistinguishable from paranoid schizophrenia.)

The almost universal employment of the drug made research difficult. The autopsied brains of schizophrenics did show subtle and more or less consistent differences from normal brains, but there was no way to demonstrate whether the differences were due to schizophrenia itself, or just from years of taking chlorpromazine. In the seventies and eighties, jazzy futuristic tools like positron-emission tomography, magnetic resonance imaging, and single photon-emission computed tomography allowed researchers to analyze the living brain in action. But they found nothing simple or universal—some schizophrenics had structural or physiologic abnormalities of the brain, but not all of them did.

When the President in 1990 declared the beginning of "The Decade of the Brain" (perhaps tacitly acknowledging a previous decade of brainlessness), the consensus among researchers was that schizophrenia was probably an umbrella term for many different diseases.

Schizophrenia is partially hereditary. The brother or sister of someone with the disorder has a ten percent chance of getting it—yet an identical twin has less than a fifty percent chance, even with an identical genetic blueprint.

The pattern of symptoms is wildly inconsistent from patient to patient. About half of them show symptoms only intermittently; for the rest, the symptoms start and will continue unabated until drug therapy intervenes, and even then there is a slow constant deterioration.

Some people recover spontaneously and some never do, having to depend on chlorpromazine the way a diabetic depends on insulin. Chlorpromazine has no effect on about twenty percent of schizophrenics, though some respond to other drugs, controversial and expensive.

The onset of schizophrenia is sometimes related to sudden trauma. (Freud originally thought that it was always caused by a specific traumatic event.) Usually it just happens.

One out of a hundred people becomes schizophrenic. No one really knows why, or why the rest of us do not.

THE CUCKOO'S NEST

Spider thanked Phillips for helping him and slumped down onto his bunk. His feet were cold. He thought about getting under the covers, for the warmth, but it had taken him so long to make the bed. And it wasn't a really great job of bed-making; in Basic it would have gotten him KP. He smiled, recalling that. Everybody was supposed to hate Kitchen Police. As if washing a few hundred dishes were harder than slogging twenty miles through the snow with a pack on your back.

Spider looked around the government-green room. Twenty beds, seven of them currently empty. Most of the men were sitting or lying down, asleep or half-asleep, many of them staring blankly ahead. Some rocked or nodded. Two were mumbling and one was crying. Two were carrying on an intense discussion of baseball.

"What was that all about?" The guy on the next bunk; Spider had said hello to him but couldn't remember his name. Serious-looking blond man in his late twenties.

"Prison, um, Fulsom. Captain Fulsom."

"'Fole.' Captain Folsom. Is he a dickhead, or what?"

"Yeah."

"He's afraid of us, you know. You can really fuck with him."

"Yeah." Spider laughed. "I started talking to him in German, in Pig Latin. He looked at me like I was crazy."

"Really." He lit up a cigarette. "If you aren't crazy, though, what the fuck are you? In the wrong ward?"

"Don't put it out." Spider shook out a Newport and used his match. "Is this really Walter Reed?"

"Yeah, trust me, flew into Edwards. Where do you think you are?" He leaned forward. "Are you really crazy?"

"Huh uh, no. Yeah. I don't know. I was in the jungle, we got the shit kicked out of us. I guess maybe I did go a little crazy. Is that why I'm here?"

The guy shrugged. "You're the doctor. You come from the 'Nam?"

"Around Pleiku, yeah. We got in this firefight and, I don't know. I got knocked out, some weird shit happened. Maybe it didn't happen. I do remember the helicopter and some hospital, I guess in Pleiku, really crowded. I was on a cot in the hall, all tied up. They'd let me take a shit and then they'd shoot me up with some shit, tie me up again. It's all just a big blur. I wound up here, in some other ward. My ears hurt and kept popping so I figured I'd been on a plane; that's one thing I do remember. Then they stopped giving me shots and I stopped sleeping all the time. When I could walk, they moved me in here. Then last night the nurse says this is Walter Reed."

"Trust me. We landed at Edwards Air Force Base. It's Walter Reed."

"But I live here."

The guy squinted at him. "We all live here."

"I mean I *really* live here. Out in Bethesda."

"Maryland?"

"Yeah."

He nodded. "They say I tried to kill my wife. That's not true. You speak German?"

"Just a few words. One semester."

"We were stationed in Germany, but I never got the lingo, you know? Like I hardly ever got off the base."

"Yeah, like I never learned any Vietnamese. *Chieu hoi. Di di mao.* Stuff like that."

"What, 'don't shoot; I voted for Mao'?" They both laughed. "No way I was gonna kill her. She come at me with a fryin' pan, man, a fuckin' cast-iron skillet."

"Shit. She's the one ought to be in here." Spider made a face at the cigarette and twisted the filter off. "So you hit her?"

"Huh uh." He didn't change expression, but tears started to run down his cheeks. "We were in the kitchen, I poked her."

"Poked?"

"Yeah, I picked up a steak knife and poked her."

"Where?"

"In the kitchen."

"Oh."

"That's how I got this." He raised his foot, encased in plaster. "She dropped the fuckin' fryin' pan on my bare foot. Broke two toes."

"Was that before you poked her, or after?"

"After. Well, just barely. About the same time. It only went in a couple inches. Maybe four inches. Then I did it again, after she dropped the skillet."

"Where?"

"Oh, I poked her in the stomach. Abdomen, if you want to get technical."

"She okay now?"

"She's a fuckin' bitch, man, I don't know. She's still in Bremerhaven, far as I know." He wiped his face with his hands. "I even took her to the infirmary, drove her there. I told her what to say. But I'm waitin' for her out in the waitin' room and in comes these three MPs with guns. I go quietly, you know? But when they started to put me in the lockup, I don't know, I freaked out." He laughed and smacked his fist into his palm. "Decked one of them. One shot, fuckin' decked 'im."

"You *hit* an MP? With a *gun*?"

"Yeah, that was stupid, I know. They got me down on the ground and cuffed me. Then they took off the cuffs and put me in a straitjacket and left me in a room with the one I'd knocked down. He pushed me off the chair and proceeded to kick the stuffing out of me. I passed out."

There was a long pause. "What, you woke up here?"

"No, hell. There was a couple of hearings and some shrink talked to me, I thought he was on my side. But then they say I'm not competent to stand trial and send me here." He coughed hoarsely. "When I'm *competent* I guess I go back to Germany and they hang my ass." He coughed again and threw his cigarette into the butt can on the wall. "The bitch."

"They'd hang you for that?"

"Shit, I don't know. Not unless she dies. She got infected with para something. Para-nitis."

Spider looked up at the door. "Here comes the Pill-down Man." Specialist Knox, a tall, heavy black man, came into the ward pushing a shiny metal cart with lots of trays and compartments. On the top there were thirteen small white paper cups containing pills, matched up to small square Polaroids of each patient's face.

Spider was his fourth customer. He emptied the cup into his hand and said, "Juice or water."

Spider looked at the pill and capsule. "These aren't what I got last time, though."

"Don't give me any shit, man, I just work here. Juice or water."

"The little orange one's Thorazine," the blond man said. "Make you behave. I don't know about the other one."

"Antibiotic," Knox said. He poured Spider a paper cup of juice.

Spider tried to hide the Thorazine under his tongue but he swallowed it reflexively. The juice was watery and acrid.

Knox handed the other man his pills but then looked back at Spider. "Yeah, you Speidel." He reached behind the cart and brought out a spiral notebook and a ballpoint pen. "Captain My Captain say you supposed to write somethin' out for him." He handed it to him and said in a low voice, "Where you from in the 'Nam?"

"II Corps, here and there. I was attached with the 1st of the 8th when I got wounded."

"Yeah, up Pleiku, Kontum. I been through there." He glanced back at the door. "Look, don't you sweat the Tho'azine. That's the smallest they got, twenty-five mikes. You been gettin' ten times that much, injected, over on the other ward. Pretty soon you be able to count up to ten."

"Oh. Thanks." Knox nodded absently and moved on down.

"He's okay for a lifer," the blond man said. "You must of been pretty much a zombie over there."

"Guess so. I don't remember much. Hell, I don't remember goin' from

Vietnam to the states." He smiled. "You sure this is Walter Reed? I mean, they could build a place like this in 'Nam and keep all us paranoids there."

The other man stretched out on his bunk. "Hey, you don't have to worry about bein' paranoid. You're in the Army. There really *is* somebody after your ass." He chuckled at his own joke and lit up a cigarette. When Spider didn't respond, he glanced over.

Spider was staring at the doorway, his face pale and waxen, mouth half-open.

"What the fuck? What is it, man?"

"Nothin'. Just a guy I see sometimes. He's not real."

"Not real?"

"He's *there* but he's not, like, not real. I mean nobody else can see him."

"You ever talk to him?"

"Huh uh." Spider rubbed his face hard and blinked twice with his whole face. He looked at the other man. "Sometimes he talks to me."

MARCH

Sarge said it was going to be a "walk in the park." Some park; some walk.

It was about local noon by the time we got our shit together, suited up, out of the ship and ready to hike, just like we'd done every other day for the past ten. But all the other expeditions had been through the grassy plain that lay between our landing site and the sea. This was our first foray into the hilly jungle to the rear.

To give Sarge some credit, there was no reason for anybody to expect trouble. All of the action on this planet had been thousands of klicks to the south, in frozen tundra. But I guess the powers that be were using us as bait, trolling us in various directions to see whether we could lure the enemy into a new environment. If that was the goal, we were to be wildly successful.

I was nervous from the very beginning. We were used to an unobstructed line of sight all the way to the horizon, and if you wanted to see further, you could just hit bounce and your suit would shoot you up about a hundred meters.

But here, you could only see a few meters in any direction. The jungle was a riotous tangle of brush and vines, knobbly vines as thick as your arm with spikes like tenpenny nails. Everything was a sickly chartreuse and brown, like the grass but more washed out. If you bounced, you'd come back down in the middle of the briar patch somewhere. Your laserfinger could cut through it easily enough, but how would you know which direction to go? (Actually, I guessed you could spin around at the top of your bounce and take a reading on the ship. I hadn't really thought it through.)

Sarge took point, cutting us a swath several meters wide with the heavy laser. The stuff was still smoldering when I walked through, at the end of the line. That was not anybody's favorite position. I spent a lot of time checking the rear, which in the cumbersome suits means lumbering around in a semicircle. The things need rearview mirrors.

I trusted the two guys in front of me. Batman was weird, an Allied observer from Sirius IV, wings and all, but he'd seen a lot of combat and was absolutely cool. Moses was from Earth like me, a Jew from Iowa, which some guys thought was funny, like in the movies the Jewish guy is always from Brooklyn. He's always the first one to die, too, him or the black dude, which in this case would have to be Batman. We kidded Moses about that (and Batman, too, but Sirians don't have any sense of humor) and he went along with it, but you could tell it spooked him. Rightly so, as it turned out.

After a couple of hours it was starting to get routine, up and down the hills, splash through the slimy sulfurous streams, every now and then see a flowering plant or one that wiggled at you. That was a little eerie, as if they were reaching out.

We came to a natural clearing, like a dell where three hills came together, and Sarge told us to take five. Moses started to say something sarcastic, and then the top half of him just disappeared. Nothing left but two legs, toppling, and a fine mist of red spray. Then Batman got it, his blood was bright blue.

I bounced, by reflex, but I didn't bounce far. I must have crashed into a tree limb a few meters up. It knocked me out cold, which evidently saved my life.

When I woke up, there was a Bug walking around the clearing, making sure people were dead. He would scrabble along sideways up to the head and use a sonic blaster, pretty messy.

I didn't move. My arm was stretched out, and he had to walk right over the laserfinger to get to me. I squeezed and it sliced him in two.

I got up and looked around. There weren't any other Bugs, but it didn't look like there were any of us left alive, either.

I went to the center of the clearing. For some reason they had sliced Sarge's suit open, I guess just to watch him die in the poisonous atmosphere. His skin was bright red.

I checked overhead and bounced. At the apex of my bounce, I turned around to locate the ship, broadcasting my emergency beacon.

But there was no one to come help. The *Roger Young* was a smoking ruin. I drifted back down into the clearing full of carnage. I guess I went a little crazy.

SEXUAL RELEASE

Spider's father stepped diffidently into the open doorway. "Dr. Folsom?"

The captain did not correct him. "Ah, Mr. Speidel; come in, come in." He gestured at the chair across the desk from him. "Have a seat. Just a minute." He returned the file on his blotter to a desk drawer and searched for another one. "Here we go."

There were actually only two files in the drawer. This was not Folsom's office. He did not like to have other people in his office; it was too small even for him alone.

He took out his pipe and pouch and began the filling ritual. "John is doing well, quite well. He responds well to his medication; there have been no further violent outbursts."

"That doesn't surprise me. He's about as *un*-violent a kid as I've ever known."

"Yes, that's interesting. Yet it did take four men to restrain him at one time." They both shook their heads. "I wanted to speak to you alone, without Mrs. Speidel, because a couple of the matters I have to discuss are sexual in nature. I saw no reason to embarrass her."

"I appreciate that."

"First of all, John's syphilis has responded dramatically to penicillin. That's lucky. There are some virulently resistant strains in Vietnam."

Mr. Speidel made a strangled sound. "Pardon me?" Folsom said.

"Good." Mr. Speidel fired up a Camel. "That's ... that's good."

Folsom lit his pipe carefully, twice. "He does still have, well, hallucinations. He hears voices, sees people who aren't there, Vietnamese. But he does know they're not real. That's important."

"People he killed?"

"As far as I know, John never killed anybody. Or if he did, he's repressed the memory. That wouldn't be uncommon.

"By themselves, these hallucinations wouldn't be enough to keep John in the hospital."

"Really?"

"As long as he doesn't think they're real, no. He understands that he's sick and that these illusions are part of the sickness. He knows not to pay any attention to what they say."

"You mean, uh, he might be coming home?"

Folsom raised his eyebrows and didn't say anything.

"I mean, look. Do you have any children?"

He studied his pipe. "No."

"A teenage son is, uh, is like a kind of wild man. It was a real sigh of relief when he went off to college, you know?"

"And now he's coming back, and crazy, too."

"Yeah. I guess that's about it."

"And homosexual. That bothers you."

"Sure it does. I mean, he's still, he's still my boy…"

"It would bother me, too." He squared the papers in front of him. "Look. There might be something we can do."

"To make him, make him normal?"

"Well, to make him prefer girls to boys. It's called aversion therapy. We'd have to keep him a while longer."

"Well, sure."

"And we'd like to give him electroconvulsive therapy, too. It would make him more receptive."

"Sure. You're the doctor."

He slid over a piece of paper. "John's still a minor, of course, and also not mentally competent. Would you sign this release for him?"

Mr. Speidel looked at it. "But he's in the Army. Can't you do anything to him you want?"

"It's just a formality. Besides, John won't be in the Army much longer. He'll be getting a medical discharge as soon as we feel comfortable about him leaving."

His brow furrowed. "But then if he has like a relapse? Can we bring him back here?"

"No, he'd go to the nearest VA hospital. We've already started the paperwork for his disability rating. If he gets a fifty percent disability or more, which is likely, he can go to the VA for anything—free medical care for the rest of his life. But no matter what, he'll always be able to receive treatment for this problem."

"His homo, homosexuality?"

"Any mental problem whatsoever. Anything that's service-connected." He set his pipe down in the ashtray and looked steadily at Mr. Speidel. "Before the Army, John was interested in girls. Very interested, you said."

"Definitely. It was a problem."

"Well, sometimes that can be a smokescreen. A man will pretend to be interested in girls so no one will suspect. You know?"

"He could get an Oscar, then."

"Well, yes. But there's also 'situational' homosexuality. A guy is in prison, or aboard ship in the Navy, or at a boarding school—or out in the jungle with a bunch of other guys..."

"But wait. I've been in situations like that. I mean, I was in the Army, too. We didn't go around..."

"Of course not. But some people, boys who have an unusually strong sex drive..." He shrugged. "All we really have to do is repattern him. Sort of make him regret what he's done—and get interested in girls again."

Mr. Speidel nodded vigorously, took out his fountain pen and signed the release and dated it. "He'll be grateful to you for the rest of his life, I know it."

Speidel nodded. "He's a good boy. We just have to put him back on the right track."

HOMOSEXUALITY

In 1991, people investigating the difference between male and female brains found that there was a region of the hippocampus that was twice as large in heterosexual males as in females and homosexual males. The next year researchers claimed to have found a gene that apparently predisposes men toward homosexuality.

Socrates and Plato, who had a love relationship as well as a scholarly one, probably would have been mystified by a supposedly advanced culture that made a big deal out of this. There have been other cultures, like the Etoro in New Guinea, in which homosexuality is mandatory for a certain period of a man's life. All primates and most mammals do it under some conditions. Only humans, presumably, worry about it.

Captain Folsom worried about it a lot. He had authority to back him up, too; the *Diagnostic and Statistic Manual*, DSM-I, still classified homosexuality at the top of the list "302. Sexual Deviation." In May of 1968, this manual would be superseded by the DSM-II. That would still call homosexuality a deviation, but would note "this diagnosis is not appropriate for individuals who perform deviant sexual acts because normal sexual objects are not available to them." Captain Folsom would ignore that. As he ignored Spider's absurd contention that he had never indulged in a homosexual act.

The poor boy was irrational about Lee, the pinko queer. But it was not too late to save him.

SUGGESTIONS

Lee and Beverly sat together on the couch, reading the paper and a text-book, the house cat scrunched impartially between them. Lee scratched the animal's head and it purred loudly. Beverly set her book on the floor and leaned back, rubbing her eyes. "I'm not going to learn this."

"Is that a prediction or a declaration?"

"Algebra." She yawned. "If I'd dropped out last week I could've gotten some tuition back."

"Why do you need two courses in algebra, anyhow? I got away with one."

"Yeah, but you're dumb." She leaned up against his shoulder. "It's for stat. Need stat for Historical Methods."

Lee put his hand on her thigh and the cat scrambled for freedom. "You ought to drop out. Larry's offer's still open."

"Sounds like fun, slap paint all day. I've seen how tired you get."

He shrugged. "It's twice minimum wage."

"Huh uh. Minimum wage went up to $1.60 on the first."

"Larry'd go $3.20 if we asked him. He'd like to have a girl on the job."

"Sure, stare at my butt all day. Larry gives me the creeps."

Lee took a pencil and scribbled on the newspaper. "Look, I get five an hour. If we both put in a thirty-hour week, we'd clear almost a thousand a month."

"Really?" She studied his figures.

"And last month I made more than two hundred dollars on the grass. We can almost live on that." She rolled her eyes but didn't say anything.

"We could put away a solid eight or nine hundred a month. Summer comes, we say fuck it and split for California." They had talked about that. "Haight-Ashbury, man. It's another world."

"Yeah," she said. She leaned over and picked up the book and opened it where a folded over sheet of graph paper was holding her place. "See how I do on this test." She stared at the page without reading.

Lee slid his hand up to her crotch and stroked lightly with his fingertip. She smiled. "I'll give you ten minutes to stop doing that."

THE FIFTH VERSION

Captain Folsom's "office" was actually one-fourth of a large office that had been quadrisected by six-foot-high government-gray dividers. He had a *Playboy* calendar up on one wall and diplomas from his two degrees framed on another. His desk blotter was an expensive-looking leather artifact embossed with the seal and motto of the University of Oklahoma.

He hung up his hat and coat and looked with mild satisfaction upon his orderly domain. There was a single piece of interoffice mail in his In box, and the person who had delivered it had taken care to center it precisely.

He sat in the swivel chair and opened the envelope and frowned. It was another one of Private Speidel's fantasies. He should never have given the boy that tablet.

•••

We didn't know what to expect when we came up out of the shelter. Nothing but ashes, I figured, even though it was a park. Washington was a prime target, not even fifteen miles away.

But it was surprisingly green. Normal-looking at first, but then you realized there weren't any big trees; there weren't any plants that looked like they were more than about two years old. We'd been in the shelter for three.

There was a sparrow hopping around in a bush, that looked bigger than a normal bird. I stared at it. It had a long curved beak and three eyes.

Sarge said the Geiger counter was going crazy, two hundred roentgens. Be thankful for the suits. We'd just take a look around and then go back down under. Lock and load and get into formation.

I got the rear position, center file, which made me nervous. We could walk a couple of hundred yards past a sniper and then he'd pop the guys in back and run like hell.

But there couldn't be anyone alive up here, I told myself. Not unless they lived underground and only came up in suits like ours. Russians? Forget it. We blew them to atoms the first day. While they were doing the same thing to us.

We walked around Bethesda for several hours, stunned by the magnitude of the destruction. Almost every building was a charred ruin, overgrown with come-along vines and honeysuckle. The People's Drug Store was half standing, though, and we raided it for cigarettes. The candy was all spoiled.

We were almost back to the shelter entrance on Highland when they hit us. Mutants, dozens of them, armed with rifles, machineguns, and shotguns. They'd been hidden behind a low stone fence. When they popped up and opened fire, I didn't even have time to raise my weapon and get a sight picture. Batman went down and then Moses, who was in front of me, just exploded. They must have hit his demo bag. I was wiping the blood off my faceplate when a big round must have hit my helmet. Bulletproof, but it was like being clubbed by a baseball bat. I went down, out cold.

I don't know whether it was minutes or hours later when I woke up. I could hear individual shots, a "pop" every thirty seconds or so. Through my smeared faceplate I could see one mutant walking around with a rifle, shooting people in the head.

He was an ugly son of a bitch. His eyes were twice the size of humans' and blood red. His teeth were long and pointed; it looked like he couldn't close his mouth. His hands had three fingers and a thumb and were covered with hair, but his head was bald, scaly.

He wasn't paying a lot of attention to what he was doing, just shooting corpses at random, sometimes stooping to take some ammo or other stuff from a utility belt. I thought maybe if I lay still, he might go on past me. My M16 was locked and loaded, but I didn't know whether it worked. Besides, if I tried to sit up and aim, I'd probably faint again. My head was pounding, vision blurry.

I was still thinking about it when he walked over to me and pointed the rifle at my head. Before I could react, he pulled the trigger—but it went *click*, out of ammo. I tipped the M16 up to point at his crotch and pulled the trigger. Eighteen rounds ripped him wide open. He fell over with a terrible high-pitched squeal.

I staggered to my feet and looked around. No mutants, but I reloaded anyway. God, it was a terrible sight. All of the platoon had been blown away, some of them literally shot to pieces. The street was slick with blood and there were flies everywhere. There were four dead mutants over by the stone wall.

I scarfed up an M79 and a bandolier of grenades and headed back to the shelter. No sign of any of the mutants, not until I got there.

The door was open, deadly radioactive air flooding the chambers. I stepped inside but didn't have to go past the anteroom, piled high with corpses. I knew there was noplace for me to go. I grabbed a box of air filters for my suit and found another bandolier of grenades. Then I went back topside to hunt mutants. I think I went a little crazy. But then I knew I was going to die.

•••

Well, it was interesting. He wondered about the two hundred roentgens. Did Speidel make that up? Folsom was embarrassed to realize that he didn't remember whether the effect of radiation was measured in roentgens or volts or what. Rams?

So he shot the enemy in the crotch. In the genitals. Speidel's father was balding and had hair on the back of his hands. Prominent teeth. At the last interview he'd had bloodshot eyes, a drinker's eyes.

Was Speidel acting out some Oedipal fantasy here? Perhaps it was something less conventional. Probably anger at his own homosexuality, since shooting is a pretty obvious symbol, and he shot at the other man's penis. Ejaculating on his father's penis? A desire for sexual domination of his father?

Folsom opened the file drawer and took out Spider's previous essay. He set them side by side and opened his top drawer, where he had 3 x 5 cards in five pastel colors plus white, in orderly stacks. It was Friday, pink day, so he selected a third of an inch of pink cards and slid all but one of them into his breast pocket. He titled one "Private S's fantasies," and read through the space-opera one, which he didn't realize was loosely modeled on *Starship Troopers*, a novel by Robert Heinlein. Captain Folsom had never read any science fiction, which he thought was trivial, nor fantasy, except for some pornography, which was of professional interest.

He printed neatly with a Rapidograph drawing pen:

> Hostility toward Authority
> Sarcasm
> "Moses" in both/anti-Semitism?
>   — Explodes in both, blood
> "Batman" in both/negro? racism?
> "I guess I went a little crazy"

in both
Hopelessness in both
Hostility, revenge

He studied the card. Actually, patterns were emerging. He should encourage Private Speidel to write some more.

He did have more pressing things to worry about; patients in worse condition. But a lot of them would never be helped. It was gratifying to work with the ones like Speidel, where you could identify the problem and see that it was amenable to solution. He took out an Interoffice Memo tablet and routed to Dr. Tolliver a request to begin aversion therapy with Speidel, augmented by electroshock.

NO NEWS IS GOOD NEWS

Beverly woke up the next morning feeling happy. She had decided that algebra was less important than working for Dr. King and saving a little money so they could go spend the summer with Lee's friends in San Francisco. The world was changing fast, and she wanted to be out *in* it, not imprisoned in a classroom.

She looked at Lee's face for a long time in the thin dawn light. He looked childlike, almost pretty, when he was sleeping. She suppressed the slight urge to wake him up. He probably didn't have much juice left after last night, and besides, they ought to save their strength. They'd volunteered to go down to the Mall and help with the construction of the shantytown that was being built for the Poor People's March.

She slipped out of bed and dressed quietly, jeans and a MAKE LOVE NOT WAR sweatshirt. She liked the defiant sexy feeling of not wearing underwear—Lee didn't so she didn't, except for her period. But she wouldn't go braless. That was a little too much, too public. And she wouldn't walk the ten steps to the bathroom naked, even though other people did.

She made as little noise as possible in the bathroom and decided not to shower; she'd be grimy in a couple of hours, anyhow. Maybe they could take a bath together when they got back.

Downstairs, she put on water for coffee and brought in the paper. It was a good news day, the 16th of March. Bobby Kennedy announced that he was going to run for president! Martin Luther King was pressing Johnson on human rights. Alexandr Dubcek was defying Moscow—a communist himself, he was declaring an era of democracy and freedom in Czechoslovakia.

Later in the year there would be sadder news about Kennedy and King and Czechoslovakia. But one important thing happened on March 16th that wouldn't make the papers for more than a year.

At 7:30 in the morning, a wave of assault helicopters landed a company of infantrymen outside of the Vietnamese hamlet My Lai-4. Told that it was a "hot LZ," they jumped out of the helicopters shooting. Nobody shot back.

This was Charlie Company, 1st Battalion, 20th Infantry, 11th Brigade—part of the American Division, the Army's newest, largest, and least well-organized division—and though the company had lost forty-two men killed and wounded by land mines and sniper fire, they had never engaged the enemy in combat. They were more than ready.

Their company commander, Captain Ernest Medina, had said that this was their big chance to "get even" with the Viet Cong. The 48th Viet Cong Battalion was holed up in My Lai, and although they outnumbered Charlie Company two to one, Medina had confidence in the Americans' superior firepower and fighting ability. All the women and children should be out of the hamlet, getting an early start for their weekly sojourn to the market in Quang Ngai, six miles away.

There was no one in there but VC. Kill them all. Destroy all crops and livestock, and burn the fucking place to the ground. It would be a lesson to the whole province.

It wound up being the wrong kind of lesson. Eventually, it would have as much effect as the Tet Offensive toward demoralizing America and losing the war. Medina was wrong about the VC and he was wrong about his men's competence: other people in the Americal Division derided the 11th as "the Butcher Brigade," a gang of undertrained thugs who beefed up their body counts with dead civilians.

The LZ wasn't hot. The only man killed in the disembarking firestorm was an old farmer, unarmed. The enemy must have been holding their fire. Charlie Company advanced cautiously on the hamlet. A few people tried to flee the village and fell in a hail of bullets: two women, three children.

The company was not fired upon as it swept into the village. Nobody knows what started it, but a couple of soldiers began shooting into the grass huts, and then more people started shooting, and the situation degenerated into a massacre. There was no return fire; there were no VC. Young women were raped and sodomized and then shot pointblank. Old men and women and children were herded into a drainage ditch and exterminated with aimed single-shot fire; target practice. Fifteen or twenty women and children were discovered kneeling, praying, around burning incense. They were executed with shots to the head.

Medina's men killed more than three hundred old men, women, and children on 16 March 1968; their only casualty was one man who shot himself in the foot. The official battle report was sixty-nine Viet Cong killed in action, with no mention of civilian casualties.

Since Spider wasn't over there any longer, Beverly didn't pay much attention to battle reports. Her Sunday *Post* the next day would report America's successful engagement in two paragraphs that had more typographical errors than facts: "Troops of the U.S. Light 41st Brigade killed 128 Vietcong on the central coast Saturday… two Americans were killed and ten wounded in the fight on the coastal lowlands just outside Quang Ngai City 330 miles northeast of Saigon. The enemy force had been softened up before the U.S. ground assault by an air attack. Helicopter gunships and artillery covered the infantrymen's advance, which began around 7:50 a.m. and ended around nightfall.

"One company of the American brigade swept into the enemy area shortly after the air attack. Then a second company landed in helicopters an hour later two miles to the north to try to cut off the Vietcong's escape routes."

About a year later, one of the men who had witnessed it would step forward to tell the truth. Fourteen soldiers were tried for war crimes. Thirteen were acquitted. Lieutenant William Calley was convicted of the murder of twenty-two civilians and sentenced to life imprisonment. The term was reduced to ten years; he served three and was given a dishonorable discharge.

The Americal Division would be deactivated in 1971. Its own people called it "the outfit that couldn't even do wrong right."

STUFF AND NONSENSE

Among the artifacts available for Folsom's analysis were a sketchy account of Spider's service in Vietnam, an evaluation form filled out when he finished Advanced Individual Training at Fort Leonard Wood, and a plastic bag with the wallet and a small notebook that he had carried with him in the field. The notebook's pages, stained with red laterite dust, had the names and home addresses of other soldiers, notations about IOUs, and several pages of Vietnamese words and phrases with English equivalents, in somebody else's handwriting. The last page had several puzzling statements, ending with "We had sexual intercourse" and "I got run over by a tank."

In the wallet there was a school picture of Beverly and another picture of Beverly and Spider at a picnic. A tightly folded-up mimeographed copy of "The Ballad of Eskimo Nell," a pornographic poem. Payment records and receipts for money orders he'd sent home. A single playing card, the ace of diamonds. There was an interesting "conduct card" issued by MACV, the Military Assistance Command/Vietnam:

THE ENEMY IN YOUR HANDS

As a member of the U.S. military forces, you will comply with the Geneva Prisoner of War Conventions of 1949 to which your country adheres. Under these conventions:

YOU CAN AND WILL

DISARM YOUR PRISONER
IMMEDIATELY SEARCH HIM THOROUGHLY
REQUIRE HIM TO BE SILENT
SEGREGATE HIM FROM OTHER PRISONERS
GUARD HIM CAREFULLY
TAKE HIM TO THE PLACE DESIGNATED BY
YOUR COMMANDER

YOU CANNOT AND MUST NOT

MISTREAT YOUR PRISONER
HUMILIATE OR DEGRADE HIM
TAKE ANY OF HIS PERSONAL EFFECTS WHICH
DO NOT HAVE SIGNIFICANT MILITARY VALUE
REFUSE HIM MEDICAL TREATMENT IF RE-
QUIRED
AND AVAILABLE

ALWAYS TREAT YOUR PRISONER HUMANELY

Folsom smiled grimly at that. He knew how humanely GIs treated prisoners. He had read all about atrocities like torturing people and shoving them out of helicopters. Some of his patients had lots of stories about such things, although most of them did not. That was probably denial, of course, and understandable.

He puzzled over the cryptic statements in the back of the notebook. If he had asked Spider about them, he would know that Spider was just continuing a practice he'd begun in civilian life: whenever he heard a joke he liked, he jotted down the last line of it, to help him remember. Those last two were from the last jokes he'd heard in Vietnam:

JOKE #1

Two GIs are in a barracks. One is telling the other about the fantastic time he had on his weekend pass:

"I take the fuckin' bus into fuckin' Jonesville and go into this bar, you know, right by the fuckin' bus station?"

"Yeah?"

"I'm not in there ten fuckin' minutes and in walks this fuckin' BEAUTI-
FUL babe, and she can go anyplace in the fuckin' bar but she sits down on
the fuckin' stool right next to me!"

"No shit?"

"No fuckin' shit. We start to fuckin' talk and it turns out we're from the
same fuckin' town—went to the same fuckin' high school, she used to watch
me play fuckin' basketball."

"I'll be damned."

"Fuckin' A. Anyhow, we go down to fuckin' McDonald's and we go to some
fuckin' movie and, can you dig it, she pays for MY fuckin' TICKET. We're
watchin' this fuckin' movie and all of a sudden she grabs my fuckin' cock
and whispers how fuckin' horny she is and can we leave the fuckin' movie
and go to her place?"

"Aw, you're fuckin' shittin' me."

"No shit, man, she's a fuckin' LIVE one. We go one block to her fuckin'
pad, man, and it is fuckin' gorgeous. She must be a fuckin' millionaire. She
pulls me into the bedroom and tears off all her fuckin' clothes and jumps
on this big fuckin' waterbed, and then we, uh, we had sexual intercourse."

JOKE #2

This new 'cruit's been in-country about a month and he's frustrated. He
goes to the Field First Sergeant and says, "Sarge, I signed up to come over
here and kill gooks and make the world safe for democracy, but I ain't even
seen a fuckin' gook. They just hide in the bushes and take a shot at you and
split. Am I ever gonna get one of them bastards in my sights?"

The sergeant smiled and said, "Son, you just been goin' about it wrong.
You got to use *psychology*! You go out in the boonies and get yourself a good
field of fire, hide behind somethin' solid, and shout at the top of your lungs
THE HELL WITH HO CHI MINH! You just shout it over an' over. Pretty
soon the dink gets so pissed at you he starts to shoot. But you're behind
somethin' solid, so you don't get hit. You just peek out and see where the
muzzle flashes are comin' from—puffs of smoke, leaves fallin'—lock and
load and empty a clip at the son of a bitch. I can guarantee you'll get your
gook that way. He might even get so pissed he'll step out in the open."

"Gosh, thanks, Sarge. I'll go do just that."

About two weeks go by. One day the Field First Sergeant is walkin' to the
tennis court—did I say he was Special Forces out in Kontum?—and along
comes two medics carryin' a stretcher, and on it is that private. He looks
like shit warmed over, man, all bloody bandages and blood bags drainin'
into each arm.

"Good God, boy," the sergeant says. "What the hell happened to you?"

He spits out some blood and teeth and says, "Well, Sarge, I did just like you told me. I got in this clearing with a great field of fire and got down behind a big fat rubber tree and yelled out THE HELL WITH HO CHI MINH at the top of my lungs. I yelled it three times and it was just like you said. Fuckin' gook ran right out into the clearing."

"Yeah? So what the hell happened?"

"Aw...the fuckin' gook yelled THE HELL WITH LBJ, and while we were in the clearing shakin' hands a fuckin' *tank* ran over us."

EXIT

Spider and two other patients were in the day room working on a jigsaw puzzle of an aerial photograph of Washington, D.C. They were all wrapped in blankets. The day room windows were open, orders from Captain My Captain, and a stiff morning breeze blew in.

The puzzle was a challenge. There was no picture to guide them; it just came out of a shoebox labeled PITCURE OF WASH D.C. They had assembled all of the border and were slowly building from there.

His blond friend, who had "poked" his wife, was named Arlo Sanders.

The other puzzler was Frank White, who was not white and not particularly frank. In fact, he was downright evasive.

"This piece gonna go here," he said, and carefully positioned a piece exactly in the middle.

"Yeah, sure." Sanders turned to Spider. "We got a fuckin' genius on our hands."

"It's the fuckin' dome, man, the Capitol Dome." He pointed around the edge. "You got you' North Capitol Street, you got you' South Capitol Street, you got you' Pennsylvania Fuckin' Avenue. Place they come together is where all you' Senators eat bean soup."

"You live here too?" Spider said.

For about half a minute he didn't say anything, rocking back and forth, staring at the empty space inside the puzzle. Then he started to croon. "Sometimes I live in the country," he sang, a hoarse imitation of Leadbelly; "Sometimes I live in the town. Sometimes I take a great notion...to jump in the river and drown." He picked up another piece and set it down a couple of inches from the Capitol. "Union Station. Got rails."

Sanders pulled the blanket tighter and looked back at the ward. "How long they gonna fuckin' take?" Everybody who wasn't bedridden had been moved into the day room while the ward was being mopped out.

"Till the day room freezes over," Spider said.

Sanders crumpled up an empty cigarette pack and tossed it toward the wastepaper basket. It missed. "Got a weed?"

Spider slid his pack of Luckies over. Sanders lit one and coughed. "How can you smoke this fuckin' shit?"

"Death wish." He offered the pack to White, who shook his head slowly and started rocking again.

Two big white aides Spider hadn't seen before came down the corridor into the day room. "John Speidel?" one of them said.

"Him." Spider pointed at Sanders.

"Fuck you, man." He held out his dog tags. "I'm Sanders. He's Speidel."

"I get confused," Spider said. "Identity crisis."

"*Give* you a crisis," the other aide said. "Come on along."

"Where to?"

"You got a date with a angel."

"Yeah, I bet." He shook out a couple of cigarettes onto the table in front of Sanders and went with the two men, shuffling, looking pale.

BRUSH WITH DEATH

Beverly had found a pair of painter's coveralls for a dollar at Next to New. They were a couple of sizes too large, baggy and shapeless, so she figured they might prevent Larry and the other guys from putting eyetracks all over her butt.

Larry had already been at the job site for an hour when they showed up at eight. He'd used the time to mask one window and set out dropcloths, ladders, and buckets of paint.

The two other guys who showed up, Vince and Haskel, were white and long-haired like Lee. Vince was nineteen and had gotten his draft notice; he was nervously killing time until he had to report for duty in three weeks. Haskel was a vet who'd been out of the Army less than a year. He'd lost two fingers from his left hand in Vietnam and wore hearing aids in both ears. He made Vince nervous.

Larry was a fortyish Puerto Rican who reminded Beverly of a fox, or a weasel. He was small, fast, and restless but graceful with tools. His intensity had scared Beverly the first time they met; his one long look that made her feel naked. But as she got to know him better, bringing lunch to Lee twice a week, she relaxed around him. He was just as intense with everybody else.

Larry sent Vince out to get everybody coffee and told the other guys to finish the first coat. They were painting the walls and ceiling of a single large warehouse room. He showed Beverly how to mask windows and paint the frames. It was rather delicate, compared to what the others were doing, and Beverly resented the implication that it was "woman's work." But the one-inch finishing brush was easier on the hand and wrist than the heavy rollers the boys were using on the walls and ceiling, and it really was the right job for her. She enjoyed taking pains and getting things right. Besides, her right wrist still ached from the weekend's unaccustomed labor, wrestling boards and hammering nails downtown.

Once everything was set up, Larry went off to another job, tacitly leaving Lee in charge. The morning went by pretty fast. Vince had a big radio, and he amiably alternated between Top 40 and WGMS, the classical station, each half hour. There were ten large windows along one wall. Beverly finished half of them before noon.

They sat on a rolled-up carpet and worked their way through a bucket of fried chicken and a sixpack. Beverly declined beer because she already felt drowsy; she also passed on the joint Lee rolled for dessert.

Haskel sat on the floor and leaned back against the carpet roll. He took one big hit on the joint, but that was all. "Can't do much shit," he explained to Beverly. "Takes me back to Nam."

"You were injured, uh, badly hurt."

He grunted and pulled up his shirt to show a long puckered scar that ran from his left breast down to his belt. "Same explosion that did my hand." He gestured. "I already told the guys about it."

"Go ahead," Lee said. Vince nodded but looked a little sick.

"It was a mortar round, might have been friendly fire, American." He blew out a breath. "Killed everybody else, the rest of the crew. We were a one-five-five howitzer."

"That's awful," she said. "Were you in a fire base?"

"Huh uh, no. That's what was funny. We were in a pussy, 'scuse me, a relatively safe position in a big base camp. We mostly did artillery demos for the new guys. I mean, this place never got hit. But then one night it did.

"We never even got a round off. Started to get incoming, maybe four in the morning, and we were hustling to get inside the emplacement where the gun was, you know, like a low wall of sandbags. About half of us, six, got in and then a mortar round popped right in the middle of us. Cooked off one of our own rounds, blooey." He took a swig of the beer.

"It didn't hurt much. I was like just numb. Couldn't get up." He fingered a scar on his throat. "Tried to call for a medic but I couldn't make a sound. It was all dark; I didn't know what the hell had happened."

His voice got flat and quiet. "Then somebody popped a star shell or illumination round, and it was really awful. I mean those guys were my buddies, and there they were. Just all over the place. I don't think there was any piece bigger than a leg. Looked down and saw my own insides and I just fainted. Didn't even notice the hand. Just fainted dead away."

Beverly felt a little faint, too. "How long ago?"

"Coupla years." He drew up his knees and leaned forward so his chin was resting on them. "It's mostly okay now. I was pretty fucked up for a while, especially since I couldn't play the guitar. Used to do a lot of rock an' roll." He wiggled the two fingers and thumb on his left hand. "Found out I can do electric bass just fine, though. Workin' on that.

"Lee says your ex is in Walter Reed."

"He's, yeah." She looked at the floor. "He was wounded but that's not it. He's in the mental ward. Something happened, I guess, that he just couldn't handle."

"He a newbie? I mean, did he have much combat?"

"I don't know. I don't think he wrote me about everything that happened. But before he was out in the field he was in Graves Registration. He said that was a lot worse."

Haskel made a face. "Ye-etch. Probably." He lit a cigarette. "I was in Walter Reed for eight weeks, rehab. Not a bad place, for the Army."

"Did you get mail?"

"Oh, yeah. Dear old Mom wrote me once a week."

"I keep writing Spider but I don't get any answers. They won't let me see him, either."

"I tell her not to worry about that," Lee said. "They probably control the mail both ways pretty tightly in a mental ward."

"Oh, yeah, yeah. Nothin' you can do. Just hang in there." Haskel stood up and stretched. "Larry gonna check in at one?"

Lee looked at his watch. "Yeah, ten minutes. Let's look busy."

Beverly was glad that she worked with her back to the others, so they couldn't see her tears. She was angry at Haskel for getting through it so well, and angry at herself for feeling mad at him. Angry at the Army and the Vietnamese. Angry at Spider.

THE SIXTH VERSION

The new suits were really uncomfortable, the way you could barely move your arms and legs, and the rubber thing clenched between your teeth. Actually, you could go anywhere by just *thinking* in a special way; the suit's arms and legs would respond. But you couldn't move your arm to take the rubber mouthpiece out.

What was the thing for, anyhow? The jungle air was breathable, but not like Earth—lots of chemical smells and something like urine—so maybe the thing was just to keep us from talking to each other. Like asking, What the fuck are we doing here? Whose war is this, anyhow? But we rolled along through the jungle, smooth like on wheels, the come-along vines snapping at our ankles, the sky green, green-on-green.

Couldn't smoke with the fucking mouthpiece on, either, and I'm thinking why are we all dressed in light blue and white, standing out against all this green, and just at that thought it happens—Batman goes down dead and there's gunfire everywhere, loud, and then Moses explodes in a spray of blood and guts and I lose it, I lose it, I try to run but the suit doesn't work anymore, I'm helpless, struggling inside the suit, and here comes the man with the skull face, he has things like batons in each hand, he jabs me on both sides of the head and I pass out.

I wake up in the clearing and the man with the skull face shuffles from body to body with his batons. Vultures walk behind him. Even the people who are obviously dead get the treatment: he touches both batons to the temples and there's this humming sound, and the guy's brains blow out the top of his head, boiling. My M16's just a few inches away, but I can't move a muscle; I'm totally paralyzed. Maybe I'm dead? I don't have the mouthpiece anymore, though I can still taste it; could I taste it if I was dead? He works his way to me and I try, try to reach the gun but all I can do is make little squeaky noises. He leans over with the batons but instead of blowing out my brains he touches them together. They make a blue spark and crackle and I smell ozone, and he's gone.

I'm sore all over. I feel like I've been in a fight. I'm tasting starch and I wake up in a bed. I guess I've gone a little crazy.

SCHIZO (3)

In 1968 there were relatively few practitioners who would prescribe electroconvulsive therapy, "electroshock," for patients who exhibited symptoms of schizophrenia. It was the treatment of choice for severe depression, and would still be so used for decades, especially with suicidal patients. It produces relatively fast results.

By the mid-fifties, most schizophrenics were given drugs, or a combination of drugs and psychotherapy, rather than electricity. Some clinics relied heavily on electroshock well into the seventies, though; detractors called those places "shock boxes." Repeated use of electroshock, especially in high voltages, can damage the brain, impairing memory and intelligence.

Some lobotomists who preferred electroshock, rather than a conventional anesthetic, prior to stirring the brain with an ice pick (see "Schizo (1)") used garden-variety line current, straight from the socket. Certain of the psychological changes attributed to transorbital lobotomy were probably due to the jolt instead.

Properly applied, it's not the electricity *per se* that affects the patient, but rather the coma induced by the shock. Injected drugs like insulin can bring on a coma with the same desired result, and in fact insulin shock was preferred, for schizophrenia uncomplicated by depression, by most therapists from the 1930s on.

The simplicity and drama of electroshock proved irresistible to some professionals, though, like Captain Folsom. His supervisor might not have approved the treatment for Spider if he had been familiar with the details of the case. But he was not particularly well-informed about any of Folsom's patients. Most of his expertise and energy went into indulging and concealing his own problem, chronic and acute abuse of alcohol and other drugs.

BETTER LIVING THROUGH ELECTRICITY

Spider had three shock treatments in a week, which made him withdrawn and tired. But he had also gotten a box from home, books and cookies. He drifted out of his lethargy enough to pass the cookies around the ward, gravely going from bed to bed with the coffee can full of homemade gingersnaps. Then he returned to inspect the books.

His old dog-eared *Handbook of the Heavens.* An introduction to psychology. *Conan the Conqueror.* A rolled-up map of the southern constellations.

He wondered about that for a minute. Then he checked the box's wrapping: it was his old Vietnam address. The box had gone to Kontum and been forwarded here. He ate a gingersnap; it lacked snap.

Interesting. Unless somebody had gone to a lot of trouble unwrapping and rewrapping, the package had not been inspected. He had a hunch they wouldn't appreciate his having a psychology book. He sat on the bed and read parts of it for an hour. When Knox came in with his pill cart, Spider slipped the book under the mattress.

He traded Knox a cookie for his Thorazine. "Food from home?"

"Yeah, dear old Mom." He washed the pill down with juice. "Knox, look," he said quietly. "Am I a schizophrenic?"

"Don't ask me that, man. I just work here."

"Don't give me that shit. You see a hundred schizophrenics a day. Am I one of them?"

Knox looked at his chart and frowned. "You want my diagnosis," he whispered, "my professional opinion, what I say is that you fucked up in the head. Now, on my way to work, walkin', I pass three or four people look more fucked up in the head than you. But just because they ain't in here don't mean *you* ought to be out there. See?"

"Okay. But am I a schizophrenic?"

"I don't know what the fuck you are. You see a guy who's not there, right?"

"Well, he is *there.* He's just not real."

"Jesus." He shook his head, hard. "You know what it's like to talk to crazy people all day long?" He laughed. "Spider, I don't know what the fuck a schizophrenic is, and I don't think Captain My Captain does either. I mean, you can say a guy who stares at the wall all day jerkin' off, he's probably schizophrenic, and you can say Lyndon Johnson, he probably isn't, but in both cases you gonna find some guy with a degree say the contrary. So what the fuck. You see little green men, you know somethin' wrong with you. The label don't mean shit. Just go with the flow; you get better, they let you out."

"And if I don't get better?"

"At least you don't got to get a job." He pushed the cart on.

Spider ate another cookie, slowly. It was the first time he'd thought of that possibility. What if they *didn't* let him out? Could he wind up like one of those zombies who just sit around and drool?

The man with the skull face appeared on the empty bed next to him, where Sanders used to be until he snapped. Spider tried to project a thought at the apparition. *Go away.* He stayed about ten seconds and then disappeared, as if to demonstrate who was in charge of the situation.

The book said that schizophrenics had auditory hallucinations. The skull guy didn't talk anymore. Did that make him more crazy, or less?

Had he ever seen the guy in real life? A clearing up on a hill. Something to do with Sarge, but Sarge was dead. That's a face he would never forget, the teeth blown out. Slick black blood all over his chest, flies, vultures. What was the deal with the clearing? He'd stuffed C-4 in a tube.

Shit, there was a lot he couldn't remember. Something real important, something Knox had said…

He suddenly stood up, cold sweat evaporating all over his skin. Jerking off. He remembered sitting in the car with Beverly, petting. And he was absolutely sure he wasn't a virgin. But he couldn't remember anything in between. *He couldn't remember fucking her!* Not Beverly, not anybody else.

Knox looked up at him from across the ward. "What's up, Spider? You okay?"

All he could do was shake his head.

DEROS

The popular illusion of the American dogface in World War II was of a determined "Willie and Joe" kind of guy, a civilian in uniform who came to war unwillingly but waged it with stubborn tenacity, year in and year out, slogging through freezing mud and steaming jungle until Hitler and Tojo were finally brought down.

Indeed, some GIs did have to survive years of combat. But most of them did not come through it well. The government's postwar analysis, *Combat Exhaustion*, said "most men were ineffective after 180 or even 140 days. The general consensus was that a man reached the peak of his effectiveness in the first 90 days of combat, that after that his efficiency began to fall off, and that he became steadily less valuable thereafter until he was completely useless."

Certainly one factor that wore these men down was uncertainty: they might be soldiers for another month or another year or just however long it took for their luck to run out. That was one thing the military thought that it could control when Vietnam rolled around. Instead of sixteen million men scattered all over the planet, they could take care of this one with a few hundred thousand working in a country the size of New Mexico. And each one of them could work for a definite period of time; twelve months or thirteen, depending on rank and branch of service.

So every soldier went to Vietnam with a magic date, more important than any date could ever be for the rest of his life: DEROS, the Date Eligible to Return from OverSeas.

It backfired. Soldiers developed "short-timers' attitudes," being reluctant to undertake dangerous missions when they only had a few weeks, or even months, left in the field. Whenever anyone was killed within a couple of months of DEROS, it added to the superstition that the closer you were to leaving, the more likely you were to be killed, which did wonders for morale. Morale was also hurt by the fact that platoons and companies tended not to develop a group identity, since people rotated in and out on a staggered schedule. If you had only a month till DEROS, you had a lot more in common with any random short-timer than with the FNG the Army had just tossed into your platoon.

APRIL

Beverly had never liked April Fool's Day. As far back as she could remember, her father had startled her with some malicious silliness that he considered good clean fun, and so for more than half her life she had tiptoed through that day, expecting the worst.

This April 1st, she was invited to be with Spider's father, not her own, going with him to Walter Reed to visit Spider for the first time. His mother had begged off tearfully, saying she would do more harm than good.

Lee wondered whether Beverly would do any good, either, and said so, but otherwise didn't pressure her. It was obvious that she was unsure and nervous about it and would probably be miserable no matter which course she chose. So he played it smart and stayed neutral.

Mr. Speidel picked her up a little before eight. She was dressed in an alien high-schoolish frock, wearing makeup the way she had when she was dating Spider. Lee watched from an upstairs window as they drove off. He skipped breakfast and went to work early.

She showed up at the warehouse while the guys were eating lunch, still in the frock, her painting clothes rolled up in a grocery bag. Larry wolf-whistled at her prettiness. She smiled nervously and said she had to change.

"Take it easy," Lee said after she disappeared into the bathroom. "Can't you see she's been crying?"

"Hokay, okay. Maybe she needs like some cheerin' up, hmm?"

"Maybe. Let's let her call the shots."

She came back out in the baggy spattered overalls, her hair pinned up, and quietly accepted a slice of cold pizza and a long-necked Budweiser, the first time she'd had a beer on the job. She gave Haskel a dollar and took a quarter in change.

Young Vince broke the silence. "So what was he like?" The other guys shot him a look.

"Oh, he was real quiet. Drugged, for sure." To Lee: "Valium and...what was

319

that one you told me about?"

"Thorazine. Use it to bring people down from bad acid trips."

"That's it. Valium and Thorazine, the doctor said. I'm not sure whether he recognized me. His dad, yeah. But even with his dad he didn't bring up anything about the past.

"He looked really out of it. Just really half-listening to what we said. But he's nervous, too. His dad's umbrella made a noise falling over, and he nearly jumped out of his skin."

"I think that's normal," Haskel said. "I still do it."

"At least he's out of the boonies," Lee said. "He's alive and has a chance to get better."

"The doctor, he give the guy a prognosis?" Larry said, the last word slowly.

"No, not the doctor. He acted half as stoned as Spider. Some other guy, a captain I talked to before on the phone, he was sort of optimistic. But he seemed goofy, too, in person. Fidgety. Maybe being around crazy people all the time gets to you." She looked at Lee. "He will be coming home, he said. In a month or two."

Lee nodded. "We'll handle that when the time comes, I guess."

She put the pizza slice back half-eaten. "I'm not sure any of it's our problem anymore. My problem. If he doesn't even recognize me."

"Well, he'll be happier at home, anyhow."

"I wouldn't count on it. His father was really pissed off at his mother for not coming along, and you can tell that there's something a lot worse than that buried away. He's really on the edge." She sipped at the beer. "It's funny. If you didn't know any of them, and you put all four of them in a room together—Spider and his father and the shrinks—you couldn't say which one of them was really crazy, you know? Spider would seem kind of dumb, yeah, but his father really comes on more nutty, like he was about to explode. He's always been a mean drunk. One of the shrinks is creepy, antsy, and the other's as stoned as any dropout hippy."

Larry laughed. "You ask me, the whole fuckin' world's crazy. Some of us is crazier than others, but it's all a big fuckin' nut house."

"Well, that explains everything," Lee said, and lit up a joint.

Neither Lee nor Beverly had seen the morning paper, which had arrived late after the biggest *Stop the Presses!* order in some years. At the end of a predictable pro forma press conference the previous night, the President dropped a bombshell. Banner headlines exclaimed LBJ TELLS NATION HE WON'T RUN.

Also in the paper, the results of a Gallup poll predicting that Robert Kennedy would beat either Republican, Nixon or Rockefeller, and a wry note saying that ex-actor Ronald Reagan had been chosen as California's favorite-son candidate.

Martin Luther King would have had the headline if LBJ hadn't upstaged him. Dr. King spoke to an audience of 4000 at Washington Cathedral, trying to bolster support for the Poor People's Campaign. The previous week's demonstration in Memphis had erupted in violence; King warned his sympathetic audience that "if nothing is done between now and June to raise ghetto hope, I feel this summer will be not only as bad, but *worse* than last year."

In years to come, not many people would see past the smoke and flames of 1968 to remember that previous summer. Dr. King had three days to live.

SWEET MYSTERY OF LIFE

Spider could smell Captain My Captain's tobacco for some hours before his appointment. He must have changed blends; it smelled a little better. He took the list out of his pocket and checked for the hundredth time what he was going to ask. He stared at the clock and wished it had a second hand. When it finally crawled to 10:29, he walked across the hall and knocked on the door. When Captain Folsom bade him enter, he walked in, hardly limping anymore, and stood at loose attention until Folsom offered a chair, waving without looking up from the file folder he was studying.

As usual, Folsom gazed at him for an uncomfortable period before speaking. "So. Specialist Knox said you wanted to speak to me about your medication."

"Yes, sir. I just can't think straight. I have trouble, um, concentrating." He tried to remember what was on the list. "My memory's shot to hell, too. Maybe that's the shock therapy, though."

"You've become an expert on shock therapy?"

"No, sir. I'm not an expert on anything. In fact, I feel pretty stupid about everything. But I do know there's things that happened to me that I just don't remember anymore. Big things."

"Such as?"

"Like sex. I know I've done it because they said I was getting pills for syphilis. Antibiotics. But I don't remember ever doing it. Not with anybody."

"Spider." He inspected his pipe, a meerschaum whose finish was an ugly dapple of off-white, brown, yellow, and black. "Sometimes we forget things because they were too unpleasant to remember."

"That just doesn't make sense."

"Sex isn't always pleasant. Sometimes it's very painful."

"If I was gonna forget unpleasant things, how come I remember every stinking body I took out of every fucking bag at Graves Registration? How come I remember everybody in my platoon gettin' blown away in that ambush? *That's* unpleasant. I can't forget those things. I think about them all the time."

"It would be worse without the drugs and the ECT."

"I don't know. If I'm gonna remember the bad shit anyhow, I'd just as soon remember everything."

"You can't say that. Don't you see? You can't know how bad the things were that you're forgetting, repressing."

"Yeah, like getting laid. That sounds really horrible." He crossed his legs and rubbed the sole of his foot through the slipper. "The bullshit with the dirty pictures and the shocks. Is that why I've forgotten having sex?"

"Oh, no, never," he said quickly. "A slight shock to your foot couldn't affect your memory." Three days before, they'd sat down Spider in a small mirrored room with a stack of 8 x 10 black-and-white photographs of naked people. Some of the subjects were standing or lying alone in various postures, and some were couples engaged in various sexual practices. Whenever the picture showed homosexual sex, or just a man alone in a state of arousal, Spider was given a shock through a pair of electrodes taped to his foot. Captain Folsom had put the aversion-therapy treatment together himself, at no cost to the government, and he was proud of it.

Spider looked at his list. "That was another thing I wanted to know. I got a shock every time I turned over a picture of a queer. Is that supposed to prove something? Does somebody think that *I'm* queer?"

"Well, we don't use that word. But you said in an interview that you had had sex with a man named Lee, and you enjoyed it."

"*What?*"

"And when you came here you had a syphilis chancre in the anus. There is only one way that could happen."

Spider looked at him for a moment and his jaw dropped. "Oh, bullshit. Me let somebody fuck me in the ass?" He screwed up his face. "I mean, ee-*ewe*. I'd kill him first. I really would."

"His name was Lee Madden. You remember Lee Madden?"

Spider looked nervously around the room, as if there might be a queer hidden someplace. "This is such bullshit! Jesus! This Lee Madden says he fucked me? You bring him here and *I'll* fuck him, all right."

Folsom sat quietly, observing. Denial, healthy under the circumstances. "You remember Beverly. You saw her in this room not long ago."

"Yeah, 'course I do. I don't remember fucking her, though."

"She's Lee Madden's roommate. You must have met him through her."

"Now, wait." He looked at the floor and thought. "She does have a room-mate Lee, but Lee's a girl. Oriental, really pretty. I remember now, some. Maybe I did have sex with her, with Lee, not Beverly."

"Lee is a twenty-two-year-old white male who got out of the draft for homosexuality."

"So I met him over at Beverly's and let him cornhole me."

"That's the word you used before."

"That's absolutely crazy. I would never do that."

"But you said you did."

"*No!*" He gripped the arms of the chair as if to restrain himself. "You believed me then, but you don't believe me now?"

"It's not a question of 'belief'—"

"The *fuck* it isn't!" He got halfway to his feet, leaning toward Folsom.

"Sit *down*, Private! If you can't control yourself I will have Specialist Knox restrain and medicate you."

Spider slumped back into the chair. "Look. Isn't there some way you can test somebody? I mean, I *know* I'm not that way. Like, the pictures of the girls, they got to me, but the pictures of the boys didn't do anything."

"That could be a defense mechanism. How do you explain getting a syphilis sore...there...and on the mouth, rather than on the penis?"

"How the hell should I know? Ask some sexologist, if there is such a thing."

Folsom pursed his lips. "Do you know what Occam's razor is?"

"Huh uh." Spider swallowed hard. "A treatment for syphilis?"

"No, it's a logical principle. Basically, it means that the simplest explanation is usually the right one. In your case, it means that you must have had oral and anal sex with a man, and willfully put it out of your mind." He leaned forward. "But you know...I hadn't thought of this...that doesn't necessarily mean you're homosexual. It could have been done against your will. Then, because you couldn't handle the memory, you blocked it off."

Spider rubbed his chin. "People do that."

"Yes, they do. Maybe there was somebody in your company in Vietnam? Somebody who was aggressively homosexual?"

"Uh, no. Not really. There were two medics everybody knew were gettin' it on together, weirdos. Not aggressive, though."

"Were either of them named Lee?"

"I don't know. They were both Doc; Artillery Doc and Engineer Doc."

He nodded blankly at that. He was thinking. "You're still having the bad dreams."

"Not every night. Sometimes."

"And the apparition? The man with no face?"

"He, uh, hasn't been around in a while."

"Well." Folsom wrote several lines on a pale yellow 3 x 5 card. Then he squinted at what he had written and tapped the card on the desk three times. "We'll discontinue the ECT for the time being, and the aversion therapy. And we'll adjust your medication downward, see whether your concentration improves. But *you must promise* me—" he stabbed the yellow card at Spider for punctuation—"promise that you'll tell the truth if you start feeling worse."

"Oh, I will, sir, I promise."

"Bad dreams, hallucinations, funny feelings about the men around you. We can fix them all, but sometimes it takes time."

"Yes, sir. Understood,"

"Well. That's all. You may go."

"Thank you, sir." Spider tried not to move too fast, leaving. The pipe smoke was really getting to him. He carefully slipped the door shut, and noticed three things:

The smoke smell in the corridor was different from inside. There was wood and asphalt. That's what he'd smelled earlier, when he thought Captain My Captain had changed blends.

Most of the patients were standing in the hall, looking toward the nurses' station.

Two white MPs were talking to the duty nurse. They carried automatic rifles.

"What's up?" Spider whispered.

From forty feet away, one of the MPs answered him, turning to face them with his rifle at port arms: "Return to your wards. The Negroes are rioting. Washington is burning."

MARTIN LUTHER KING AND JAMES EARL RAY

Martin Luther King had returned to Memphis in April to try to straighten out the sanitation-worker strike that had escalated into violence, the disturbance possibly started by undercover police infiltrators.

King's party had made reservations to stay in a white-owned hotel. A newspaper story berated him for that, so he changed to the black-owned Lorraine Motel. There was a 205-foot clear shot from the bathroom of a nearby rooming house to King's motel-room balcony. A man named John Willard checked into the rooming house the same morning King checked into the Lorraine. He chose a lousy room whose only saving grace was that it was near the bathroom.

He locked himself into the bathroom and waited.

King stepped out onto the balcony and exchanged a few words with Jesse Jackson and a musician friend. His chauffeur hollered up from the parking lot that it was getting chilly; King ought to get a topcoat before they left for dinner. He agreed and started to return to his room and was struck by a .30-06 bullet on the right jaw. The round is designed for much larger game. He died at St. Joseph's Hospital an hour later, throat torn open, spinal cord severed.

The weapon was immediately recovered, a Remington Model 760, coincidentally the weapon of choice for Marine snipers in Khe Sanh, who routinely attempted head shots at fifteen times the distance between King's balcony and the rooming house bathroom.

There were no fingerprints in the bathroom, none in Willard's room. There was one on the rifle, but it was never linked to anyone. Right after the single shot, two white Mustangs took off in opposite directions from in front of the rooming house. An abandoned white Mustang was later found in Atlanta, ultimately traced to James Earl Ray, an escaped convict who was going to bartending school in Los Angeles under the name Eric Starvo Galt. He had recently undergone plastic surgery and had bought the Mustang with two thousand dollars cash, though he had no legitimate source of income.

Ray was not exactly a cunning criminal. He was eventually arrested in London's Heathrow airport when he accidentally showed two passports with different names on them and—oops!—was found to be carrying a loaded .38 pistol.

The case was quickly closed, but there were loose ends that indicated at least one other person was involved. Ray was a non-smoker, but the floors of the rooming house and the Mustang had been littered with Viceroy butts. Clothes found with the rifle were not the same size as the clothes in the Mustang trunk that led, through Los Angeles laundry marks, to James Earl Ray. Witnesses' descriptions of John Willard varied wildly, though admittedly that's not uncommon. But there were those two white Mustangs.

A lot of people wanted Martin Luther King out of the way. Twenty years after the assassination, his soft-spoken son, County Commissioner Martin Luther King III, said, "That's what he was killed about: redistributing the wealth and resources. And if anybody could have gotten the masses to say 'We want the wealth redistributed,' he could have. So the powers that be said, 'Well, he's got to be removed.'" The son went on to exonerate Lyndon Johnson specifically, saying "It could have been the Mafia, it could have been a number of forces. Anyone who felt threatened that their wealth could be... diluted."

In 1978, the House Assassinations Committee reported that "there is a likelihood that James Earl Ray assassinated Dr. Martin Luther King as the result of a conspiracy." Circumstantial evidence linked Ray with the New Orleans Marcello Mafia family, who might have financed the hit as a favor for the Ku Klux Klan. James Earl Ray apparently had no racial or political reason to murder King himself; he was just a pusher, forger, smuggler, thief, and evidently a better marksman than, say, Lee Harvey Oswald.

Or was he? Ray, who was discharged from the Army for "ineptness," claims he didn't fire the shot. He took money and orders from a man named Raoul, but claims he was set up, and doesn't have any idea as to who actually did the deed.

A deliciously paranoid *frisson* to this tragic crime is that FBI Director J. Edgar Hoover detested Martin Luther King. He had agents tail King and make tapes of an extramarital affair, and then—three weeks before King was to receive the Nobel Peace Prize—mailed the tapes anonymously to King's wife, along with a note suggesting that the only honorable action for King would be suicide. When that bit of blackmail produced no results, he released the tapes to reporters.

Hoover had close personal ties with Mafia figures for most of his life, though until the sixties denied that the Mob existed. He continually blocked Bureau action against organized crime until he was forced into it by the very public opposition of his boss, the attorney general Robert F. Kennedy, whom he also despised.

J. Edgar Hoover planted the news story that made King change his reservation to the Lorraine Motel.

THE FIRE THIS TIME

The television in the lounge was almost always on, but the nurse never allowed it to be tuned to a news program. That was probably smart, since most of the boys and men on the ward had psychological problems relating to Vietnam, and the networks had discovered how profitable it was to provide the public with daily war footage.

But the lack of local news was suddenly disconcerting. They could smell the smoke and when the sun went down they could see the flickering reflection of flames on the low-lying clouds. Were there lunatic mobs ranging around the city attacking white people? Did they survive Vietnam just to be killed by Americans?

Frank White was playing solitaire with Spider. "You have relatives in town, White?"

"Not anymore. Moved out." That was unusually direct for White. "Landlord sell the building fuckin' right out from under 'em, they go back to Sou' Carolina."

"White guy?" Spider asked. "The landlord?"

"Nah. White nigger, is what he was. Jive-ass son of a bitch, he doin' it all over town, is what my father say. Rippin' off the brothers, the motherfucker." He shifted three cards. "You worried about you' folks?"

"Yeah. I tried to call but can't get out."

"They live out Bethesda?" Spider nodded. "Shit, they ain't gonna let 'em burn Bethesda. Gonna be like L.A. a couple years ago. Long as the black folks burn out our own neighborhoods, nobody give a shit. They move in on fuckin' Whitey the fuckin' cops gonna mow 'em down."

"Guess so." Spider built the hearts up from seven to Jack. "Look, I'm sorry."

"What, you kill fuckin' Martin Luther King? You got nothin' to be sorry for."

Knox had moved quietly behind Spider. "Wish you guys wouldn't be talkin' this shit."

"We talk what the fuck we want, motherfucker."

"You want a shot, Frank? That what you want?"

"Get off my fuckin' case, motherfucker." He stood up. "I give *you* a fuckin' shot!"

"Come on, White," Spider said. "You can't beat him."

"Oh, fuck this shit." White flipped the card table over suddenly and dove toward Knox, clutching for his throat. Knox sidestepped and kicked him behind the knee. He went down hard and Knox pinioned both arms behind his back. "Nurse," he said, voice only slightly raised, "Code Blue."

Two other black patients stalked over. "You let go the brother," said one, even bigger than Knox. "Whose side you on, anyhow?"

"Get back in bed, Royce. You want a shot, too?"

"Yeah, whose side you on?" the other one said. Two more black patients joined them.

"You stop this 'side' shit. Need that Blue, nurse."

"Don't get no nurse." Royce stepped forward and aimed a kick at Knox's face. Knox raised one hand to block it and White squirmed away. Three of them piled on Knox and Spider stood up.

"Come on, guys. This won't—" Someone kicked him in the balls and, when he doubled over, rabbit-punched him into oblivion.

FIRES

By mid-afternoon on the 5th of April, there were more than seventy fires raging in Washington, and open looting was going on two blocks from the White House. That building and the Capitol were protected behind cordons of soldiers.

Seventy-five thousand National Guard troops were spread through 110 cities; "controlling" the rioting, arson, and looting that had broken out in black neighborhoods all over the country, and would eventually result in 2500 casualties, 39 deaths.

For some blacks it was an explosion of bottled-up rage. For some, well-publicized by the white press and television, it was just an opportunity to raise hell or go shopping without the inconvenience of cash. (A London *Times* reporter caught in the Washington looting claimed "most of the

youngsters had never heard of Dr. Martin Luther King, let alone his murder.")
For a few, it was an unprecedented political opportunity.

Martin Luther King had not been admired by all blacks. His Nobel Peace
Prize didn't cut any ice with people who perceived America as the battle-
ground in a lopsided race war.

King had followed his idol Gandhi in a belief that nonviolent resistance
would eventually prevail against the white power structure, as it had in India.
His Southern Christian Leadership Council was joined by the mainstream
National Association for the Advancement of Colored People in that belief.
But not many young blacks were listening. Even the pacifistically named
Student Nonviolent Coordinating Committee was moving away from King
and toward the violent radical Black Panther party.

The Black Panthers themselves were split by conflicting ideologies and
personalities at the top. Stokely Carmichael called for a pure color-line
division, blacks of all classes united against all whites. Blacks who didn't
cooperate would be "offed." Eldridge Cleaver didn't think that Black Power
could prevail without the cooperation of sympathetic whites; he called for
a united front of all radical forces against the Establishment, who were not
themselves all white. Both leaders were forceful, charismatic, educated, and
unbending. One party wasn't big enough for both of them.

The Establishment's police almost simplified the problem for the Panthers
on April 5th. Cleaver had hated King, but wasn't above using his death for
political ends. He exhorted a rally in Berkeley to avenge their fallen leader.
Later that day, police surrounded Cleaver and a fellow Panther in a burning building in Oakland. According to Cleaver, they came out with their
hands up, but the cops opened fire anyhow. His companion was hit five
times and killed. Cleaver was spared but was beaten up in the ambulance
and later in jail.

By the end of 1968, Cleaver and Carmichael would flee the country, finding asylum in Algeria and Guinea, respectively. Black resistance to the white
Establishment became more and more fragmented, less effective.

The ghetto fires burned down and in some places neighborhoods were
rebuilt. In some places, they were rebuilt for black people and businesses
to move back in. In Washington, D.C., a couple of blocks from where the
London reporter had talked to the black looters, the new FBI building rose
up from the ashes, a brooding fortress for J. Edgar Hoover, its architecture
jarring in a graceful city. Albert Speer, Hitler's architect, might have liked
it.

BOY HERO

Bright glare and ammonia and a pounding headache. Spider woke up in a hospital bed in a room that was beige, not green. "No concussion," said the voice behind the glare. "You hear me, Speidel?"

"Yeah, yeah, shit." The room started to come into focus. A stranger in a white tunic, holding a doctor's light. Another stranger in a gaudy Hawaiian shirt, green and red and orange.

"What happened? God, I feel like shit." It felt like he'd been kicked in the testicles. He remembered he had been.

"Here. Take a couple of Darvon." He accepted the capsules from the doctor-or-whatever and washed them down with ice water. "You take it from here, Mike. I got a lot of customers."

The other man loomed like a garish jungle cartoon and put a cool hand on Spider's forehead. "You'll be okay, John. Spider."

"Captain Folsom?" Spider hadn't recognized Captain My Captain, out of uniform.

"I came on duty as soon as I heard about the riot," he said gruffly. "An extra pair of hands."

"A riot? That fight in the day room turned into a riot?"

"Well, the duty nurse had to lock herself inside her station and call the MP's. Several of the patients went to the stockade."

That'll cure what ails them, Spider thought. "What happened to Knox?"

"He suffered a broken nose. But he dealt out a good deal more than that."

"Old White jumped him. Never would've thought he could move so fast. Then a bunch of other guys piled on."

"Knox says you stood up for him; that's why you got creamed."

"Uh huh." Actually, Spider didn't think that was exactly what had happened. He did remember standing up, true, and saying something. But nothing heroic.

"I think it would be well to speed up your release rather than put you back on the ward. You know, with all the, uh, Negroes. I'll be calling your parents tomorrow morning. You can rest here for a couple of days while we outprocess you."

"Home?"

"That's right, home and a civilian. You'll outrank me!" He stood up to leave and Spider shook his hand and thanked him numbly. Home? Was he well enough?

A pretty nurse came in with pills. His usual Thorazine and Valium, and a little blue one she said was a sleeping pill. He took them all and then regretted the sleeping pill when he heard the theme from *Star Trek* come from the TV. He watched about fifteen minutes of an episode he hadn't seen before, but couldn't keep his eyes open.

LIFE IS BUT A DREAM (2)

Spider is standing on the walk that leads to his home in Bethesda. Behind him, a jeep pulls away.

He has a heavy duffle bag and, inexplicably, his M16. No, it's Sarge's M16, the one that works, with two magazines taped back-to-back. The selector is on AUTO. He clicks it back to SAFE, but then resets it back to fully automatic. This only looks like home. He knows where he is.

Spider is wearing tattered jungle fatigues, spattered with blood and brains. He goes up the walk slowly, dragging the duffle bag behind him. Checking the ground for boobytraps. The trees for snipers.

He reaches for the doorbell but the door is slightly open. Inside, he hears dinner sounds: murmured conversation, clinking silverware and glasses. Smell of pork chops.

He silently eases the door open with the muzzle of the rifle. Louder noise, stronger smell. He leaves the duffle bag and stalks through the entrance hall, the living room, unchanged in any detail but subtly different.

The dining room. As expected, his parents are chatting amiably with the man with no face. Everyone is eating human parts.

Spider fires from the hip, emptying a magazine into the man with no face. He explodes in a cloud of bone fragments and dust and dry shreds. The head falls onto the dinner plate and stares at him sideways. His mother is screaming.

Spider ejects the magazine and reverses it. He releases the cocking lever and shoulders the rifle, aims, puts a burst of three into his mother's chest. She fountains blood, still screaming, and tips over backwards. His father stands up and throws his dinner napkin down on the table and says something stern. Spider empties the rest of the magazine into him, blowing away his face, stitching his chest and abdomen. He sprawls forward over the table.

Spider sits down to a plate of pork chops.

BAGGAGE

There was no need to take winter clothes to California. Beverly left most of her warm things with Penny. It did not make her happy to see that all her future life would fit into two cardboard boxes and a suitcase.

Of course it was good not to be a slave to material things. Lee didn't even own a suitcase; all of his stuff fit into a knapsack and a canvas shopping bag, plus another bag for his painter's tools, the good brushes and rollers, the spattered cap and coveralls.

Both of their worlds fit with room to spare in the trunk of the Thing, Lee's beat-up old Buick. At the Army-Navy Store they picked up a Boy

Scout camp cooking kit and a Sterno stove; they made up a "chuck wagon" box with cans of beans and stuff and a couple of plates and cups long ago liberated from the University. They turned the back seat into a bed so that one could sleep while the other drove. They would save a fortune on motels and restaurants.

It was more than a month before they'd planned to leave, but there wasn't much reason to stay. After King's assassination, white people weren't welcome at the Poor People's March headquarters, and it wasn't safe for them to be down in that part of the city anyhow. The warehouse job was over, and although Larry promised he could get them more work in a couple of weeks, they figured they could paint in California as easily as Maryland, and the vibes would be a lot better. Washington was nothing but bad karma, death and hate and destruction.

Besides, they didn't need a lot of money. Lee had a large Prince Albert can of primo Columbian and, as the saying went, "dope can get you through times of no money better than money can get you through times of no dope." That was more literally true with Lee than with most hippies, because of his talent for turning grass into cash. You could drop him blindfolded into a one-horse farming town in Idaho, and in ten minutes he'd find the town's only doper and make a deal that left them both feeling good.

Meanwhile, Beverly did not feel good, on several related levels. She had missed a period and was discreetly sick after breakfast almost every morning. She hadn't said anything to Lee, and he evidently hadn't noticed. She wanted to get out to California and get it over with. It would be easier to get an abortion out there, and no way that her parents would find out.

She hadn't stopped thinking about Spider. But she told herself that it was probably best for her to disappear before he was released from the hospital. Nothing was going to happen between them. No need to add to his problems.

The idea of an abortion made her sick with horror and fear. But the alternative of having a child, even if it could have been legitimate, was unthinkable. She was still a child herself, not ready to be a parent. Lee would never be ready. She would lose him.

Besides, she rationalized, who could ever want to bring a child into a world like this? America, Amerika, on the eve of destruction; the black-power fanatics and rednecks facing off with torches, the pigs with clubs and tear gas, the National Guard with guns—and Brezhnev waiting offstage with his finger on the button.

HOMECOMING (1)

They laid out a uniform of ironed starched khakis and new dull black dress

shoes that had never been polished. Nothing quite fit. Spider felt like a display
dummy. There were brown plastic vials with thirty days' supply of Valium
and Thorazine and a prescription for another thirty days' worth. He had an
appointment on May 6th with a Dr. Taupo at the Baltimore VA Hospital.

He got through Outprocessing in a surprising ten minutes. They had his
completed DD 214, the basic document that proved he had once been a
soldier and now was not, and a message from his mother that Aunt Phyllis
was going to pick him up at 2:00. They also gave him a back-pay envelope
with $147 cash. He would much rather have blown ten bucks on a cab ride
than wait around for two hours to be locked up in a car with his least favorite
relative. But neither his mother nor Aunt Phyllis answered the phone, so he
took his stuff down to the canteen to kill time with lunch and coffee.

Among his effects was a black cardboard box containing a Purple Heart, a
lush purple ribbon from which hung a golden heart bearing a stern likeness
of General Washington. He hefted it: anodized aluminum.

Could you get a Purple Heart for running into a tree? Maybe it was for
getting kicked in the nuts defending a medic. No, the typed orders tucked
underneath said:

> Date action: 29 January 1968
> Theater: USARPAC
> Reason: Wound received in action.
> Authority: By direction of the President and under the provisions
> of AR 672-5-1.

The President, wow. That and a dime would get you a cup of coffee.

Actually, Spider knew it was potentially valuable. The medal gave him a
ten-point preference for Civil Service jobs, if he ever wanted to work for
the U.S. Government again. That didn't seem likely. Did they use the point
system for astronauts? Astronaut or president, those were the only jobs he'd
take. No, scratch president.

Captain My Captain had dropped off two science fiction books, Van Vogt's
The Pawns of Null-A and Heinlein's *Starship Troopers*. He'd read both of
them already, but thought the Heinlein would be interesting to reread in
light of his recent experience.

It took him about an hour, since he'd read it only a few months before
being drafted, and it was still pretty clear in his memory. It described a
strange future where only veterans were allowed to vote or hold office. Spider
wondered about certifiably insane veterans like himself.

No one in the book was driven even slightly insane by combat. All the
soldiers were either heroes or cowards, but fortunately all the cowards were
weeded out in training.

Well, it was just a book, and the enemy involved were alien Bugs, not humans, so the soldiers were exterminators rather than murderers. Bugs, slopes, gooks, dinks. He wondered what the VC called Americans, to make them easier to kill. "Round-eye" and "capitalistic running dog" lacked punch.

Maybe they didn't need to call us names to dehumanize us. If Vietnam were a science fiction novel it would be clear who the invading aliens were, complete with inexplicable motivation and futuristic weapons. He remembered bringing that up in a bull session once; how Killer had gone along with him, but the other guys thought it was all flying-saucer bullshit.

It came at him like a physical blow: it doesn't mean shit anymore because they're all dead now. Coffee surged up into his throat and he choked it back. It was a blow that came at odd times, once or twice a day. Sweat trickled down his ribs and he swallowed hard, staring into the jungle. Into the white room with the roadkill smell. Get a fucking grip on yourself. He snapped the top off a bottle and tore out the cotton and shook out two Valium capsules. His ears rang with the rattle and roar and scream of the ambush. He carried the pills to the water fountain in front of the latrine but he realized he'd better not use it; if he leaned over he'd probably vomit. He walked carefully back to the end of the serving line and got a glass of water. He didn't look at the woman at the cash register because he knew she had become the man with no face. He swallowed the Valium and walked cautiously back to his table and lit a cigarette. When he set it in the ashtray he saw there were already two there, smoldering, a short one and a long one. Well, you didn't have to be crazy to do that. A lot of people do that.

He carried his stuff outside and stood under an awning in the April cool. A thin drizzle was not washing away the smell of the smoke from the riots. What a sorry fucking world. He stepped to the end of the awning and closed his eyes and let the rain wash his face.

After a while the door behind him opened. "John Speidel?" He spun around and almost dropped his stuff, trying to salute the pretty woman with captain's bars. She returned his salute and smiled and took his arm. "Come on. Your aunt's waiting for you up in Reception." He walked along with her across the canteen floor and up the stairs, replying to her polite conversation with monosyllables, carefully not looking at her face.

Aunt Phyllis looked old under crusted makeup. Phony smile with perfect false teeth. She kissed him on the cheek and gave him a brittle hug.

Was she still his aunt now that Uncle Terry was dead? Had she still been his aunt after the divorce, before the suicide? She got along well with Mother. They had known each other since high school, and the presence or absence of husbands was probably not a big factor in their friendship. She had always given Spider the creeps.

It was a long ride home. Spider had decided not to mention Uncle Terry, but that was what she wanted to talk about. How could he do this to her, to the family? It made them all look bad, as if they hadn't cared. As if they hadn't put up with him year after year, him and his lunatic fantasies. He should have gotten help. He knew he needed help; he talked about it all the time. But the one time he went to a doctor he wound up yelling at him and then dropping out of sight on a six-week drunk. Spider knew the story, the litany. Men in his family did not go on six-week drunks, not as a rule. Maybe he would be the second.

His father, as it turned out, may have been in the process of beating him to it. When he'd heard that Spider was coming home, he'd driven off to the Moose for a drink. He had been gone for two days. Aunt Phyllis said she didn't know what had come over him. Did he want to lose his job?

Spider's mother had scissored a sheet in half and lettered on the fat banner WELCOME HOME JOHN in red, black, and blue Magic Marker. It was thumbtacked over the front door, bleeding slightly in the rain.

Aunt Phyllis said she would love to come in but she was late for the garden club. Spider thanked her for the ride and balanced the duffle bag on his shoulder and tried to look sharp as he walked down the flagstone path, feeling like a sixties perversion of a World War II Norman Rockwell painting.

The front door was slightly ajar. From inside, the tinny sound of a small radio, chirping Walker & Scott's theme song: "We are the Joy Boys ... of ray-dee-oh ... we chase elec-trons to and fro-oh-oh." He pushed the door open.

His mother was lying on the couch with her shoes off, a hand over her eyes, listening to the radio. On the coffee table was a tall glass with an inch of slightly amber water and the small round ghost of an ice cube.

Spider eased the duffle bag down and she heard it and sat up suddenly. "John! Oh, John!" She tottered over to him and clasped him in a fierce hug. Her kiss was bourbon and ginger ale. "Your father, uh, your father has the car..."

"Aunt Phyllis told me."

"Oh." She looked around. "Phyllis couldn't come in?"

"She had garden club."

"Of course, Tuesday." She pulled him toward the dining room. "You must be hungry."

"No, no, Mother." There was a horrifying radiation of déjà vu as he resisted. He didn't want to see what was on the other side of the door. "Really, I'm not hungry, I ate at the canteen, the cafeteria, just now."

"Well, you can have a drink." She kicked the door open and it was just a dining room. "Beer or bourbon or what?"

"Just a, just a beer." Each of the four chairs around the dining room table shimmered with bad luck. He took the chair closest to the kitchen and turned it around to face his mother, his back to whatever might appear in the other chairs. "Have you heard anything from Dad?"

The refrigerator had two solid rows of Budweiser cans. She studied it and picked one. "No. I called the Moose and Kerry Daniel, he was the bartender night before last, he said that he had drunk too much to drive and had Kerry call a cab. But he didn't come home, and the next day the car was gone." She popped the beer open and got a glass out of the dishwasher.

"Call the police?"

"Oh, I wouldn't, no, not yet." She brought the beer out with two coasters. "It's like when he lost the job with Woodie's, remember?"

"Vaguely, yeah." Spider had just turned ten. He had noticed his father was not around, but hadn't thought too much of it, since he wasn't around all that much anyhow. Years later, he found out that the old man had holed up in a Baltimore hotel room, down on The Block, and stayed drunk for a week, probably with professional female sympathy.

"I just don't understand." She rattled ice cubes into a glass. "This should be a happy time. But you know, he wouldn't even say a word about it? He just ate dinner and left."

"Well, he was kind of funny about the whole thing. Me not wanting to go, getting drafted and all. As if Ho Chi Minh was fu ... was Hitler or something. As if we belonged over there."

"John, please don't talk to him that way." She poured a jigger of bourbon into the glass, hesitated, then measured out another jigger.

"He still believes all that crap?"

"More than ever. Ever since that Tet Offensive." She poured a little ginger ale into the glass and joined him in the dining room. "You can tell me anything you want. Just try not to argue with him."

"Sure. Don't worry. I won't be around that much anyhow; soon as I get a job I'll find an apartment."

"Oh no; don't rush. The doctor said...it would be good for you to stay at home."

"Not if I'm going to—"

"Besides, I fixed up your old room." They'd rented it out when he left for college. "It's just the way you used to have it."

"Really?" That gave him an odd feeling. Safety. "Let me go see it."

"Sure." She stood up quickly. "You probably want to lie down."

"Yeah, maybe." After the long ride with Aunt Phyllis. They walked upstairs to his room, twelve feet square with a dormer window.

It did feel safe, and odd. It was the first time he'd had a beer in this room without having to sneak it in past his mother. All the science fiction books were in place, although in random order, in the brick-and-board shelving he'd dismantled for college. Guitar on the bed. His telescope stood in the corner, in front of the taller shelves with the science books. The Lick Observatory Moon photographs, now totally obsolete.

He moved the guitar and sat down on the bed. "Guess I would like to lie down." His mother made nervous polite noises and left him alone.

He stretched out and looked at the constellation charts he'd pasted on the ceiling seven or eight years ago. Anxiety drained away. This was a place where the man with no face could never find him.

EINE KLEINE NACHTMUSIK

Lee had indulged himself in the luxury of a new pair of wiper blades before they took off, and they made all the difference in the world. The old ones had made night driving a dangerous pain in the ass if it was raining. It was five in the morning and the Beltway was nearly deserted, but with every pair of headlights that whipped by, he remembered squinting through blear and glare, and was happy. He quietly hummed a few bars of "In the Early Morning Rain," his left fingers chording on the steering wheel. Then he thought of Beverly asleep in the back and sang on silently, subvocalizing. She usually had a sweet disposition, but it was not wise to wake her up before she wanted to get up.

The idea was to drive well out of the Washington area before the morning rush; stop for breakfast somewhere around Frederick. He was already hungry, but the food box with its bag of apples was on the floor in the back, great planning. He took the cold joint out of the ashtray and sucked on it just to do something with his mouth. No smoking while driving. People did do it; he did it, but Beverly thought it was dangerous, like drinking and driving. Well, dope affected her a lot more. It was a good rule, but one that Lee would have broken if he were alone in the car. A couple of tokes would make the time pass faster. He heard her moving and put the joint back in the ashtray.

"You doin' okay?" she said behind his ear.

"Fine. We'll be almost to Shady Grove by the time it gets light."

"I want to come up."

"Pull over?"

"Huh uh." She angled one leg over the front seat and then the other, and squirmed over with girlish gracelessness. It made her t-shirt ride up to the bottom of her breasts, braless for sleeping. She tucked the shirt back into her gym shorts. Then she leaned back over the seat to retrieve the pillow and blanket. All the activity filled the stuffy car with female musk. Lee suddenly had an insistent erection. He reached inside his jeans to adjust himself.

"Aw...got a problem?" She stroked his thigh. He laughed. "Pull over and I'll suck it off."

"What? Are you serious?"

"Well, you don't have to pull over." She started to undo his zipper one link at a time. "It would be safer, though."

•••

Spider woke up early, rain drumming in the darkness, a bad dream fading, sheets clammy with nervous sweat. He fought the sure feeling that there was somebody in the room with him, fumbled with the reading lamp and snapped it on. Books, guitar, telescope, microscope, pictures.

He padded over to the dresser and opened a drawer to select his first civilian outfit since October. He had put on his army costume on Halloween. The night before, his last day of pre-Vietnam leave, he'd sat with Beverly and his parents, watching a dumb horror movie on TV. Not knowing that in two weeks he would suddenly face the real thing, a white room full of decomposing corpses, reek of chemicals and rot. There was someone behind him in the mirror. He wouldn't look. He studied his feet and let his hands find jeans and a shirt. He dressed facing the door and then opened the door slowly. There was no one in the hall. He walked down the pool of light to the stairs, switched on the light, walked down to the kitchen and reached inside to switch on that room's light before entering.

He surprised two cockroaches. He watched them run for safety, then got a beer from the refrigerator and repeated his trip in reverse, leaving dark rooms behind him. He locked the door to his room and turned on all the lights. He opened the dormer window and enjoyed the cool humid breeze, the smell of civilized suburban vegetation. Smoking and drinking the beer, it felt so good. He was going to be all right. It would take time. But he was safe.

He uncovered the microscope and got out his collection of prepared slides. He looked at all the mineral specimens without any particular plan, just for the satisfying familiarity of them.

After the horror movie, his parents had gone to bed, leaving him and Beverly on the couch for their final goodbyes. She had used her mouth on him, the first and only time. There was something else, just on the edge of memory, but he did remember her mouth, the surprising coldness of it because she'd been panting, and then the warm moist envelopment, the small pain from her teeth.

He unzipped and looked at his erection, standing like a stranger in the bright light, growing out of civilian jeans. His collection of pictures from *Playboy* was still where he'd left it, hidden in the middle of a large biology text. He set them out on the dresser and studied their new familiarity, every curve and mound, the silly expressions, the perfect hair. He looked at them and at himself while he stroked as slowly as his hunger would let him.

Then he cleaned up and put the pictures back and left one small light on, the microscope's stage illuminator, and lay down and turned the radio on low, an all-night classical music program. He stared at the ceiling and smoked.

Tomorrow he would call Beverly.

THE SEXUAL REVOLUTION

History records a constant, if uneven, ebb and flow of society's tolerance for sexual enthusiasm and oddness. Spider's chronic masturbation, in pre-anesthesia England, would have been "treated" by cauterizing the prostate gland and cutting the nerves of the penis. Lee's bisexuality would have raised no more eyebrows in Imperial Rome than it did in Haight-Ashbury. Chaucer's fourteenth-century Wife of Bath would not have been shocked by Beverly's straightforward lust—though Beverly's mother would have been!

Beverly's parents, and Spider's, were in their twenties during World War II; their icons for sexuality were The Man in Uniform and The Pin-up Girl. Both women had boyfriends overseas; both men were soldiers with girlfriends back home. When they thought or talked about their future mates, it was likely to be in terms of love and children and a house with a den and a nursery, a neatly mowed lawn and a white picket fence, rather than specific sexual geometries.

Soldiers will be soldiers, of course. In his narrative history of America, *The Glory and the Dream*, William Manchester records this classic conversation between a World War II soldier and a war correspondent:

Correspondent: "What's the first thing you're going to do after the war?"

Soldier: "Hump my wife."

Correspondent: "And the second thing?"

Soldier: "Take off these goddamned hobnail boots."

But it was a time of terrible insecurity, at home and in the foxhole, and people didn't want more excitement. They wanted normality.

They got the Eisenhower fifties. The desire for security ossified into conformity and conservatism. Anyone who was overly eccentric in public was scorned as a "beatnik," though actual pot-smoking, dirty-word-using, free-loving beatniks were always a rare and endangered species.

A non-beatnik person coming of sexual age in the fifties had to contend with obstacles more profound than a forest of crinoline, a prison of girdle. Nice girls didn't do It. They just plain *didn't*. If they wanted It, they were nymphos. If they loved a boy enough, or were passionate enough, to do It, they were promoted from nympho to slut.

The double standard was absolute and unquestioned. Boys cajoled and pleaded and promised, but if a girl finally did give in, they would in all probability have sex with her for a month or two and then wander off looking for fresh blood, or meat, meanwhile telling all the other guys about how easy she was. She was a slut but he was normal, he was a man.

A 1954 Gallup poll asked, "Should a wife's adultery be more condemned than her husband's?" Four out of five of the women polled said yes.

The sexual revolution was partly a reaction to this hypocrisy and suffocating conformity, but it was more complex than a simple reaction. Many factors combined and converged: women's liberation, a growing permissiveness toward sexual content in books and movies, pharmaceutical and technological breakthroughs in birth control, the drug culture that evolved from the isolated beatniks into a pervasive hippy community. The young sexy presidency of John and Jacqueline Kennedy fueled the movement and, in a curious way, so did the culturewide body-blow of his assassination, with the subsequent Generation Gap that gave young people a mandate to rebel against their parents' conventional morality.

In the fifties, a girl's virginity was a carefully guarded treasure, as it had been for her mother and grandmother: a trophy that her husband-for-life would be awarded on their wedding night. By 1968, most girls considered their virginity an encumbrance, even an embarrassment, and some didn't bother to wait until they were in love, let alone married, to get rid of it. In the sector of society that Lee and Beverly inhabited—white, middle-class, educated—peer pressure had made a complete about-face in half of a generation. A lot of girls and women had sex even if they didn't much care for it, or for the boy or man they happened to be with. They didn't want to be "out of it."

Any revolution produces casualties. The epidemic of venereal disease hit both genders, but of course women had to pay the bill for unwanted conception. Botched abortions caused infections, sterility, even death. Sudden single motherhood stopped some lives cold, even though being an "unwed mother" wasn't the social stigma it used to be.

There was a lot of sex, but not much reproduction. In 1968 America's birth rate fell to 17.9 per thousand, the lowest since the Great Depression.

The word "revolution" had its astronomical meaning in Chaucer's time; it was not to be a political term for another two centuries. When scholars began to use the word to describe a sudden transfer of power in government, they chose the term ironically, from an appreciation of history: the excesses of monarchy lead to democratization; the excesses of democracy lead back to monarchy. What comes around, in the words of a later generation, goes around.

Eisenhower begat the Revolution, but the Revolution begat Ronald Reagan.

SOLDIER'S HOME

Spider didn't feel like talking to Beverly's parents, since he didn't want to answer questions about his own, but he didn't have her new phone number. Ma Bell's Information didn't have it, unsurprisingly, but the house mother at her old dormitory gave him both address and phone. He called and there was no answer; probably at class.

It was ten o'clock and his mother still wasn't up. He left a note on the refrigerator, took a couple of beers, and split.

His old Chevy was balky but did finally turn over. His father was supposed to have run it for a few minutes every week. He probably missed every now and then. When he could put the choke in without it going too ragged, he eased the car down the driveway and pointed it toward town.

There was one bit of Army business to do. He had to go down to the Selective Service Office and turn in his draft card. He found a parking place in back of Forty Alleys and crossed over to the nondescript chalk building. There were three clerks on duty, but as it happened, the one he handed the card to was the same old lady who had sent him off to his near-fatal induction. He remembered her as a vicious old crone who had been visibly elated that he had flunked out of college and fallen into her clutches. But now she saw that he had a medical discharge and a Purple Heart and got all choked up about how proud she was of him. She said she'd lost sons in both World War II and Korea.

Spider was slightly stunned by that. He wanted to grab her by the scrawny shoulders and shake some sense into her—didn't she know how they had wound up? Rotting grinning corpses feeding flies and worms. After a few hours or weeks of screaming festering pain, you bitch you fucking bitch you lost your own sons so now you murder other people's sons? But he stood there shaking silently and dropped the card on the desk and scrawled his name on a release. Then he sat in the parking lot and drank the two beers he'd brought from home, keeping the cans out of sight under the dashboard, pouring the beer into a coffee cup. He killed them both in about two minutes and then smoked until he'd stopped shaking.

Breakfast/lunch was a half-dozen bitesized hamburgers at Little Tavern. The price had gone up but they were still good little greaseballs. He took a lap around Hot Shoppes for old time's sake and swung by B-CC, Bethsheba Cheddar Cheese. In both places the high school kids were milling around on lunch break, looking unbelievably young, giggling children who had somehow acquired secondary sexual characteristics.

Don't be crazy, he thought. Two years ago you were one of them.

He went back down Wisconsin Avenue to the Beltway. It wasn't the shortest route to College Park, but he wanted to get the Chevy up to seventy; blow it out a little bit. It responded pretty well, missing for the first mile or so but then settling down to a purr. He throttled back to a legal sixty and cruised around to the Route 1 exit.

He still had a little buzz from the two beers and wanted to renew it, so he pulled into the Starlight Lounge for a truly surreal conversation. He had a perfectly good fake ID, a Maryland driver's license, but the bartender demanded to see his draft card. Spider said he didn't have a draft card; he'd been discharged from the Army and turned it in just an hour ago. The bartender didn't believe him. Everybody has a draft card, unless they were one of those hippies who burned theirs, protesting the war. Spider insisted that he'd just come from Vietnam. The bartender said bullshit, he'd been in the Army himself, in Korea, and he could tell. You just don't want to fake your draft card because it's a federal offense. Spider got pissed off and went out to the car to get his DD 214, but then realized it had his real birth date on it. So he drove on into town, beerless.

He had to calm down before he went to see Beverly. When he got to the University he pulled into the Maryland Book Exchange—Maryland Book & Crook—and idled in the parking lot until he was able to snag a space. Then he went inside and walked along the aisles of books, sampling one every now and then, which always calmed him one way and excited him another. More than the University itself, the bookstore seemed an infinite fount of accessible knowledge. No tests, no lunatic graduate assistants; just the raw materials. He picked up a Dover book about meteors and a new Heinlein novel, *The Moon Is a Harsh Mistress*. He'd read a short version in a magazine before he got drafted, but it looked like there was enough new stuff to make it worth rereading.

Somewhat illegally, he left his car in the Book & Crook slot and crossed over to the drugstore. He bought a carton of cigarettes, stunned at the price after dollar-a-carton Vietnam, and worked up the nerve to ask the woman at the pharmacy counter for a pack of Trojans. Beverly would probably want to go slow, but why not be prepared?

Going back to the car he was transfixed by a small Oriental co-ed who walked by him chattering with a friend, laughing brightly. He stumbled over the curb and almost fell. Did he know her from before? The sight and sound of her had triggered a wave of desire as strong as a physical blow.

He decided they must have been classmates. The damned shock therapy had taken out blocks of memory, most of which he would supposedly get back. He resisted the temptation to run after her and ask if they'd met.

Li, that was her name. Some parts of him remembered her; he hurried to the car holding the shopping bag discreetly in front of his crotch. Could they have dated? She hadn't made any sign of having recognized him, and he didn't remember dating anybody but Beverly. Maybe it was some weird association, brought on by buying rubbers. Maybe he *should* go after her.

He swung up onto Route 1 and drove slowly, but she wasn't on the sidewalk. For no reason, he suddenly remembered the stranger whimpering with the bloody bandages at his crotch, his friend holding out the bloody scrap of his dick, and then a couple of nights later, the guy from Bangkok… his erection wilted. Those were two memories he could afford to lose. Why couldn't the shock therapy be more selective?

He had a vague idea where Chillum Heights was, or thought he did, but wound up totally lost. He went into a 7-Eleven and studied a map, then bought the map after a clerk cleared his throat and shot him a dirty look.

Eventually he found the place, in a rundown student-ghetto neighborhood. It was a two-story clapboard house that might look all right with a fresh coat of paint and a lawn instead of a thicket.

He knocked on the door, waited a minute, knocked again. He was about to leave when the door opened a crack. "Yeah?" a man's voice said from the darkness.

"Is Beverly here?"

"No man, she's gone."

"When do you think she'll be back?"

"I mean like she's like *gone*. Who are you?"

"Old friend. John Speidel, Spider."

The door opened to reveal a skinny young man in jeans, shirtless and barefoot, holding a joint. "You're the guy from Vietnam, like Spider."

"Yeah, that's right."

"You kill any babies?"

"What?"

"I mean like in Vietnam, did you kill any babies?"

"Hey, yeah, all the time. What the fuck are you talking about? I never killed anybody. I was fuckin' *drafted*."

"Sure, yeah." He waved his joint hand in a vague gesture. "Nothin' personal, just curious…you didn't burn any villages?"

"Yeah, that's all I did all day, is burn villages. Wore out three Zippos. So what happened to Beverly?"

"Don't get hostile, man. She went off with Lee. You know about Lee?"

"Her roommate, yeah."

"Well, okay. Okay." He opened the screen door. "Come on in. We got some Coke, maybe got a beer left."

Spider followed him down the hall. The place looked more than lived in; it was somewhere between grubbiness and squalor. Beverly lived here? "How long has Beverly lived here?"

"Oh, Lee brought her over, what. Two months ago? Three months?" They entered the kitchen and he went to the refrigerator. "I own the place but my old lady takes care of the details. Split the last beer with you."

"Thanks."

He sat down at the table and filled two jelly glasses with beer. Spider sat across from him and felt an odd tingling connection: Beverly must have sat right here. He took a sip of the cool beer. "So when will she be back?"

"She said somethin' about when classes start."

"What, Monday?"

"No, man, when *classes* start." He relit the joint off a wooden match and took a deep drag and passed it over. Spider did a shallow hit and set it in the ashtray between them. The landlord held the smoke in for as long as he could and then exhaled in a puff. "Like September."

"September? She moved?"

"Sure. You didn't know, sorry. They put all their shit in the Thing From Detroit and went off to California."

"Oh. Gone, shit." He picked up the joint. "Why California?"

He shrugged. "Where the action is. He's got some connections out there."

"He?"

"Yeah, that's where Lee came from. San Francisco, Haight-Ashbury. Leary Land."

"Lee's a guy?"

"Sort of. He switch-hits." He extracted the joint from Spider's frozen fingers. "You thought Lee was a girl?"

Spider shook his head slowly. "I don't know. Everything's all fucked up."

"Oh yeah." He took a puff as if it were a normal cigarette and passed it back. "She said you were in a mental thing, up in Walter Reed. You must of got better."

"Yeah, must've." Spider stood up. He had to leave before he hit this guy, and it wasn't his fault. "Look, man, I gotta go."

"Okay. She calls, I'll tell her you came by."

"Thanks. You don't have a number for her out there?"

"Huh uh. They were just gonna go see what happens."

Spider held on to the chair back until the room calmed down. It was sort of glowing. "Yeah, right. Thanks."

"Look, I didn't mean it about the babies, killin' babies. I just got a sick sense of humor."

"That's okay. You can't laugh, what the fuck can you do?" He walked fast out into the sunlight and air. He stood by the car for a minute and then sat in the driver's seat, gripping the wheel.

Then he started to pound the wheel, saying "shit" over and over. He *knew* that Lee was a guy; Captain My Captain had said so. That had been after the shock treatments, too. He didn't want to believe it and so he had willfully forgotten it. He trembled uncontrollably and everything around him seemed to shimmer.

That glow usually meant the man with no face was coming. But it was just an overgrown lawn, some birds, the sun and sky. The hippy looking at him through the inch-wide gap between curtains.

The Valium was on his dresser at home. Well, he wasn't supposed to take another one until dinner, anyhow. Good idea not to carry it with him. But he needed something. Beverly running off to Haight-Ashbury with a goddamned queer.

He didn't look at the map, but just headed roughly south until he hit Route 1 again, and drove a couple of miles, across the District Line. In Washington the drinking age for beer was eighteen. He bought a cold sixpack at the first liquor store.

The cans were poptops. They hadn't had them in Vietnam. When you open them they sound like a grenade being armed. Spider popped one in the parking lot but didn't drink from it. He drove off with it nestled in his crotch and took a sip every now and then, when there were no cars around. The cops used ghost cars in Washington, he remembered, unmarked cars with plainclothes officers. He had a Maryland license but if he got busted in Washington he was pretty sure they could pull it.

He drove across town to Rock Creek Park and found a small deserted picnic area by the water. He took a coffee cup full of beer and sat on a big flat rock and watched the stream swirl by. He and Beverly had had picnics here, just south of the zoo.

So Lee was a guy. Did Beverly ever say he wasn't? Probably not. Mail in Vietnam wasn't all that reliable; he probably missed a crucial letter or two where she explained about him. A hippy, though? A hippy *queer*? Beverly was so *normal*.

He tried to sort through his feelings honestly. By the third beer he had gone past forgiving her, to seeing that there was nothing to forgive. Life went on. She met a guy and fell for him. Now he had to meet a girl. He took the rubber out of his pocket and felt it, slippery inside the foil. He had used one. He was sure of it. When Beverly got settled in California maybe he could call her. Hey, how's the weather out there, did we ever fuck?

Maybe it was that Chinese girl Li. No, he would remember something about her. He was sure he hadn't dated anyone but Beverly since twelfth grade. Maybe he'd had a class with her and fantasized. He had a ghost of a memory of her in a position that you wouldn't see even in *Playboy*, bending over naked and smiling at him from between her knees. It certainly was an effective fantasy, still. He had a sudden erection, painfully urgent.

He got back in the car and put on the rubber and beat off fast, before somebody could come by. The rubber did feel familiar, exciting. His body again remembering things that his brain didn't.

He wrapped the rubber up in a Kleenex and disposed of it in a trash barrel. With the fourth beer he didn't bother with the coffee cup. He sat on the rock and drank it from the can, warm like in Vietnam.

He felt sad and angry with himself. Is this what the rest of your life is going to be? Beer and beating off and bad dreams? He threw away half the can and drove carefully home. Tomorrow he'd go down to the Administration building and talk to somebody about the GI Bill. Maybe he could start classes in summer school. Take a couple of classes and get a night job. Get his shit together.

LET IT ALL HANG OUT

The last thing Beverly wanted to do when they arrived in California was party. It had been a pretty rough four days' drive, two flat tires and a starter replacement, and what she really wanted to do was soak in a tub and then fall unconscious for a day or two. But Lee had some friends who were science fiction buffs as well as dopers, and they were all in Berkeley for a four-day convention weekend.

Beverly had read three science fiction books because Spider was so far into it, and she knew it was magical for some people, but it didn't do much for her. Spending a long weekend with people who were addicted to the stuff sounded like an extended exercise in diplomacy. She didn't feel diplomatic. She felt shell-shocked.

At least the hotel was pretty, a large white wooden mansion on a hill outside of town. And there was a tub in their room, an old-fashioned one with claw feet. She filled it with water as hot as she could stand while Lee went out to "make connections." He'd better make good ones. She read the rate sheet on the door; the room was costing almost forty dollars a night.

She made a mental note to buy some bubble bath, undressed, and slipped into the water up to her chin. It was stupefyingly comfortable. She had brought a magazine into the bathroom but didn't have the energy to pick it up. She just gazed sleepily over the steaming water at the strange refracted image of her body, foreshortened like a funhouse mirror, stretched left and right. Wow, look at those tits. Not getting a belly yet.

And then a guy walked in. He was wearing funny pointed ears like Mr. Spock on *Star Trek*. He said "hi" and Beverly returned the syllable. She started to cover herself with her hands but the guy was politely not looking at her. He urinated for an impossibly long time, which was probably normal for Vulcans, flushed the toilet, checked his ears in the mirror, and left. She could hear him and Lee talking in quiet urgent tones, and then there was the unmistakable rustle of money, and then the door to the hall opened and closed.

Lee came into the bathroom. "Jesus," he said. "Can you believe it? That dope *came* from Berkeley, and I just sold him two hundred dollars worth for four hundred bucks!"

"He came in here and took a pee," Beverly said.

"Yeah, sorry about that. What, I'm supposed to send him next door? He really had to go."

"He sure did. He must've been in here five minutes. Taking his time."

"Oh, come on. He's gay. He wasn't interested in you."

"Thanks. Thanks a lot."

He leaned forward. "Look..." Beverly took a wet hand and slapped him hard on the cheek.

He sat back. "What the fuck?"

"You...you..."

"It's your goddamned period."

"No, it's not!" She was finally able to cry. "Not for another eight months, you careless son of a bitch."

MAY

John sat in the doughnut shop and went through the brochures and forms he'd picked up at the VA office at the University. It looked like a pretty good deal. If he went to school full time, they'd pay him a couple of hundred a month. He could easily live on that, his tuition deferred with a standard Student Loan.

Spider had only been in the Army for a little less than eleven months, so a strict reading of the rules would give him only fifteen months of GI Bill. But the VA counselor was pretty sure the Purple Heart and service-connected disability would get him more; perhaps the full forty-five months. That would be plenty enough to finish his degree and get a start in graduate school, if he wanted.

He got another doughnut and a coffee refill. Tomorrow he'd talk to a freshman advisor, but he was pretty sure what he wanted to take. Two courses would qualify for full-time in the summer. He wanted to take Intro to Psychology and Observational Astronomy, the only astro course he could take without Math 11. He'd gotten a B in Math 10, but didn't feel like tackling a math course in summer school. Not German, either; that was bad enough when you had plenty of time.

The fat gruff man who ran the shop came over, wiping his hands with a towel. "Just get out of the Army?"

Spider ran his fingers through his military crewcut. "Yes, sir. I guess it's pretty obvious."

"Well, I saw the VA stuff, too. Look, you wouldn't be after a job, would you?"

"Uh, depends. I'm starting school next month, full time."

"Guy who's got the job now's a full time student, too. It's just three hours a day." He gestured at the display case. "Makin' doughnuts, three to six in the morning."

"Pretty early." Actually, Spider used to get up around four, anyhow, when

347

he was in the dorm. "How much would it pay?"

"I'm givin' the guy nine dollars a day, six days a week. I got a Jew friend takes over the shop on Sundays."

Spider's brow furrowed as he tried to calculate nine times twenty-four. The man evidently took it as hesitation. "Since you're a vet, I'll make it ten. Plus all the doughnuts you can eat, though I can guarantee you won't eat many after the first week."

"Well...well, sure." An extra $240 a month would make him almost rich. If it didn't work out, he could quit and still have the GI Bill. "When you want me to start?"

"Guy wants to quit next Wednesday, finals, then he graduates. You come in and work with him Monday and Tuesday, learn the ropes." He reached into his shirt pocket and pulled out two business cards. He turned one over. "Put your name and phone number on that. Give you a call if there's any change."

Spider had a doctor's appointment on Monday, but it wasn't until ten. He printed carefully. "You want my Social Security number or anything? I've got my DD 214 here."

"Nah." He stuck out a palm as if to ward off monsters of paper and government. "The wife takes care of that stuff. She'll get the forms together by Monday."

They shook hands and Spider left, thoughtful. It would be an interesting schedule. To get here by 3:00 a.m., he'd have to leave home every morning a little after two. Make it 2:15, with no traffic. So he ought to be in bed by nine each night. But twice a week, the astronomy class met at night, eight to eleven; have to catch a nap here and there.

He might be better off getting a room in College Park. He could easily find one in the summer for fifty or sixty bucks a month. Maybe he should rent Beverly's old room. Maybe not.

• • •

"Move *out?*" His mother actually turned pale. "I promised Dr. Folsom I'd watch out for you."

"He's not a doctor," Spider said, "and you've done a real good job."

"You've only been home two weeks."

"And I feel fine." He felt stupid, actually, standing in front of the refrigerator with a beer in one hand, a salami in the other, and a jar of pickles under one arm. He set down two of them and opened the third. "I'll try commuting for a while." He returned to the refrigerator for mayonnaise. "Do we have any peanut butter?"

"I'll get it." She bustled off to the pantry. "It's not that far."

"Eighteen miles." He got the cutting board from beneath the sink. "That's a gallon of gas, two gallons both ways." He cut three thick slabs of salami and sliced two pickles into strips.

"So what's that, eighty cents a day?"

"Twenty-four dollars a month. That's half what a room would cost."

"Well ... you could use my Esso card for gas. Your father wouldn't mind."

Spider refrained from pointing out that his father had been gone for two weeks, and probably *would* mind. He put mayo on one slice of bread and crunchy peanut butter on the other and stacked the salami and pickles together into a thick pregnant woman's sandwich. His mother handed him a plate. "You don't like mustard anymore?"

"Not with pickles. You eating?"

"No, I had an egg." There was no evidence that she'd had anything but bourbon and ginger ale. Spider put the stuff back in the refrigerator and carried his sandwich and beer to the dining room table.

"Dad call last night?"

"Yes. He's in Gettysburg." Spider had overheard a teary drunken conversation between his mother and Aunt Phyllis two nights before. All the collect calls were coming from the same number in Baltimore. His father was supposedly out "checking prospects" for his insurance company in western Maryland and southern Pennsylvania. She'd checked with the company, though, and he was on an indefinite leave of absence. He was with *that girl*, his mother had said. Aunt Phyllis had said that she was hardly a *girl* anymore.

What Spider wanted to say to his mother was that it was obvious his father was not coming home as long as Spider was there, for some mysterious reason, and they were probably running out of money, and pretty soon his father wouldn't have a job to come back to. The best thing in the world for all of them would be for Spider to pack up and move out to College Park. But he wasn't sure he wanted to. This house was secure, especially the room upstairs. And in some screwy way he liked the family the way it was, having his mother to himself. Maybe it was an Oedipus Complex.

• • •

Spider went to bed early and set the alarm for 2:00 a.m., partly to get used to it, and partly so he could use his telescope after moonset. He'd wrestled the heavy instrument downstairs and set it up in the back yard while there was still light, covering it with a plastic tarp to keep the dew off. He'd gone down for a few minutes after sundown to look at the crescent moon and Jupiter, which wouldn't be visible later.

He dressed in the dark to preserve his night vision, and felt his way down-stairs in the darkness. He had a red-light astronomical flashlight, the lens dimmed with thick coats of fingernail polish, but he'd left it down on the back porch, with the star map and eyepiece box.

The sky was black and brilliant with summer stars, just a faint horizon glow in the direction of Washington. The Milky Way rolled from Cygnus overhead down to Sagittarius in the south and Cassiopeia in the north. Spider stood and looked up at the sky for a minute, drinking in the familiarity and the alien aloofness of it.

He slid the tarp off and enjoyed the faint smell of the machine, the pungent Bakelite telescope tube and the grease-and-cutting-oil whisper of the heavy mounting. He'd built the telescope in junior high, half a year's worth of weekends and a red ribbon in the Science Fair. It was a six-inch Newtonian reflector. The workshop leader had persuaded him to build a mounting sturdy enough for a bigger machine, since most people go straight back to the workshop and start grinding an eight-inch mirror, and then a ten- or twelve-inch, and so on up. Spider had never contracted "aperture fever," though. Puberty struck, instead, and his weekends were spoken for.

He rocked the mounting around a few inches so it was in line with Polaris, and then used bright red Antares to adjust the viewfinder, a modified rifle-scope. He inserted the high-power eyepiece to lock in the focus, switched back to the low-power one to look at the globular clusters in the south, and then slowly cruised up the Milky Way. He paused for the blue-and-gold double star Alberio and the four jewels of Epsilon Lyrae. He found the tiny O of the Ring Nebula, and started to switch eyepieces, to get a close-up look. He saw a light out of the corner of his eye and looked up.

It was a brilliant meteor, rolling slowly down to the west, coruscating white and yellow and red, leaving behind a pale gray glowing trail. For some reason it was terrifying rather than beautiful. Spider dropped the eyepiece. He heard it click against the tripod leg and thump in the grass some distance away.

Spider set down the eyepiece box and picked up the flashlight, hands shak-ing. The batteries were dead. He crawled out into the darkness on his hands and knees, patting the damp grass in careful arcs. His heart was hammering. He thought he heard a noise and looked up, and saw he wasn't alone.

There were vague figures everywhere, motionless in the dim starlight. And right by the telescope, not six feet away, the familiar slumped posture of the man with no face.

Spider did know there was no one there, no one real, but his legs would not be convinced. He ran straight for the porch steps, slipped on the damp wood and almost fell, rushed through the door to the kitchen and locked it. Then he turned on both kitchen lights and got a beer out of the refrigerator and drained it in three fast gulps. He pulled out two more and trudged up toward his room, leaving a path of light behind him.

DECISIONS

Roe v. *Wade* was still five years in the future, but it wasn't hard for a woman in California to get an abortion. The three-room clinic friends had recommended to them was clean and modern; the gynecologist and nurse they talked to were casual, reassuring. It would cost $575, cash on the barrelhead—feel free to shop around, but you get what you pay for. Beverly said they had to talk about it, and took the release form down the block to a coffeehouse.

Beverly took one sip of cappuccino and let it turn cold as she read the form over and over.

"You don't have to do it," Lee said. "I'll stick by you."

"You said that already."

"WELL, IT'S TRUE."

"I know you think it's true."

"What do you mean by that? Don't you think I'm a... you think I'd back out on—"

"Shut up," she said quietly, not looking up from the paper. "Would you please shut up and get us a couple of beers?"

The waitress brought two drafts and centered them on souvenir blotters that said STEAL ME BUT LEAVE THE GLASS. Beverly put the paper down and reached for the beer, but then stood up suddenly. "Have to go barf. Save my place?" She put a hand to her mouth, looked around quickly, and darted toward the sign that pointed to the restrooms.

She came back pale. Her hand trembled as she picked up the beer.

"I'm sorry about the morning sickness," Lee said.

"That wasn't morning sickness." She took a slow sip and made a face. "That was thinking about that old man sticking a vacuum cleaner up my cunt and sucking the life out of it. Wouldn't that make you puke, if you had a cunt?"

Lee made a helpless gesture.

"But you do have a cunt. You're stuck with me."

"Not stuck with. I do love you, Beverly."

"Uh huh." She unfolded a paper napkin and pressed it to both eyes. "I feel so shitty. I don't know what to think, I don't know what to do." She balled up the napkin and looked at the ground. "Whatever I do is going to be wrong for both of us. And the baby, too, or whatever you call whatever it is now."

"We could raise a baby. There's that commune up in Oregon—"

"Oh, stop. You've already fucked half the women in that commune. You'd fuck the other half while I was changing diapers."

"I wouldn't. I'd promise."

"I guess you would. Promise." She took a big drink and set the heavy mug down silently. "How much money do we have?"

"About six hundred, plus whatever's in your purse."

"Twenty and two ones." She looked straight at him. "We better do it now."

"He said a month wouldn't make any difference."

"Not to him. I think we better do it now."

"You don't have to rush into it."

"You're right." Her face tightened with the effort of keeping tears back. "Let's finish these beers first."

PTSD

If Spider had presented his symptoms a few years later, he probably would not have been misdiagnosed as a paranoid schizophrenic. In 1968, people mumbled about shell-shock and neurasthenia, but there was no actual medical term for the malady that eventually affected about a third of the men and women who were exposed to combat in Vietnam.

There was nothing new about Post-Traumatic Stress Disorder. Odysseus shows symptoms of it in Homer's banquet scene. The disease is accurately described in *Henry IV, Part I*, when Lady Percy complains to her soldier husband Hotspur:

Tell me, sweet lord, what is't that takes from thee
Thy stomach, pleasure and thy golden sleep?
Why dost thou bend thine eyes upon the earth
And start so often when thou sit'st alone?
Why hast thou lost the fresh blood in thy cheeks;
And given my treasures and my rights of thee
To thick-eyed musing and cursed melancholy?
In thy faint slumbers I by thee have watch'd
And heard thee murmur tales of iron wars…

Hotspur can't answer. Lady Percy presses him, and he blows up:

… Love! I love thee not,
I care not for thee, Kate: this is no world
To play with mammets and to tilt with lips:
We must have bloody noses and crack'd crowns…

Psychologists note that veterans like Hotspur, who were able to respond to the terrors of combat directly, by killing the enemy, later also respond with violence when confronted with the more mysterious anguish of PTSD. Those like Spider, who witnessed the terrors but never fought back, tend to retreat into more passive states of anxiety, panic, and depression.

Captain My Captain's DSM-I, the diagnostic manual that classified homosexuality as the prime sexual perversion, didn't have any description of psychological problems caused by combat stress, although individual physicians had been reporting them at least since the Civil War. Years after that war broke Walt Whitman's heart, tending the wounds of "O my soldiers, my veterans," he described PTSD's characteristic recurrent dreams:

> In midnight sleep of many a face of anguish,
> Of the look at first of the mortally wounded, (of that indescrib-
> able   look),
> Of the dead on their backs with arms extended wide,
> I dream, I dream, I dream...
>
> Long have they pass'd, faces and trenches and fields,
> Where through the carnage I moved with a callous composure, or
>   away from the fallen,
> Onward I sped at the time—but now of their forms at night,
> I dream, I dream, I dream.

The 1987 DSM-III(R) does list PTSD, and its description of the cause and symptoms fits Spider well·

> A. The person has experienced an event that is outside the range
> of usual human experience and that would be markedly distressing
> to almost anyone, e.g. serious threat to one's life ... or seeing another
> person who has recently been, or is being ... killed as the result of
> an accident or physical violence.
>
> B. The traumatic event is persistently reexperienced in at least one
> of the following ways:
>   (1) recurrent and intrusive recollections of the event
>   (2) recurrent distressing dreams of the event
>   (3) sudden acting or feeling as if the traumatic event were
>   recurring
>
> C. ...numbing of general responsiveness...
>
> D. Persistent symptoms of increased arousal...

(1) difficulty falling or staying asleep
(2) irritability or outbursts of anger
(3) difficulty concentrating
(4) hypervigilance
(5) exaggerated startle response

Spider always had been a little antsy, as his mother put it, but now he was a constant nervous wreck. He jumped at the slightest noise. If a car backfired he would dive for the ground. He'd done it twice indoors, frightening her—once in the grocery store, when someone dropped a large can, and once at home, when she drew the living room curtains shut. He had picked himself up sheepishly and explained that it sounded like an artillery round coming in.

She didn't know how to act. He got agitated when he realized that she was tiptoeing around him. But if she tried to "act natural," it was even worse. He drank beer all the time, but of course she couldn't say anything about that. He'd found an old BB pistol that Terry had given him for his twelfth birthday. She remembered how relieved she'd been when he lost interest in it. Now he spent an hour or more every day down in the garage, listening to the radio and shooting Necco Wafers that he propped up on a Scrabble rack. (She'd hated the smell of the little candies ever since his uncle had shown him how the BB made them explode.)

He kept talking about leaving, getting a room near College Park, and she half wished he would. But that would be like deserting him. And she didn't want to be left alone, herself.

MAGAZINE ISSUES

Spider decided to investigate reality as a kind of research project. At the hospital they'd only had a limited range of magazines, like *Reader's Digest* and *National Geographic*, and even those had articles missing if they were potentially disturbing. He stopped at a newsstand and bought a couple dozen magazines, from *National Review* and *Harper's* to various journals of observational gynecology.

One article really got to him, a supposedly factual thing called "What Every Vietnam Veteran Knows." It was a catalogue of horrors—GIs mutilating Viet Cong bodies, making necklaces of ears and even genitalia, fragging officers, massacring civilians, running amok on heroin and speed. There was a kernel of truth in all of that. Everybody did know about the necklaces of ears, though to his knowledge nobody had ever seen one; unpopular officers died and there were whispers; civilians got in the way of bullets and bombs; men took dope and some got addicted. But things like that must have happened in every war; it was basically an unsavory and dangerous dehumanizing activity. This writer acted as if Vietnam vets were something out of a grade-B horror movie, soulless zombies out to destroy anything that got in their path. Killer was the only guy he'd known who was crazy, and even he wasn't *that* crazy.

Spider started to write a letter to the magazine, but after half a page he saw that it made *him* look like a raving maniac. And he reminded himself that he hadn't exactly been in the hospital with the flu; he wasn't the world's most reliable authority on sane soldiers.

And then his father came home.

HASHBURY

Beverly suffered no physical complications from her abortion. She was upset, especially after the doctor insisted that she look at the fetus, but after only a couple of days of lying crying in a dark room, crammed with cotton and full of Valium and pain pills, she was ready to sample the wonders of Lee's spiritual home, the Haight-Ashbury district of San Francisco.

Haight-Ashbury wasn't the only concentration of hippies in the area. The Pine Streeters could lay claim to more solidarity. Virginia City, Nevada, was probably more drugged-out. But the Haight drew media attention and became symbolic of the youth revolution characterized by particular kinds of rock and folk music, dope smoking, interest in Oriental religion, weird clothes, and sexual liberation.

The term "hippy" was originally a derisive name applied by the few surviving Beatniks to these young and uncool upstarts—"hipsters" who didn't quite make the grade. Since the mid-sixties, beatniks and hippies alike had been moving out of their traditional North Beach digs, which had become fashionable and expensive. Haight-Ashbury attracted them with its big cheap Victorian houses and funky atmosphere.

When Lee had left the Haight, early in 1967, there were already signs of trouble in Paradise. He was part of the January Be-In, more than ten thousand "Love Generation" youths wandering around Golden Gate Park absorbing Krishna consciousness, stoned on marijuana and Owsley Stanley's new White Lightning LSD and each other. The Diggers passed out free turkey sandwiches (from dozens of turkeys donated by dealer Owsley) and the Hell's Angels kept the peace. Free music from bands like Airplane, Loading Zone, and the Grateful Dead. Two mounted policemen moved through the crowd, ignoring violations of drug laws.

But there were problems, for the ten thousand and for Lee. At one end of the crowd, fights broke out between the hippies and a group of local blacks and Chicanos. When the horde left the stadium, the waiting police arrested nearly fifty for obstructing traffic. Lee saw it happening and slipped away through side streets, wandering around while his high dissipated. When he came back a few hours later, though, the cops had towed his car away. He'd left it in gear, and so they'd kindly wrecked the transmission in the process of towing it. Fixing the transmission would have cost more than he'd paid for the junker. He bought The Thing From Detroit from a friend and headed east, just to be away for a while.

He didn't know that the Be-In problems were just a pale foreshadowing of the storm that was building. The new governor of California, Ronald Reagan, was not exactly a friend of the Movement. His campaign had been pro-Vietnam, pro-police, and anti-student. One of the first things he had done upon taking office was to fire the president of the University of California, who was coddling the student radicals. Police stepped up drug and obscenity busts.

But the Haight would have been going to hell without any help from the government. Lee had left before the widely publicized Summer of Love began. Nearly a hundred thousand people from all over the country converged on Haight-Ashbury, most of them high-school dropouts and other rootless youngsters. Marijuana and LSD became relatively scarce; speed and heroin became problems. Drug-related hospital admissions quintupled. Stoned teenagers wearing what their hometown newspapers said hippies wore wandered around the district grokking it in its fullness and asking, "Spare change?" of the hordes of tourists who came down to look at them.

By the end of summer, the tourists and media went away, and most of the stoned children went away, but the hard elements stayed. The police began to sweep the streets for runaways and undesirables. Any male who couldn't produce a draft card was in trouble. Most of the actual hippies drifted out into the country.

Lee hardly recognized the place. The glittering bohemia had become a dangerous slum. They drove around for an hour, Lee quietly describing things as they used to be, and then headed back to Berkeley for the night. Lee might have spent a few days in the Haight out of curiosity and nostalgia, but Beverly was in no shape for it.

Some Berkeley friends let them crash for grass and groceries, and Lee found a two-week housepainting job. Beverly sought out the local Kennedy-for-President campaign office and spent a few hours a day stuffing envelopes and being a gofer. It helped her state of mind to be doing something useful, and she was excited at the prospect of actually meeting Robert Kennedy. He was scheduled to come to California in a few weeks.

HOMECOMING (2)

Spider was sprawled across his bed upstairs after dinner, immersed in Delany's *The Einstein Intersection*, when he heard his father's car pull up in the driveway.

He wasn't sure what to do. Go downstairs and greet him? Hi, Dad. How were things in Gettysburg? How was *that girl*?

The front door opened and his father called out, "Midge, I'm home," as if he was just getting home from work. Spider heard his mother's running footsteps and then muffled sobs, and decided to wait until he was summoned. He lay back on the bed and pretended to be asleep.

After a few minutes his mother came to the door. "John? John, wake up." He sat up and made a show of rubbing his eyes. "Your father's downstairs." She didn't look very good, slumped against the door jamb, tired red eyes and crooked smile.

He followed her down to the living room, where his father was centered on the couch in front of a tall glass of bourbon, already half gone. That was how and where he sat when he wanted an audience. Spider and his mother would sit and listen on easy chairs facing the couch. For a second he felt like a kid again, having to explain a report card or that broken window.

But he kept his cool. This is my father but there's not much he can do to me now. This is my father but it's also a man who just deserted his wife for two weeks of drinking and adultery.

"You're still at home," he said. "That's good. We've hardly had any chance to talk."

Spider nodded and sat down and took the beer his mother brought. His father's speech was slow and slurred. He had dark circles under his eyes and his skin was pasty. "Was it a good trip?" Spider asked.

"Oh yeah, yeah. Good trip." He gulped at the bourbon. "We have to talk about what you did in Vietnam."

Why? Spider almost said. "Handled bodies for a while, humped the boonies for a while, got hurt, came home. I pretty much wrote you everything that happened."

"But not everything. You didn't write everything."

"I held back a little. Didn't want to upset Mom and Bev."

"Bet you did. Hold back." He looked up at his wife. "Carrie, this is man talk."

"PhooeY on that. *Man* talk! He's my son, too."

He looked at her for a long moment. "You've had a lot to drink."

"And you, you've been on the wagon for the past couple weeks."

He swiveled back to Spider, like a man aiming a weapon. "Okay. You tell me and your *Mom* just what you couldn't put in those letters."

He looked straight into his father's face. "Couple of guys got their dicks blown off."

At first he didn't move a muscle, but his face turned red, dark red. "You just wade right in, don't you."

"You asked."

He picked up his drink slowly, thoughtfully, and hurled it straight at his son's face. Spider ducked; the glass bounced off the carpet and hit the wall without breaking.

His mother stood up unsteadily. "What on Earth—"

"Your *son*'s a *fuc*king *queer!*" he roared, stabbing his finger toward Spider as he rose in sodden wrath. "You don't even know what 'blow' means, do you?"

Spider was wiping bourbon sting from his eyes. "What the hell are you talking about?"

"Your own doctor said so! He said he was trying to cure you."

"Oh, that. Folsom's not a doctor. And he admitted he was—"

"By God you don't have to be a doctor to tell a queer!"

Spider turned to his mother. She was staring at both of them with dumb astonishment. "It's not true, Mother."

"Has he been on a date since he got home? Has he even *looked* at a girl?" She shook her head slowly. "No."

"I *have*. I tried to find Beverly."

"She ran away," his mother said, voice shaking. "Her father says she ran away to California with a hippy, a ho… a homo hippy."

"You see? You *see*?"

"If he's a homo," Spider said, "why is he interested in Beverly?"

"Why don't *you* tell *me*," his father said. "I don't know a fucking thing about that kind of… thing."

He looked at his father and wondered why he didn't feel more anger. He didn't feel fear or hate or much of anything. Just tiredness, and frustration. Probably the Valium. "Dad, why don't we talk in the morning? You're tired and you've had too much to drink."

"You can't tell me how much to drink."

"I guess not." Spider stood up and headed for the door. "I'll see you both later."

He was wrong.

LIFE IS BUT A DREAM (3)

Spider stopped at the light where East-West Highway crosses Wisconsin, a long light, and a man walked by and looked into the car at him. His face was melted, scar tissue from a terrible burn.

And suddenly Spider was not in the car. He was back in the cold white room with the smells, and today, his next-to-last day, there was a new smell, like roasted pork.

It was already out of the body bag, lying on its side on the porcelain table. The image of a human being crudely sculpted out of carbon char.

"Saved this one for you, John," the black man said, but his voice was serious and strained. "You never got a napalm before. Crispy critter."

"One of ours?"

"Uh huh. Air strike, Fang said, guy was in a LP cut off from the rest of the unit. You wanta check his dog tags?"

Spider moved toward the corpse as if through thick glue. Its mouth was open impossibly wide. Even the tongue was burned, blistered. The face was not a face. There were cheekbones and holes that had been eyes and two slits marking where the nose had been and one melted ear. The black stumps that had been arms were drawn together across its chest and its knees were pulled up. All the clothes were burned off and it had the charred fossil of an erection.

The dog tag was warped by the heat, and oxidized. Spider bent it back into shape and scraped the crud off it with his thumbnail, and wiped the thumbnail on his trousers. When he tried to talk no sound came out.

He coughed twice. "Ramble, John NMI. RA377664598."

"Stupid prick joined up."

"Yeah. Baptist. Type A."

"See if there's a unit designation on the body bag."

Spider bent over to look at the body bag and his knees buckled and he fainted dead away. Almost a year later, the incident triggered a chorus of automobile horns.

THE GREAT WHITE HOPE

Robert F. Kennedy had run John F. Kennedy's presidential campaign, and as a reward for that success was appointed to the office of Attorney General at the age of thirty-five. After his brother was killed, RFK sought the vice-presidential nomination in 1964. Lyndon Johnson said no, so RFK ran for a Senate seat in New York and won. He bided his time. In 1967 and early 1968, Johnson's popularity slid and then, after Tet, nose-dived. In mid-March, six weeks after Tet, "Bobby" threw his hat in the ring.

Like a lot of Americans of her generation, Beverly was hypnotized by Bobby's youthful energy and Brahmin charm, and saw in them the possibility of reclaiming JFK's Camelot. Never mind that much of the world had seen JFK as a saber-rattling bully, threatening nuclear war over Cuba and sending American troops to support a corrupt regime in Vietnam; never mind that RFK had cut his political teeth on Joe McCarthy's vicious Permanent

Subcommittee on Investigations. Both men had personal magnetism and liberal credentials that overshadowed not-so-liberal actions.

It was another McCarthy, Eugene, who had Lee's vote. "Clean Gene" was going to fire Secretary of State Dean Rusk, the Selective Service's General Hershey, and J. Edgar Hoover. (Like both Kennedys, McCarthy's record was not in harmony with his rhetoric: he had voted for the Tonkin Gulf Resolution that put us into Vietnam, and voted in favor of every Vietnam war appropriation bill.)

McCarthy, much more than Kennedy, pushed Johnson into the decision not to run in 1968. The President was humiliated by the Wisconsin primary, which went to McCarthy, fifty-seven to thirty-six percent. Right after that, LBJ gave the famous 31 March television speech that ended "I shall not seek and I will not accept the nomination of my party for another term as president."

Bobby moved in for the kill. He was less worried about McCarthy, whom he assessed as a fringe protest candidate, than he was about Vice President Hubert Humphrey, who was shedding his liberal principles fast, in order to secure the party's centrist nomination. Bobby was generous in his public praise for LBJ's wisdom and magnanimity; his great achievements for racial harmony and economic opportunity—forgetting the beware-the-warmonger rhetoric of previous months—but Johnson was unmoved. He hadn't liked Bobby in 1964, and he certainly had nothing to gain by appearing to like him now. LBJ would endorse his vice-president as the lesser of two evils, and the Democratic Party machine would fall in behind him.

Kennedy campaigned hard through April, and in early May won his first primary victory, Indiana, with almost twice as many votes as McCarthy. He won handily again in mid-May, in Nebraska, but at the end of the month was edged out in liberal Oregon, McCarthy taking forty-five percent to his thirty-nine.

California would be the make-or-break test, with its large liberal population and crucial 174 convention delegates. Both men moved toward Los Angeles for the showdown.

MOVING IN, MOVING OUT

Spider parked the car more or less legally and went uphill to the Language Building, where he'd seen a bulletin board full of notices of apartments and rooms to rent. There was a furnished attic room for sixty-five dollars that was only a few blocks from the doughnut place. He called from a pay phone and a woman with a dry whispery voice said it was still available.

It actually looked better than he had expected. It was smaller than his room at home, but it was clean and had an interesting mix of Salvation Army furniture. The man who showed him the room was not your ideal landlord, though; old and deaf and querulous. He asked if Spider were one of those "hipsters." When Spider said no, he'd just gotten out of the Army, the man was monumentally unimpressed. He'd been Field Artillery in double-you-double-you-one, now that was a *war*. Spider agreed with him.

No pets, no girls, no parties. Mrs. Remington will fix you one egg and toast in the morning; if you want more than that you have to get it somewhere else. Laundromat two blocks away, but Mrs. Remington will do your sheets every Saturday for an extra two dollars a month. No food stored in your room but you can have the bottom shelf of the refrigerator.

Spider looked at the money he had left over after the deposit and realized he would have to budget it. He hadn't asked the guy at the doughnut shop how long it would be until he got paid. Figure a couple of weeks, anyhow. There was a place in Riverside where he could get Budweiser in returnables for $1.99 a case. Otherwise, he could live on peanut butter and pickle sandwiches and canned beans. It wouldn't be any worse than his mother's home cooking.

He went out and stocked up and filled the bottom of the refrigerator with beer and pickles and cans of tuna fish that had been on sale. He decided to wait a day before going back home, at least a day. Give his dad some time to cool off. Or leave.

The Remingtons had an old balloon-tire bicycle in the garage that he could use. He pumped up the tires and oiled it and set out squeakily to explore the neighborhood. Mostly quiet and residential. He came to a park and watched some girls play softball for awhile. They were fun to look at but probably too young for him, and anyhow none expressed any interest. They were absorbed in the game, awkwardly intense, but the worst of them could probably outhit and outpitch Spider. He could probably outrun them, but none of them chased him.

A few blocks away, he found a large ramshackle used bookstore. They had unbelievable deals on old science fiction magazines and paperbacks, two for a quarter. He re-evaluated his budget and dropped four dollars. That was about as much literature as the bicycle's front basket could manage.

He went back to his new home and sat on the porch drinking beer and reading *Mercenary*, a Mack Reynolds novel about a future where wars were fought by corporations and televised as entertainment. That didn't seem so far-fetched. Parts of the book made him nervous, so he took an extra Valium. He fell asleep in the last chapter and dozed until dark, his butt growing numb and cold on the porch swing.

He woke up famished and polished off a can of tuna with two slices of bread and a dill pickle. He read in bed for a while and then turned off the light and worried about tomorrow until he fell asleep.

•••

His father's car was gone when he pulled into the driveway in the morning. He peeked in the garage and saw his mother's car was gone, too. He let himself into the quiet house.

He got a beer out of the refrigerator and walked around the rooms, remembering. They had moved here when he was six; nothing earlier was actually real to him.

For some reason it was easier to remember things, walking through alone. He didn't have to reconcile his memory of his mother, or his father, with what they were now. The memories were mostly good.

He found three liquor boxes in the garage and filled them up with books. He opened the biology book and got an insistent erection from the *Playboy* pictures, but decided not to do anything about it until he got to his new place, a sort of christening.

He swaddled the microscope in clothes and packed it with the slide collection, but decided against hauling the telescope over. It would take up an awful lot of room, and he wouldn't be able to use it anyhow, until he got better. The memory of that night still spooked him. He took all the astronomy books, though, and the star charts.

He looked at the chart of the southern skies and had to sit down on the bed. That terrible night with the guy moaning kill me, kill me, just shoot me in the head. His legs and dick blown off, or was it just his dick. Bang cock. And then his father thinking he was talking about blowing a guy. Sucking someone's dick, ugh. Thanks a lot, Captain My Captain. Thanks for everything.

He filled a suitcase with school clothes and threw in a bathing suit and his gym shorts and jockstrap from high school. The catalogue said he had to take swimming and two other gym courses to graduate. Maybe swimming was co-ed; that would be all right.

At that moment he realized it wasn't Beverly he missed, not Beverly specifically. He just desperately needed a girl, any girl, to talk to, to look at. God, to hold her softness and smell her hair. He remembered that like a blow.

He wasn't crying but his eyes were leaking, and his nose filled up. He went down to the kitchen to get a paper towel. His mother's bourbon bottle was there and he poured half a tumbler full. He added a couple of ice cubes but it wasn't even cool when he choked it all down, medicine drinking. Just like dear old Dad. He shouted at the empty kitchen and loaded up his car and drove slowly, grimly, back to College Park.

A GOOD MAN IS EASY TO LOSE

Lee's Thing From Detroit had a flat tire on the way to the Ambassador Hotel, so they showed up for the Kennedy party an hour late. Beverly was in a rotten and contentious mood anyhow, since McCarthy had won Oregon the week before, and Lee was doing a bad job of hiding his pleasure at that. He dropped her at the hotel and went off in search of a free parking place. He'd find a place to wash up from changing the tire and meet her upstairs.

The Embassy Room, where Kennedy would make his victory or concession speech, was packed solid; a brace of firemen blocking the door sent her downstairs to the overflow area, the Ambassador Ballroom.

There was no point in getting pissed off at the firemen, and the flat tire actually wasn't Lee's fault, and McCarthy wasn't such a bad man. But she really felt like biting somebody. She went into the ladies' room instead, and sat in a stall for ten minutes, reading a *Cosmo* someone had left behind.

At least the ballroom wasn't so crowded. Up in the Embassy Room, she would have had to wait for hours in the crowd crush, and probably never actually get close to Kennedy. She'd probably see him better on the TV monitors here.

Volunteers were hurriedly setting up punch bowls and tubs of soft drinks. Beverly volunteered to join the bucket brigade for ice. She went upstairs to the ice machine five times, and each time she went by a row of three stainless steel warming tables under a sign that said THE ONCE AND FUTURE KING. Tomorrow she would see them in a newspaper photograph and faint dead away.

Lee showed up tired but determined to be friendly, and they commandeered a table with eight chairs close to one of the monitors. The table filled up fast and they chatted with the others while the TV moved from network to network. Lee didn't mention his own heretical affiliation; on his grease-smudged shirt he wore a couple of RFK buttons as well as the Volunteer Guest badge.

The punch was slightly spiked and one of the volunteers came up with a bottle of vodka to help it along, so the wait wasn't too onerous. The results should have been in before ten, but Los Angeles County, with forty-three percent of the votes, was having computer trouble. One by one the networks predicted a Kennedy win.

They heard the cheering from upstairs first, and then the TV screens all switched to the Embassy Room. Kennedy gave a rather long, rambling victory speech, thanking everybody under the sun, including Eugene McCarthy. His last words were "Now on to Chicago and let's win there."

Lee wanted to get out fast and beat the crowd. That was all right with Beverly; it was past her bedtime and the vodka was making her heavy-lidded in spite of all the excitement.

The Thing was parked about ten minutes from the hotel. Beverly got to the bathroom before the line started and Lee hustled her out.

They were alone on the sidewalk, approaching the car, when a tan ambulance went screaming by. "Hope no one's hurt," Beverly said, without logic.

· · ·

There was no Zapruder film to document the assassination of Robert F. Kennedy; only a room full of eyewitnesses. Most of them agreed on one central fact: Sirhan Sirhan fired a pistol at RFK, and RFK fell mortally wounded.

Sirhan eventually was convicted of the crime. Investigators found a notebook that he had filled with weird stream-of-consciousness ravings, repeating "RFK must die." He sometimes acted quite sane, but was irrational often enough to make it seem convincing that the assassination had been a combination of obsessive planning and lunatic impulse.

There are two problems with that straightforward explanation. One is that Sirhan was standing in front of Kennedy, but Kennedy was struck by three bullets fired from *behind* him. Sirhan's revolver only held eight bullets; either ten or thirteen were retrieved from the scene.

The fatal bullet was fired point-blank, less than one inch from Kennedy's skull, behind the right ear. Sirhan was never closer than eighteen inches. A bullet taken from his body was compared to one taken from a bystander wounded by Sirhan while people were attempting to disarm him, and two forensic examiners agreed that the bullets came from different weapons. (A 1975 review board was not as confident as the earlier examiners, saying that the two-weapon theory was a possibility, not a certainty.)

Conspiracy buffs are quick to drag in the Mafia, since Kennedy had given a lot of grief to organized crime as Attorney General. The previous month Jimmy Hoffa, serving time in a Pennsylvania federal prison, had been overheard discussing "a contract to kill Bob Kennedy." There are tenuous links between the Mob and Sirhan (racetrack acquaintances) and the Ambassador Hotel (where racketeer Mickey Cohen had run a gambling operation in the forties) and Kennedy's bodyguard Thane Eugene Cesar (vague "connections"), who was the only other armed person in the room.

Cesar carried a .38-caliber revolver, not a .22, which would seem to exonerate him. But several people reported seeing Cesar pull out a pistol and fire several times, supposedly at Sirhan, and no .38-caliber bullets were recovered from the scene. (Cesar did have a Harrington & Richardson nine-shot .22 pistol registered under his name, but he claimed to have sold it months before the assassination. Years later, a bill of sale surfaced dated *September*

1968, three months after the deed; police tried to track the pistol down, but it had been stolen.)

The odd resonances with RFK's brother's assassination can be taken two ways, of course. It could be that both men were murdered by a conspiracy involving organized crime. It could be that if you probe deeply enough into any murder that's not a domestic affair, you'll find oddities galore, including connections with criminals, some of them more or less organized.

Maybe our desire to see these assassinations as the work of large mysterious forces beyond our control is a way of denying the simple truth: in America, any nut case with the price of a gun obviously has a fair prospect of killing any public figure he dislikes.

That said, there are other strands of coincidence and malice to be added to the web that connects Martin Luther King, Robert F. Kennedy, and J. Edgar Hoover. It was Kennedy who authorized Hoover's snooping on King, that led to the taped evidence of adultery being sent to his wife. But Kennedy was of course on King's side politically, and it was Kennedy who chartered the plane that transported King's family and his body from Memphis to Atlanta. In a eulogy for King, Kennedy had the weirdly prophetic line "No one can be certain who next will suffer from some senseless act of bloodshed."

As noted earlier, James Earl Ray was apprehended in a theater-of-the-absurd confrontation with the customs people at London's Heathrow—presenting two passports with different names; trying to smuggle a concealed weapon aboard a plane—but Hoover asked the British authorities to keep it quiet. He delayed the news of Ray's apprehension for a day so that King's widow would be told of it during her attendance at Kennedy's funeral.

ONE DAY ON THE JOB

Spider bicycled through the morning darkness to the doughnut shop, peering intently at the pool of light thrown from a flashlight clipped to the handlebars. It had rained earlier and now the air was pleasantly heavy and cool. Crickets chirped back at his squeaking wheels. When he got to Route 1 he switched to the sidewalk, enduring the cracks and puddles rather than trust the night vision of truck drivers high on Benzedrine and coffee, trying to make New York before rush hour. Why didn't they use the Beltway? Speed traps, he supposed.

He got to the shop a few minutes before three. (On the other coast, Robert Kennedy was taking a short-cut through the hotel kitchen.) The bright fluorescents inside flooded the small parking lot with a ghostly glare. There weren't any customers. The guy behind the cash register was squinting at a thick textbook and taking notes on a spiral pad. While Spider locked up the bike, a rattletrap van pulled into the lot and parked next to him. It dieseled, the engine coughing and sputtering after the driver turned it off. Spider could hear him pump the accelerator, grumbling in some foreign language. The engine stopped with a minor explosion and his boss got out.

"Early, that's good." He shook Spider's hand and ushered him into the shop. "Hey, Kerry, studyin' on company time."

Kerry looked up heavy-lidded. "So you want a doughnut?"

"Huh uh. You gotta stop bein' a student and be a teacher." The boss introduced them.

Kerry had been expecting him. "Yeah, that's mainly why I'm going into grad school, stay out of Vietnam. Hope it'll be over in a couple of years."

"God knows. They stop fuckin' around in Paris and get down to business." Spider saw the boss wince. "Sorry. Watch my language."

"Jus' when customers around. You got the Fryolater up?"

"I'd give it a few more minutes," Kerry said. "Thermometer's been running low, I mean high. It'll say the oil's hot enough but they won't brown up."

"Well, show Spider the batter stuff. I gotta inventory and go down to the warehouse, shoulda done it yesterday."

"We just have enough four-ex for one more batch, maybe two."

"That's what I figured; apples, too. Check everything out, I'll be back by five."

Kerry took Spider back to the Mixing Station. It was not too challenging for a person who was able to read; there was a fifteen-step menu taped to the mixer head. It took about ten minutes for Spider to go through the process for vanilla. He carried the heavy steel mixing bowl to a sideboard and started over with an empty one for "fudge." Kerry was a good mentor, supplying information when Spider needed it, but mainly letting him go through the steps on his own.

The doughnut gun was fun to learn, but Kerry guaranteed it would get old fast. You filled the cylinder up with batter and then fired it into the Fryolater's tub of hot fat, firing close to the surface so the hot oil didn't splash on you. One cylinder produced about twelve doughnuts. You refilled and emptied it fast and fried two dozen at a time. (Too many and the temperature of the oil would go down and make the doughnuts greasy. But you didn't want to make too few, or you'd be standing by the Fryolater all morning.) The doughnuts floated. After they'd fried for a little less than two minutes, brown on one side, you turned them over with a long fork and let them go until that side was brown, maybe another minute. Then you threaded them onto a cooling rod and racked them, and started over.

The hot oil made Spider nervous. He had been badly burned as a kid, trying to help his mother fry chicken. The back of his right hand was slick with scar tissue from the accident. The napalm memory was there, too.

Kerry studied while Spider did five racks. Then he initiated him into the mysteries of powdered sugar, which was pretty obvious; honey-dipped, which used no honey and weren't dipped; and the panoply of combinations possible with sprinkles, coconut shreds, and chopped nuts, combined with glazes of chocolate, cherry, hard sauce, and butterscotch. Spider ate three of his creations and thought they were great. Kerry went back to his books and ate half a ham sandwich.

Spider started the process over. They wanted to do all of the regular batter before they fried the fudge ones. His boss came back and approved of his new expertise, and manned the Fryolater while Spider and Kerry unloaded the van and stacked the boxes in the storage room.

This is how things happen. Spider was dragging, so he poured a cup of coffee to perk him up. He went to relieve his boss at the Fryolater. The boss finished turning the current batch and told Spider to give them a little extra time.

He studied the doughnuts turning lazily in the sizzling oil. He didn't notice his boss go outside through the storage room and get into the van, parked right by the open window. When he tried to start the old thing, it backfired, one loud bark like a hand grenade. Spider's whole body jerked in a spasm of hypervigilance, and the coffee cup sailed into the Fryolater. He just had time to throw up his hands to shield his face.

Spider staggered back from the explosion of boiling oil, knocking over a rack of doughnuts but staying upright himself, sagging back in agony against the wall. The left side of his face was badly burned: forehead, eyelid, cheek, and ear. But he didn't notice. He was staring at his hands, watching angry blisters form on the palms and fingers and on his forearms halfway down to the elbows.

His boss did one good thing, calling the Rescue Squad, and one bad thing, smearing the burns with Crisco. Then he went outside to lean on the van and stare at the charcoal sky.

Spider wept, but not from pain. "Why me?" he asked Kerry, who was cradling his head and dabbing at his face with a paper towel wetted with ice water. "I go through all this fuckin' shit and now this. Why me?"

• • •

The paramedics gave him morphine and, after they found the bottle in his pocket, a shot of Valium. He still cried out in agony when they got him back to the ER and cleaned the Crisco off and dressed his burns. They gave him more morphine and he fell asleep.

From his wallet they got his home phone number and called it. There was no answer. He wasn't carrying any record of the place where he was currently living, of course; he hadn't even given the address to his boss yet.

They found the purple ID that identified him as a disabled veteran, and called the Baltimore VA hospital to arrange for a bed in the burn unit. The clerk there noted that John Darcy Speidel had an appointment that morning in Psych. Could the wound have been self-inflicted? The medic said he didn't know, but it seemed unlikely. There were a lot of more direct ways to hurt yourself.

He slept through most of the ambulance ride to Baltimore. When he woke up the nurse who was riding with him gave him a pill. When he realized he couldn't even hold a glass by himself, he began to cry again, and ask her the same question that Kerry couldn't answer. Sobbing herself, partly for him and partly from the shocking news about Kennedy, she held him for a minute, carefully, and in her softness and sadness he quieted down.

SUMMER

For weeks the pain was always there, but it never came to the surface, smothered under layers of medication. Spider felt like he never slept and never quite woke up, either. He lay on a bed, naked except for a t-shirt and socks, with his palms taped permanently to his thighs. He was growing a new layer of skin on his hands, they told him; try to keep them still.

He couldn't feed himself or wipe himself. He didn't talk to anyone. He was in a corner bed, and the man in the bed next to him didn't say anything; he just moaned and whimpered, his face a blistered molten ruin. Spider wondered what his own face looked like. They'd asked him whether he would rather let his beard grow out than have someone shave him, and he nodded. He could feel it on the pillow, scratchy at first, then more like hair.

Every few days a male orderly would unbutton the soft buttons along the side of his t-shirt and give him a sponge bath. It mortified him, because he always had an erection, but there was no way he could *think* it away! The orderly always worked around it without comment. Once, after a couple of weeks, an older female nurse gave him his bath, behind a screen, and with a whispered lame joke ("Don't point that thing at me; it might go off.") helped him with three or four merciful strokes, and cleaned up afterwards.

A WORLD OF HURT

The summer that followed Kennedy's assassination was a season of anger all over the world, citizens' protests answered with clubs and guns and cynical politics.

In Czechoslovakia, the promise of a "Prague Spring" of liberalization was crushed under the treads of Soviet tanks. The coalition of students and workers in France was beaten down by truncheons and tear gas. Students and police exchanged blows in Mexico, Japan, Yugoslavia, England, Spain, Germany, California.

369

In Miami, the Republicans selected their ticket, Richard Nixon and Spiro Agnew, who would eventually become the only executive pair ever forced from office for criminal dishonesty. While the Republicans were celebrating with their noisemakers and confetti and balloons, Miami police were trying to contain a race riot downtown that had escalated from shouts to sniper fire.

Nixon was less worried about the Democrats than the American Independence Party's George Wallace. His straightforward campaign—keep the niggers in their place, put the students in jail, untie the hands of the police, go in and *win* that goddamned war—was not going to siphon many votes from Hubert Humphrey, but it could dangerously split Nixon's far-right bloc.

(By November, Wallace's campaign—following the usual pattern of third-party politics in America—would weaken to where he only cost Nixon fourteen percent of the popular vote, dropping "Tricky Dick" down to an equal forty-three percent tie with "The Hump." But Nixon would win handily in the Electoral College, with thirty-two states and the District of Columbia.)

Nixon may have taken a few votes from Humphrey with his claim that he had a "secret plan" to end the war in Vietnam soon after he took office. The plan would still be secret when he left office in disgrace, six years later.

. . .

A week after the Soviets invaded Czechoslovakia, the Democrats invaded Chicago. It was hostile territory for liberals.

After Kennedy's death, Beverly had joined Lee in working for McCarthy. Their labors in the Los Angeles office were similar to what they had done for King in Washington—slipsheeting mimeos, stuffing envelopes, talking to strangers on the phone—but the spirit was completely different. In Washington the fuel had been rage. In Los Angeles it was righteousness, which burns with a paler flame. It didn't help that a lot of workers felt there was no realistic chance of their winning the nomination, let alone the election, but you did have to do *something*.

At the end of August a lot of the workers convoyed to Chicago to show their support for Gene. Lee's Thing was one of the few plain American cars in the group, which had a preponderance of Volkswagen bugs and buses, many with amateur paint jobs in floral motifs.

The trip was a lot of fun, eight carloads stopping together for lunch and camping out, Lee playing and singing protest songs, half of the people high on politics and half on other painkillers. Some version of the experience was duplicated thousands of times as the counterculture converged on Chicago. Chicago would be ready for them.

Beverly and Lee, planning to demonstrate with the National Mobilization to End the War in Vietnam, were on the sedate end of the counterculture's political spectrum, closer to the mainstream than the Students for a Democratic Society and the Student Nonviolent Coordinating Committee (many of whose members were neither students nor pacifists). At the far ultraviolet end were splinter groups like the White Panthers and the West Side Motherfuckers, into violent anarchy.

The best organized far-left group was the Youth International Party, the Yippies, led by Abbie Hoffman and Jerry Rubin. Rubin and Phil Ochs had scoured the Illinois countryside for the ugliest pig they could find; they named it Pigasus and offered it as the Yippie candidate.

The Yippies got a disproportionate amount of media coverage, especially television, since political conventions are basically boring and repetitive. The reportage had to be sanitized, though, with a "Look at what these crazy kids are up to now!" slant, because most of what the Yippies did and said was not suitable for the six o'clock news or family magazines. For instance, they circulated a leaflet demanding that the city of Chicago set up free medical clinics, to prevent a plague of VD—otherwise "We will fuck the police and their horses! NOTHING will be SAFE from STREET FREAK GERM WARFARE if the city does not allow us to disarm ourselves!"

The L.A. contingent had heard about a Yippie gathering in Lincoln Park the Sunday they arrived, August 25th. It was a good place to relax after the long drive. A couple of thousand young people, rock music, dope, street theater. There was a nervous edge to the festivities, but the expected trouble with Mayor Daley's police didn't materialize. After sundown, the more affluent went out into the suburbs to find motel rooms. Lee and Beverly found a quiet side street and slept in the Thing.

They were not sure where to head after the convention. Beverly sort of wanted to go back to Maryland and resume college, and maybe get in touch with her mother, but she liked California, too. Lee was bummed out over what the Haight had become and never had liked L.A. much. If by some miracle McCarthy won the nomination, he wanted to go back to the Washington area, to be where the action was. They wound up deciding not to make a decision just yet.

They wandered around the park the next day. Beverly found a couple she'd known at the University, who had brought along a hibachi grill. They pigged out on cheap hot dogs and then followed the crowd, several thousand, to the Chicago Coliseum for music and speeches. Dick Gregory and Phil Ochs entertained the troops, and the air was thick with antiestablishment solidarity.

Things started to unravel Tuesday night. The city ordered everyone out of the park. In response, the various groups organized a sit-in vigil, people wearing black armbands and singing hymns.

Plainclothes police surrounded the park. The uniformed cops took off their badges and nameplates. Around 12:30, they struck, first raining tear gas and Mace on the crowd, and then wading in with nightsticks. To Beverly and Lee it looked like a hopeless situation; they managed to slip out unharmed except for eye and nose irritation from the gas. On their way back to the Thing they stopped and watched a convoy of National Guard trucks roar toward the park.

They talked about leaving, but both of them were more angry than scared. The morning news said that Mayor Daley had given the Mobilization a permit to assemble at Grant Park. They decided to stay at least for that, since that was one reason they'd come: to assemble and march ten thousand strong to the Democratic Convention Amphitheatre. Confront the delegates with the fact that most of the people they represented wanted the United States out of the war.

The permit was to assemble, though; not to march. By dusk, nearly fifteen thousand people had poured into the park. The police tried to cordon them off. They broke through the police line and surged downtown.

Lee and Beverly went with the crowd. For the first half-hour it was fairly peaceful, if not exactly orderly. But as they approached the Conrad Hilton Hotel, where the delegates were staying, the police attacked with a sudden ferocity that made Tuesday's harassment look like a mild dress rehearsal.

Norman Mailer, watching from a hotel balcony, later said "lines of twenty and thirty policemen striking out in an arc ... attacked [the crowd] like a chain saw cutting into wood." Lee and Beverly saw clouds of tear gas and Mace coming toward them. They tied bandannas soaked with Coke over mouth and nose. People were running in every direction, screaming, as anonymous police worked through the crowd swinging their clubs at random.

Lee was holding Beverly's hand, both of them trying to stay upright in the stampede, when she received one of those impersonal blows. Neither of them saw it coming. She was struck from behind, whacked on the crown, and fell forward onto her hands and knees, blood streaming. Lee went to help her and someone kicked him in the ribs. As he fell down, a big cop grabbed one foot and held his legs apart, laughing, while his partner beat him three times hard in the groin with a nightstick. He stayed conscious just long enough to crawl over to Beverly and curl protectively around her.

The rescue squad people who cleaned up after the police gave Beverly twelve stitches. There wasn't much they could do for Lee other than cold compresses and reassurance. His scrotum was bruised and bleeding and swollen to twice normal size; he was in so much pain he could only grunt in monosyllables. They would later find out that he had two fractured ribs as well.

The police had destroyed every camera they saw, but they didn't get all of them. The riot was on prime-time news Wednesday night, before the tear gas had even dissipated. Walter Cronkite, whom a poll had named "the Most Trusted Man in America," told viewers, "I want to pack my bags and get out of this city."

That's exactly what Lee and Beverly did, she steering the big car out to the interstate while he lay curled up in the back, washing painkillers down with beer. As soon as they were out of the city, she exited onto a random country road, pulled over onto the shoulder and had some pills and beer herself. They spent the next ten hours in drugged sleep and then woke up and pointed the Thing From Detroit toward the rising sun.

HEALING

Spider watched the Chicago police riots on television with some interest, but the big thing in his life was that he was going to be released from the hospital. The skin grafts had been successfully completed weeks before, but his arms and hands were weak from the long period of immobility. He spent most of his day either doing physical therapy or recovering from it.

They found out he played the guitar and got him one from the Red Cross. It was especially good exercise for his left hand, which didn't get as much casual use as his right.

There was a beautiful well-shaded lawn in front of the hospital, and when the weather was nice he would sit on a park bench there and play, practicing songs out of the hospital's Joan Baez and Bob Dylan songbooks.

(Once he'd worn a straw hat outside to keep the sun off his head, then took it off when clouds came up. A passerby threw a quarter into it as he sat there playing. Amused, he moved it to the grass at his feet, and after a couple of hours had collected $1.87—a new career!)

The world didn't look too bad. He'd given up smoking, rather than ask people to sit and hold a cigarette for him, and he felt a lot better for losing the chronic cough and sinus problems. He was still taking Valium, but only two-thirds of his prescription (he palmed the morning pills and sold them to a more strung-out patient). He was in some pain most of the time, but it was a healing pain, tolerable.

He was apprehensive about going home. The VA had notified his parents as to what had happened to him and where he was, but there had been no response. He'd called home daily since his hands had been free, but never got an answer.

FALL

The VA released Spider on 14 September, and put him on a dawn bus to Washington. All he had was the clothes he'd been wearing when he reported for work at the doughnut shop, a hospital ditty bag, and a couple of beat-up books from the Red Cross box. He was fairly flush, though, with $216.76, and another VA check due in two weeks.

At the Washington terminal he called home and listened to it ring twenty times. The ticket lady gave him directions and he caught a city bus to the District Line (that would have been the #9 streetcar when he was a kid; they were all gone now). He was tempted to walk the five miles home, to put off facing whatever was there, but he took a cab.

The ride was reassuring. Bethesda was unchanged. It felt like he'd been hospitalized a long time, but it had only been a couple of months. Maybe there was something wrong with the phone, or he had the number wrong.

He paid off the cab and got out to stare at a FOR SALE sign. The grass had been cut but half of it was brown patches, and the flowers that used to border the house were all dead.

There was no car in the driveway. He peered into the garage and it was empty—not only was his mother's car gone, but so was all the years of crap that should have been piled on the shelves all around. He peered into the living room and there was no furniture, just fresh paint and new carpeting. He tried his key in the front door and it just got stuck.

"What the hell do you think you're doin'?" Spider turned around. One of the neighbors—Mr. Menzel, Manville?— was standing there with a baseball bat.

"It's me, Spider." The man took a step toward him and Spider cringed back. "John. John Darcy."

"Good God, boy." He peered at him. "You look like hell."

"I was in an accident at work. Been in the hospital."

"Didn't know you was back from Vit-nam." He gestured with the baseball bat: the lawn, the house. "What happened with your folks?"

"I was gonna ask *you*. What is this?"

"I don't have the faintest. You know your dad was gone for a while. Then he come back two days, Mrs. Marvell says, or at least his car's back. Then he goes away again and about a month later your mom goes away, too. Then a coupla weeks ago this movin' crew comes in and cleans the place out and they paint it inside and mow the lawn—I mean it was a *foot* high—and put up the For Sale sign."

Spider shook his head. "Jesus."

"You got any relatives could tell you something?"

"One aunt. Tried to get her from the hospital. She's got an unlisted number, though, and the phone company wouldn't give it to me."

"I was you, I'd call this real estate company on the sign. You can use our phone."

Spider wrote the number down on the back page of *The War Against the Kull* and went inside the Marvells' home. It was oppressively neat, doilies on top of plastic on the arms of furniture.

The real estate lady said the owner of record was the Bank of Bethesda, and gave him a number. The woman at the bank said they couldn't give him any information unless he showed up in person, with identification.

"Maybe you better shave and dress up before you go to some bank," Mr. Marvell suggested.

"Yeah, maybe." Spider wasn't going to shave. He didn't want to know what his face looked like. "My stuff's all over in Riverside. Mind if I call a cab?"

The cab took about ten minutes, while Spider and Mr. Marvell engaged in excruciating conversation on the front porch. He directed the cab to the doughnut shop, since he didn't remember the Remingtons' address.

The shop had a new paint job, an awful shade of pink, and a new neon sign. Inside, it had a new owner. He was Indian or Pakistani, friendly and earnest but without much English. Spider was able to make out his explanation that the previous owner had retired to California and "Would like old job back, please? Boys we need two." No, thanks. He'd had a lifetime's worth of doughnut shop experience in one night.

The Remington's bicycle was still locked up where he'd left it, but both bike and lock were rusted solid. He walked the few blocks to their house. His car wasn't parked outside.

Mr. Remington talked to him without opening the door for a minute, unconvinced that he was who he said he was. Finally, Spider held up his driver's license up to the peephole.

He opened the door a foot. "We thought you'd took the bike and gone. Kids do things like that."

"Like I say, I had an accident at work. I didn't have any way to get in touch with you."

"Well, that ain't my fault. What about the damn bike?"

"It's still down at the doughnut shop. I would've brought it up, but the lock's rusted shut."

"Hmm. Figured you were gone for good."

"That's okay. Can I just get my stuff? My car?"

"Cleaned out the room when we got a new tenant. Down to the Goodwill. Police took your car away."

"You gave away all of my things?"

"We ain't no storage company. You go down to the Goodwill, it's likely mostly there."

"But the car, my car...it wasn't illegally parked."

"Couldn't have it clutterin' up the curb. New tenant, he had a car, too. You go down to the Riverside Police Station and they'll have it there." His brow furrowed. "One thing we still got is that guitar. Mrs. Remington kept it for her grandson, but he didn't want it. Said it was a piece of junk."

Spider knew that. "Could I have it back anyhow?"

"I don't know. You want the room?"

"I thought you had a tenant."

"Didn't work out. Foulmouth kid."

"Look, that guitar's *mine*. Could I please have it back?"

"Don't you raise your voice at me, young man." He walked away. After a couple of minutes he came back, but with a hacksaw rather than a guitar. "Now you bring back that bicycle. Then we'll see about the guitar." Spider took the saw and the man shut the door.

He went about a block and threw the saw behind a hedge. Then he headed for the police station.

• • •

Spider would never find out what had happened to his parents. His father had one last drunken confrontation with his mother and then left, picked up his Baltimore girlfriend, and went out west to "make a new start." That lasted less than a year. She testified against him and he wound up in a Phoenix prison, doing time for assault and battery and assault with a deadly weapon, a tire iron.

His mother grew increasingly depressed and ineffectual. Her sister stopped having anything to do with her, and on impulse she drove up to New Hampshire, where she had a half-sister from her father's first marriage. The older woman, recently widowed, took her in, but they weren't good for each other, both alcoholic and depressed. She stopped making sense and her half-sister had her committed, and then sort of forgot about her, and then died.

Spider didn't know the half-sister existed; he didn't even know his grand-father had been married twice, a dark family secret.

. . .

The police didn't give Spider any trouble about his car. They even offered him a lift out to the private lot in College Park where it was impounded, pending auction. He had to pay the lot fifty-eight dollars for towing and storage, but they did help him jumpstart the car.

He gassed up with the engine still running and took it out to the Beltway for a half-hour of high-speed aimlessness, just charging the battery and *moving*. Then he drove back to Riverside and parked it on a hill overlook-ing the Goodwill store.

The lady there was apologetic that she couldn't just give him his things back, under the circumstances. She did let him have anything he was sure was his for half price. He found the suitcase with his name on it and a few changes of clothes, including a set of fatigues left over from Basic Training, and almost all of his books except for the science fiction. The microscope was long gone; she remembered it selling the same day it came in.

The whole thing came to twenty-eight dollars, but she only took twenty. She said she would pray for him and things would get better if he would only try to look on the good side. He thanked her and lugged the suitcase and box of books up to the car. When he opened the trunk a very skinny rat jumped out.

The car started okay. He drove downtown to Ninth Street and got lunch from a hotdog stand, then wandered from pawn shop to pawn shop for a couple of hours, looking at guitars and trying them out. He finally settled on an old F-hole Silvertone, mainly because the guy behind the counter was a fellow Vietnam vet. They saw each other's brass bracelets and traded a few tales, and he offered to knock twenty bucks off the sixty-dollar price tag.

Spider drove back toward Maryland and stopped at a bar that looked halfway clean, and took the suitcase in. He ordered a beer and went into the john to change clothes. School clothes with a sport coat; that should be good enough for talking with a bank clerk. He combed his hair and briefly considered shaving. No. With the beard he just looked sort of like a student, hair not long enough for a hippy. The beard would be less conspicuous than the scars.

He drank the beer standing up and bought a roll of breath mints from the bartender. Three o'clock; better move along.

He sucked on the mints as he drove slowly down Wisconsin Avenue. He didn't really want to talk to the woman at the bank. What could she tell him that was good news? Sorry, it was all a mistake, your mom and dad are vacationing in Florida, it was somebody else's house we were supposed to gut and paint and put on the market. I'll just open the vault here and let you take all you want, okay? Feel better?

Florida. That's where Killer was from. They were going to meet in Tampa and go down to the Everglades and hunt alligators. You could make a lot of money and it would be a damn sight easier than humpin' the boonies.

He parked on the street a block from the bank and checked the name he had written in *The War Against the Rull*. Mrs. Daintith. A woman with an extra tit, right in the middle of her name. His hands were shaking.

The bank was all marble and dark wood and brass. High heels clicking and echoing, the smell of expensive cigars.

He found Mrs. Daintith's cubicle: Mortgages. She was a fairly young woman, attractive, trying to look neither. No makeup except lipstick, small square eyeglasses, ash-blond hair pulled back in a bun, dark blue dress with high neck and long sleeves. Spider tapped on the wood and she looked up over the rims of her glasses. "May I help you?"

"I'm John Speidel. I called you this morning about my house, my parents—"

"Yes. Please sit down." Spider perched on the hard wooden chair and she flipped through the manila folders on her desktop. "Here, Speidel. You have identification?"

Spider fumbled with his wallet and handed over his driver's license. She studied it and looked at him and then looked at the picture again.

"I was sixteen then; I look a lot—"

"Do you have some other ID? Draft card?"

"No, they took that when I got back from Vietnam."

"Oh," she said. "Ah." She looked at the license again and passed it back. "I guess this will do. How can I help you?"

"I just want to know what happened to my parents. I was in an accident and they put me in a hospital up in Baltimore, and by the time I was able to call home, nobody answered the phone. I got back this morning and the house is empty and for sale. What happened?"

"Have you talked to relatives?"

"There aren't any."

She studied the file. "I'm afraid I can't be of much help. All I can tell from this is that your parents stopped paying their mortgage three months ago. They didn't respond to letters or phone calls. A loan investigator went out and found the house deserted."

"So you put it on the market? Just like that?"

"No, first some inquiries were made. Police, hospitals, funeral homes. We found that your father had emptied out his savings account, and the checking account was overdrawn. So yes. We put the house on the market."

"But they owned it for fourteen years!"

Mrs. Daintith took off her glasses and folded them. She didn't look at Spider. "John, you don't understand. Your parents never owned the house. The bank owns the house. Your parents paid fourteen years of a thirty-year mortgage. Some people put insurance on their mortgage, so that if something happens to them it will be paid off. Your parents didn't do that."

She tilted her head toward him. She had lovely blue-gray eyes, almost purple. "Is it possible that your father lost his job?"

"More than possible. He was fu...he was not showing up, not making any sales. My mother was worried."

She shrugged. "Something happened. I'm sorry." She closed the folder and tapped it to even the papers inside. "If I were you I'd go to the police and file a Missing Persons report. You might run an ad in the Personals section of the *Post*."

"Look, what if I got a job — could I pay off the missing three months and then pick up the mortgage payments until they came back?"

"If you were twenty-one and had a power of attorney. You aren't and don't, though. I think your best bet is to find your parents before the house is sold."

He sagged back in the chair. "Yeah, maybe. No. They didn't even tell the neighbors. Just left."

"I wish I could help...oh, there is one thing." She opened the file again. "It's not much. Here." She opened a white envelope and took out three certificates. "Your father bought savings bonds for you on your birthday in 1958, '59, and '60. They're worth $92.16, if you want to cash them in."

"Hey, yeah, I'd forgotten about that." He looked at the ornate documents. "These'll get me where I'm goin'."

"Where is that?"

"Florida," he said, making up his mind.

THE UNIVERSE IS QUEERER THAN WE CAN IMAGINE

Beverly and Spider were in Bethesda at the same time, and they both got money from their parents, at the same bank.

She showed up at her parents' house right at noon, without Lee. Noon because she wanted to catch her mother in a good mood (it took her a few hours to get moving), and because her father would be out to lunch and un-phoneable until 1:30 or so.

They had a tearful reunion and Beverly related a sanitized, not so terrifying version of what she had been doing the past five months. No abortions or police brutality. Her mother had been a secret fan of Robert Kennedy, so they had that sadness to share, and she'd always wanted to go to California. (Her husband called Bobby Kennedy the White Nigger and thought California was part of the Soviet Union.)

The big news was that, on their drive back from Chicago, Lee had asked her to marry him.

That threw her mother for a loop. She was pouring coffee, and the spill gave her a chance to do something before responding. She rushed to the kitchen and came back with a whole roll of paper towels.

"But darling..." She carefully stripped off two towels, setting one on the small puddle of coffee on the end table and using the other to soak up the coffee that had splashed into the saucer. "Darling, how can that possibly work out? Your father says that he's a, a homosexual."

"Oh, *Dad*! Like, *I* would know if anybody did."

"You mean you've been..."

"Of course we have, Mother. What did you think?"

She blushed. "I guess I, guess I just didn't want to think about it. I mean, I know you're a modern girl and all, and I guess I *knew*, but you know. You're still my little girl."

She hugged her mother, feeling manipulative. "Always will be, Mommy."

"But your father got it from John's father, who talked to John's doctor at Walter Reed."

"Got what?"

"About your Lee, that he was homosexual."

"What would a doctor at Walter Reed know about Lee? He's never been in the Army."

"John's father said that he was in the Army but he was kicked out because he was queer."

"No. Not possible. I mean, maybe he could lie to me about being in the Army, but he couldn't lie about liking girls. I mean, obviously." Her mother nodded, looking at the floor. "And he just wouldn't lie. Not about the Army, not about the other thing. He's fiercely honest, which doesn't make him the easiest man to live with, but I love him."

"None of them are easy, baby." She looked up with a strained expression. "I can't tell your father about this. He'd go after him with a shotgun."

"I know. That's why I came over when he wasn't home."

"What can I do? Do you need money?"

"Well, Lee has a job. But it won't start for a couple of weeks. And I'm going back to school." That was mostly true: Lee had an outside job coming up with Larry in a couple of weeks, but Beverly would be painting alongside him. She was going back to school, yes, but only night school, one math course. When they'd saved enough she would go back full time.

"I'll write you a check. I'll make it out to cash, so don't you carry it around. Go straight down to the bank and cash it."

"Dad won't find out?"

"He never looks at the checkbook anymore. He was always making mistakes." She took the checkbook out of her purse and scribbled quickly. "Let's call it a wedding present." She handed it over. "Give me a call when you set the date. Make it a weekday so I can come?"

"Of course I will." She kissed her mother and sneaked a look at the check. Three hundred dollars!

The phone rang. "That'll be your father. Run along now. Keep in touch."

Beverly said she would, and meant it, and went out to steer the Thing toward the Bank of Bethesda. If she had disobeyed her mother and dawdled for a couple of hours, she might have met Spider there. But they might not have recognized each other, him all bearded and shaggy, her tanned and blonde, long hair swept back into a barrette to cover the shaved spot and scar from the nightstick.

She couldn't wait to tell Lee that he was a queer.

TRAVEL BROADENS

The great trek south didn't require much advance preparation. Spider changed the oil in his car and got a pup tent, mess kit, sleeping bag, and a small cooler at an Army Surplus store. Some munchies and Cokes. He went across the District Line to buy a couple of cases of beer and, on impulse, a bottle of Old Crow. What would the drinking age be in Florida?

Spider hadn't been able to get his VA check early; didn't really expect to, but they did agree to send it to him c/o General Delivery in Tampa. He didn't know one part of Florida from another, but on the map Tampa looked far enough south for winter not to be a problem. He thought he would check out the state and national parks; just camp out for a while. Maybe go down to the Everglades, like they'd planned.

Pity he didn't know Killer's real name. He could look up his parents. The last time I saw your son, a Chinaman in black pajamas blew his brains out with an AK47. But that's okay; I think he was already dead.

He pulled the car over onto the shoulder and sat for a few minutes with his eyes closed, forehead against the steering wheel. He got a Valium out of his shaving kit and cracked a beer to wash it down. When he felt steady enough, he drove across town to Route 1 and headed south.

• • •

Spider didn't quite make two hundred miles the first day, but he wasn't trying to break any records. There was a fish camp outside of Emporia, Virginia, that had a few campsites and a million mosquitos. The grizzled black man who ran the camp sold him a mosquito net and a serviceable old folding cot to keep his sleeping bag off the damp ground. The pup tent was a lot more complicated than the hooches they'd slept under in Vietnam, but he managed to get it standing, after a fashion, just before dark. He built a small fire and drank whiskey, swatting mosquitos, while he warmed up a can of spaghetti.

He went to bed feeling pretty good, but woke up just after midnight with a growing sense of panic. It was too dark. He could hear things rustling in the woods.

He got a bright fire going and fed sticks to it while he drank beer. A dark form loomed out of the night and Spider jumped up, expecting the man with no face, but it was just the old black guy, who said he was checking to see if anything was wrong.

Spider gave him a beer and they talked about the army for a while. He'd been in an all-Negro battalion in World War II. Fought in France, got a Bronze Star and a Purple Heart, and came home to find that his wife and kids had flat disappeared. It took him two years to track her down, and by then he didn't care much about her one way or the other. He took a job at this fish camp, and when the white owner died, he left it to him in his will.

Spider got up at dawn and used an improvised Sterno stove to heat a canteen cup of water for coffee. While he was taking down the tent, the old man came out with some ice for his cooler and a souvenir postcard, a faded aerial photo of the camp.

The weather was perfect, clear and cool, and Spider figured he could angle over to the interstate and make it to Georgia by dusk. He didn't, quite. After a long day of cruising along uneventfully at sixty to sixty-five, the engine started to make a loud clattering sound and various idiot lights glowed.

He pulled over and popped the hood. The fan belt was intact and the engine didn't seem to be overheating, but that just about exhausted his car repair expertise. He left the hood up and trekked back a mile to the Bamberg exit. There was a service station right there, and the mechanic was glad to come down and have a look.

He listened to the clatter for one second and told Spider that the engine was a total write-off; it had sucked a valve. You could rebuild the engine, but it would be cheaper to just pull it and drop in a replacement. Maybe seven or eight hundred bucks. When Spider said he didn't have that kind of money, the mechanic offered to hold on to the car until he could come up with it. Alternatively, he could buy the car as a junker, two hundred bucks, no, two-fifty.

The guy looked honest, and he offered to let Spider call around town to see whether anybody could come up with a better deal. I'll take the $250, Spider said, if you throw in a ride to the bus station. What the hell; he'd expected something like this to happen. He just wanted to get to Florida and start living.

It wasn't too bad a deal, he told himself. He only had about seventy-eight dollars left; he'd probably have to sell the car in Tampa, anyhow.

The mechanic pulled a fat roll of greasy bills out of his pocket and counted the money out in damp twenties, tens, and fives. They emptied his stuff out of the car into the back of the tow truck and made a bumpy U-turn across the median grass—legal in South Carolina, the mechanic said, grinning—and went into town, where there was a Greyhound pickup point at a Shell station. A bus to Jacksonville, Florida, was due in about two hours.

Spider watched his car roll away and then set about trying to consolidate his pile of possessions. He managed to stuff the whiskey bottle and six of the beers into the suitcase, and another half-case of the beer into the sleeping bag, zipped up into its canvas bag. He took the rope from the pup tent and lashed the rolled-up tent and sleeping bag to the bottom of his suitcase. Most of the mess gear fit in the cooler.

So all he had to leave behind was a case of beer and the cot. He sold the beer for half-price to the Shell gas jockey, but he didn't want the cot.

So when the bus pulled in, Spider staggered up like a poorly loaded beast of burden: suitcase in one hand, cooler in the other, sleeping bag strapped to his left shoulder and guitar to his right. He checked everything to Jax except the cooler and the guitar, and sat in the dark of the back of the bus, strumming softly and drinking beer. He felt pretty good about the trip, all things considered. It was probably a good thing that he would never know that, tomorrow morning, the mechanic would spend thirty minutes adjusting his car's valves and then sell it for a thousand dollars.

SETTLING IN

Beverly and Lee were able to rent the upstairs of a small old house for seventy-five dollars a month, provided they would clean it up and repaint the inside. It was a shabby mess, but reclaimable, and Lee had two weeks before his job started. The rental agency, which occupied the floor below, put up the money for paint and cleaning supplies, and asked that they keep the noise down during the day.

Lee found out in a local bar that the place had been a whorehouse until it was busted in '66. That explained why the pile of debris in the living room included five moldy mattresses. He borrowed a pickup from his former and future employer Larry, and was able to take all of the garbage to the dump in two trips.

They spent two days scrubbing the place down and then another three days painting. Lee rented a floor sander and buffer; the old wood flooring was comically warped, but had a beautiful grain. They got most of their furniture from the Salvation Army and Goodwill stores, but sprang, so to speak, for a brand new mattress. The landlord provided a small refrigerator and gas range, which had to go into the living room. Whorehouses don't have kitchens.

They had five days' rest between finishing the apartment and starting work. They made a lot of use of the mattress. Beverly set out to become pregnant. She knew it was partly atonement for the abortion, partly wanting to bond Lee to her with more than a piece of paper. Most of it was that she wanted to be a mother, and she wanted it now.

They were married by a justice of the peace in Hyattsville, with Beverly's mother and six assorted hippies in attendance. Her mother took them all to lunch at a decent Italian restaurant, but declined to attend the reception, at the Chillum Heights crashpad where Bev and Lee had once lived in sin, perhaps rightly intuiting that there would be a lot more marijuana than champagne involved.

Once they were settled in, Beverly called Spider's parents to see how he was doing, and was surprised to find the number no longer in service. Information didn't have a new number for them. There was a new listing for John Speidel, but she called and it was an old man, not Spider.

In a mood for detective work, she called Walter Reed, and was surprised to find out that Spider had been released about the time they left for California. She checked her diary and found that it had actually been the day before they left. She called the guy who owned the old crashpad and he said yeah, Spider'd come looking for her the day after they left. Had a joint with him; he seemed pretty shook.

She called the University and found out that he had begun the registration process for summer classes but hadn't turned in the completed forms.

So he could be anywhere. She felt a little guilty. If they'd stayed in town another day or two, she could have talked it out with him.

Maybe, like her, Spider had wanted to stick around College Park even though he wasn't enrolled. She called *The Terrapin*, the college newspaper, and arranged for a week of SPIDER CALL BEVERLY, followed by her phone number, in the Personals section.

That was all she could do for the time being. She'd keep her eye out for him around campus, but no telling what he looked like now. He'd looked so strange in the hospital, drawn and pale. And in one of his letters he'd said that as soon as he got out of the Army, he was going to grow a beard.

EXPENSIVE BEER

Spider's beer ran out just before Jacksonville, so when he arrived in Tampa, at noon the next day, finding a bar was high on his list of priorities. He stashed his gear in a locker at the bus station after putting half his money in the suitcase, and went outside.

In Maryland it had been cool and dry, a few leaves starting to turn. Tampa was a sauna, ninety degrees and muggy. It wasn't unpleasant, though, with the salt sea smell—actually Tampa Bay—mingling with a whisper of tropical flowers. He could learn to like this kind of winter.

Second order of business, buy some shorts. First, find a bar.

There was a grungy-looking place across from the bus station that had a faded sign advertising twenty-five-cent drafts. Why not?

It was cold inside, smell of stale beer and nicotine, and so dark he could barely make out the bar, illuminated by a single red bulb. A pool table bulked in the darkness.

The barmaid was half again as large as Spider, with huge swaying breasts. "What'll it be, Coach?" she said in a scratchy baritone.

"Draft and a Polish sausage. And one of those pickled eggs." Health food for lunch.

She peered at him. "You old enough?" Spider reached for his wallet and she waved a meaty hand at him and went to pull the beer. She put the egg and sausage on a saucer with a stack of saltine crackers and set it out with salt, pepper, and Tabasco. "Wanna fork?" she said.

"Say no," someone said from the dimness on the other side of the circular bar. "Hold out for a blowjob."

The barmaid grabbed her crotch. "Hold out for *this*, motherfucker." Nice place.

She gave him a fork and a napkin and then lit up a nonfilter Camel. The smell made Spider's heart hammer with narcotic nostalgia. There was a cigarette machine in the corner.

No. That was the only good thing he'd gotten out of his hospital stay.

"So you just get off the bus?" the barmaid said.

"Uh huh. What, I sound like a Yankee?"

"Naw. Just most of the dorks come in here are regulars."

"Regular *some*things," the other voice said.

The bartender clicked a switch and a jukebox lit up. The fluorescent lights over the pool table blinked on. Spider could suddenly see. The other three customers in the bar were wearing dresses, like the bartender.

The bartender had cut her chin shaving.

Spider paid close attention to his egg. He sliced it in two carefully and applied salt, pepper, and Tabasco.

Everybody watched him in silence.

He was carrying the copy of *Playboy* he had bought in the Jacksonville station. He opened it up and studied the pictures. He ate rapidly.

One of the customers came around and looked over his shoulder. "Oh, my *God*. She's so beautiful. Look, Henry."

The barmaid scrutinized the Playmate of the Month, who was well endowed. "Ah. No tits."

Spider looked around and made a decision. "Any of you guys shoot pool?"

• • •

A man in a paisley frock squeezed Spider for fifteen bucks at a quarter a ball. During the course of play he told Spider that he was not homosexual, but just liked wearing women's clothing. Two other denizens said the same thing. Spider didn't believe any of them, but didn't care one way or the other, so long as nobody made a pass at him. He didn't really understand why a man would want to have sex with another man, but after his treatment at the hands of Captain My Captain, he had a certain amount of sympathy for them.

Anyhow, the beer was ice-cold and the company was congenial. The paisley guy didn't hustle him; he was just a better pool-player. It was an enjoyable afternoon, and Spider was feeling no pain as he ambled out of the bar to go get his stuff and start looking for a place to stay.

"Hey, faggot." Two cliché hard guys lounging on a white '57 Chevy, nosed and decked, chopped and channeled. The one who spoke was sitting on the trunk, long and skinny, deeply tanned, toothpick balanced on his lower lip and a box of Marlboros rolled up in the left sleeve of his white t-shirt.

Spider looked back at the door to the bar. "You. Faggot."

"You talkin' to me?"

The other one stepped forward. He was a head shorter than Spider but solid with weightlifter muscles. Sleeveless t-shirt and cut-offs. Like Robert Mitchum in the movie, he had L-O-V-E tattooed on one set of knuckles and H-A-T-E on the other. He hustled his balls. "Want some, fag?"

Spider didn't know what to say. He just shook his head.

"Let ya blow me for twenty-five bucks." He was standing right in front of Spider. He unzipped his fly. "Come on. Just get in the back of the car."

"Look," Spider managed to croak, "I don't swing that way."

"Sure you don't." The little man smiled and hit Spider in the solar plexus with stunning force. Spider bent over, retching, and the man pulled down his head by the ears and his knee jerked up to smash Spider's mouth and nose. He staggered sideways and the man kicked him in the side of the head. He was unconscious before he hit the ground.

When he woke up it was dark. His mouth was full of blood. When he spit it out, it carried a fragment of a front tooth. His nose felt broken.

He was lying behind a line of garbage cans. His wallet was gone and his pockets were turned inside out. He tried to stand up and sat down hard, almost losing it. He waited for the world to stop spinning and stood up again, carefully.

He saw the neon Greyhound sign and oriented himself. He was behind the bar. He staggered around and into the front door.

A couple of dozen people suddenly fell silent. Then the bartender Henry recognized him. "Oh my God. It's Spider."

Two men helped him to a chair. Henry came over with a mug of beer and a wet rag. "Hold still." He dabbed at the blood caked on his face. "God, you're a *mess*! What did you get into?"

"Shit. I got jumped. Right outside of the bar." Spider's voice sounded strange to him. His tongue was swollen and the new gap where his front tooth was chipped made his sibilants whistle. "Two guys. Called me a faggot and beat the shit out of me."

"*Are* you a faggot?" a stranger asked.

"Oh, can it, John," Henry said. "He just came in for a beer."

"Gotta call the police," Spider said. "They got all my money, got my wallet."

"Maybe you don't want to call 'em." Spider recognized the voice but not the man. It was the one who had looked at his *Playboy*, but he'd traded in the dress for Esso coveralls. "You might get beat up again, they find out where you were."

"That's right," Henry said. "Use the phone over at the bus station."

Spider slapped his pockets. "Shit. I don't even have a dime."

Henry pulled a bunch of change out of his pocket and put it in Spider's hand. "Look, how much did Taylor take you for this afternoon?"

"Fifteen bucks. But that was fair and square."

"Yeah, I'll fair-and-square him tomorrow." He selected a ten and five from his wallet and stuffed them into Spider's shirt pocket. "Coop, you go with him. Don't let anybody fuck with him."

"Right." The Esso coverall had "Cooper" sewn into the breast. Coop looked pretty tough when he wasn't wearing a dress. "You want to drink that beer first?"

"Yeah. 'Scuse me." Spider went to the men's room and rinsed the blood out of his mouth. He looked bad in the mirror, black eye as well as everything else. Big purple bruise over his solar plexus. He stood over the toilet for a minute but didn't puke, thank God for small favors.

He went back out and drank the beer. Henry offered him a shot to go with it, but he declined, thinking about facing the police with whiskey on his breath.

"You were in the 'Nam," Coop said, pointing at his bracelet.

"Yeah." Spider laughed, a grunt. "I know all about ambushes. Just didn't expect one here, in broad daylight."

"What these guys look like?" Coop asked.

"Coupla JDs. Mutt and Jeff. One guy over six feet, skinny, the other, I don't know, five-four. Little guy's the one who got me; looked like a goddamn prizefighter."

"Tattoos on his knuckles?"

"That's right. You know him."

"Shit," Henry said. "Everybody knows him. Name's Sonny. You don't fuck with him."

"Speak for yourself," someone said.

"Yeah, you *fuck* with him. You just don't fuck with him."

"I'm gettin' lost," Spider said. "You mean he's a fa... he's a homosexual?"

"Ah, he ain't homo or hetero," a black man said. "He just fuck anything don't move fast enough. He stick you with a knife and fuck the fuckin' *wound*."

"Jesus."

"And can't nobody fuck with him because he's fuckin' Family."

"That's what he says," Henry said. "I think he just has an overactive imagination."

"And a gun, man. I seen his fuckin' gun."

"What, nobody here has a gun?" Henry pulled up enough skirt to show the Derringer strapped to his calf.

"Hold it," Spider said, rubbing his face. "Is all of Tampa like this? Might as well go back to Vietnam."

"This the *nice* part of town," the black man said.

"Oh, bullshit," Coop said. "This is the same kinda part of town you always find the bus station. Drink the beer and let's go over there."

"Good idea," Spider said. He finished the mug and stood up.

Crossing the street, Cooper told Spider he had done a tour in Vietnam. "That was '65, though," he said. "Not much goin' on. Just teach the gooks about M14s and such."

"You were an advisor?"

"Green Beret, all the way. Fuckin' crock a crap. Shouldn't of been there then and double shouldn't now."

"Damn straight." They went into the bus station. "Oh, shit." Spider crossed over to where his locker was standing wide open.

Coop came up behind him. "Least they left your guitar."

"Yeah. Knew how much they could get for it." His suitcase was unzipped and the money was gone. They had taken *The War Against the Rull*. Otherwise everything seemed to still be there.

Spider sat down on the suitcase. "Shit. I had over three hundred dollars."

"So you gonna call the cops?"

"Yeah. Maybe get the wallet back."

"Maybe. I wouldn't finger Sonny, though, the knuckles. That Mafia stuff is probably bullshit, but he's one hard case. Be back on the street in a week and lookin' for you."

"Yeah. I'll tell 'em I didn't get a good look at him." He stood up and stretched. "Big black guy. Jumped me in the men's room here."

"Okay. Then what? You call the cops and then? You got a place to stay, know anybody?"

"Huh uh. Sleep in a chair here, I guess. Go look for a job tomorrow."

"Spend a night here, you probably *will* get mugged. You come on to the Esso station with me, you can sleep in my truck. Tomorrow... you got a tent and a bedroll, I know a place you can stay for free, pretty safe."

"That'd be okay. I wanted to camp out some anyhow."

"Yeah." He laughed. "This place is some kinda campin' out."

WINTER

THE END OF SOMETHING

Beverly kept running the ad for Spider until November, when she missed a period and decided it would be prudent to save the money. Lee was resignedly happy about the prospect of becoming a father. He took another part-time job, teaching guitar in Montgomery Mall. The manager wanted him to cut his hair, but he charmed her out of it.

School went well for Beverly. She decided she would take a full load next semester, then leave for a year after the baby was born, then continue part time at least to the B.A. level.

On one wall of their converted whorehouse there were large pictures of Kennedy and King, of Chicago in riot and Washington in flames, of black athletes with their fists raised high in Mexico: a kind of 1968 in review. But when the ROTC building burned, they were not in attendance. Beverly walked through tear gas to get to class, but she wasn't among those who threw the gas grenades back at the cops and wore football helmets against their clubs. When a news program came on television, she would turn it off or leave the room.

Sometimes she would sit alone and cry for no reason, or for reasons beyond counting.

JOHN IN THE BOX

Hooch City was a vacant lot near the railroad tracks where a floating population of forty or fifty men hung out: mostly young, mostly Vietnam vets, mostly not working. All of them fucked up one way or another. Spider fit right in.

The police didn't bother them, probably because it was convenient to have them all in one place. They kept the area pretty neat and didn't flagrantly break laws other than the obvious one of vagrancy.

Those who, like Spider, got disability checks or occasional money from home went in together on a post office box. Dinners were communal, fixed by two guys who lived together in a packing crate, Red-eye and Deros. Their home was everyone's pantry, stocked with big sacks of rice and dry beans, which were the basic staple, along with odds and ends that people scavenged or shoplifted or sometimes bought. When the VA checks came in, those fortunate enough to be disabled put together a monthly party of beer, wine, and whiskey. There was not much regularity to their lives other than 7:00 dinner and the first-of-the-month party. Some of them worked odd jobs or begged, and others just sat around, waiting. Every now and then someone would tire of waiting and play a round of "Kiss the Train."

Spider lived in his tent for two weeks, and then inherited an eight-by-eight-foot packing crate when its owner, Radio Jon, got bitten by a scorpion and had such a severe reaction he had to be taken to the hospital. Spider paid the cab fare, so Radio Jon said he could have the hooch if he didn't come back. He did come back, two days later, but just to pick up the big Japanese radio on his way to Georgia, where he figured there wouldn't be any scorpions. Spider missed the radio but was glad to have a dry place to sleep.

The University of South Florida wasn't too far from Hooch City, so Spider went up there and got a set of catalogs and registration materials. He really ought to get back into school and start collecting the GI Bill money, but he had plenty of time before classes began in January. He could use the P.O. box as an address; it would be funny to be living like a hobo and going to school at the same time.

He was actually in a kind of twilight zone between respectability and bumhood. When he got his first disability check, he opened a bank account, mainly because he was afraid to carry a large amount of money. That put him so close to the economic mainstream that American Express sent him an application, which he thumbtacked up on the wall of his crate for everybody's amusement.

He did have a sort of a regular job, playing guitar on the street. He usually wore his fatigues from Basic Training and a boonie cap from Vietnam that a guy traded him in exchange for a sixpack. Every now and then someone would give him a hard time about Vietnam, but he'd just smile and nod until he or she got nervous and left. Twice he was spat on, but he let that go by, too. After his experiences in Walter Reed and outside the gay bar, the last thing he wanted to do was get into a fight.

He went out every day it wasn't raining, at least for a couple of hours. He had a regular route, mostly bus stops, and even wound up with some regular customers, who would say hello and give him a dime or a quarter every time, and sometimes ask for specific songs.

He also made a little money as a small-scale purveyor of pharmaceuticals. He picked up his Valium every fourth Friday at the VA hospital dispensary, and it was twice as much as he needed, so he sold half of it on the street through a hippie who came through Hooch City now and then.

He wasn't bothered by dreams as long as he could wash his evening pill down with whiskey. Beer if it was cold. Warm beer tasted like Vietnam; he couldn't swallow it.

He knew it was no health pill, whiskey plus Valium, but figured it was temporary. He was saving a few bucks here and there. When he started school in January, he might have enough to rent a room for the semester. Get off the street.

And this is how he ended the year, 1968:

On December 31st he was kind of broke but not unhappy. He had made good tips the couple of weeks before Christmas, having learned a few carols on the guitar, but had spent most of it. He'd spruced up his packing crate with a carpet remnant, an aluminum folding cot, and a wool blanket, and had bought a smoked turkey for everybody, Christmas Eve. He had eight dollars in his pocket earmarked for a couple of bottles of cheap champagne to take back to the hooches tonight. Bring in the New Year like real people.

It was cool that day but not too cold for playing guitar. He had some woolen army gloves modified by snipping off the fingertips. He couldn't do anything fancy, like barre chords, with them on, but eight plain chords sufficed for most of his repertoire.

One of his most lucrative spots was a bus stop in a poor section downtown; he went there just before five and played while people came home from work. On this last day of the year, he was almost to the bus stop when a carload of laughing teenagers went by him and threw out a holiday firecracker. Spider didn't see it bounce off a parked car and roll between his feet.

The Valium, and maybe the whiskey, helped Spider with anxiety in general, but they didn't do much about his hyperreactivity; his startle reflex.

The firecracker was a red 2-incher Salute. It was about as loud as a single shot from an AK47. When it went off, Spider hit the dirt, hard. He landed on his guitar, which made a bad "crunch" sound.

Spider turned the guitar over and looked at it. The back was pretty much caved in, the wood split lengthwise in two places.

He tried to play it but it just kind of buzzed. He tried various ways. If he held it really tightly against his chest and plucked the strings down by the nut, he could pick out a recognizable melody, but chords still sounded like shit. He held his face tightly, too, holding in words more than tears.

One of his regulars, a tall skinny Rastafarian with tight greasy braids, got off the bus and walked up to where Spider was sitting on the sidewalk.

"Spidah? You gonna catch cold down there." He reached down to help him up but Spider shook off his hand. "What the fuck, man?"

Spider tried to speak but all he could do is shake his head. He turned the guitar around and showed the man its busted back.

"Somebody stove it in? Be some tough shit, man." This time Spider did let himself be helped up, and then led to the bench by the bus stop. "Ah, shit." The man looked around. "You wait here."

He ran across the street, dodging traffic, and went into a pawn shop. A few minutes later, he came out with a guitar similar to Spider's old F-hole. He pried the old one away from Spider and gave him the new one.

Spider strummed a couple of chords. It was in tune and sounded crisp and beautiful. He found his voice. "I can't let you do this, Royce. I can't take this."

"Ah. What you can't do is you can't tell me what to do, white boy." He held out the broken guitar and admired it. "Some day you be a famous music dude and I sell this mother for a million bucks." He walked away laughing, the old guitar jaunty over his shoulder.

For a long time Spider played the same chord over and over, staring at a spot on the sidewalk. Then he snapped out of it and put his hat down at his feet. He salted it with three quarters and began to sing a song about a man in trouble.

LIFE IS BUT A DREAM (4)

The tall, older man who had been given the job of making sure the dead were dead, and killing the wounded, was being punished. Punished for being Chinese, punished for being a scholar, punished for hating war and showing compassion.

Shi-Jung Han was born in the Cholon district of Saigon in 1941 to Chinese parents who had emigrated from San Francisco in the thirties. They spoke a little English around the house, and he studied it in school. At university he studied Chinese literature and took a few courses in English, and was delighted with his graduation present: his parents sent him San Francisco in the summer of 1961. He stayed with relatives in Chinatown and wandered through the city, revelling in its strangeness.

When he returned to Saigon, Han took a job in a bank, and amused his fellow clerks with tales of the cool foggy city, its hills and cable cars, its bridge and bay and beatniks. When American customers came in, Han was the one who had to figure out what they wanted and respond, which embarrassed him. He understood English well but spoke it terribly, and usually had to communicate by written notes.

The bank failed in a cynical takeover during the disastrous year of 1964. Han's parents were thrown out of their house, and the three of them lived in a succession of mean rooms, just making enough from sewing and labor to cover rice and rent. Han detested the puppet government that had brought him and his family to such a state, and so, like many of his friends, he joined the Viet Cong.

For some reason he was not allowed to stay in Saigon. They sent him a couple of hundred miles north, to Tay Ninh, where he had two weeks of arduous training in a secret camp, and was then assigned to this company, which moved around in the forests and mountains of the Central Highlands between Dak To and Pleiku.

He was supposedly the company's translator, but they had never taken a prisoner. In fact, he had never seen a live American soldier, since he was not exactly a front-line rifleman. (His marksmanship training had consisted of twenty rounds fired with a rattly old bolt-action rifle, the Chinese Mauser that he carried now.)

He had never fired an AK47 before. He clicked the selector switch to single-shot and stepped up to the first dead American. The shot was a flat sound, muffled, and the result was as horrible as he had expected. His boots were spattered with blood and brains. He wiped them off on the dead soldier's tunic.

He had never seen a live American soldier but he had felt the fury of their weapons. His company specialized in harassment, hit and run, and what they ran through was often a hail of artillery and air support. A few months ago a napalm strike had blossomed only a few tens of meters away, close enough to singe his hair. He had been stung by small bits of shrapnel several times. None of his wounds had been serious, but he had no illusions. He was not going to survive this war.

He stepped up to the next body and swallowed bile.

He had no doubt that an American bullet or bomb would kill him, but he couldn't hate the Americans. The ones he had met in San Francisco had been sometimes foolish, always friendly, never malicious. "Laid back," as they said. He had seen the newspaper accounts of peace marches and draft-card burnings. He knew that most of the black and white men who lay strewn across this bloody clearing had been sent here against their will.

This time he didn't close his eyes when he fired, and he didn't bother to wipe his boots. They would just get dirty again.

This last action had been pure serendipity. A messenger returning from the headquarters bunker had seen the small American unit crossing the stream and knew they would probably come up the trail toward the company's bivouac. He took the ridgeline trail and got to the bivouac an hour before them. The company set up two heavy machineguns in a cross-fire covering the clearing, along with riflemen and grenadiers. The Americans never stood a chance, evidently.

Han had not watched it. He stayed a couple of hundred meters away, by a bunker, along with two reserve squads and some supernumeraries, notably

Lieutenant To, the unit's political officer.

It had been obvious from the sound how one-sided the engagement was, and when the first men ran back with their accounts of how complete the butchery had been, Han showed more honesty than intelligence. He remarked to the medic how terrifying it must have been and what a horrible price was paid for even a complete victory such as this; they were just men like us, after all.

Lieutenant To overheard. He gave Han a quick, loud tongue-lashing and then switched rifles with him, and ordered him to do the cleanup. All the others would fall back to an assembly area a couple of kilometers away, to avoid the inevitable artillery and helicopters.

Where was the artillery? Maybe they hadn't had time to call in. Third body.

As Han lowered the muzzle to this one, he started to rise up feebly, not quite dead. He jerked the trigger reflexively and the bullet blew the top of his skull and a mass of brains back into his helmet, which rocked back but remained attached by its chinstrap. Dying, the man threw his arms up as if in supplication. Han yelled at him furiously in Chinese, the first man he had ever killed. Until now there had been a chance he would never have to live with that.

He slumped, looking at his handiwork. He could just wait here for the artillery, for the gunships. But that would be suicide. One new sin per day was enough.

The next two he could skip. One was in a sitting position, slumped over staring at the cooling blue coils of entrails piled in his lap, on his hands, like a Japanese warrior contemplating the results of his pride. The other had no head to shoot.

A big black man, chest-shot, rigid, eyes open and filming, lips drawn back in a grimace. He shot him in the mouth for no reason.

A pair of legs with no body attached; that was a rarity, he supposed. There was a lot of bloodslick on the ground, and small bits of flesh, a length of vertebrae, most of a hand with a gold ring. It was as if the man had burst. Han reached toward the ring and pulled back, disgusted with himself.

Two together, one a medic killed while wrapping the other's shattered arm. The medic had flopped over on his patient, flinging the gauze out in a stark white ribbon. The patient may have been slightly alive; he shuddered when the bullet shattered his forehead. The medic was firmly dead, two matching exit wounds in his back exposing lung tissue and ribs. He shot him in the back of the head anyway, leaving a relatively clean round hole.

Now three together, who had all died while operating, or trying to set up, a belt-fed machinegun. A fortuitous rifle grenade had landed close enough to destroy the weapon and kill all three men, boys. One must have been very handsome, in a movie-star way. His jaw had been blown off, or blown into his neck, but Han could block the gore off with his hand and see the perfect nose, the high cheekbones, the strange blue eyes and the pale hair. He had drawn a complex mandala on his helmet cover, ornate lettering spelling out "San Francisco Hippy."

There was a faint squeaking sound. The boy was trying to breathe through his shattered jaw and throat.

"I'm sorry," Han said in English, and killed him. He shot the other two quickly.

For a minute Han wiped his eyes and studied the clearing. Had he missed anybody? There, one over by the trees.

He walked toward the body. At first it looked as if he could skip this one, dead of a head wound, but on closer inspection he could see that the blood was superficial, from a cut on the forehead. He carefully set the muzzle on the center of the line that joined the man's eyebrows, slightly higher—

When the hot muzzle touched his skin, his eyes opened wide. Han could read the terror there, and felt a moment of sympathy and self-loathing, but he pulled the trigger.

Nothing happened. But there was plenty of ammunition. The AK47 had jammed.

The boy's eyes were closed again. He was waiting to die. Han had no idea how to clear the AK47 and make it fire. He had little inclination to experiment.

He remembered a thing a beatnik poet had said to his audience in San Francisco, six summers before. He'd been amused because the poet had said it was an ancient Chinese curse, and Han had never heard of it.

He spoke it softly to the boy in nine flat syllables of bad English, and moved on. For the rest of his life, Spider would hear that phrase in his dreams, and never decipher it:

"May you live in interesting times."

ACKNOWLEDGEMENTS
AND DEDICATION

A lot of Vietnam veterans helped me with this book. Thanks to Bill Hutchinson and John Chambers for checking me out on ground combat memories; special thanks to Bob and Patience Mason for their expertise in helicopters and PTSD. Their books *Chickenhawk* and *Recovering from the War* were especially valuable.

There's not much science fiction in this book, but I got a great deal of help from the science fiction readers and writers on GEnie's SF Bulletin Board, who saved me a lot of library footwork when I needed to know the color of the walls in Walter Reed in 1968 and how doughnuts are made. It's pretty science-fictional to have a group mind of over a thousand brains just one modem call away.

And then there are two veterans whose names I never learned.

On the 4th of October, 1968, I was in the Army hospital at Tuy Hoa, Republic of Vietnam, my first day on crutches after being confined for several weeks to bed and wheelchair with multiple bullet and fragment wounds.

The hospital was suddenly crowded to overflowing with injured Vietnamese civilians, mostly women and children. It had been Election Day, and the Viet Cong decided to demonstrate against the election by simultaneously attacking various polling places.

The hospital was a madhouse, a charnel house. Orders came down to transfer to other areas every American patient who could be moved. I hobbled aboard a crowded DC-3 borrowed from Air America, the CIA's airline, and as I moved toward the rear I passed the man who would become the rough draft of Spider.

Most of the passengers were obviously wounded or ill, but this man was tanned, healthy-looking, smiling—and strapped down to a stretcher, confined within a straitjacket, staring, evidently Thorazine-ed to the gills. Pinned to his straitjacket was a tag saying "paranoid schizophrenic." I sat down behind him and wondered about using him in a story—maybe you *had* to be crazy, to make sense of this crazy war. This crazy time.

Two years later, happily out of uniform, I was visiting patients in the neurological wing of Bay Pines VA Hospital in St. Petersburg, Florida. There were some sad cases there, and no doubt some of them are still there, but the one who sticks in my mind is certainly dead by now. He was about ninety, the hospital's only patient left over from the Spanish-American War. He was legless and blind. They said that for forty years he had done nothing but call out for his mother.

This book is for those two men, obviously, and for men and women everywhere who are trapped day and night, locked away in the dark prison of their memories of war.